THEIRS TO PLEASURE

A Marriage Raffle Novel

STASIA BLACK

For Bobby Kim, the crazy mofo genius
who changed my life

In the not too distant future, a genetically engineered virus is released by an eco-terrorist in major metropolitan areas all over the globe. Within five years, almost 90% of the world's female population is decimated.

In an attempt to stop the spread of the virus and quarantine those left, a nuclear war was triggered. It's still unclear who began attacking who, but bombs were dropped on all major US cities, coordinated with massive EMP attacks.

These catastrophes and the end of life as people knew it was collectively known as *The Fall*.

MAP OF THE NEW REPUBLIC OF TEXAS

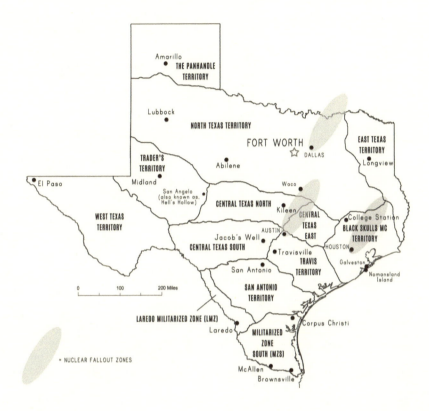

Amarillo
THE PANHANDLE
TERRITORY

Lubbock

NORTH TEXAS TERRITORY

FORT WORTH
☆ DALLAS

EAST TEXAS
TERRITORY

Longview

TRADER'S
TERRITORY

Abilene

El Paso

Midland

San Angelo
(also known as
Hell's Hollow)

CENTRAL TEXAS NORTH

Waco

Kileen

CENTRAL
TEXAS
EAST

College Station

BLACK SKULLS MC
TERRITORY

WEST TEXAS
TERRITORY

AUSTIN

Jacob's Well

HOUSTON

CENTRAL TEXAS SOUTH

Travisville

San Antonio

TRAVIS
TERRITORY

Galveston

Nomansland
Island

0   100   200 Miles

SAN ANTONIO
TERRITORY

LAREDO MILITARIZED ZONE (LMZ)

Laredo

Corpus Christi

MILITARIZED
ZONE
SOUTH (MZS)

McAllen

Brownsville

= NUCLEAR FALLOUT ZONES

CHAPTER ONE

CHARLIE

Charlie blinked blearily at the sunlight coming through the window where it wasn't boarded up. The sun was setting. Another day gone.

He looked at the wall where he'd just finished scratching a line into the cinderblock with a small rock he'd found on the ground, briefly glancing up at all the similar hash marks.

Three months. It had been over three months since he'd woken up in this very room—covered in his own blood, with a headache so bad he'd been convinced he was gonna die. He had no idea where he was. A tiny office in a really old building, he thought. Cream-colored painted cinderblock walls. It had an institutional feel. Maybe a hospital?

There was a thick wooden door with a tiny rectangular plexiglass window, but all it showed was the end of a dark alcove, so no clues there. Through the limited view out the window, he could only see the plumbing of another building.

When he'd first woken up, part of him had wanted to just give up and die. Because no matter how many times he shouted questions at the guards who occasionally delivered food and water, no one would tell him anything about his sister Audrey.

Had those bastards killed her right there by the spring where they'd knocked him out? Or did she manage to run away after all?

In the end, he'd fought for consciousness and clung to life as hard as he could. Because what if she was here? What if these mother-fuckers had her too? What if they were—

He cut that line of thought off just like he did every time it sprang up. He'd go fucking insane if he let himself go there.

Voices sounded in the hallway and he scrambled to his feet. Well, as much as he could with the handcuffs and connected ankle fetters. He shuffled hunchbacked toward the door and the small plexiglass window.

And saw *her*.

He thought she was a mirage the first time she came and pushed his tray of moldy bread and sour mush through the skinny two-inch rectangular hole that had been sawed in the door.

She was tiny with long blond hair, wearing a faded white dress. Like some sort of angelic apparition.

But then she got closer and he saw that no, she was a flesh and bone woman. Because surely an angel wouldn't be walking with a limp and have a black eye and a split lip.

She refused to approach with the tray until he backed up to the opposite wall. Then she slid it through and ran away as fast as she could.

Charlie couldn't even be mad that the tasteless bowl of mush spilled all over the floor. If he were her, he wouldn't voluntarily get within three feet of a man either.

He hadn't spent the last eight years hiding Audrey away from the world for nothing. Which was when it hit him—*Audrey*. If Audrey was here, this woman might know her.

It was all he could think about. So the next time the woman came, he ran for the door and started firing questions. "Do you know a girl named Audrey? She would have been brought here the same time I was. Two months ago."

The woman was so startled by his voice she'd dropped his tray and fled.

"Wait!" he'd shouted after her. "Audrey. Do you know her? She's my sister. Please!"

But all he heard was the sound of rapidly fleeing footsteps. And then nothing.

She didn't come back for three days.

It wasn't unusual to go that long between meals. They gave him a gallon of water once or—if he was lucky—sometimes twice a week. But meals were hit or miss.

Still, the next time he heard light footsteps approaching, he backed away to the farthest wall and raised his hands in surrender.

He didn't dare say a word. If Audrey *was* here, this girl could be the key to getting information about her and he wasn't going to fuck it up again.

She was cautious as she approached. Hesitant.

He waited as patiently as he could manage.

She shoved the tray through the hole, sending the bowl splattering again, and then ran away.

As much as it killed him, he did the same thing the next three times she came.

And on the fourth, he said in his calmest, gentlest voice, "I won't hurt you."

She startled so much she almost dropped the tray again.

But she didn't make a run for it.

Considering that a win, he continued, still not moving from the wall and keeping his hands up and visible. "My name's Charlie."

He didn't push any further than that.

She didn't say a word. Just shoved his tray through and skittered away.

But the next time, he started talking about Audrey. "I have a sister about your age. Her name's Audrey. She drove me crazy growing up. Little sisters, you know? Always coming in my room and bothering me and my friends when we were playing video games. Trying to tag along when I'd go to the mall." He shook his head. "Jesus, it feels like a million years ago."

The woman hadn't bolted. The tray was paused halfway through the slot.

Charlie didn't move an inch but he kept talking.

"Dad and I couldn't believe how lucky we were when all the girls and women in town got sick but she stayed healthy. It was like a miracle." Charlie huffed out a sad laugh. And then, when the woman still didn't leave, he told her about what happened with his dad and the mob that came to the front door, and how he escaped with Audrey out back.

"She's dead now?"

Her voice was so soft at first Charlie thought he might have imagined it.

He sat up straighter and she flinched backwards, tray clattering against the slot as she yanked it back.

"Sorry, sorry," Charlie said, chains rattling as he lifted his cuffed hands again and put his back flush with the wall. "I didn't mean to scare you. I— I don't know where she is. She was with me when—" He swallowed, looking down. "The men from here, they attacked us when we were getting water." He lifted his eyes to hers where she watched him warily through the plexiglass. "I thought if they brought me here, then maybe they brought her too."

Her eyes dropped and Charlie's heartbeat sped up. What did that mean?

"Is she here? Do you know her?"

Her eyes flicked back up to his. "A lot of girls come through here."

Nausea hit Charlie fast and hard. She was confirming his worst fears. No, his worst fear was that Audrey was dead. But what this woman was describing was a close second.

It was an open secret that girls were trafficked all over the territories. The president had officially outlawed it, but there was a reason Charlie chose to stay with Audrey in an underground bunker for almost a decade. Law and order were so far from a reality yet, it was fucking laughable. The Wild West looked like a picnic compared to the New Republic of Texas, and the New Republic was actually way better than most places in the former US.

Charlie bit his cheek against the million questions he wanted to ask. *Don't press it. She's just opening up. Push too hard and she could bolt again.*

But then those big doe eyes of hers came back to him. "I could maybe... ask around."

"Yeah?" The word came out half-strangled. Was she really just— Just offering like that when he'd— "Cause that would be— It'd be fuckin— Sorry, I just, it would mean everything—"

"I'm not promising anything," she said sharply. Then, as if she'd just remembered the tray in her hands, she gestured down to it with her eyes. "Here. Take this."

And, though she watched him warily, she stood still as he approached. He came slow, careful. She was skittish as a deer. When he got close enough to take the tray, he saw her hand was shaking.

And for the first time since she'd shown up, he thought about her. *Really* thought about her, and not just in relation to the info she might be able to get him on Audrey. What was life here like for her? She said girls came through. But not her? She obviously had some sort of position here. Maid? Servant? Slave?

While her split lip was healing, she had a fresh bruise on her cheek.

"Who hurts you?"

Her eyes shot up to his through the glass and he realized too late how harsh the question had come out.

He didn't apologize, though. Or look away. For a second, neither did she.

In spite of the bruise and her too pale skin, she was undeniably beautiful. So, so fucking beautiful. She had huge, translucent green eyes that looked far too sad for the rest of her angelic face.

What the fuck had happened to this girl to bring her here?

"I have to go," she whispered. "If I can find anything out about your sister, I will."

And then she was gone.

She didn't come back for a week. The longest goddamned week of Charlie's life. And when she did, she didn't have any news about Audrey.

"It doesn't mean she's not here, though," Shay whispered.

Shay.

That was her name. Like the sound of a sigh.

"Travis Territory is big and there are several processing facilities."

All thoughts of beautiful names and sighs fled at that. Charlie's blood went ice cold.

Processing.

Facilities.

For.

Women.

Even though he hadn't eaten in a week he wasn't sure he was gonna be able to get down the food on the tray Shay brought.

"But I'll keep asking around," she rushed to add, obviously seeing her words upset him.

One of the guards who came through sometimes walked by then so she yanked back and scurried away.

And it continued like that for weeks. Quick, stolen conversations broken up by long, endless days of nothing.

But during the moments she was there, Jesus, it was more than a lifeline. Charlie lived for the sound of her soft footsteps on the tile outside his door.

Though she didn't yet have any information on Audrey, Shay filled in so many gaps. He was being held in Travis Territory. To the southeast of what used to be Austin, Travis Territory centered around a township where a good-sized river sprang up from the Edwards Aquifer. Before The Fall, Charlie had even visited the place. You used to be able to take glass-bottomed boat tours on the river and watch the springs bubbling up from the source waters.

And now it was home to one of the most powerful and corrupt governors in the country. Arnold Travis.

The building where Charlie was being held used to be a faculty office in the English building of the old college campus.

The one thing Shay wouldn't talk about, though?

Herself.

Anytime Charlie asked anything about her, she clammed up and scurried off. So he learned not to. Because every second talking to her through the door was like being able to breathe after days starved for oxygen.

Thinking of their brief moments together helped get him through the hard days.

And there were plenty of hard days.

Because as much as he tried to hold out hope, in his darkest moments, it was too easy to believe the worst about Audrey. They'd been in the middle of fucking nowhere when they'd gotten ambushed. Even if Travis's men didn't get her, what were her chances out there all alone in the world?

She wasn't even safe on her own *uncle's* fucking property.

Some days, if not for Shay, it would have been too easy to give into the dark thoughts. Take this week for instance.

Audrey's twenty-third birthday was coming up in a couple weeks and he couldn't get this one memory out of his head. Audrey'd been maybe six and it was before The Fall. Before Xterminate, before any of it.

He was eight and playing with his friends in the backyard. He'd already told her to go away but instead she just went over to the swing set and started swinging, staring longingly at him and his buddies where they were playing armies by the back fence.

Little sisters were so *annoying*, he remembered thinking.

He'd been climbing a tree when all the sudden she started up an unholy wailing. Just looking for attention, like always. He shook his head and ignored her, climbing higher.

But she just kept crying, louder and louder until she was screaming bloody murder. He kept waiting for Dad to come out of the garage and take care of it, but he must have had that stupid old rock music he liked playing. And Dad *had* made him promise to look out for his sister for the afternoon.

So with a huff, he climbed down from the tree and went over to the swing set, face flaming in embarrassment at having his friends see him have to deal with his sister who was such a freaking *baby*. She was six but here she was wailing her head off like a two-year-old.

She was even laying on the ground by the swing set, like she'd thrown herself on the ground to throw a full out tantrum.

"Come on, Audrey," he muttered as soon as he got close. She just wailed even louder. He rolled his eyes and knelt down on the ground beside her. Her face was cherry red and fat tears ran down her cheeks.

"Audrey, stop crying." He hated it when she cried. It was loud and well... he just didn't like it. "Come on, sit up." He held out a hand and hiccupping, she took it. He put his other hand to the back of her head and helped her sit up.

"All right. You're okay now. Calm down. It's okay."

And then he pulled his hand away from the back of her head.

It was covered in blood.

Like, *covered*.

Blood dripped off his fingers, even.

Charlie's stomach cramped just at the memory. He'd been playing with his friends, having *fun*, and she'd been lying there, seriously hurt. Crying—no, *screaming* for him—and he'd just ignored it, for what? Five minutes?

The sound of those screams kept him awake at night. Filling the silence of his office prison.

Look out for your sister.

His Dad had made him promise the same thing he had so long ago when the bad times came. *No matter what happens to me, look out for your sister.* And Charlie had sworn, *sworn*, both to his dad and to himself, that he would never fail her again like he had that day in the backyard.

But he had. And ten thousand times worse.

Because whatever she was going through right now, wherever she was, wouldn't be solved by a trip to the emergency room and twelve stitches to the back of the head.

And he was stuck in this fifteen-by-ten-foot room, fucking *useless*. She was out there, with God knew what happening to her, screaming and screaming for his help and he couldn't get to her—

"Let *go* of me. This is for the prisoner!"

Shay.

Charlie jerked to attention and ran to the door, ankle fetters yanking taut and tripping him halfway there. He hit his knees hard but then stumbled back to his feet and scrambled to the door.

It was almost dark out now but there was a single candle burning in the hallway of the alcove. Charlie got to the window just in time to see the big, bald guard who sometimes patrolled yank the tray of food out of Shay's hand and then backhand her.

"No!" Charlie roared, pounding the door with his fist. "Shay!"

Her body was knocked to the ground where she lay crumpled like a ragdoll. "Shay!"

The bald bastard nudged her with his big, booted toe, then chuckled and walked off, tray in hand.

Charlie was about to pound at the door again but fisted his hands and bit back his curse. Because goddammit, he didn't want to do anything to bring the guard back. Yet again, he was fucking useless. Another woman he cared about was laying out there hurt and he was here, just feet away, and he couldn't do a goddamned *thing* to help her.

As soon as the guard's footsteps were gone, he dropped to his knees to look through the tray slot.

"Shay. Shay! Can you hear me? Are you okay?"

But she just laid there.

Fucking lifeless.

Fuck. *FUCK.*

Charlie grabbed at his hair, wanting to yank it out by the roots and—

But then he heard a noise.

The smallest groan.

"Shay!" He smashed his face to the hole in the wall and thank God. She was moving. He shoved his fingers through the small slot. "Shay, Jesus, are you okay?"

What the fuck, obviously she's not okay.

"Sorry, that's stupid. Can you sit up?"

She rolled over and dragged her body farther into the little alcove where the office was, out of the path of the main hallway.

When she finally sat up, he expected tears. He expected a bitter grimace. He even expected to see blood.

And she did have a fresh split lip, blood trickling down from the corner of her mouth.

But what he didn't expect?

For her to be fucking smiling.

She was grinning. Huge.

"Shay?" Charlie asked uncertainly. "Are you feeling okay? He hit you pretty hard."

When a small giggle escaped her lips, Charlie really started getting worried. But then she hopped to her feet.

And when she came near, there was a light in her eyes he'd never seen before.

"Shay, what's going—"

"I know where Audrey is."

Charlie coughed in shock, hand going to the plexiglass. "Where? Is she okay? Who has h—"

"Back up." Shay gestured impatiently for him to move back.

He frowned, totally fucking bewildered.

"Back *up*."

He took a couple steps away from the door.

That's when her grin got even wider, though he wouldn't have thought that was possible. And, with one quick glance back toward the hallway, she produced a keyring, holding it up briefly so he could see through the plexiglass.

Holy sh—

He didn't even have time to finish the thought before he heard the click of the lock turning. Then the door pushed open.

He could only stare in shock as Shay slipped inside. Her dark head was bowed as she flipped through keys on the keyring. Then she reached for his hands.

"Shay," he gasped. "How did you—"

She didn't look up from unlocking the shackles around his wrists. "I stole them off Carl when he was grabbing for the tray. I'd scrounged up some butter for your bread and made sure to pass by him. I knew he wouldn't be able to resist."

"But he *hit* you."

Shay just shrugged it off as if it was nothing. She got his wrists free and then dropped to his feet. The sight of her, crouched down at his feet, was just too much.

"Shay, Shay, stop."

Charlie leaned down and put his hands on hers, taking the keys.

Those endless green eyes of hers flashed. "I know where Audrey is.

And I'll tell you. Better yet, I'll take you there." Then her face went flinty with determination. "As long as you help me get the hell out of here."

He felt his eyebrows shoot to his hairline. This woman was full of surprises. But everything she was saying was music to his fucking ears.

"You've got a deal." He'd protect her. Yes, they'd only recently met, but he was *not* going to let her down.

In another half minute, he had the shackles off his feet. The chains dropped to the floor and he stood fully upright for the first time in three months.

Then he reached out a hand to Shay.

"Let's go."

CHAPTER TWO

CHARLIE

"Get your hands off me," Charlie roared as the giant with the scar down his face wrestled his arms painfully behind his back and shoved him forward. After all they'd done to get here to Jacob's Well? "Shay! Shay, are you okay?"

They'd escaped Travisville and traveled all night on a stolen four-wheeler to get here—not to mention walking the last two miles when the four-wheeler ran out of gas—and now these motherfuckers were going to treat them like *this*?

Charlie strained to look over his shoulder at Shay. Another soldier in dark fatigues led Shay forward with a hand at the small of her back. How dare the bastard fucking touch her?

"It's okay, Charlie," Shay said, hurrying up to his side. "Trust me. Everything's going to be okay."

How the hell could she say that? They were met with hostility almost the second they'd arrived at the Central Texas South border five minutes ago.

Charlie asked about his sister and one of the guards radioed it in on a walkie talkie.

Then, *bam*, next thing Charlie knew, he was eating dirt with a knee in his back and his arms wrenched behind him. Bastard had him zip tied in thirty seconds.

If only Charlie weren't so damn weak from three months in that prison... He'd tried to work out back in the cell when he had the energy so if he ever had the chance at escape, he'd be strong enough to make the most of it, but still. Some days he was living on what had to be maybe eight hundred calories a day if that and others they didn't bring him any food at all.

How the hell was he supposed to protect Shay if he couldn't hold his own against some prepubescent guard with more muscles than brain cells? But that was how it went, wasn't it? When it counted, he always failed at protecting the people he cared about.

Then he had to endure the humiliating experience of being thrown on the guard's horse to be taken into town with a black bag over his head. At least before everything went dark, he'd seen the other guard helped Shay on his horse in a decently respectful manner. But relying on the chivalry of a stranger in a strange town was not what Charlie had in mind when he'd vowed to protect Shay.

There was nothing to do other than stew furiously about it while he was jostled ruthlessly up and down on the back of the horse for the ride into town, though. Finally they stopped in front of a building that turned out to be some kind of security headquarters.

That was where this dickhead with the face scar had taken over.

When Charlie demanded to see his sister, the guy totally lost his shit. He shoved Charlie up against the wall by his throat.

It was only Shay's screaming that stopped the crazy bastard from choking him to death. Then another man stepped up and said the Commander should decide what to do with them. So the scarred guy—*Nix*, Charlie heard someone call him—let go of Charlie's throat only long enough to start marching him across the street and town square into what looked to be an old courthouse.

People in the street all stopped to stare.

As soon as they got in the building, a man's voice echoed off the granite walls. "—the rules apply to every woman who enters the township."

"What if I said I was a lesbian?" an angry woman's voice challenged.

There was a pause. Then, "Are you?"

Another long pause. "Yes. Yes, I *am*. So no matter how long you give me to *acclimate*," the word came out acidic, "to the idea as you call it, it would still be rape. No matter what."

What in the holy fuck was going on in this place? Even the huge oaf dragging him around had paused in the corridor outside the door as the shouting continued.

Charlie's eyes shot to Shay. Some woman in there was talking about being raped. Coming here had been a bad idea. He never should have risked it. He was so blinded with excitement about seeing his sister again and Shay had been convinced it would be a safe place. But they were obviously so, so wrong.

"You're being impossible."

"Me?" the woman sounded absolutely enraged. "I was the commander of a sovereign territory and you brought me here against my will. Now you try to impose your *barbaric* polygamic practices on me, and *I'm* impossible? This is all bullshit nonsense anyway. What we need to be discussing is organizing a rescue mission to go back for the rest of the women still being held at Nomansland—"

Charlie's whole body jolted. They knew about Nomansland?

"I told you, I've put the request in to President Goddard multiple times. But he doesn't feel it's a priority at this time considering our limited resources—"

"Not a *priority*?" the woman all but roared.

"We'll be out here all fucking day if we wait for these two to stop," Nix said, rolling his eyes and knocking. Without waiting for a response, he pushed the door slightly open and said loudly, "Bad time?"

He slid it open wider, revealing a woman with long blonde dreadlocks standing toe to toe with a tall, distinguished looking man who was dressed in similar military fatigues as the guards.

"I was just leaving," the woman said, still glaring at the man for another long second before turning on her toe with a grand flip of her rope-like hair.

She stormed past them, only pausing when she noticed Shay. "Oh. Hi. This bastard gives you any trouble," her eyes flicked back toward the man by the big oak desk, "you come find me."

"Drea," the man said sharply, but the blonde just squeezed Shay's arm and then left without a backward glance.

The man by the table sighed heavily and waved them in. "What is it now?"

He stood up straighter when Shay moved out from behind Nix, though. "Oh. Hello. I'm Commander Wolford."

He smiled and walked toward Shay like there was nothing at all unusual in the world.

"Don't you fuckin' touch her," Charlie snarled, yanking to get away from the big ape who had a tighter hold on him than ever.

The Commander leveled a glare over Charlie's shoulder, presumably at Nix. "Who is this? What's he done?"

"He's a stranger. He showed up at the border today asking about Audrey. Claiming he was her brother." He jerked one of Charlie's arms up and back in a way that almost had his bone snapping. "Her *dead* brother. The only fucker who'd even know her name and to say he was her brother would be her fucking cousin, who tried to—"

Charlie jerked his head around to look at Nix, his eyes wide. "She's here?" Jesus, it was true. She was really here. He hadn't let himself really believe it. But the only way Nix could have known any of what he'd just said was if Audrey was really here.

"I *am* her brother," Charlie said. "That day by the spring when we were attacked. I was hit over the head and the last thing I saw was those bastards going for her. Is she okay?" The man had relaxed his grip on Charlie but his face was impassive. "Just tell me if she's okay," Charlie demanded.

"She's fine," the Commander said from behind him.

Charlie swung around. "I'll believe it when I see it. Where is she? Take me to her. Now."

"You're in no position to be making demands," came the growl from behind him.

"Oh yeah?" Charlie challenged. He was tired of this bastard's attitude. "And who the hell are you to even get a say in it?"

"I'm the Security Squadron Captain. And her husband."

Her... *what?*

"You son of a bitch," Charlie yelled and launched himself at the larger man even though his hands were still zip tied behind his back.

He hit a solid wall of muscle and all but bounced off. Motherf— As soon as he got his strength back, he'd—

"Nix," the Commander snapped. "Enough. Go get Audrey. You know how happy she'll be to see her brother's alive."

"*If* he's her brother." Nix glared at Charlie.

"Well the quickest way to find out would be to go get Audrey, wouldn't it?"

Nix's mouth went tight but he finally sent a sharp nod in the Commander's direction. He didn't leave before directing a harsh, "Watch him," to the other guard, though.

"What the hell is going on here?" Charlie moved further into the room toward the Commander. "That woman when we came in. She was talking about polygamy and rape and now I find out my sister has a *husband* after only three months."

The Commander let out a heavy sigh and put a hand to his temple. "We live in a new world. Things couldn't go on as they were or—"

"Look," Shay said, cutting in and stepping between the Commander and Charlie, eyes on Charlie. "I probably should have clued you in to a few things before we got here. Then again, we were escaping Travis Territory on a four-wheeler and didn't exactly stop for snacks or to chat along the way, so..." she lifted her shoulders in a helpless little shrug.

"What?" Charlie took a step toward Shay. "What aren't you telling me?"

"Charlie! Oh my God!"

Charlie whipped around. Audrey. The relief of seeing her safe and healthy made him stagger a step backward. She came running toward him, a huge, disbelieving grin stretched across her face.

She flung herself at him, wrapping her arms around him. "How? You were dead! The blood. There was so much blood!"

Then she pulled back, face stricken. "Oh my God. You weren't dead and I just *left* you there. Oh God, Charlie. How can you ever—

Oh my God, why are your arms tied behind your back. Nix, cut him loose. He's my brother!"

Nix did as she said and Charlie didn't even take a swing at him, that's how relieved he was to see his sister again. He pulled her back into his arms, shuddering with relief.

"Hush." He pulled her back into his arms. *Jesus*. After all this time, she was safe. She was here and she was safe. He hadn't failed her completely. She was alive. Unless he was dreaming. Oh God don't let this be a dream.

"Are you real?" she whispered and he laughed.

"I was just wondering the same thing."

She giggled against his chest and it was the most wonderful sound he'd ever heard in his life.

He pulled back just so he could get another look at her. It had only been three months but she seemed so changed. She wasn't as skinny for one. Her cheeks were rounded out. And her hair looked... softer, or something.

And well, she was smiling. Like she couldn't stop. And Charlie didn't think it was an act for the other people in the room. Audrey never could act for shit. She'd done a play when she was in Jr. High and it was so painful he felt the audience cringing around him during her speaking parts.

But that was part of what made Audrey Audrey.

"Jesus, where are my manners?" Charlie ran a hand through his hair. "Audrey, this is Shay. She helped me escape and get here." He ushered Shay forward.

Shay held out her hand but Audrey threw her arms around her just like she had Charlie. "Thank you, thank you, thank you, *thank you*. You've won a devotee for life."

"So the border patrol agents said you claimed to have come from Travis Territory. That you were detained there against your wishes?" the Commander broke in.

Charlie nodded absentmindedly, still too focused on his sister.

"Yes," Shay answered, and Charlie realized the Commander had been speaking to her all along.

"And I always heard talk about this place," she continued. "No one watches what they say in front of the help. So I knew you treated your women well here. And I don't have a problem with the lottery system. I just want a place where I can finally be safe."

The Commander's face softened but Charlie could only look back and forth between them in confusion. What in the holy fuck were they talking about? "Lottery? What is she talking about?"

"Charlie, calm down," Audrey said, putting a hand on his forearm. "Just give them a second to explain. It sounds bad at first, I know it does, but it can actually turn out really—"

Why were they all suddenly acting like a bomb was about to detonate?

"What. Is. She. Talking. About?"

"It's a lottery to see who I'll marry," Shay said calmly.

Charlie all but choked, sure at first he'd misheard her.

But then she went on. "There aren't enough women to go around anymore. Everybody knows that. So Central Texas South Territory came up with a solution. Each woman marries five men. The only way for it to be fair is to have a lott—"

"No fucking way." Charlie's head whipped around to his sister. "Aud. Tell me you didn't."

Audrey's face was screwed up in that way she did when she used to come home with a bad report card she knew would disappoint her parents. Fuckin' hell.

"Look, Char, it sounds worse than it is. Once you get to know the guys themselves, you'll understand. They have protections in place. Not just anyone can enter the lotto."

"You don't believe that," Charlie scoffed. "You're a shit liar. Why are you protecting them, Aud? Are they holding you here against your will? Cause I'll—"

"No," Audrey breathed out loudly in frustration. "Okay, look, I still have some reservations about the whole thing. My husbands treat me like a queen but there was one case of abuse discovered recently."

Charlie's jaw tightened and all he wanted to do was grab Shay and Audrey, steal one of the trucks he'd seen outside, and get the hell *out* of here.

"But we've cracked down on the vetting process since then," the

Commander broke in. "It's more rigorous than ever. Any man raises a hand against a woman, he loses the hand and then is exiled."

"Oh yeah? Did that happen to whoever abused that woman?"

The Commander's gaze stayed rock steady. "Yes, it did. To four of the husbands. Unfortunately, the crowd got to the fifth before we could. Jacob's Well does not tolerate mistreatment of women."

"No, you just treat them like objects to raffle off with no say in the matter. They're human beings," Charlie said incredulously. He couldn't believe he was having to explain this fucking concept. "They have the right to choose how they live their lives. Who they live their lives with. You can't just—"

"You think *you* can solve all the world's problems?" the Commander cut him off, obviously out of patience. "You want to restore law and order in the midst of anarchy?" He held out a hand. "Go right ahead. Be my guest. This is the best we can do in imperfect circumstances. But your own sister has found happiness here. And so have a lot of other people."

"This is what I want," Shay said, stepping forward again. "But I've seen enough in my life not to just take some stranger's word for it, okay? So let's wait a little bit before we pass judgement. Take a look around. Meet everyone."

Charlie nodded. Good. So she'd call a stop to this nonsense as soon as she saw for herself how insane—

"I want protection I trust. Which is why I'll only agree to a lottery if it's for four husbands," her eyes flicked his way, "with Charlie as the fifth."

Wait.

WHAT?

CHAPTER THREE

SHAY

Shay clocked the exits as she followed Sophia, the Commander's eighteen-year-old daughter, to the room where Shay was supposed to sleep for the night. In the Commander's own house.

"Oh my gosh, I'm just *so* excited you're here," Sophia said, clapping in excitement. "We haven't had a new girl in ages. Well," she rolled her eyes. "There was Drea, but she barely counts."

Drea. The name was familiar. Oh right, she was the woman they'd overheard arguing with the Commander when they'd been first brought into the courthouse.

"I don't think that woman would understand the concept of fun if it walked up and bit her in the—" Sophia broke off, eyes going wide like she'd just realized what she was saying. "Oh, um. Anyway." She laughed and held out a hand, gesturing at the room. "*Ta da.*"

Shay glanced around. Wow. That was a lot of... pink. Sort of like a bottle of Pepto-Bismol had thrown up all over it.

They were on the second story. A quick glance showed the window wasn't barred. After Sophia left, Shay would check if there was a trellis or drain pipe she could climb down if need be. If the last eight years had taught her anything, it was to always have an escape route ready. "Nice place."

Sophia laughed. "It's atrocious. You don't have to pretend. The style of my eight-year-old princess-loving self is going to haunt me forever, seems like. But it's a waste of resources to repaint and redecorate when so many other homes need *actual* repair so..." she held out her arms, eyebrows scrunched, "welcome to my pink palace...?"

Shay pulled her lips up at the side in what she hoped passed for a smile. That looked natural, right? She hadn't been around... well, *people*... in a long time.

And this girl was a little *too* bubbly and friendly. In Travisville, they had girls like her to greet any new female arrivals who were brought in. *Welcome, welcome. You're finally safe. Travisville is a wonderful place to make your new home!*

Then—after the girls were fed and back in good health—came the bait and switch. They were sold off to the highest bidder, often after six months of 'training' at the processing center.

Jacob's Well wasn't supposed to be that kind of place.

Then again, neither was Travisville. Officially, at least. Slavery was illegal in the new Republic of Texas, but that had never stopped anyone in Travisville. Especially Colonel Travis himself, who had a reputation as the best flesh trader in Texas. Among certain circles at least.

Then again, it was from the higher ups in Travisville that she'd overheard the rumors about Jacob's Well. And since the monsters there didn't like the Commander here—and that was putting it mildly —that only said good things for him. Colonel Travis himself and the Commander were enemies. Apparently it was personal, too, though she'd never heard the whole story.

But Colonel Travis's temper was legendary and he didn't make a secret of his animosity for Jacob's Well's Commander.

And the enemy of my enemy is my friend, right?

She wasn't the naïve girl she'd once been, though. She didn't trust anyone in this township farther than she could throw them.

Which, considering how large the border guards and that huge scarred man, Nix, had been, wasn't very far at all.

So how come all she wanted right now was to run downstairs and throw herself in Charlie's arms?

You don't know that he's any better than anyone else in Travisville was. Not really. Bringing him a few meals here and there didn't mean she *knew* him.

Yeah, they'd been helping each other... but escaping had been in his own interest. It wasn't about her at all. They'd used each other. Plain and simple.

Still, even as she thought it, it felt wrong.

She'd decided a long time ago that the only thing she could ever trust from another person was that they'd always be looking out for their own self-interest.

But Charlie... if he was just looking out for himself, then why did he object so much to the marriage thing? It was the perfect opportunity if he wanted to fuck her.

Then again, he *had* been trying to get her to leave Jacob's Well almost as soon as they'd gotten there. Maybe he wanted her all to himself and didn't like the idea of sharing?

Again, the thought felt wrong though.

Maybe it was the way he'd followed her directions so unquestioningly as they'd snuck off the old college campus where he'd been kept prisoner in Travisville. She was so used to Jason grabbing her elbow and jerking her back if she took even a step ahead of him on the rare occasions when they walked anywhere together.

Stay at my back, bitch. Who do you think you are? Bitches walk at their master's heels.

But Charlie had just waited patiently for each whispered direction as she led him down to the river. It had been a new moon last night, so there'd barely been any ambient light. Just the little bit from the few buildings powered by solar panels whose batteries had been charging all day.

When Charlie took her arm, Shay had almost jumped out of her skin. But his touch had been gentle. He was reaching for her so *she* could lead *him*.

She couldn't remember the last time someone had touched her without it being—

A knock came at the door and then Audrey peeked her head in. "Hey guys."

"Hey hon." Sophia's face brightened, which Shay would have said was impossible just a minute before. Shay'd never met anyone so damn... *smiley*. And she had been in a sorority back in college before The Fall, so that was saying something.

"You and Charlie been reconnecting?" Sophia asked.

Audrey nodded with a wobbly grin and a sheen of tears coating her eyes. "I just can't believe he's really here. That he didn't— That he's—"

"Oh honey." Sophia jumped up from where she'd been perched on the edge of the bed and hurried over to her friend, wrapping her up in a hug.

Shay felt awkward and out of place watching the affection between the two friends. Everything since breaking Charlie out of his cell had felt a little like a movie—like she was outside her body watching all these things happen without really being part of any of it.

If she closed her eyes, she'd wake up in the little broom closet where she slept. It would be another day of arduous and never-ending routine.

Cooking. Cleaning. And waiting—always waiting in case *he* felt in the mood to call for her. Jason liked her to be at his beck and call, any time of day or night. Sometimes for himself, sometimes to entertain friends...

But God, she was being such a fucking princess about the whole thing. She'd had it so much easier than most women in Travisville. She'd never seen the inside of the Women's Processing Center. She hadn't been sold off to some stranger as a sex slave.

Back in the beginning, when she was just a stupid, stupid girl, she'd even given herself to Jason willingly. He'd been handsome, charismatic...

So who could she blame except herself for everything that followed?

She was too old to have been that naïve—nineteen when the

bombs were dropped. That was old enough to have recognized Jason for the psychopath he was.

The strong will always take advantage of the weak.

It was one of the most basic facts of life. But she'd been stubbornly walking around like a romantic little fool. She might as well have painted a target on her back announcing: Stupid and Desperate: Please Take Advantage Of.

Love will conquer all, she had told herself in the beginning. And later, she thought, *my love can change him*. It was far too late when she realized that he'd never change and finally understood that fighting back was futile.

But she'd helped Charlie escape. She was here, in Jacob's Well, wasn't she? She'd really done it. Those weren't things a weak person did.

Maybe, just maybe, she could wrestle back some control over her own life. One way or another, this was a new chapter. It all depended on what she made of the opportunity.

"And you," Audrey said. Shay looked up to see Charlie's sister coming toward her, arms outstretched. "Oh my God, I can never thank you enough."

Before Shay could really register what was happening, Audrey had her wrapped in a hug so tight Shay had a hard time breathing. "Charlie told me how brave you were. How you risked everything to get him out of there." She squeezed even tighter for a moment before pulling back and looking Shay in the eye. Tears spilled down Audrey's cheeks, but her smile was so wide and full of gratitude, Shay immediately wanted to jerk away.

These people didn't know her. If they did, they wouldn't like what they saw. She wasn't a good person.

But that was fine, she'd made her peace with the fact a long time ago. She did what she needed to do in order to get by and to take care of what needed taking care of. Freeing Charlie had just been a means to an end, not something she'd done out of the kindness of her heart.

"It was nothing," she mumbled, pulling back.

But Audrey just scoffed. "You gave my brother back to me from the dead! That's not nothing."

"Yeah, well." Shay tried for a smile and lifted a hand to the back of her neck, grabbing her hair and twisting it into a loose bun before securing it with a hair band Sophia lent her. "No big deal."

"She's modest, Audrey, leave her be," Sophia said. "Besides, the real question is who's gonna be chosen in her lottery. I saw Daddy leaving about twenty minutes ago. They could be drawing the names right this moment." She clapped excitedly. "Who do you think would be a good match for her?" she asked Audrey. "You've been here long enough to get a feel for the town."

But Audrey just laughed and held her hands up in surrender. "I leave that to the town gamblers and the romantics. All right, I've got to head out. Nix gets grumpy when he doesn't have a warm body to snuggle up to at night."

"Swoon," Sophia said with a longing little sigh, holding her hands to her chest. "I want a Nix."

Audrey laughed. "Hands off. He's all mine."

Sophia rolled her eyes. "I don't want *your* Nix. I want *a* Nix. Someone strong and manly and capable like him." She made a little squee noise and hopped up and down. "Just four months away from my nineteenth birthday now. I can barely sleep some nights I'm so excited!"

Audrey just shook her head good naturedly and dropped a kiss to Sophia's forehead. "Take care, sweetie." She looked to Shay, her gaze warm. "So good to meet you. I'm sure we'll see a lot of each other." Her smile broadened. "A little birdie told me we're about to be sisters-in-law, after all."

Shay nodded, again attempting what she hoped came off as a natural smile. She'd just gotten away from one controlling man. And here she was, marrying five more.

But it was all part of the plan.

And it *wouldn't* be the same. Not at all. She wasn't the naïve girl she'd been eight years ago when Jason first walked into town. She'd learned the lessons that had been beaten into her and she'd learned them well.

She'd be the strong one now.

And she could give them her body, that was nothing. She'd given it a hundred times before. The difference was, this time it was *her* doing the giving, not Jason. And that was everything.

Plus, in return she'd gain everything she'd ever wanted. *Family*. It was the only thing worth fighting for in this shitastic world. She was done with being alone. Nobody could survive alone, not for long.

"So," Sophia said after Audrey left, pulling out a big binder and a purple glitter pen. "Let's make a list of potentials and then we can put down pros and cons for each of them."

When Shay just kept standing there, Sophia waved her forward again as she settled in on the bed, back against the plush pink headboard. "Come on, silly."

Sophia's forehead scrunched in concentration. "All right. There's Sebastian, he's the town's chief engineer." She glanced up at Shay and smiled, one eyebrow lifting. "He's handsome. And smart. That's two in the pros column already for him. And, let me think. Oh! Ryder. He's the blacksmith, and just between you and me," she leaned in, "I've daydreamed about those huge muscles of his more than once."

Shay shook her head and laughed. See, she could pull off being a normal girl. No problem.

"Oh my God," Sophia said, pulling back. "I can't believe I forgot about Diego! He supervises all Central Texas South's construction crews. He's tall, has the most gorgeous black hair, and—"

As Sophia went on, scribbling names and attributes about man after man, Shay could only think about one. Charlie. If Audrey and her husband, Nix, had finally left, did that mean Charlie was downstairs all alone?

Was he thinking about her? Or was he just happy to be reunited with his sister? She knew she'd taken him by surprise demanding that he be one of her husbands.

That had *not* been in the plan.

You don't really *know him*, she reminded herself for the umpteenth time. *He's no more trustworthy than any other man.*

But he'd seemed so concerned about her, staying close the whole time they snuck from the college down to the river. He'd helped her down the river bank and gestured her to get in the river first, holding out a thick branch to make sure she didn't get swept away too quickly.

Even as they floated the few miles down river, he'd make sure to always stay within a few feet of her. And when they reached the small dam that marked the border of Travisville? Without a word, he'd been the one to sneak onto the river bank and take out the guard there, securing them the four-wheeler they'd ridden all the way to Central Texas South's border, right at Jacob's Well.

He hadn't minded the fact that she'd climbed on and taken the controls.

She'd been relying on a map she'd overseen, along with her memories of the area from long ago. Shay had lived in Travisville for almost a decade, and she knew it like the back of her hand. Back before The Fall, she used to drive all over the hill country in the area because she loved the views.

But Charlie hadn't known that. He'd just climbed on the four-wheeler behind her and wrapped his strong, steady arms around her waist in complete trust.

Maybe it was that he reminded her of how she used to be. A thousand years ago... And it made her want to smack him and shout, "Wake up!" before the world crushed him.

She shook her head and looked toward the window. It was still dark out. What time was it? Ten or eleven at night?

"I think I'm going to try to get some sleep," she said, cutting Sophia off mid-sentence as she listed another guy.

"Oh of course, I'm sorry. You must be exhausted and here I am rattling on." Sophia immediately hopped off the bed. "I just get so carried away. Like I said, we don't get a new girl very often." She paused, tilted her head to the side, and grinned at Shay. "I'm just *so* happy you're here."

Shay shrank a little under Sophia's intense consideration. "Yeah. Um. Me too..."

Sophia grinned even wider and Shay's face hurt just looking at her but then Sophia was bouncing over and throwing her arms around her. Shay went immediately stiff but Sophia just kept on squeezing.

Finally Sophia pulled back, laughing. "Sorry, I'm a hugger. Dad's always trying to remind me of a little thing called *personal space* but I usually only remember after I've violated it."

"No, it's fine," Shay said, voice as stiff as her spine.

"Oh good," Sophia said. "Because you know how sometimes you just have so much happiness and excitement pent up in you and it just has to come out somehow?"

Shay could only stare at the girl and blink. "Um..."

But Sophia just laughed again and pulled her into another hug. It was much quicker, though. Thankfully.

"Sleep tight," Sophia said as she pulled back. "Don't let the bedbugs bite. And just think, tomorrow you'll get to meet your new husbands. So exciting!"

And on that ecstatic utterance, Sophia flounced out of the room.

Leaving Shay feeling a little shell-shocked. While she'd prepared herself for a lot of different scenarios on this little adventure, she could genuinely say that Sophia Wolford was something she'd never expected.

Shay thought she'd feel relieved to be alone. It was the first moment of solitude she'd had since before she'd broken Charlie out. But instead, the room felt... too quiet.

She glanced at the door Sophia had exited through and immediately hurried over, trying the knob. It turned easily and when she pulled on the door, it gave with no problem.

So she wasn't locked in. Okay. Good. Her hammering heartbeat slowed, but only marginally. She went back to the bed and changed into the sleep clothes Sophia had laid out for her—an oversized shirt and some short girly boxers with hearts on them.

After changing, she sat on the bed, back against the headboard, eyes darting around at every little sound.

Sophia said her father was out conducting the lottery right now. What if Shay's new *husbands* decided they didn't want to wait for tomorrow and came for her in the middle of the night?

Yes, she was committed to seeing this through—but only on *her* terms.

When had any man she'd ever known been willing to let her have anything on her terms, though? Never. Not in recent memory.

Except for one.

So before she fully realized what she was doing, she was bolting for the door and down the stairs.

Charlie might be naïve but he was strong. Even after losing weight from not having a normal diet, she'd seen him working out in his cell regularly. He'd taken out that guard at the dam like it was nothing. And she'd felt it when he'd wrapped his arms around her on the four-wheeler.

And in a world where she didn't trust anyone, for some reason, she trusted that he genuinely wanted to protect her.

Foolish probably.

Even after all these years, maybe she hadn't learned her lesson after all.

CHAPTER FOUR

CHARLIE

10 Minutes Earlier

"So, you just, what?" Nix asked Charlie, eyes hard. "Up and walked out of Travis's camp? Just like that?"

Charlie's jaw was so rigid, he was sure he was about to crack a damn tooth. Reconnecting with Audrey had been more than he could have ever dreamed of.

Except.

Except for the fact that her damn *husband* had been breathing down their necks the whole time. Charlie had only had a few minutes alone with his sister when they first got to the Commander's house. Nix and the Commander were stopped outside by another soldier in fatigues to discuss something. Charlie dragged Audrey into the house and asked in a rush, "Aud, tell me the truth. Are they holding you against your will? Because I swear, I can get you out. We'll find a w—"

"What?" She'd sounded flabbergasted. "Charlie, no. I love my life here. I love my husbands."

Husbands. Fucking *plural*. Charlie flinched when she'd said it but she just kept repeating that once he got to know her husbands, he'd understand.

Well, he'd spent all evening with the son of a bitch currently sitting across the living room from him, Nix, and he was no less tempted to murder him. The whole time Audrey sat on the couch opposite Charlie, the fucker had kept a hand on her knee, rubbing circles with his thumb. And every time his thumb traveled in that little looping path, Charlie fantasized ways of killing him. He could use the fire poker. Or there was that carving knife he'd seen in the kitchen. Really there were all sorts of things he could use as a weapon. A man could get inventive with enough motive and Charlie, he was motivated.

"Seems awful convenient to me, you just showing up out of the blue like this."

Charlie shot up out of the armchair where he'd been sitting. "You got something you wanna say, just say it."

Nix stood up too and took a step toward him. "I'm saying your story sounds like bullshit. I know Arnold Travis and no way you just walked out of the center of his encampment."

"I never said I was in the center." Charlie's eyes narrowed. "What the fuck do *you* know that you're not saying?"

Nix scoffed like Charlie was an idiot. "I'm the Captain of the Security Squadron. It's my business to know about the layout of our chief rival's town."

"Oh yeah? Just like it was your business to fuck my sister and brainwash her into thinking she's happy here?"

"You better watch your mouth." Nix jabbed a finger his direction, "before I shut it permanently."

"Aw, what's wrong? I'm not a vulnerable, impressionable young girl, so you can't mind-fuck me, is that it?"

"You son of a—"

Right as Nix started toward Charlie, Audrey came bounding down the stairs. "Hey guys, I'm ready to—" She paused on the last step, eyes shooting back and forth from Nix to Charlie. "What's going on? Is something wrong?"

Nix's face, which had been hard with menace only moments ago, turned suddenly soft as he looked at Audrey. "No problem, babe. Your brother and I were just getting to know each other better."

Audrey's head swung Charlie's way, like she was looking for confirmation. Charlie could see by the hope in her eyes that she wanted what Nix had said to be true. And if he was going to help her, he needed her to trust him. He couldn't alienate her right out of the gate. It would take time to see what sort of conditioning they'd done to her so he could figure out how to *undo* it.

"Yep. He used to be a big Cowboys fan. Just like Dad." Charlie slapped Nix on the shoulder a little harder than was strictly necessary. "Say, Nix," Charlie looked over at him, "how old did you say you were again?"

"I didn't," Nix growled.

"Oh good," Audrey said, either missing the tension between them or choosing to ignore it. She pulled both of them into a group hug. "Now my family is complete," she breathed out happily, eyes closed in contentment.

Charlie and Nix just glared at each other over her head.

Then Nix put an arm over Audrey's shoulder. "Bedtime, wife." And he all but dragged her toward the door.

"Oh," Audrey said, and then giggled and swatted at his hand when he pinched her ass. Right there in front of Charlie. Fucking bastard.

"See you tomorrow, Charlie," Audrey called over her shoulder. Then she was gone, the door shutting behind her with a resounding *slam*.

Charlie dug his hands into his hair and pulled, leaning over to growl in frustration through clenched teeth. This was so goddamned infuriating. To be so close to his sister and then for her to be acting like, like...

He shook his head. He couldn't believe this was how he found her after all these months. Was he glad that she was healthy? Of course he was. But while she might be in great physical condition, her mental faculties were another story entirely.

What in the holy fuck had they *done* to her? Okay, so she had seemed normal enough all evening. Over dinner, she'd laughed and joked just like she was... well, the old Audrey.

But she couldn't be. She'd been married off to *five*... Jesus, he couldn't even wrap his head around it. And they thought they were gonna do the same thing to Shay? Over his dead fucking body.

His eyes went to the stairs. The house was quiet. He had no idea what time it was. It had been dark for hours. The Commander had gone out a while ago and who knew when he'd be back. Could Charlie sneak up there, grab Audrey, and get out, or were there soldiers on guard outside the house watching in case they tried to do just that?

I know it all seems weird and too good to be true, but it's real. Audrey's words from earlier came back to him. At which point he'd looked at her like she was crazy. One woman having to marry five guys was not his idea of 'too good to be true.' The fact that she was even saying that shit was worrisome. Then she went on, *I'm not saying it's perfect here or some kind of utopia, but these are good people.*

Yeah, well, he'd feel better with a knife strapped to his belt just the same. He slipped into the kitchen and looked through the knives in the block on the counter. The butcher's knife might be a little bit overkill, but he grabbed it anyway, along with several smaller steak knives. He stowed the butcher's knife underneath the couch cushion and then made up the couch with the sheets and blankets Sophia had brought down earlier.

One knife he put under his pillow, the other underneath the couch, still easily accessible. Only then did he turn out the lights. He'd scope out the situation in the backyard in a few hours. If it was all clear, then he'd go get Shay. The bastards had shoved a black bag over his head on the way in to town, but they obviously had horses, and those shouldn't be that hard to find—

A noise had him sitting up straight and reaching for the knife under his pillow.

Until he saw the feminine figure coming down the stairs by the light of a single candle still burning on the mantle.

A feminine figure wearing only what looked like a long t-shirt.

Charlie gulped.

"Shay?" he whispered. When she didn't answer, for a second, he was horrified that it was the Commander's daughter coming to, like, seduce him or something.

But then Shay's soft voice came through the darkness. "It's me."

He relaxed but only for a moment. "You ready to get out of here? I haven't had a chance to scout the grounds yet, but if you just give me a second, I can check the yard and see if—"

"Shh," Shay said, coming and sitting down on the couch beside him. "Lay down." Tentatively, she extended a hand and touched his shoulder. Then she ran it down to his elbow. "I just..." she trailed off, pulling her hand back like she'd suddenly been burned. "It's stupid but..."

"What? What is it? Did something happen up there? I swear, Shay, I'll—"

"No, no, nothing like that."

Then she grabbed his hand and after another second, tentatively toyed with his fingers. Charlie's skin felt electric everywhere her skin touched his. And not just because she was a beautiful woman... or because of all the years it had been since touching a woman was even a possibility.

Touch from Shay seemed like a privilege. Every time she touched Charlie, he got the feeling it was a big step for her somehow. There was always a hesitancy to it, like she was proving something to herself or pushing a boundary.

So he kept his own hand slack, not wanting her to pull back like a skittish deer.

"I just didn't like being up there alone," she whispered it like she was confessing a personal failing. "I mean, I spent plenty of time alone in Travisville. But now that I'm here, it's different. I don't know how to explain." Her head twisted as she looked back and forth from the front door to the doorway that led to the kitchen.

Charlie was close enough to her that he felt the small shudder go through her body. She dropped her face. In the darkness he couldn't make out her features but he could imagine the distress on her lovely face.

"Do you think I could... I don't know. Maybe sleep with you down here tonight?"

"Oh." Charlie swallowed. The truth? Her being so close already had him fighting a stiffy. Which made him the world's biggest douchebag. Especially because as soon as she'd sat down in just that t-shirt, her long legs on display in the light of a sputtering candle on the mantle, he'd had the overwhelming thought: *she said she'll marry you. Which means you might get to have sex with her sometime soon.*

"Shay." He shook his head, shifting so he could sit up—but her hand shot back to his forearm to stop him. Her grip was so forceful it took him by surprise. This time when she looked at him, the angle was just right that her eyes caught and reflected the candlelight.

And he could see the fear there. Real, terrible fear. "Please. Can't we just lie here together tonight? Leave everything else till the morning?"

Her looking so afraid had taken care of his hard on at least. But it ripped his chest open to know terrible things had probably happened to her to put that fear there.

"Yes." He shook his head and laid back down, opening his arms. "Yes, of course. Whatever you need."

As she laid down, head in the crook of his arm and back against his chest, he vowed, "Always. Whatever you need, I'll always be here for you."

This was one vow he swore he would never break.

CHAPTER FIVE

HENRY

Henry had a picture of the life he wanted for himself. Riches, wealth, and a beautiful woman standing by his side.

A beautiful woman he was only moments away from meeting.

He swallowed hard. Damn, was he nervous? When was the last time he, Henry Sutherland, had been nervous about anything? He'd faced down the meanest mob bosses, traded with MC presidents, had even traveled to the Mexican front and made a back deal with a colonel of the 5th Mexican brigade to smuggle solar panels into the country. So no, he was *not* afraid of meeting his future wife.

Then why on earth was his hand shaking as he lifted it to the brass knocker?

He stood up straighter and banged on the door.

Sophia opened it, standing there in her pajama pants and an oversized pink t-shirt with a picture of a kitten on it. She grinned huge with surprise when she saw Henry.

"Henry." Her voice was full of pleasure. "What are you doing here at this time of day?"

Henry smiled back in amusement. She was less than subtle about her schoolgirl crush on him. Never mind the fact that he was the same age as her father. Granted, he and her dad, Eric, were only forty-one, but still, math was math.

"I come bearing breakfast." He held up the basket he'd prepared.

Her eyes got even brighter.

Oh dear. He softened his voice, knowing there was no real good way to break the news to Sophia. "For my betrothed. I was one of the lottery winners."

Sophia's face went pale so fast Henry thought she might pass out.

"Sophia," Henry reached for her when she stumbled sideways.

"Oh," she gasped, regaining her balance and waving him away. "I'm fine." She kept her face averted. "Fine. She's— Shay is— that way." Sophia pointed toward the living room and then fled up the stairs.

"Sophia," Henry called, stepping into the house but all he heard was the sound of light footsteps and then the slam of a door.

He sighed and wiped his feet on the welcome rug. Poor girl. There was nothing he could do about it. He'd tried to dissuade her affections over the past few years but this was probably the only thing that was going to do the trick.

"Um, hello?"

Henry's attention turned to the living room and—

Good Lord. The most gorgeous women he'd ever seen stood up from the couch and Henry couldn't help the grin from stretching across his face. "Why hello, beautiful. I come, your humble suitor, bearing gifts." He held up the basket and bowed slightly.

"Who the fuck are you?"

Beside the beautiful woman popped up a man's head. He was a decidedly *less* pleasant sight, and not just because his hair was mussed and he had a dark, tangled beard.

Still, deciding that discretion was the better part of valor and all that, Henry dipped a small bow to the man as well. "Henry Sutherland, at your service. I am betrothed to this beautiful young woman. If you are Shay Monroe, that is."

The woman nodded, eyeing him warily. *Shay.* Henry grinned. She was beautiful enough to be a queen. She would more than do.

Henry had always liked the finer things and it wasn't something he'd apologize for. He'd worked hard every day of his life because that was the promise he'd been fed all growing up—work hard and you can achieve whatever your heart desires.

Well, his heart desired a winter chalet in Paris and a Jaguar XLJ and he'd worked his ass off to get them. From the trailer park to a chalet. He couldn't count the number of people who'd told him his dreams were ridiculous. Impossible, even.

He'd proved them all wrong. Every. Single. One.

He'd had it all. He worked at the most prestigious investment firm in Dallas. Headhunters from New York were always trying to scoop him up, but like he told them whenever they did, Texas was his home. Where else did churches only *barely* outnumber strip clubs? Sin and hellfire and tits and ass were the Texas way. Hypocrisy and bacon, mmm, they just tasted like home to him. If there were other reasons... well, he preferred not to dwell on the past, even if it meant he had a connection to this land he couldn't seem to shake no matter how many vocal coaches he'd hired over the years to help him get rid of his white trash twang.

So yes, he'd turned down every New York offer and stayed in the Lone Star State, doing what few could ever claim—living the life he'd always dreamed of. He finally made top partner at the firm, which meant the years of eighty-hour work weeks were at last behind him. He could enjoy his success at last.

Then, one week later, the first cases of Xterminate were reported.

Cause life was a bitch like that.

"I brought spinach omelets. I suggest we hurry to eat them. Actually having eggs only to eat them cold would be a tragedy too great for words."

Henry strode into the house and set down the basket on the dining room table. The house had an open floor plan, with the dining and living rooms visible from the kitchen. Henry busied himself with checking cabinets and pulling down plates and silverware.

"Gabriel is working and will not be here until later," Henry said conversationally, not looking over his shoulder to see where Shay was or if she was watching him even though he was dying to.

He certainly wanted to stare at *her* for hours like he used to at the expensive artwork he collected in his past life. He doubted he'd find a single imperfection and even if he did, it would only serve to make her more unique and precious.

A woman truly worthy of the man he had been and strove every day to become again.

"But I do not know where Jonas and Rafael are." Henry looked down at his watch and frowned. "Rafael is a former Air Force pilot and—"

A clumsy knock sounded at the door, cutting him off. The door pushed open before anyone could move toward it, and there stood Jonas in the rectangle of morning light.

Jonas, the former golden boy. Beloved preacher. All-state track star back in high school. The man who could do no wrong in the town's eyes.

No matter how much of a fuck up he was these days.

Jonas held a joint to his mouth, his cheeks hollowing as he sucked in one last hit before stubbing it out on the side of the doorjamb and tossing it into the shrubs by the porch. Then he stumbled inside, his eyes bloodshot and his hair standing up on one side like he'd just rolled out of bed. He probably had.

Henry stood up straighter and smoothed his hands down his suit-vest. Jonas was an affront to all things civilized. How was the world ever supposed to recover if slobs like Jonas kept walking around like they were extras in some old *Living Dead* TV show?

"*Jesus*." Henry tipped his nose up. "This is how you come to meet your future wife?"

Jonas gave a sardonic grin. "Not in the Jesus business anymore."

Henry expelled an annoyed breath and turned back to Shay.

He finally gave himself permission to look at her. She had stood up. And hot *damn*. She had on a large shapeless t-shirt similar to what Sophia's. But instead of pajama pants, she was wearing the tiniest little short shorts that exposed *acres* of thigh.

He forced his eyes back up to her face. He didn't want to be caught ogling. Granted it had been a long time since he'd properly been with a woman, but he remembered enough to know that being caught staring never went over well.

The noise of feet on the stairs had Henry looking up again. It was Sophia. She was dressed for the day in jeans and a tight-fitting top that bared more than a little cleavage. She shot only the quickest glance Jonas's way. Did she hope to find him watching? He wanted to shake his head at her. Oh Sophia.

She jerked her gaze away like she could hear his thoughts and steadily avoided looking at him or anyone else as she hurried past. "I'll be at the Food Pantry all day. Double shift. Bye."

Then she was out the door. But not without pausing on the threshold and shooting one last lingering glance Henry's way.

But Henry only had eyes for Shay. Who looked awkwardly back and forth from Sophia to Henry.

"Sophia, wait," Shay said when Sophia's head whipped back toward the door and she all but fled.

"It's all right. Let her go." Henry stepped forward and put a hand on Shay's shoulder from behind and she jumped a mile.

"Get your hands off her," the man beside Shay growled, grabbing Henry's wrist and jerking it back.

Dammit, that hurt. But Henry just smiled. He hadn't gotten where he had in life by letting it show when things hurt.

"If you're quite done," Henry said dryly, leveling the man with a cool stare. "Kindly let go of my arm."

The man tossed Henry's arm back and Henry just continued smiling. "Charmed, I'm sure. And you are?"

The man glared.

Henry had met plenty of men like this one before. Big on brawn. Intellectually inferior. They liked staking their claim on things the same way dogs did. By effectively pissing circles around them.

"This is Charlie," Shay said, stepping between them. Her eyes dropped for a moment before lifting to meet Henry's. "And it's Henry, is that right?"

She was utterly enchanting. Henry took her hand and lifted it to his lips. "Indeed. So lovely to make your acquaintance. You have no idea how incredibly fortunate I consider myself to have been chosen as your betrothed."

"Is this guy for real?" Charlie turned to Jonas. "Who the hell talks like that at," his eyes searched the wall, settling on the wind-up grand-father clock, "eight-forty-five in the morning?"

"Fuck if I know," Jonas said from where he was leaned against the wall with his eyes closed like he could catch a nap while he waited for something interesting to happen.

Henry rolled his eyes. Some people wouldn't understand class if it came up and smacked them in the face with a can of beluga caviar.

"Should I go after Sophia?" Shay's eyes went to the door, a crease appearing between her eyebrows. "She looked upset."

"She'll be all right," Henry said. And, as much as he wanted to reach out to her again, he kept his hands to himself. She seemed a bit jumpy. Besides, all in good time.

He did step close so she could still hear him when he lowered his voice, though. "It was just a schoolgirl crush. Nothing serious."

Shay's eyes were still trained on the front door. "I doubt that's the way she saw it. Her lottery is only a few months away."

She finally turned to Henry and he felt slugged in the guts by how the morning sun made the green of her irises almost translucent. Like the finest peridot gemstone. He made a mental note. He had a line with one of the best jewelers in Texas. He wasn't Trade Secretary for nothing. He'd talk to the man about acquiring some peridot earrings that would make those gorgeous eyes pop even more. Shay deserved to be draped with jewels.

Henry pushed a stray lock of hair out of her face and tucked it behind her ear and this time, while she trembled slightly, it was far from a flinch. "I'm with you now. And like you said, Sophia will have her own lottery in a few months."

It wasn't just a line either.

He was with Shay. As soon as his name had been announced at the lottery last night, Henry had barely been able to sit still but for think-ing: *finally, finally, his life was getting back on track*.

A life far, far away from the grimy trailer his mother shared with her pimp when he was a boy.

After Xterminate hit, he'd been back there for a while.

Slogging through mud with a hundred other refugees fleeing the west Dallas suburbs. It was just sheer luck the fallout cloud blew northeast instead of west. There'd been no way to know that at the time, though. When it stormed the day after the bomb fell, the fleeing crowd went crazy, sure it was toxic nuclear rainout.

Men turned into animals, beating each other off for the smallest scrap of plastic tarp to try to stay dry. They killed one another so they could hide from the rain under the dead bodies.

It was Henry's childhood all over again except a hundred times worse—and there was no closet to hide in this time.

Day in, day out, he'd had to rub shoulder to shoulder with those animals, fighting tooth and nail for resources. He thought he'd known sacrifice the first time he crawled out from the gutter to the heights of wealth. But it was nothing to the wits and sheer determination to never give up that it took to get where he was today.

Finally, *finally*, he was poised on the threshold of resuming the closest thing this post-Fall world had to his former wealth and success.

And Shay would be the shining jewel in his crown.

CHAPTER SIX

SHAY

Henry was unexpected. He wasn't big or brutal looking. And he was clean. All plusses if she was filling in pros on Sophia's little chart.

Then again, sometimes it was the charmers who were the most dangerous. And he was handsome. He had blond hair and dark eyes. It was like a model had stepped off the pages of an old GQ magazine and into the Commander's living room. Even though it must have already been nearing eighty degrees at nine in the morning, he was dressed like he was headed into a chic big city pre-Fall office. He was wearing a well-cut suit, complete with a vest and a shining silver tie.

Shay distrusted good-looking people on principle. She always had, starting with her mother who was too beautiful for her own good. A hundred broken promises later, Shay had still somehow been an optimist by the time she left for college.

A few days in Travisville was enough to cure the most ardent optimist though, and she'd spent eight *years* there. So consider the lesson officially learned.

Another knock sounded at the door and this time Charlie went to get it. He yanked it open. "Who the hell are you?"

Guess she knew *his* feelings on the whole situation.

She moved to look over his shoulder to see who was at the door.

"You must be Rafael," she said. "Hi. I'm Shay." She pushed past a still glaring Charlie and held out her right hand to the dark-haired man standing there.

He'd had an easy grin but it dropped as he looked down at Shay's hand and a second later she saw why.

His right shirt sleeve hung loosely from his broad shoulder. Because he was missing most of his right arm.

Oh.

She pulled her hand back, eyes flying up to his. She thought she saw a pained look flash there before a wide grin stretched his face.

"Call me Rafe. All my friends do." He leaned in conspiratorially and gave her a wink. "Since you're gonna be my wife, I'd say you earn the privilege."

He reached for the hand she'd dropped back by her side with his good one and lifted it to his lips, a cocky grin on his face. "It's great to meet ya, babe."

His lips brushed her fingers and ridiculously, Shay felt a blush rise on her cheeks. Henry had kissed her hand when he'd introduced himself, too, but somehow the two experiences felt completely different. Henry's gesture had seemed formal and romantic, like a courting gesture from the nineteenth century. Whereas the caress of Rafe's lips sent a hot tingle racing down her spine.

While Rafe didn't have Henry's polish and wasn't as strictly handsome as either he or Charlie, he had a rakish charm. He was maybe 5'11 with a broad chest and thick, corded muscles that were visible through his t-shirt. It was clear he kept his body in top shape in spite of whatever accident had taken his arm.

"Tell me I didn't miss the party." Rafe looked past them to the basket of food on the table. "Right on. Is that breakfast that smells so good?"

Henry nodded and before he could even say anything, Rafe plucked the basket Henry had set on a chair and took it to the table.

"Damn, are these real eggs?" Rafe asked, lifting the lid on the plastic container he pulled out of the basket. "Like the kind an actual chicken shits out? Not that powdered protein reconstituted crap?"

Henry looked beyond exasperated. "There is so much wrong with that statement I do not even know where to begin. I am going to get us all something to drink." He was still shaking his head as he walked into the kitchen.

It did smell good but Shay was too busy taking in her fiancés. Jonas finally pushed off from the wall and headed for the dining room table as Rafe leaned over and took a deep inhale of the food.

Shay couldn't help her eyes ping-ponging between all four men as Henry came back with a large pitcher and several stacked glasses. She hurried to help him with the glasses, taking the opportunity to get a closer look at each man as she handed them a glass.

They all couldn't be more opposite if they tried. The threadbare gray t-shirt Jonas wore looked like it might have once had a logo on the front but it had long since faded. It also did little to hide his lithe and muscular physique. He wore cargo shorts slung low on his hips.

But he'd been standoffish and moody ever since he'd come in. Nothing like Rafe's open and easy charisma or Henry's eloquent charm.

The only thing Henry and Jonas had in common might be their age —they both looked to be in their mid-thirties. Maybe Henry was slightly older? He did have a little bit of gray peppering his hair at his temples but somehow it only made him more attractive.

Shay studied Rafe as he grabbed a chair, flipped it around backwards and sat down, straddling it. He looked to be around her and Charlie's age—maybe twenty-seven or twenty-eight.

When Shay started for the table, Charlie was right there at her side, cutting in front of Henry. She frowned. Was Charlie being territorial? Or protective?

Back in Travisville, Jason had considered her his property. Even though sometimes he was the one to invite other men into their bed, he was still quick to turn violent and jealous if he felt she was sharing her attentions too freely.

She kept her eyes narrowed on Charlie as he held out a chair at the table for her. Again, she couldn't tell... gentlemanly, or controlling?

She grabbed a different chair at the table and sat down, watching his expression carefully. But there was no flash of anger on his features. No tightening of his jaw like happened with Jason whenever he was displeased with her. Usually followed by a blow. Whether it was a slap or a fist depended on his mood.

Charlie didn't seem perturbed, though, he just moved to sit down beside her.

But his hand didn't come down on her thigh. He didn't squeeze her flesh so hard it bruised to remind her who was in control. He just moved the Tupperware of omelets closer to her. "You hungry?"

She blinked. He was offering it to her first? He had to be starving. She knew exactly what they fed him back in Travisville. Or rather, what they *didn't* feed him.

She just nodded and he forked an omelet onto her plate. Only after serving her did he serve himself.

It made her chest feel funny—like, *ache* in a strange way. Her throat felt too tight all the sudden.

But then Rafe took her attention, leaning across her, all the way over the table to grab an omelet from the container with his fingers before dropping it onto his plate. A second later, he shoved a huge bite in his mouth, still without using a fork.

"For fuck's sake," Rafe groaned while still chewing, "This is the best thing I've ever fucking tasted in my life. You guys here in town live like kings, huh?"

Jonas nodded in agreement, leaning back in his chair and closing his eyes while he chewed, his eyes closed like he was savoring every bit of the eggs.

"I cannot believe I am wasting my real eggs on your case of the munchies," Henry muttered sourly. "Who smokes reefer at eight-thirty in the morning?"

"Judge not lest you be judged," Jonas opened his eyes and picked up his fork, pointing it at Henry before spearing another bite of eggs. "And no one calls it reefer anymore."

Henry held up his hands. "Judge away. I live a life beyond reproach.

Some of us have priorities. You know, things we actually want to accomplish in a day."

"I have things I'll accomplish today. My plants need watering and weeding, after all." Jonas lifted his arms behind his head and pushed the chair up on its back two legs.

"The weed needs weeding?" Rafe joked, chuckling as he shoved the last of the omelet in his mouth. "Fuckin' priceless." He slapped the table and kept laughing.

"Is this really the first impression we want to be making on our wife?" Henry asked sharply, cutting Rafe off before he could open his mouth again.

Jonas let out a scoffing noise. "Like you don't just love trading my Purple Kush for all sorts of luxury shit. Now you're gonna bust my balls?"

"Wait," Shay said. She wasn't sure what to make of Jonas. "You used to be a preacher? And now... you grow marijuana?"

Jonas just shrugged and dropped the front legs of his chair back down to the ground. "Weed's not that different from religion. It expands our understanding of the universe, right?—but without all the guilt. Sounds pretty damn perfect to me."

Then his eyebrows lifted as he glanced Shay's direction. "Sorry, I'm bad at this whole..." he waved a hand, "human interaction shit." He ran his fingers through his hair. It only made it stand up more. But when he looked back at her, his dark eyes were so striking her fork paused on the way to her mouth. Which was saying something because Rafe was right. The omelets were fantastic.

She put the fork down and tilted her head at Jonas. "So how did that happen?" she asked. "Why'd you stop being a preacher?"

She hadn't ever been especially religious but she had always been fascinated by those who were. Believing in something bigger than herself... it seemed like that would be comforting. There had definitely been times she wished she had some sort of faith.

But Jonas's eyes only darkened further. "I saw the light," he said with a sarcastic smirk. "Literally. Ka-*BOOM*." He made an explosion motion with his hands. "I was hiking up on Enchanted Rock when the bombs dropped." He shook his head, his eyes going distant. "The blast cloud looked just like it always did in the movies."

He finally looked back at her, crossing his arms over his chest. "You see a thing like that, well," he huffed out a bitter laugh, "it's a little hard to go back up into the pulpit the next Sunday and say God loves you and has a beautiful plan for your life."

Shay frowned, knowing even as she asked her next question that there would inevitably be a sad answer to follow. Between Xterminate and D-Day, everyone had lost somebody. "Did you have family in the city?"

"Hmm?" Jonas looked up at her. "Oh. No," he shook his head. "But I just realized, what's the point, ya know? The toxic rainout's gonna fall on the good and evil alike. And we're all gonna die. Question is, how soon you gonna take that dirt nap? And what's the best way to distract yourself in the meantime?" He pulled a joint and a lighter out of his pocket, at the last second pausing and offering it to Shay.

Shay put her hand out palm up to stop him before he could hand it to her.

It was official.

She didn't like husband number three.

So he'd watched the bombs drop and it had given him an existential crisis. Boo hoo. That was a pretty damn privileged issue to have if you asked her.

Some people had *real* problems.

Henry reached over and snatched the lighter out of Jonas's hands before he could toke up. "I will not allow that filthy habit in my presence. Or the presence of our future wife."

Jonas shrugged. "Whatever man." He put the joint back in his pocket and took a long drink of water.

Yeah. She really didn't like him. She went back to her food.

Rafe let out a quick burp. "*Damn*, that was good. Are there seconds?" he asked, reaching for the container again.

Henry yanked it back before Rafe could touch it, glowering at him. "There is one left but it's for Shay."

Shay was about to tell Henry it was fine—after all, she was almost half the size of some of them—when more banging on the front door startled her so much she almost knocked her glass of water over.

"What now?" Charlie said, dropping his fork onto his empty plate and turning toward the door. Apparently the delicious food hadn't done anything to improve his mood.

"I will get it," Henry said when no one else moved. The Commander must have already left for the day because whoever was banging on the door was not going about it quietly.

Shouting voices filled the air as soon as Henry cracked the door.

"The preacher here?"

"Let us in. We heard Pastor Jonas was here. We need him."

Henry looked irritated, Shay could tell from all the way across the room. "Do you have an appointment with him?"

"Well no, but this bastard here stole my—"

"Hey! Danny said we'd both get to say our side. You're predispo— prendis— makin' him turn against me before he's even heard my side."

"You don't got a side. You stole my ration card. I saw you with extra bread and I swear I'm gonna—"

There was a brief scuffling noise and then a third voice shouted, "Men!"

The door was pushed open and Shay could finally see the three men standing on the door step. One was huge—absolutely a gigantic bear of a man—but very young. He couldn't be more than twenty-five, if that. He was physically holding the other two men apart. They were smaller and while they were all wearing paint and dust-spattered clothing that marked them as construction workers, the denim shirts of the arguing men were far more threadbare and ratty.

"Sorry, Jonas, but I didn't know where else to take them," said the huge blond man. "If I haul them in to the Security Squadron Head-quarters, Nix'll just kick them both out of camp for stealing and fighting. They about tore up their dorm room. It's Cam here's third strike." He jerked the slightly larger of the two men forward.

"It's not my fault this time, Danny," Cam said. "I told you, he stole my ration card. I was just trying to retrieve my property. All I ever asked for was a fair shake, Danny. But is anyone willing to give me that? No. They aren't. And I'll tell you why. It's because—da"

"That's *Mr. Hale* to you," Danny cut him off, a warning in his voice. The other man stopped talking. *Damn*, Shay thought. Cam looked like he was a decade older than Danny, maybe in his mid-thirties, but Danny was layin' it *down*.

Shay looked back at Jonas to check his reaction and was surprised to see his face had gone hard. "Danny, I told you the last time. I don't do this shit anymore."

Danny sighed. "Come on, you really gonna do this to me? Make me drag these two to Nix? You know he'll kick them outta town. You want that on your conscience?"

Jonas's gaze only went flintier. "Sounds good to me. Don't need any troublemakers in town. And my conscience is doing just fine, thank you very much."

Danny crossed his arms, which, considering how huge they were, was intimidating. "I didn't want to have to do this. But you owe me. Remember three summers ago?"

Jonas's nostrils flared and he stood up straight. "Fine, *Daniel.*"

Then he stood up even straighter. Shay blinked as the lounging slouch completely disappeared from his posture. Like he'd been playing a character in a movie before and now he was stepping back into real life.

He walked over to where the three men by the door stood, his shoulders military square. He looked between the two men with the dispute. "Tell me what happened, from the beginning."

"He stole my—" Cam said right as the other guy started, "I was just minding my own business when he jumps me—"

Then they both looked at each other and shouted, "Liar!"

"So this missing ration card," Jonas questioned, his voice clipped and commanding. "It hasn't been found?"

Both men shook their heads.

Shay watched in fascination as Jonas's focus narrowed in on the smaller of the two men, the one whose name hadn't been said yet.

"Are you certain?" Jonas's face was stern but as he continued, his voice gentled. "Because it's understandable. You're new to camp, aren't you? What's your name? Anderson? Am I remembering that right?"

The man looked surprised but then his mouth went hard again. "What's it to ya? How do you even know—?"

Jonas waved a hand. "I have a good memory and the Commander has me look over new resident applications. Correct me if I'm wrong, but you arrived to town two and a half days ago with the refugees out of Oklahoma, right?"

The man just nodded and Jonas continued. "Now, I think about a man like you. A man used to making his own rules up as he goes. And if you've only just come here, well that means you spent a helluva lotta years out *there*," Jonas jerked a thumb toward the door. "And I've heard plenty of stories to know the things that go on outside Central Texas South are enough to break a man."

Anderson stared at the floor, refusing to look Jonas in the eyes.

"So I guess what I'm saying is that it'd be more than understandable for you to come into the township and expect more of the same you found everywhere else. But I'm here to tell you, this place is special. Special in how we treat our women. And special in how we take care of one another. I promise you this—whenever you're in Jacob's Well Township, you're—"

"What?" Anderson asked with a belligerent scoff, "Let me guess, when I'm here, I'm *family*?"

"No," Jonas said, standing even taller and glaring the man down. Shay was a little taken aback by the authority that emanated from him. He seemed taller and... intimidating all of the sudden.

But at the same time, the way he was talking, well... Could Central Texas South and Jacob's Well really be everything Jonas was saying it was? She'd had her own reasons for coming here and yes, the rumors about how well they treated their women were part of it. But she'd lived long enough in the post-Fall world to be suspicious of anything that sounded too good to be true.

"Family, you have to *earn*," Jonas continued, dark eyes penetrating. "You have to work your *ass* off for the privilege, in fact. What I was going to say was, whenever you're in Jacob's Well Township, I promise that you'll be afforded more dignity than anywhere else I've seen post-Fall."

Shay swallowed hard at his words.

Dignity. It was a rare commodity these days. *It's probably just propaganda*, she told herself. But she couldn't look away from Jonas as he went on after a short pause.

"On your application to the Township," Jonas said, "didn't you mark down you had a son, recently deceased?"

Anderson's face jerked up toward Jonas at that. His mouth was pursed, brow furrowed. He was angry. Defiant. But Shay read the sadness underneath, worn into every line of his face. Shay had no idea how old he actually was, but he looked ancient in spite of the fact that his hair was still dark brown. It was clear the world had made him old before his time.

"My boy made it so long. Eight years." Anderson swallowed hard, but he didn't look away from Jonas. "He was so little when it all started. And I kept him safe. Fought when we needed to fight. Hid him when we needed to hide. We feasted and starved together." He shook his head, a distant sort of shock on his face. "Then he gets killed by an infected scratch on his leg he was too proud to tell me about till it was too late? How is that *fair*?"

"It's not," Jonas said swiftly. "It's not fair. Nothing will ever make what happened to your son right. Or fair. And for that, I'm so, so sorry."

By the devastation in Jonas's eyes as he said it, Shay thought he really meant it too. It was as if... as if he was taking the man's pain into himself. Either he was a sociopathically good actor or he was the real deal. She could see how he must have once been a powerful pastor.

He was the kind of man other men followed.

"And I won't feed you some bullshit about how your son—what was his name?"

"Aaron."

"I won't give you some bullshit about how Aaron's looking down on you from heaven and ask how you think it would make Aaron feel, watching you screw up your one chance in a lifetime at landing in a safe haven. I won't ask what the point of all those years of struggle were worth if you just give up now. Or why you'd negate all those grueling years getting you and Aaron through the mud and shit and piles of bodies and the burning Texas heat."

"So what the fuck *are* you sayin, preacher?"

Shay held her breath. Was Jonas going to start in again about how shitty life was and that dirt naps were all they could hope for?

But the groove between Jonas's eyebrows only grew deeper. "I'm saying there's no good reason for any of it—the bombs, your son dying, all those people—" Jonas's voice cut off and he swallowed hard, face dropping for a moment before he looked Anderson in the eye again.

"If there *is* a God, I'll *never* forgive him for all that he's allowed to happen. And if there's a heaven, I'd rather go to hell than ever meet him face to face." The last words came ground out through clenched teeth and Shay felt the hairs on her arms rise at the vehemence in his voice.

"What that means is that all we have is today. This moment. Right *here*." Jonas jabbed a finger toward the floor. "We can either live it or we lay down and die. That's the choice. This here—Jacob's Well—it's a place you can live like a man and not an animal. So you'll get one more chance if you choose to stay."

Anderson's eyes had grown wary and thoughtful as Jonas spoke but he slowly gave a nod.

Jonas walked over to where Charlie stood by Shay. Charlie started to say something, but before he could, Jonas reached behind him and yanked a knife from the back of his belt.

"Hey," Charlie said but Jonas ignored him, walking back toward Anderson, knife raised.

"Whoa, preacher man." Anderson held up his hands and started backing toward the front door. "I thought we was coming to an understanding. I—"

"Hold him," Jonas said, voice suddenly cold. All the compassion from moments ago was gone. What the hell? Shay started to step forward but Charlie put his arm out to block her path, his face tense.

Shay's head swung back and forth between Charlie and Jonas. God, was Jonas actually a sociopath after all? Was this all just some terrible sort of cat and mouse game?

Shay's stomach dropped out. She'd seen that sort of thing before. Too many times to count, in fact. She stumbled backwards a step. Jason had liked to play with his prey.

Charlie reached out to steady her but she jerked away from him.

Anderson started yelling as the big man, Danny, and the other one, grabbed both of his arms and held him in place as Jonas approached.

Shay wanted to squeeze her eyes shut, but no, she'd learned over the years it was far better to look the devil in the eye and know what you were dealing with. Your nightmares might be worse, but at least you were prepared when the monsters in human form came for you.

But then, something extraordinary happened.

Because when Jonas got to Anderson, all he did was use the knife to cut down the center of the man's shirt and then—

Wha—

Shay squinted to get a better look. Was that some sort of little pocket sewn on the inside of his shirt?

With one swift slash, Jonas sliced through the edge of the little makeshift pocket. Then he reached in and slid out a small yellow ration card.

Shay's mouth dropped open as Jonas stepped back from Anderson and the two men on either side of him let him go.

Anderson immediately dropped into a fighting stance, twisting back and forth to look at the three men who had him surrounded.

But Jonas held the knife loosely now, pointed toward the floor. "Mourn your son. Do your work. Keep your head down. That's all we ask. And I'll give you the choice one last time—stay or go? But know that if you choose to stay, you're agreeing to abide by our laws. This will be your last warning."

Jonas's face was hard again. "The world's short on mercy these days. Don't abuse ours. If you're caught stealing again, you'll be taken straight to Security Squadron Headquarters and your hand will be cut off. Do you understand?"

The man was visibly shaking, but he nodded.

"I said, *do you understand?*"

"Yes, sir."

"And what is your decision? Stay or go?"

A moment of silence. And then, "I'll stay."

Jonas gave another decisive nod. "So be it. And you." Jonas pointed at the other man, the one who's ration card had been stolen. "Captain

Hale will toss you out on your ass if he catches you fighting again. Was getting thrown out of the Security Squadron not enough for you?"

"But it wasn't my fault this time," Cam repeated his earlier protest. "He—"

"A man steals your ration card, you report it to your superior," Jonas cut him off. "Especially considering that you already have two strikes."

"But I—"

"The right answer here is *yes, sir*," Jonas cut him off with a glare.

Cam stared at the ground, looking like he was just barely biting back his true thoughts. "Yes, *sir*."

"Now get out of here, both of you."

They both turned and left out the front door.

The big blond man, Danny, breathed out and clapped Jonas on the back. "Thanks, Preacher. Don't know what we'd do without you."

Jonas's glare didn't soften. "Stop bringing me this shit. I'm not in this business anymore."

Danny just shrugged. "You're the best at it, though."

Jonas turned away from him. And in the time it took for Danny to follow the other men out the door and close it behind him, Jonas's posture went from hulking intimidation back to slouching stoner again.

If Shay hadn't seen it with her own eyes, she wouldn't have believed it. She *had* seen it, and she still could hardly believe it.

"Well," Henry said with a clap of his hands, "that was eventful. Now, onto the rest of the day. Do you want a tour of the town, Shay? Or are you interested in anything in particular?"

It took Shay a moment to wrap her head around what Henry was saying. Her eyes were still on Jonas, who'd gone back to leaning against the wall like when he'd first come in the house. He'd crossed his arms and closed his eyes, head leaned back against the wall as if he was taking a nap standing up.

"Some women like to take up an occupation of some kind until children come," Henry continued. "I know Julia has been needing some help over at the school if you are interested. The children are—"

"No," Shay cut him off sharply, her attention suddenly snapping back to Henry.

Small faces flashed in her mind. Tiny hands fisting around her fingers.

Mommy, look what Nicky and I found! It's a frog. Look Mommy. A frog! Can we keep it?

"Not the school." She swallowed and stood up, turning as she grabbed her empty plate from the table. She wasn't sure she could control her facial features at the moment.

She would share her body with these men. But her secrets were her own.

"Well, there is the library," Henry continued, oblivious to her inner turmoil. "And Sophia works at the food pantry."

"Here, let me get that," Charlie said when Shay reached for his plate. He pulled the one she was holding out of her hands and then proceeded to go around the table picking up everyone's dishes. Which was gentlemanly and all, but now she didn't have anything to do with her hands. She toyed with the bottom hem of her overlarge sleep shirt and tried to focus on what Henry was saying.

Sophia. Food Pantry.

Shay thought of the dark, almost betrayed look Sophia had shot her way as she left this morning and wilted. Shay liked Sophia, but she did *not* have the energy for girl drama today.

"Any other options?" she asked Henry.

"Well, there's candle and soap-making. And the clinic."

The hospital was a possibility. Though in all honesty, she'd seen enough dead and dying bodies for a lifetime, thank you very much. She'd been pre-med for a while in college but mostly just so she could keep her scholarship. She'd filled every elective she could with art classes instead.

"What, do you have something else in mind?" Charlie asked.

Shay looked up at him and bit her lip. Then she nodded. "I do, actually. Is there somewhere you put all your trash?"

She was met with confused faces on all sides.

"Like plastics and the non-organic stuff you can't compost?"

"Um, are you thinking of starting a recycling program?" Henry asked. "Because I am not sure we have the equipment to—"

"No, no," Shay waved a hand. "Nothing like that. I want to make art out of it. You know, like found object art. Ever heard of it?" She looked from one blank face to another. "It was a thing before The Fall. Like, a big thing."

Charlie was nodding as if he was totally with her even though she could still see the skepticism he couldn't quite hide.

"It'll keep me busy while, you know—" Just force the words out. Say it. *Just say it.* "—we wait for you guys to knock me up." The last half of the sentence came out in a rush, but she managed it. She tried for a smile but she was pretty sure it came out a grimace.

"So anyway, got any place like that I could collect supplies?" She looked at the table and let her long hair fall in her face. Gotta love built in camouflage.

"Looks like you're comin' to work with me then, babe," Rafe said. When she looked his way, he shot her another wink. "What you're looking for is the Scrapper Yard. We got everything from old electronics to cars to refrigerators to old toys. Everything anyone looking for old junk could want."

Shay perked up. "Sounds perfect. Can we go there?"

"You bet, babe. I'd be happy to give you your own personal guided tour."

Henry's nose was wrinkled. "Are you sure you would not like to go see the hydro-electricity project our chief engineer has set up by the river? Or I can show you the extensive inventory of luxury items I have accrued for trade the next time I visit the President's Palace—"

"What's the matter?" Charlie asked. "Is Cinderella afraid his pretty, pretty shoes will get a little dirt on them?"

Shay thought she ought to tell Charlie not to pick but she couldn't help an inadvertent glance down at Henry's shoes. They were a very shiny, perfectly buffed leather that looked new, right out of the box.

"It is called having pride in one's appearance," Henry said, lifting a haughty eyebrow. "Acting civilized is the first step toward attaining civilization."

"I don't know," Charlie said, "I'd have said the bronze age or opposable thumbs or the Magna Carta."

"What?" Henry asked.

"The first steps toward civilization, old chap," Charlie said, adopting a British accent and slapping Henry on the shoulder as he passed by and held out his arm for Shay to join him. "So, we going to look at some junk, or what?"

"I need to change," Shay said, but before she started toward the stairs, she paused. "One last thing."

"Yes, lovely?" Henry asked, affecting his most charming smile yet. Dimples. Even as her stomach did a funny swoopy thing, she couldn't help asking herself how she was ever supposed to trust a man with dimples.

You don't have to trust him to get what you want out of him. Her eyes traveled slowly down his body. And it was one *fine* body beneath the perfectly tailored suit.

"I, um." Shay forced herself to move her eyes off Henry. Only for her gaze to snag on Charlie. She quickly looked away. She knew he wouldn't like what she had to ask.

"So, um. When will I meet the last one? My last fiancé?"

Henry and Rafe exchanged a glance. Even Jonas had opened his eyes and stood up straighter again.

"Well," Henry said, drawing out the word, "we were thinking about having dinner tonight all together. Over at the house. The one that will be ours once we are married."

Shay could feel Charlie's blood boiling from across the room.

Rafe broke in before he could erupt. "But if that's too much at once, babe, we can wait. There's no r—"

Shay just shook her head, though, waving their concerns away. "When does the marriage become official?"

Another significant glance was exchanged.

But Charlie was apparently done holding his opinions to himself. "This is insane. There's no way we're letting them force you into any of this—"

"Charlie," Shay said, loud enough that it stopped his tirade before it really got legs. "I want to hear what they have to say."

This was going to happen *her* way or not at all. The sooner she got them all on an equal playing field, the better.

Charlie ground his teeth together, a vein standing out in his neck.

Shay took a deep breath and looked back to Rafe and Henry. "Well?"

Rafe held out a hand for Henry, like *this one's all yours*. Henry narrowed his eyes in return, but he spoke up, looking back to Shay. "The wedding usually takes place a few weeks after the lottery. After we've all had a chance to get acquainted with each other and feel comfortable enough to share a living space." Henry held up a hand like he was anticipating resistance. "That doesn't mean we're expected to share a bed right away, though."

"But it is expected eventually," Charlie growled, turning on Henry.

Henry shrugged reluctantly but Shay spoke over both of them.

"All of that's ridiculous anyway."

That got everyone's attention. They all looked her way. Charlie was smiling, while Henry just looked confused. Shay couldn't read the expression on Jonas's coolly appraising face and Rafe simply looked interested.

"Wha—" Henry started to ask but Shay spoke over him, impatient to have this part done with.

"It's ridiculous to wait that long. We should get married as soon as possible. Tonight even." The moment the words came out of her mouth, she knew it was exactly what she wanted.

"Shay!" Charlie exploded. "What the hell are you thinking?"

Shay let out a long breath and walked over to him. She took both of his hands and looked up into his worried, green eyes.

"I'm not your sister." She felt his flinch, but it had to be said. "I don't need you to protect me. I knew what would be expected of me before we even left Travisville. And I was fine with it. I still am."

She was more than fine with it. Looking between the four of them, she felt the quiver start deep in her sex. Wrong as it probably was, she looked forward to fucking these four men. And the fifth who was still a stranger.

You're my whore. Jason's words rang in her head. *My perfect little fucking whore.*

Not tonight. She squared her jaw. Jason wouldn't be anywhere nearby as she took these men into her body. Tonight she'd belong to herself. And she'd take as much as she gave. More, maybe.

But Charlie just kept stubbornly shaking his head back and forth. He leaned down and whispered fervently in her ear. "We don't have to *stay*. I've seen Audrey. I know she's alive. I can get you out, get you somewhere safe, then come back for her and—"

Shay let out an exasperated huff. Why wouldn't he *listen* to her? Men never listened. They just assumed they knew best and, because there were more of them, they got to run everything. It was crap.

She spun on Charlie. "So everything you said last night in the Commander's office—about how a woman should be able to choose. Was that just bullshit?"

"What? Of course not. That's my whole point. This lottery system gives you no ch—"

"*This* is what I choose," she spoke over him. "Sex isn't a big deal to me. If it is to you, fine, you don't have to join us—but that's your problem, not mine. I want you there, but if you can't handle it, let me know now."

Charlie's mouth dropped open. "Shay..."

But she just shook her head. "What's waiting around for three weeks going to get me? It'll just drive me crazy. I know what I want and I'm ready. So we do it tonight."

She looked over to Jonas. "You're a preacher, right?"

"*Former* preacher." He watched her with a dark, intense look. She couldn't tell if it was disapproval or attraction.

She waved a hand. "Whatever. Can you still do wedding ceremonies?"

He nodded solemnly.

"Good. Then after dinner, when the last man gets there, I want you to perform the ceremony. Just something small and intimate. Only the six of us."

One after the other, she looked each of them in the eye. "But we get married tonight."

CHAPTER SEVEN

JONAS

The day showing Shay around town went by too quickly. Which meant Jonas had been enjoying himself.

Which pissed him the fuck off.

He wasn't supposed to like her this much. He hadn't put his name in the marriage raffle to get a wife he *liked*.

Eat, drink, and be merry cause tomorrow we die, right?

Well, maybe in his case, eat, drink, *smoke*, and be merry... but blah, blah, the idea was the same. He'd figured, since he was all about celebrating the pleasures of the flesh now, why not toss his hat in the ring to get some pussy on the regular?

A man's hand could only get him so far for so long. So into the marriage raffle his name went. And fuck him, he'd won the damn thing.

But *liking* the wife?

That had never come into his estimation.

He'd tried the whole wife-thing once before and that was enough to cure him of ever wanting anything to do with the institution again.

So no, he didn't want to like Shay.

It would help if she weren't so goddamn beautiful. But okay, a beautiful wife, he could deal with—if that were the only thing.

But it *wasn't* the only thing. They'd passed by the medical clinic on their way into town and she decided she wanted to stop in to see it after all.

Dr. Kapoor hadn't had time to talk or show her around, though, because a few construction crew guys had been in an accident. A heavy beam had broken loose from a pully and fallen on them, smashing them up pretty good. The doc and nurses were all working on them, leaving the rest of the clinic short-staffed.

So Shay went and volunteered to help with rounds. Apparently she'd been in nursing school back before The Fall and had done some field work in Travisville too.

She was competent and kind as she moved from bed to bed. She chatted up patients, changed bedpans without flinching, and listened with compassion to the complaints of everyone whose illnesses didn't justify the few sparing meds the clinic did have on hand—which was most of them. Meds were only given out in the most severe, life threatening cases, and too often, Jonas knew they didn't even have them then.

Jonas donated a fourth of his crop to the clinic every other harvest, sometimes more if something happened and the hospital needed it. But cannabis could only go so far. It couldn't replace insulin or blood pressure medications.

As Shay sat there patiently holding the hand of a stroke victim, Mr. Randal—a man ancient enough to have known the world before the internet existed—Jonas knew he was fucked.

Shay was just the kind of woman Jonas had been looking for to join him in his ministry back when he'd first been an eager seminary graduate looking for his first church assignment.

The kind of woman he *thought* Katherine was.

Katherine was pretty and vivacious and Jonas had proposed to her after only knowing her a month. She kept talking about how it was God's plan for them to meet and how she'd been praying for years to meet a godly man like him.

He took it as a sign that God meant her to be his wife.

Turned out he should have been looking closer. Cause yeah, in reality, he'd missed all the *actual* signs. It wasn't like they weren't there.

Katherine's nails always had to be perfectly manicured. She followed the Fall fashion trends like a damn slave. Then there was how she loved to be on his arm when he guest-pastored a couple times at a big Dallas mega-church. But when he volunteered at the soup kitchen? She was nowhere to be found.

And after his dad died and he moved them back to Jacob's Well to take over the parsonage here... It only took a few months of marriage for him to realize Katherine loved the attention and praise that came along with being a pastor's wife waaaaaaaaaaay more than she loved ministering to the poor and needy... or in the end, even loving him.

Whatever. He'd grown used to their cold marriage. To Katherine's obsession with appearance and status.

It was all fine.

Fine.

That was the defining term for his ministry.

His marriage.

His whole damn life.

Just *fine.*

Then he found out Katherine had been cheating on him for almost their whole marriage with the fucking accountant. Who was also a deacon at his church.

Then Xterminate hit.

Katherine died.

Hell on earth was more than just a saying. It was fucking reality.

And God?

He was nowhere to be found.

"So what are we having for dinner?" Rafe asked, cutting into his thoughts as he, Shay, and Charlie came back into the dining room off the open plan kitchen. They'd gone in to wash up for dinner after their day around town.

Jonas had washed up in the bathroom and only just walked back into the dining room. It was their first night in their new clan house. It was furnished but still had a very unlived in feel. Everything was clean and pristine, well, as much as a hundred-year-old house could be. But the crew had done a nice job preparing it for them. Hardwood floors, fresh painted cream colored walls. Even some fresh-picked wildflowers in a small vase on the mantle.

"Henry said he'd bring dinner," Charlie said.

"Well hopefully he gets here soon," Rafe said, rubbing his stomach. "I'm a growing boy."

Jonas rolled his eyes and moved off to the side of the room to lean against the wall. There'd been a period of time in his life where he'd forced himself to be outgoing and chat everyone and their grandson up, but if there was one thing he didn't miss about the pastor gig, it was that. He'd always hated that shit. This was exactly where he preferred to be. Off in a corner, no one expecting anything from him, not having to perform like some damn show pony.

At Charlie's words, Jonas looked toward the front door. He was hungry too.

Henry had begged off Shay's tour earlier as soon as bodily fluids became involved at the hospital, claiming he had *urgent* business he'd forgotten about that he had to go attend to. Jonas would have called him out on that bullshit, but by that point, the prospect of having Shay's attention divided between only him, Charlie, and Rafe without the addition of Henry was too attractive to pass up.

Which again, was a fucking problem.

Jonas's eyes zeroed back in on Shay. Even after a long day out in the sun, she still looked good enough to eat.

And all the sudden he didn't care about dinner. He just wanted to drag her upstairs and devour her.

Cause fuck him, this morning when Shay announced she wanted to get married *tonight?*

His cock had about split his cargo shorts down the middle he'd gone so hard. Hot damn.

He couldn't help the question that flashed through his head before he shut it down: *Did that mean she wanted to...?*

No. No way she meant she wanted to consummate the marriage tonight. But she would at some point... right?

And damn, Jonas would be more than happy to explore every inch of that beautiful body. Those legs that went on for-fucking-*ever*.

She flipped her hair and smiled as she, Charlie, and Rafe chatted about some of the things she'd picked out of the Scrapper Yard today for her art project.

Shit. Jonas went to the bathroom to clean up because he'd needed a moment alone to clear his thoughts. Not that it had worked.

Which pissed him off again. What the fuck? Could he not control himself for ten goddamned seconds?

He used to be the king of discipline.

He used to wake up at five a.m. every morning for an hour and a half of scripture study and prayer and meditation, followed by a five-mile jog.

Even before he converted to Christianity in college, he'd always followed rigorous routines. He'd been a weird kid, he knew. His dad was a county judge and was gone a lot and his mom had died when he was really young. Cancer.

His earliest memories were of sitting with her on her hospital bed, her reading books to him. He thought all mommies were bald. He remembered being confused by the moms on TV who had all their hair and didn't spend all day in bed.

Then she died and it was just him and dad. Except Dad worked all the time so really it was just him. The neighbor supposedly 'looked after him' but she just sat watching soap operas online the whole time and never said two words to him.

So yeah, he'd been a lonely kid. He had to find creative ways to pass the time. And the best way was to cut the hours into twenty-minute chunks.

It was scary looking at the clock and seeing it was five hours to bedtime when you knew you'd be spending all that time completely alone.

But if he just had to think about it twenty minutes at a time, well, that wasn't so bad. So for twenty minutes, he'd go play in the backyard. And when the little alarm on his watch went off, then he'd come back in and play Legos.

His dad only let him play on his computer an hour a day and of course that was the one thing the neighbor lady *did* pay attention too. The rest of the time she took away his laptop and put it underneath the couch where she sat to watch her shows. Those three twenty-minute blocks always *flew* by, so he tried to save them up to spend when he really needed them.

He took twenty-minute showers.

He took twenty-minute bike rides around the neighborhood.

When he was a little older, he'd work out in twenty-minute intervals, sometimes linking together two or three at a time, like he'd go jogging for forty minutes or an hour.

Then he'd come back and take a twenty-minute shower.

Jerk off for twenty minutes.

Take another shower. Jerk off for another twenty-minutes while the water ran down his body.

He couldn't remember when exactly he'd let go of the twenty-minute thing. Probably in high school when he'd gotten really into track and his coach had forced him to start thinking in terms of pacing and long-distance.

But yeah. Discipline.

It was all he'd known. Till the world went to shit and he said, *fuck it*. Fuck God and fuck routine and fuck ordering every little part of his life around what he was *supposed* to do. It hadn't gotten him anything but a cheating and eventually, dead, wife.

And apparently eight years of shitting his discipline to the wind meant he couldn't just pick it right back up again, because no matter how he tried not to, his eyes drifted right back to Shay.

She'd let her long, blonde hair down from the ponytail she'd kept it in all afternoon while she'd picked through the Scrapper Yard and it cascaded over her shoulder in the prettiest way.

Just looking at her now reminded him of the way her face had scrunched adorably every time she came across whatever piece of total junk in the Scrapper Yard caught her fancy. It was the most random shit. Ancient laptop keyboards, broken plastic pieces of all kinds, metallic bits, old kitchen utensils. But she caressed each piece she picked up like it was the finest jewelry from Tiffany's.

Katherine wouldn't have come within fifty feet of a junkyard like that. She'd have been too afraid she'd scuff her pumps or break a nail.

Not Shay though. Her nails were grimy by the end of the afternoon but she didn't even seem to notice.

Jonas turned away.

He was *not* going to like her.

He'd fuck her. If not tonight, then whenever she was ready.

The other guys could do the wooing. He'd just be another body on the bed when the time came. That was all.

Right then, the front door opened and Henry came in.

"Thank Jesus," Rafe said, all but running him down as he made a beeline for the basket he was carrying. "What have we got tonight?"

Henry tried to yank it back at the last moment but Rafe was too quick. He pulled out a loaf of bread and then had the top off of a container inside the basket by the time he reached the dining room table. He made an ecstatic face as he leaned over and inhaled. "Spinach, and, holy shit, is that brisket? Sweet Jesus, please tell me that's brisket."

Henry's lips went tight in a displeased line but when all eyes focused in on him, he nodded. "It is brisket."

Okay. Even Jonas had to admit that was impressive. "How?" he couldn't help asking.

Henry looked smug. But considering he'd gotten them fucking brisket, he had the right. Any meat the township got was usually strictly rationed among all residents, put in stews and spread so thin you could barely taste it.

But the town nutritionist said the taste wasn't important, that it was all about the animal protein it provided for their diet that mattered. Jonas would have begged to differ, but that would have meant getting involved. Which he had a strict policy against.

Oh look, he was still disciplined in one area of his life.

He was disciplined at not giving a fuck.

"Sit, sit," Charlie said, ushering Shay over to a dining room chair. "You've been on your feet all day.

Charlie went into the kitchen and got plates out of a cabinet. Looked like the prep crew had really fitted this place out.

Jonas had heard that hitting the lottery was really like... well, *hitting the lottery*, but damn if they didn't do everything up *sweet* for the clan families.

As soon as Charlie came back, Rafe snatched a plate off the top of the stack and started piling food on it.

"Hey," Henry snapped, grabbing the lid to the container and slamming it down on top of Rafe's fingers as he reached for more. "Rationing."

Rafe just narrowed his eyes at Henry, but then a commotion at the door had everyone's attention.

"Sorry we're late!"

The screech of little kids voices filled the foyer.

Jonas looked over to see Gabriel Herrera and his two boys coming in the door. Gabriel was a good guy—he worked the corn fields six days a week and sometimes came on his day off to help Jonas with his grow fields for extra tokens to spend at the mercantile. All so he'd have a little extra to get his kids a slightly bigger ration of food, a few more toys, and keep them in nicer clothes. He lived his whole life for those kids.

"Boys! What did I tell you on the walk over?" snapped Gabriel as he chased after his two young sons. Jonas looked the boys over. Maybe not so young anymore. The oldest had to be what? Eleven or twelve by now?

Gabriel finally got a hand on both their shoulders. "*Best* behavior. We're meeting your new mama, remember?"

The oldest glared up at his dad. "I don't *want* a new mama." Then he ran past Gabriel and up the stairs.

"Where are you going?" Gabriel called, throwing his hands up. "You don't even know which one is your room."

"Wait for me!" called Alex, the younger boy, chasing after his brother. But Gabriel was faster, scooping him up before he could get more than a few steps.

"Sorry," Gabriel said, looking over to where they all were watching on. "You must be Shay." He smiled her way. "I'm Gabriel. And this squirmy worm is Alejandro. Alex for short."

He flipped the boy in his arms, exposing his belly so he could blow a loud raspberry on it. The little boy let out a giggling shriek and started wiggling even harder to get out of his dad's arms.

Jonas smiled. He'd liked Gabriel ever since he and his boys had shown up to town six years ago. Alex was just a toddler then. Always had been a cute kid.

Jonas looked over at Shay. She had to be relieved to meet her last husband. Gabriel was the kind of guy who'd set anyone at ease.

But instead of looking happy or relaxed, she'd gone pale as a sheet.

"I want to go play with Tim," Alex said, squirming even harder.

"Okay, okay," Gabriel gave a heavy sigh like it was a huge imposition. He let Alex down, but not without a light smack on his bottom. "But I'm gonna bring up a plate for you and your brother in a few minutes and you have to promise to eat everything on it, not just the bread. Pinky swear?" He held out his pinky.

The little boy looked over at the spinach on Rafe's plate and made a face, but he finally let out a sigh that was humorously similar to his dad's and linked his pinky. "Pinky swear."

Then Alex was off in a streak toward the stairs.

Jonas glanced at Shay again and saw her eyes locked on the stairs. "No one told me there'd be..." Her voice trailed off.

"They're good boys," Gabriel hurried to say as he shut the door and came over to the dining room. "They won't be any trouble. Promise."

But it was like Shay didn't even hear him.

She looked haunted. Like she'd just seen a ghost, not a little boy. What the hell?

"Shay," Jonas said her name firmly and her head turned his way. Her eyes were still distant, though.

Jonas's frown deepened.

She wasn't telling them something. Okay, sure, he hadn't spoken more than a few sentences to her so it was hardly surprising she hadn't opened up.

But it suddenly bothered him.

A lot.

And for the first time all day he realized exactly how much of an asshole he was.

He was tired?

He was disillusioned with life and the human race?

He wanted to seek what pleasures he could in life before *he* died?

What about *her*?

He blinked. Trying to put himself in her shoes and think about what all this must be like for her felt as awkward as trying to flex an unused muscle.

Empathy.

Compassion.

She'd shown it so easily to the patients at the hospital earlier today. But when was the last time anyone had given her any?

Jonas tugged at the collar of his t-shirt. Was it hot in here?

Everyone looked out for themselves. That was the law of the apocalypse, right? You looked out for *numero uno* and fuck anyone else.

So why, an hour later, as he spoke the same wedding ceremony script that he did for every new clan, did the words strike him so viscerally?

Just the six of them had gathered in a circle in the dining room. Gabriel's boys were still playing upstairs. Used to handling wedding details, Jonas had asked Shay if she wanted him to go get Sophia as a bridesmaid but she'd just looked at him like he was some strange creature she didn't understand.

"No," she'd responded, "I just want it to be us. You can do whatever paperwork you need to later. But I don't want to deal with other people. Besides, all that matters are the promises we make to each other, right?"

Right after she said it, it was like both of them had realized the weight of it. She quickly made an excuse about needing to go change. But her words had stuck with him.

All that matters are the promises we make to each other.

"Marriage provides a stabilizing unit..." Jonas said before trailing off and swallowing hard, his eyes shooting over to Shay.

Shay looked beautiful. She wasn't wearing a wedding dress or anything. She'd changed into a fresh t-shirt, but still had on the jeans she'd been wearing all day. Her long blonde hair tumbled over her shoulders, honey colored streaks shining from the sunset streaming in through the window.

Jonas blinked. Shit. What was the rest of the script? He'd done this a hundred times over the years and *now* he forgot the words? At his own damn wedding?

He wracked his brain and finally blurted loudly, "Marriage establishes rights and obligations between all spouses."

He felt everyone watching him and he continued, in spite of feeling the back of his neck heat. He swallowed hard and looked to Shay again. "Marriage is meant to be a safe haven. Both for you and your husbands."

Her green eyes locked on his at this, like she realized he was really talking just to her.

And suddenly he wanted more than anything for the words he'd just said to be true. He wanted to be her safe haven. He had the terrible feeling it had been a long time since she'd had one.

"You're safe with us," he repeated softly, never breaking her gaze.

She swallowed and looked away, and only then did he continue with the ceremony. Jonas couldn't take his eyes off her the rest of the time, though.

He'd spent the last eight years of his life embracing nihilism and hedonism, figuring that nothing mattered so he might as well get as fucked up as he could and stay that way as long as possible.

But one day with this woman had him feeling... well, that was the point—she had him *feeling* again.

And all the sudden it hit him with the weight of a hundred-pound rock.

He was a fucking hypocrite.

He hadn't been chasing pleasure the past eight years.

He'd been fucking running.

Trying his damndest to numb himself to feeling *anything*. Ever. If he felt his high start to wear off? Fine, just toke up again. One joint wasn't enough to get the job done? Okay, he'd eat some edibles *along with* smoking.

And any time something threatened that numbness in the tiniest way, he'd do even more until he spent days so goddamned high he detached from his own damn body.

But now...

Now there was her.

And she deserved better.

She deserved so much better than a fucked-up loser like him.

Why the *hell* had he put his name in that goddamned lottery?

But you did, asshole. And now you're gonna make *her* pay for it?

Jonas's throat was so clogged up, he barely managed the final words. "And do you, Shay Monroe, accept the men before you as your wedded husbands, for as long as we all shall live?"

He held his breath as he waited for her answer, part of him wanting to yell at her—*no, don't do it. You can do so much better than us. I'm totally full of shit. I don't deserve y*—

"I do."

Jonas felt her clear, confident words echo all the way down to his soul. And as Henry slipped the ring on her finger, Jonas knew—knew with as much certainty as the prophets of old—that nothing would ever be the same again.

CHAPTER EIGHT

CHARLIE

"I now pronounce us husbands and wife, christening us Clan Cole," Jonas said as they all stood in a circle in the center of the living room. Henry smiled extra wide at that since it was his last name they'd all be taking.

And then Jonas continued, "We may now kiss the bride."

Every cell in Charlie's body rebelled at what was happening. But Shay? She just smiled good-naturedly at all of them.

"How about we head upstairs instead?" she said. "No point in kissing and getting started down here since we're just going to go up and... you know." Her cheeks went pink as she waved a hand toward the stairs.

Holy shit. She meant she wanted to— *Tonight?*

Charlie's heart started beating double time as he watched her more carefully than ever. But she genuinely didn't look afraid or upset. Maybe he did have old-fashioned ideas about sex. It was just— He was so used to being afraid and constantly vigilant for Audrey. He guessed it was hard to turn that protective instinct off.

"I think that's my cue to go get the boys," Gabriel said. "I told them I'd take them camping in the woods out back tonight."

"*You're* going to take them?" Shay asked, obviously confused. "But what about... Don't you want to—" She broke off, eyes going to the stairs.

But Gabriel just smiled easily as he took a step toward her. "I didn't put my name in the lottery for myself. I did it for the boys. So they could have the life they deserve. A house. A mother." His eyes gentled but Shay jerked back like she'd just gotten stabbed with a hot iron.

If Gabriel noticed, he didn't let on. "I don't plan on sharing the marriage bed. I'll sleep in the boy's room downstairs. But that doesn't mean I'm any less honored to be your husband or that I take the vows we just made lightly."

He leaned forward and dropped a quick kiss to her cheek. "All I ever wanted for my boys was safety, family, and a future. You're giving them all three." He took Shay's hands in his and squeezed. "Thank you." Then he let her go and stepped back.

Shay blinked rapidly and Charlie realized there were tears in her eyes. And even though Gabriel had made her almost cry, he was the one guy Charlie'd met in this place he thought he could actually like.

After Gabriel brought the boys down, Shay was the first one up the stairs. Was she nervous? She had to be nervous. They were strangers.

Charlie followed the stoner ex-pastor up the stairs. He couldn't get a solid feel for the guy. Charlie knew he didn't like the way he couldn't stop staring at Shay all day. At the same time, any time Shay tried to really engage him in conversation he pulled back, or went to take what he called a smoke break. Except he came back smelling like weed, so obviously it wasn't just cigarettes he was lighting up. Then he'd go mellow and a little distant for a couple hours.

Which, all in all, was fine with Charlie. It meant he'd been able to stick by Shay's side all day. Watching and helping her with the patients at the hospital had been amazing. Then he'd had a blast helping her pick through odds and ends at the Scrapper Yard. It was kind of magical just watching as her intelligent eyes assessed what looked like absolute *junk* to him like it held some secret value only she could see.

And now they were headed upstairs to— to— he swallowed, his

hand shaky on the rail as he hit the top of the stairs and followed Shay and Jonas down a dark hallway. This already felt completely surreal. The sun had just set and the candle Shay held only made it even more dreamlike.

Charlie glanced over his shoulder at Henry and Rafe. All of them lined up like this, Charlie had the oddest moment of deja vu like he was back in school, following the teacher.

Except his teacher had never whipped her shirt off over her head the way Shay did when she got to the master bedroom.

Charlie gulped hard even as his cock jumped in his pants. He'd been hard all through dinner and had been glad for the waning light outside.

There was light in here though. He didn't know who'd lit the oil lamps all around the room, but it gave a soft, otherworldly glow.

And Shay was fucking luminous.

Her skin looked so soft. Perfect.

At least until she turned to pull her pants down, leaving just her cream-colored lace panties on.

"Shay," Charlie cried, striding forward and turning her to get a better look at her back. "Fuck, who did this to you?" He lifted a hand to the marred flesh on her upper shoulder in the shape of a T.

She'd been fucking branded.

Shay pulled away from his touch and turned around, covering her breasts with her arms. It was the first time all night she'd looked anything other than easy and confident.

Her eyes were locked on the floor as she mumbled. "It happens to girls in Travisville."

Travisvi— Son of a motherfuck— If it was the last thing he did, Charlie was gonna burn that fucking place to the ground. He pulled Shay into his chest both to cover and comfort her.

"I'm so sorry, honey."

"It's fine," she said, shaking her head as she pulled back. "It's the past." Her gorgeous green eyes lifted and searched his. "I'm more interested in my future." Her voice was breathy and soft. "This is my wedding night after all."

Then her eyes dropped to his lips. Fuckin' hell, was she trying to kill him here? And when she lifted up on her tiptoes he couldn't help himself in spite of all his reservations. How long had he been dreaming of this? He had to taste her.

He dropped his lips to hers and she immediately opened to him.

It was his first kiss.

The first kiss of his entire life.

He'd been a pimply, shy fourteen-year-old kid when the world went to hell in a handbasket. When he got older and went on hunting trips with his Uncle Dale, well, it wasn't like they were stopping in the city brothels on their way back home. Even if that had been something his uncle wanted to do, Charlie would have let him go on his own.

Call him old-fashioned but, well, he'd grown up watching his mom and dad love each other. After she died, Dad was never the same. But even that was sort of beautiful, because Dad loved Mom that much.

Charlie just always assumed when he grew up he'd have a relationship like that. Then there were barely any women left and Charlie figured the closest he'd get to a woman were the fantasies in his head and the nudie magazines he occasionally got his hands on.

But here was this gorgeous creature, naked in front of him. Rubbing her hands up and down his chest, her tongue teasing along the tip of his in a way that, holy *shit*—

He grasped her hips and pressed his erection into her, groaning into her mouth. Even through his jeans and her tiny little panties, goddamn, he'd never felt anything like it in the world. She was so hot and responsive in his hands.

Or was she?

Maybe she was squirming like that because she was trying to get away from him? Or because he was doing it wrong?

He felt immediately stupid. He didn't even know how to *kiss*, so how in the holy fuck was he going to—

But then Shay rolled her hips against his erection and grabbed his shoulders, going up even higher on her tiptoes.

Instinctively, he leaned down like she seemed to want and she whispered in his ear, "I want you to be the first of my husbands to have me."

Charlie went immediately stiff.

Shay obviously felt it because she pulled back, her eyes suddenly guarded. "Do you still think I'm bad or wrong for wanting this?"

"No," he said in an explosion of breath, glancing over her shoulder at where the other three men stood watching them. Only Henry glanced away. Jonas and Rafe just kept looking. Charlie breathed out again and then leaned down to Shay's ear. Goddamn this was embarrassing but there was nothing for it except to just say it.

"I— This is my—" He huffed a frustrated breath out and it fluffed the hair around Shay's ear. God she was beautiful. Her silken hair. Her elfin little ears. He pulled back so he could look her in the eyes. "I've never done this before."

Her eyes went soft and she bit the edge of her lip as she blinked up at him. Then she smiled. She smiled so beautifully and took his hand, pulling him over to the bed with her.

And—because he wasn't a fucking idiot—he followed.

"Take off your shirt," she said.

He half strangled himself he pulled it off so fast. Shay giggled as she scooted over to the middle of the huge bed. Charlie felt his eyebrows lift as he looked at the bed. It was way bigger than king-size.

Damn, why the hell was he thinking about mattresses when he had the sexiest woman he'd ever laid eyes on all but naked in front of him?

He wet his lips as her eyes went to his jeans and she motioned for him to take them off. Shit. She'd see how hard he already was. Or was that a good thing? Like, it would show her how hot he thought she was?

Fuck it. It was what it was. Not like he could do a damn thing about it at this point. He had to reach in his pants and readjust his dick, pulling it up toward his stomach to even get his jeans off.

From the way Shay couldn't seem to pull her eyes away from his cock, he thought maybe he was doing it right after all. He sat on the bed beside Shay after he kicked his jeans off.

Right as he was about to lean in to her, movement from beside him had him glancing to the right. Henry was slowly unbuttoning his shirt and shirking out of his suit vest. Rafe kicked off his boots.

And Charlie immediately went on alert.

Shit.

He'd been so overwhelmed by Shay that he'd forgotten about the bigger problem with this whole fucked up situation. And he swore, if any of them tried anything Shay wasn't ready for or hadn't *expressly* given her permission—

Before he could say anything, though, Shay reached forward and took Charlie's jaw in her hand, directing his face toward hers.

After this morning's come to Jesus moment where she'd laid it all out clear for him, he promised himself he'd do anything she wanted, no matter what it was. It *was* her choice and he'd respect it.

So he followed her lead and let her pull him until he was half crouched over her.

And then they were kissing again. Goddamn. He thought he'd been hard before? When her tongue did that little thing right there? Tangling with his like that while her breasts arched against his chest? Fuckin' hell.

He groaned into her mouth and kissed her harder. He still didn't know if he was doing it right. At the moment though? He didn't care.

He tried to mirror her movements. He wanted it to be good for her. And goddamn, he just wanted more. *More.* Of all of it. All of *her.*

He had his hands planted on the mattress so he could lean over her, but when he felt her small hand tugging on his right arm, he shifted all his weight to his left.

And daaaaaaaaaaaamn.

Because the hand she'd tugged on?

She drew it down to her plump, perfect breast.

His breath caught as he brushed his thumb over her nipple. And then he squeezed gently, testing the weight and feel of her in his hand.

Fuckin' *hell.* He'd imagined it so many times. *So. Many. Times.* And none of his fantasies compared to this. A real woman.

And not just any woman. Shay. This was Shay's breast.

He squeezed again. It was so much... softer... and *squishier* than he'd expected. He wasn't sure what he thought it would be like. One older guy he and Uncle Dale used to trade with said boobs felt like squeezing a grapefruit.

Shay's tits were nothing like a grapefruit. Cause, uh, yeah, Charlie might have squeezed a few over the years after hearing that.

"I want your mouth there," Shay said, breaking from their kiss and putting her hands on the top of his head to urge him down.

"I'll show him everything, gorgeous," said a voice to their left. Charlie glanced up only long enough to see Henry sit down on Shay's other side. "You lay back and let us worship you."

Charlie felt a flashing stab of jealousy when Henry leaned down and kissed Shay's perfect lips. The same he'd just had his on. But then her breast was in front of his mouth and she was squeezing it and feeding him her nipple.

He couldn't help sucking it into his mouth. And fuckin' hell, it hardened right up like an unripe berry. Her chest arched up into him.

She liked it. She put more pressure on the back of his head, forcing more of her breast into his mouth. He sucked harder and her hips bucked up into him. God— He just— He'd never imagin—

He reached to shove his underwear down.

The only barrier between her and his aching dick was the tiny slip of her panties. The head of his cock bobbed against her and he groaned.

He wanted to shove her underwear aside and push inside her.

He wanted it so bad.

He'd never wanted anything more in his life.

Never fucking *needed* something more.

He moved over her, lining himself up as best he could. Shay had pulled away from Henry and she pushed her panties down. Charlie moved to one side, helping her yank them off her legs.

Goddamn, he was almost there.

He was about to have sex.

With Shay.

Charlie grabbed his cock, stroking himself once up and down before positioning himself at her pussy. He got even harder as he rubbed his tip up along the wet lips of her opening. Holy *God*. It was nothing like the faded magazine pictures he'd seen. It felt like fucking *heaven* on the sensitive head of his cock. Like nothing he'd ever—

He pushed in a little further. He didn't know exactly where her entrance was. But as he pushed forward, his cock seemed to be built to seek her center.

All thought, sensation, and purpose dropped to that one place in his body—his cock breaching Shay's entrance.

Get in her.

Penetrate.

Sex.

Sex sex sex *sex sex sex s*—

"Wait, are you sure you got her ready enough?"

Charlie was in such a cock haze, so ready to thrust his hips forward, that at first, Henry's voice barely penetrated.

"Stop, you idiot." Hands grabbed Charlie's shoulders, pulling him back when all he wanted to do was lunge forward.

Charlie jerked his head toward Henry. Not the fucking sight he wanted to see when he was about to have sex for the first time. "What the hell?"

"I'm ready," Shay said. "Let him be."

Charlie glared at Henry and jerked away from him but Henry already had one hand on Shay's hip, caressing her up and down.

Charlie growled when Henry's hand moved toward her center, running it down between those sweet and mysterious pussy lips and then—goddammit, the bastard moved right past Charlie's cock and slipped his forefinger up inside her.

Shay's stomach flattened and flexed at the move as her breathing picked up. Charlie glanced toward her face and found her biting her lip in pleasure.

Well damn, he liked seeing her like that. So no matter how much his cock felt like it was about to explode if he started pushing in again, he paused and moved a little to the side so he could see what Henry was doing with his fingers.

Henry had two in her now, twisting them round and round and stretching her as he pumped in and out. With the fingers of his other hand, he stretched her pussy lips wide so Charlie could see exactly what he was doing.

Charlie swallowed hard. He had no idea a woman's sex was so... complicated. He lifted off of Shay completely so he could sit beside her and get a closer view of what Henry was showing him.

There were so many... layers and folds. It was like the petals of a rose. His eyes zeroed in on the opening where her body greedily sucked Henry's fingers in and out, though. He licked his lips as his cock throbbed. He'd be fucking that hole soon.

Fuckin' hell, if he kept thinking about that, he'd spill on the bed and miss his chance to make love to the most beautiful woman he'd ever seen. He clenched his teeth and was about to shove Henry out of the way and climb back over Shay when Henry started talking again.

"Now when you are taking her," Henry said, "make sure to grind your hips down on this part of her pussy." Henry spread her lips wide and rubbed his thumb around a tiny little pink pearl of flesh at the top of her slit.

Shay's entire body shuddered and she let out a cry of pleasure.

Charlie's eyes shot to her face and then back to Henry's thumb. Whatever Henry had just done was important.

"What is it?"

Henry just smiled indulgently. "This, my friend, is her clitoris. It is one of two ways to bring her to orgasm. You need to get very, very familiar with it. Watch how she reacts when I do this."

Henry dropped his head and Charlie watched in fascination and yeah, a little jealousy, as Henry's tongue snaked out and traveled all around the little pearl.

And damn, the way Shay reacted? Charlie thought she'd been responsive when he'd sucked on her nipple, but it was nothing to the way she thrashed and shuddered when Henry licked and then latched his mouth around her clitoris.

Her little whining breaths came out higher and higher pitched. Holy shit. She was going to orgasm. Charlie was going to get to watch a woman orgasm for the first time in his life. He slapped at his cock, trying to keep himself from getting too excited.

But then Shay pushed Henry's head away.

Charlie blinked. Had she come? Did he miss it?

She was breathing as heavily as ever though when she looked down with lust filled eyes. "I don't want to come the first time as a married woman without being fucked. I'm ready, Charlie."

Charlie didn't need to be told twice. He shoved Henry out of the way and positioned himself over her again. He took his cock and rubbed his tip through her folds. Goddamn, she was *soaked*. His cock slipped back and forth through her slick flesh.

"Don't tease me," she groaned. "Fuck me with that big cock of yours."

Did she just—

"Fuck me, Charlie. I need it now. I want to know what it feels like with your big cock in my cunt."

Charlie's spine lit with her crude, sexy as fuck words. His cock found her slick entrance all on its own. He immediately pressed forward and within moments, he was sliding inside her.

Fuckin'—

Damn, this was—

The way her hot body clenched on him, it was—

Fuuuuuuuuuuuuuuuuuuck. Charlie felt like his eyes were gonna roll back in his head, she felt so damn good.

His hips met Shay's, his cock buried as deep as it would go. And damn, he'd never felt anything like— He didn't even know it could feel this—

Then Shay shifted restlessly underneath him. She wanted him to move. And the clitoris. He'd already forgotten about it. He pulled back out and Jesus, he wasn't sure which felt better, pushing in or the slide of his cock dragging along her walls as he pulled out.

But then he shoved back in again and was positive that was better. Until he pulled out and thought he'd die from the pleasure of it.

Next time he pushed in, he made sure to grind his hips up against her pearl, which made her shudder underneath him.

"Shay," he gasped. "God, you're so beautiful. You're perfect. The most beautiful thing I've ever seen."

He would have leaned down to kiss her but Henry had moved up to take her mouth. Rafe was leaning over the bed too, pinching her nipple between his thumb and forefinger.

Jonas stood off to the side, watching all of them, his hand in his boxers stroking himself.

And Charlie didn't know how to feel about it. Here he was, having the most intimate, amazing moment of his life. Feeling more connected to another person than he ever had before.

But to her, he was just one of many bringing her pleasure.

His rhythm slowed even as he told himself he was being a fucking idiot. Shay hadn't asked him to be one of her husbands because she *loved* him. They barely knew each other. But she did trust him. And then she'd trusted him again tonight, asking him to be the first to lay claim to her body. Was he going to ruin that by getting petty and jealous?

He rolled his hips into her again and her back arched, her cry of pleasure lost against Henry's lips.

And when Charlie let go of his jealousy and focused only on Shay and her pleasure, in one second he went from seeing the woman he wanted being mauled by several men when he wanted her all to himself —to seeing the woman he wanted to pleasure getting exactly that. There was almost no part of her body that wasn't being attended to.

Jonas even came forward and began massaging one of her feet even though her legs were wrapped around Charlie's back.

Charlie had set out to worship her and they were helping him do it.

But it was his cock inside her.

Him grinding against her perfect little pearl.

He dropped his head down and sucked her free nipple into his mouth. He teased his tongue back and forth along the tip as he continued driving in and out of her.

"Harder," Shay cried out, her body shuddering so much she was all but thrashing underneath him.

But did she mean she wanted him to suck her breasts harder or to fuck her harder? Or was she not talking to him at all and she meant she wanted the other guy to pinch her nipple harder?

Charlie let go of her breast with a sucking *pop*. "Which do you mean? Me or—

"All of you. Everything," she gasped, reaching a hand down and grabbing Charlie by the back of his head, shoving him toward her breast again. "I need it all harder. Fucking *harder*."

Fuckin' *hell*. Was she trying to kill him? He was barely holding back as it was. And every single word that came out of her mouth had him threatening to shoot his load far earlier than he wanted.

But he couldn't deny her. So he sucked and he fucked like his life depended on it. Because in that moment, it felt like it did. All that mattered was pleasuring her. All that mattered was taking her over the edge with him.

The way her hips drove up to meet his every thrust had him thinking that maybe she was as close as he was.

Hold it off. Not yet. Not fucking *yet*.

But with every thrust and retreat it was that much harder. He felt it in his spine. God, he was gonna fucking lose it.

"Harder," she cried again, moving her hips even more violently against his every time he pushed up to the hilt in her glorious, glorious cunt.

And then she squeezed around him harder than ever and he just fucking lost it. He sucked on her nipple as the orgasm flashed through him.

He shoved his cock in and held.

Fuck—

Damn—

He was— He could—

Cum pumped out of him. So deep inside her. He was so goddamn *deep*.

Her legs shook violently and when she started going crazy underneath him, it cut through his haze just enough for him to understand that she was coming too. He pulled out and shoved back in, the last of his cum spurting as he rode that final crest of the most amazing fucking orgasm he'd ever had in his whole damn life.

And when he looked up at her, she wasn't kissing Henry or paying attention to the guy still playing with her nipple.

No, her eyes were locked on Charlie. If he'd thought she was beautiful before, it was nothing to how she looked in this moment. Freshly fucked, her eyes bright and lazy with fulfilled pleasure.

Charlie wanted to grab his cock and start jacking himself so he could get hard and they could do it all over again.

But, though he was still half-hard, he knew realistically he needed recovery time. And as much as he might be uncomfortable with the fact, he wasn't the only husband looking to consummate the marriage tonight.

Still, he wasn't ready to give up his moment with Shay yet. He moved up to her face and for a second just hovered there, his eyes searching hers.

Her eyes grew a hair wider, almost like she was afraid of what he'd find if he looked too close. Silly woman. He brushed some mussed hair out of her face and tucked it behind her ear.

And then he leaned down and brushed his lips over her forehead, then her left eyebrow, then her right, then down her cheeks and finally, finally, he dropped his lips to hers.

"You're the most exquisite person I've ever come across in my life," he whispered when he pulled back, again looking into her fathomless green eyes. She blinked and looked down but he just put a finger under her chin and tilted her head back up so her gaze met his again. "I'll never forget tonight so long as I live."

He kissed her one last time, a long, sweet kiss, before rolling to the side and making way for whoever would take his place next. His initial plan had been to stay in the room and ignore whatever was happening on the bed unless Shay needed his help. But now he knew he'd stay as close as possible, with Shay through every step of it.

He wouldn't miss a single moment of her pleasure.

Never again in her whole life if he had his way.

CHAPTER NINE

SHAY

Shay knew she'd have to have sex with them. She'd known it ever since the plan was first formed. And it genuinely hadn't bothered her. Sex was a commonly enough traded commodity in her experience.

And yes, she'd trained her body to enjoy it even in the worst sorts of situations. Something that had saved her life on more than one occasion. Her body was just that—a body. It had nothing to do with what was on the inside.

Or so she'd thought.

But then came Charlie. So sweet. And a *virgin*, of all things.

That simple fact said so much about his character. Sure it was a little more difficult to get access to a woman these days, but there were plenty of brothels in any major city. And a strong, good-looking guy like Charlie? He was just the kind of resident Travisville was always trying to recruit.

Colonel Travis—a title he bestowed on himself—was big on rewarding the men in his service with women. And unlike the brothels, well, the legal ones at least, the women were rarely willing.

But that was all in the past.

She was here now.

Be present. Live in this *moment.*

Besides, this moment was quite a lovely one. She'd just had one of the most earth-shattering orgasms of her life. Charlie had been a little awkward at first, sure, but his natural instincts for lovemaking were spot on and soon their bodies were moving in sync.

Her legs still shook with aftershocks as Charlie kissed her one last time and then moved to the side.

"How do you like it babe?" Rafe kicked his pants off, fisting his cock and pumping it up and down with a brutal grip. "Nice and easy," his voice dropped an octave, "or hard and rough?"

Shay looked up toward Rafe, her breath hitching at his gruff, growled words. He'd left his shirt on, but his powerful thighs, and good lord, that cock—he was one of the sexiest things she'd ever seen. Did he keep his shirt on because he was self-conscious about his arm? He didn't have to be. She knew it wasn't what was on the outside that made a man a monster.

"Hard," she whispered, throat going dry. It was the only part of her that was dry. She was already shuddering, anticipating the feel of that powerful cock inside her.

"How hard?" Rafe asked.

She felt Charlie tense on the other side of her but Shay's stomach only tightened in anticipation. Everything about her time with Charlie had been perfect. She wouldn't have changed a single moment.

But as she licked her lips and met Rafe's dark eyes, she instinctually knew that here was a man who could give her a different flavor of fuck. She didn't flinch as she repeated, "Hard."

Rafe didn't waste any time after that.

He hauled her toward the edge of the bed by her ankle and then rolled her over onto her stomach. This wasn't the playful flirt who'd winked at her over omelets. This was something altogether different.

"Hey!" Charlie said but Shay held up a hand to him.

"It's good," she said. And then, the next moment when she felt a huge cock impaling her from behind, her words were a groan, "It's *soooo* good."

Her eyes had dropped closed at the sensation but she opened them again, wanting to find Charlie. Was he disgusted by her? Did he think she was a slut for liking the fact that there was another man's cock inside her only moments after taking his?

But Charlie didn't look disgusted. He did look... conflicted, though. Like he wasn't sure what to feel.

And maybe it was stupid but she didn't want to lose his respect. She reached her hand out across the bed toward him.

Would he take it? Or pull away?

Almost as soon as she reached for him, though, he was meeting her halfway. His strong hand closed around hers.

And then he crawled across the bed to get closer to her while Rafe started to just absolutely *pound* her from behind.

"Oh God," she cried. "Yes!" The bed frame was tall and the tips of her toes barely touched the ground. It was the perfect height and it provided *just* the right angle to be fucked from.

And fuck her Rafe did. His strong arm wrapped around her waist and he pistoned in and out of her pussy, the loud slap of his balls echoing throughout the room, along with the headboard banging against the wall.

It was so raw and dirty and— *ohhhhhhhhhhhhhh*.

She was already primed from her first orgasm with Charlie and here she was, already on the cusp of a second. Rafe's cock was punching that place up inside her that few had the skill or size to reach. His was a cock she could quickly get addicted to.

Then there was Charlie, whispering in her ear and playing with her hair. "You're so fucking beautiful, do you know that? Watching you take his cock so good, *fuck*. I'm gonna come again just watching you."

"Touch yourself," she gasped, eyes flying wide open as Rafe hit her G spot in such a perfect way that her whole body lit up. She fought back the orgasm though. She wasn't ready for this to end yet.

She looked around for Henry and Jonas. She might not feel as comfortable with them yet, but well, she didn't know Rafe any better and look how well that was working out. "Closer," she panted when she found them watching from the other side of the bed.

They didn't have to be told twice.

Jonas crawled across the bed, totally naked, his long, hard cock swinging between his legs. He put his hands on her shoulders. At first she didn't understand what he was doing, but when Rafe next thrust upward, she got it. Jonas was helping to brace her so Rafe could fuck her even more deeply.

"Oh God," she cried out, wriggling her ass back against Rafe as he pulled out and then shoved back in again.

And then it was just too much—all of them working together to bring her to the heights of pleasure. She couldn't hold back. She bore down as tightly as she could around Rafe's cock and screamed out her release.

Rafe roared as well. So loud she thought it shook the walls. Or maybe that was just her. Because holy *shiiiiiiiiiiiiiiiiiit*. The spasm that rocked her body from so deep— It was hard and deep and just, *God*. She felt like she'd been flipped inside out by it.

She was still gasping for breath when Rafe finally withdrew. She felt his cum spilling down her legs and her sex gave another involuntary spasm. Even the aftershocks were so intense she had to drop her chest down to the bed because she didn't trust her legs to hold her up at the moment.

Then hands were lifting and rolling her back to the center of the bed. She didn't know who and she let her eyes drift close. She knew she still had two to go. She should open her eyes and see who was up to bat next.

Maybe they wouldn't mind if she just laid here with minimal participation on this one? It had been a long day.

But as hands began caressing down every inch of her body, she didn't feel anyone climbing over her. She cracked her eyes open.

Jonas, Charlie and Henry were perched all around her. She didn't see Rafe. Where had he gone?

But then she was too tired to think much more about it. And *God* did their hands feel good. Jonas and Charlie massaged her feet. Henry had moved around behind her head to massage her shoulders.

But that was all.

No one was pressing for anything more.

Then she saw Rafe walking back toward the bed from the bathroom. He was carrying a cloth. She watched drowsily as he bent over and started cleaning her pussy with it.

She could only see the back of his head—he had thick dark hair that at some point she wanted to bury her fingers in while he pounded her. God, even the image had her sex clenching. Rafe paused in his gentle ministrations and she wondered if he could guess at what she'd been thinking.

How come when most people touched her, she flinched and could hardly stand it—but all night, every time her husbands had touched her, it had only felt *right*? And now... so *relaxed*. Even though they were still all but strangers to her.

It didn't make any sense.

None at all.

But it felt so nice.

So... very... n...

Her eyes dropped closed as she fell asleep.

CHAPTER TEN

HENRY

Their angel napped for over an hour. Henry meant to let her sleep all night. He really did. They'd covered her with a light blanket. Mostly, anyway.

It was just a crime to cover up those beautiful breasts. The nipples were such perfect little hard peaks. Henry sat beside her on the bed where she'd flung one arm over her head.

He traced one finger down from her collarbone to the valley between her perfect breasts and then around to circle her right areola.

Jonas was reading a book in the corner and Charlie and Rafe were quietly playing cards, but Henry hadn't been able to draw himself away from Shay.

She was *his*.

Finally, after all these years.

It was all coming together. The life he was meant to have. This woman. This town. Everything had been leading to this.

He dropped and his tongue traced the same trail his fingers had just taken.

Right when he flicked his tongue back and forth across her nipple, Shay woke with a small gasp.

Henry only paused for a short second, then he sucked her nipple into his mouth. And he took a long sucking pull on it.

She arched into him and her hands flew to his head.

But not to pull him away. No, she was holding him in place.

She really was the perfect woman.

What if he pushed it even further? He grazed his teeth around the hard bud of her nipple and she gasped, all but flying off the bed. Her fingers dug into his hair, she was shoving her breast into his face so hard.

His cock pulsed almost painfully.

If she reacted like this with him just sucking her nipple, how would she respond if he—

Suddenly, he had to know. He let go of her nipple, ignoring her dismayed gasp. He chuckled at her as he grasped her waist in both hands and kissed down her body, crawling between her legs.

When she realized his intent, she spread them eagerly.

He glanced up and saw her sleepy eyes heavy with lust. He didn't break contact as he extended his tongue and took a long, leisurely lick up her slit.

Her little cry attracted the attention of all the other guys. They dropped what they were doing and hurried back to the bed as Henry tongued around her clit.

Her high keening cry was his reward. He grinned and latched onto her pleasure bud. He was merciless. He suckled on it hard, then teased the tip of his tongue back and forth across it in his mouth, never letting up on the suction pressure.

He wanted her to come hard and fast. She should get to experience every kind of orgasm tonight. The quick, sharp kind. The long, slow building kind. The ones like she'd already had, first with Charlie's gentle, eager sex and then getting her brains fucked out by the brutal, one-armed guy, Rafe.

His technique was effective. Only moments later her knees were up, thighs clenched around his head as she screamed her release.

She was still gulping for air when Henry wiped his mouth on his forearm and climbed up over her. "You taste fucking amazing, lovely," he whispered, then kissed her deep.

She kissed him back voraciously. Like she loved the thought of tasting herself on his tongue. His woman was a dirty one, wasn't she? Fuck but he liked that.

He pulled back, reaching down to palm his hard cock. "Would you like to taste me?"

She grinned and Henry thanked all the heavenly host that she was his.

He moved up the bed, arranged some pillows, and sat with his back against the headboard, stiff cock standing straight up.

Shay got up on her hands and knees and crawled toward him. Right before she dropped her head down to his cock, though, she looked over her shoulder. When her eyes zeroed in on Jonas, she swayed her ass at him.

"Come and get it," she whispered.

Henry's cock jumped at her brazen words and the thought of another man fucking her while she sucked him off.

Good *Lord*, that was hot as hell.

Jonas had still been sitting on the chair in the corner, cards abandoned on the table in front of him, lazily stroking his cock. But he wasn't a fool. At Shay's words, he jumped to his feet and the next second, he was on the bed behind her. He dropped his hands to her hips, eyes on her ass.

Henry glanced down at the man's dick. Any guy who said they didn't compare dick sizes when they were around other dudes was a fucking liar. And Henry was gratified to see that he had at least an inch, maybe an inch and a half, on Jonas.

At the same time though, the man was as thick as a goddamned elephant. Thicker than any of the rest of them. She'd definitely be feeling it. Maybe even for a couple days afterwards.

Shit, the thought had Henry going even harder.

Especially when he thought about her swallowing his cock down her throat while Jonas fucked her with his elephant cock.

Henry put his hands to the back of her head and he directed her mouth to his cock. She gasped at his action and he paused. Shit. Was that too much? But when he looked down, he just saw her eyes flash up at him. They were dark and full of want. Fucking hell. It turned her on.

"Suck me," he growled out, barely able to speak the words he was so fucking on edge. "Deep."

She did. She didn't tease with her tongue. She just swallowed his knob and immediately started up with the most glorious suction.

"Fuck yeah," he hissed out, dropping his head back to the wall.

Good Lord, how long had it been since he'd had a woman in this position? Far too long, that was for damn sure. And never any as perfect as Shay.

Meanwhile, Jonas had taken up position behind her. He ran a hand down Shay's spine, ending with a quick swat to her ass.

She coughed in surprise around Henry's cock and he smiled. Well, well. Looked like there was more to the ex-preacher than met the eye.

Her bobbing rhythm stuttered when Jonas thrust into her. Henry tapped on the back of her head to bring her attention back to him. He wanted her present, with both him and Jonas. She wouldn't miss a single moment of what they were doing to her body, not if Henry had his way.

Jonas smacked her ass again and this time, she swallowed Henry deeper than ever. Jesus, she could deep throat. He thought it was something he might have to teach her. But she was swallowing his cock down her throat like she'd been a sword swallower in another life.

It was a tight fit because, while he might not have Jonas's girth, his cock was still sizeable. But Shay swallowed him down until her lips were at his groin, green eyes blinking up at him. It was the hottest fucking thing he'd ever seen in his whole life.

Before The Fall, women had only been accessories on his rise to wealth and power. One day, he'd settle down, he'd told himself. One day, he'd have the time to invest in something like a relationship. After he made partner at the firm. After he was certain he could give any family he had a life completely opposite the one he'd had growing up.

And now finally, ten years later, everything was coming together. Here was this goddess and soon she'd have their children and...

It was too much. He tapped at Shay's jaw.

"Lovely, I'm gonna—" he barely managed to groan. But she didn't pull off or move away. She just kept bobbing up and then greedily sucking him down her throat again.

His hips pistoned up and he shot his load down her hot throat.

She swallowed and the feel of her throat working on his cock—Jesus *Christ*—he'd never had better head in his whole life. None had even come close.

He'd known it the first time he'd seen her. She was the one for him.

He ran his hands through her hair, smoothing it back from her face as she continued suckling on his still half-hard cock, licking around the crown, back and forth across the slit in a way that had his cock clenching all over again.

All the while her body bounced, bounced, bounced with the rhythm of Jonas fucking her hard from behind, his fingers digging into her hips. She gasped as she let Henry's cock out of her mouth, bowing her forehead to his thigh even as she thrust her ass back at Jonas.

But Henry hated to lose her eyes. Not so soon after sharing... well, okay, it was a blow job, but it felt like so much more.

"Shay."

She tilted her head to the side on his thigh, looking up at Henry. Her lips were plumped and red from sucking his cock and her blonde hair falling over her shoulder.

"Gorgeous creature," Henry whispered.

She smiled up at him for a second before her eyebrows scrunched and her mouth dropped open in an O of pleasure.

Jonas must have felt her coming because he upped his pace, faster and harder than ever. Jesus, Henry was starting to get hard again already just watching them. Was she squeezing around his cock? How tight? What did it feel like to be balls deep in her? He'd been the first to have her mouth and tomorrow night he'd be first up for her pussy.

Jonas wrapped an arm around Shay's waist and then crawled up on the bed. He pulled her to lay sideways in front of him, spooning behind her. Her eyes dropped closed in ecstasy when Jonas lifted her leg and slid back inside her cunt.

Henry moved slightly so he could watch the spot where Jonas's massively fat cock disappeared, in and out, in and out.

Good Lord the guy was stretching her tight little hole. Just watching it made all sorts of filthy thoughts flit through Henry's head. Like, could she fit two cocks in there at once?

Jonas's hand snuck around Shay's waist from behind and then his middle finger zeroed right in on her clitoris where he started rubbing in small circles. It was already engorged from their previous play but that only seemed to make it more sensitive because she was quickly writhing and crying out.

Finally Jonas stilled, face contorting.

But Henry just kept watching Shay. Lord, was she still orgasming? How long had it been now? Ten seconds? Fifteen?

Rafe had moved in and had a hand between her legs, stroking her clit as she continued to ride the wave, higher and higher until she dropped her head back down to scream her pleasure into Henry's thigh.

It was official. Henry was going to die. His hot as fuck wife was going to kill him, right here, right now, she was so fucking sexy.

He reached down to pinch her nipples and she thrashed even more, gripping the sheets in her fists so hard it looked like she was going to tear them in two. And goddamn, if she did, sheets had never been sacrificed to a worthier cause.

Her orgasm went on and on, and when it finally, *finally* finished, Henry wanted to crow in triumph.

Because, *goddamn*, he'd wedded and bedded the most beautiful, perfect, passionate woman in the entire New Republic of Texas.

CHAPTER ELEVEN

SHAY

Shay was a restless sleeper. She always had been. Well, it seemed like that anyway. Maybe she'd slept soundly as a child? She couldn't remember. Too much had happened in the meantime. Besides, that was another world—someone else's life—it felt like. Most people she knew felt that way about life before The Fall.

So she wasn't surprised when she woke in the middle of the night, especially considering her new surroundings. Actually, what surprised her was that she'd fallen asleep in the first place. Her survival skills were usually better honed than that.

She sat up slowly, barely breathing. She had to slide out from underneath Charlie's arm that was wrapped around her stomach and Henry's leg slung over hers.

One candle was still burning. The four men sleeping around her looked like ferocious lions at rest, asleep on the savanna.

She'd enjoyed herself tonight. There was no denying that. Nothing compared to a good fuck. And she'd had three of them—four, if she counted the mutual oral she and Henry had given each other. She'd lost count of the amount of orgasms she'd had, actually.

It was far and beyond the best sexual experience of her life. Not that the bar was set very high... but still.

It had been wonderful.

And far more intimate than she'd expected.

Which, in the moment, had only added fuel to the fire. But now? She blinked in the cool room, the candlelight casting dancing shadows on the walls.

Charlie stirred on the bed, muttering something and moving his arm like he was searching for her.

And a big part of her wanted to snuggle back up to him and let him curl that arm back around her.

Too big a part.

Which was the last straw.

It was official.

She needed a goddamned breather.

How could everything be going according to plan and yet at the same time feel like it was running completely off the rails?

Careful to shift the mattress as little as possible, Shay crawled to the foot of the bed and then over the footboard. She eased one foot onto the hardwood, squeezing her eyes shut and wincing as the floorboard creaked.

She glanced around but other than Jonas shifting ever so slightly on the couch, no one moved. She let out the breath she'd been holding and tiptoed over to the closet to grab her robe off the hook. She wrapped it around herself, grabbed the oil lamp and a couple matches from the top of the dresser, and then headed for the hallway.

She shut the bedroom door behind her and gave herself a small moment to enjoy the sense of freedom at finally being *alone*. She hadn't been alone since she'd gone to Charlie's cell to free him. God, that felt like a million years ago but in reality, it had only been a little more than twenty-four hours.

Funny, at the Travisville compound, she'd always resented having to sleep alone in the broom closet rather than being able to bunk in the family dorms. What she wouldn't do for a little of that solitude now.

It was just... after months and months of waiting, *years* even, here it all was, actually happening. And it felt like time had become an adrenaline junkie, burning through minutes like they were seconds.

Shay shook her head and headed downstairs to the kitchen. She hadn't been able to eat much at dinner before the wedding. Nerves got to her in spite of herself.

Still, she'd seen one especially juicy orange in the fruit basket on the counter at dinner. She walked downstairs, still enjoying the quiet of the house. That was another thing she hadn't had in, well, she couldn't remember when. At Travisville's central compound where she'd lived— what used to be the college—there was activity at all hours of the night and day.

There was the brothel and the casino that Colonel Travis liked to pretend were much classier than they actually were. God forbid anyone tell Colonel Travis though. He had dreams of Travisville becoming a premiere destination city in the New Republic, second only to the capitol, Fort Worth.

Even if he did manage it, though, Colonel Travis was so ambitious, he wouldn't be happy with second place for long before—

"Mama?"

Shay almost jumped out of her skin at the small voice.

"Dad said you're my new mama."

"What are you doing in here?" She spun on her heel and stepped back as soon as she saw Gabriel's youngest son, Alex. He couldn't be more than eight, if that.

"Dad said we could come back inside. It was so dark and there were noises." He looked down, his round moon-face tilting toward the floor. "Tim was too scared to stay out there."

Mm hmm. *Tim* was scared. She bet.

Shay almost smiled in spite of herself.

"Will you tell me a story? Tim says our old mama used to hold us in the rocking chair and tell us stories when we couldn't sleep."

His huge puppy dog brown eyes were so open and guileless as he gazed up at her.

The rush of emotions struck so hard and fast, Shay could barely manage a few words, "I'm sorry. Not tonight," before turning and fleeing back up the stairs.

She couldn't bear to see the disappointment on his sweet little face. As soon as she got upstairs, she hurried to the bathroom and splashed cold water on her face from the bucket on the counter.

And then she looked at herself in the mirror. It wasn't her reflection she was seeing, though.

No, it was the memories from eight years ago playing out on an unending loop—starting back when the most stressful thing in her life was worrying about uneven tan lines and trying to stay awake in her morning Statistics class.

At least until the day she missed her period. Her eyes dropped shut as she remembered.

She was usually regular. Like clockwork. Still, when she'd run to the drugstore and bought the pregnancy test, she hadn't really thought there was any actual chance. She and her boyfriend, Andrew, used condoms. Well, most of the time. There had been that one night they'd been drunk and... but no, she couldn't be pregnant.

She was singing a different tune twenty minutes later in her dorm bathroom when the little pink plus sign came up in the window on the plastic stick. She thought it meant her life was over.

She couldn't help laughing bitterly now. God, she'd had no clue.

It was the one thing her mom always warned her against. "You better never show up on my doorstep teenage and pregnant. I'm not doing it again. I already lived through it once when I had you. You can bet your ass I'm not doing it again," she repeated.

Mother of the year, her mom was not.

The timing couldn't have been worse, either. Xterminate had just hit the states, with cases showing up in Texas a couple weeks before.

But back then, everyone was still in denial, though. The casualty figures had to be wrong. There was no way it could *really* be killing *that* many women. Like, maybe in Africa and underdeveloped parts of East Asia, sure.

But *America*? America had the CDC. They had DARPA and the CIA and a ton of other agencies with impressive acronyms that would save the day if push came to shove.

As soon as she saw the result of the seven pregnancy tests she'd taken—all positive—she rode her bike over to Andrew's apartment.

Only to find him packing. He was rich, she'd always known that. His dad was loaded because he was some Dallas oil bigwig.

Andrew barely looked her way when she showed up and tried to tell him about the baby.

"Look, Shay," he cut her off right before she was about to tell him. "I've been meaning to say this for a while but I just didn't know how to break it to you."

He threw a pile of undershirts in a suitcase. "This just isn't working for me anymore." Then he finally paused to look her way. "It was fun while it lasted and you're a great girl. But I gotta go. My dad's waiting outside." Then he turned back to his luggage, zipping it shut.

For a second, Shay could only gape at him like an oxygen-starved fish. But then she got her wits about her and ran after him, grabbing his arm and spinning him around. "I'm pregnant, Andrew."

He froze, eyes about popping out of his skull. Then he scraped his hands through his hair. "Shit," he swore. "Look," he dragged his hands down his face, not looking Shay in the eye. "Jesus, I can't deal with all this."

And then the coward little fucker scurried out of the room to his dad's car. He drove off without a single glance back.

What was she supposed to do? Where was she supposed to live? Thankfully she'd prepaid at the beginning of the semester so she still had a couple months in the dorm to figure it out. She remembered being so stressed out about it.

But then Xterminate really hit hard in their area. According to the way the scientists said the virus worked, it had probably been in the state for months and people had just been asymptomatic.

But when it went live, so to speak, it was... God, her stomach still curdled thinking about those days. The college town had sixty-thousand people, forty thousand of which were students.

A few weeks in, the quad looked like the scene of a massacre. The National Guard couldn't keep up with aid and supplies, and the body-burying brigades were quickly overwhelmed.

She'd been fighting morning sickness, fighting to get food for herself, and all-around fighting to survive. She didn't like leaving the dorm because people had gone crazy.

There weren't any monsters like in zombie apocalypse movies. No, it was the men who were the monsters.

But shutting herself away in her room, just waiting around to see if she'd get the telltale boils that meant she was infected made her want to scream.

So she decided to put her paltry nursing skills into practice. You couldn't even get through on the 911 line anymore—there were simply too many people making the very same calls.

So Shay and a couple other girls who didn't have symptoms sectioned off floors of the dorm as quarantine areas. She became the de facto leader, she wasn't even sure how. Maybe because she just never stopped working, she so desperately needed to keep busy?

Anyway, she organized them to separate out the healthy girls from the sick ones. There were about four dozen or so healthy girls still in the dorm of six hundred. So they set up a rotation of 'nurses' to attend to the sick and dying, even if all they could offer was the most rudimentary of care and comfort. And another crew to get rid of the bodies.

Those were gruesome, terrible days.

Endless, thankless hours caring for and cleaning up after girls going through the most horrific stages of the disease. To this day, Shay remembered the smell of the death rooms. No matter how long she showered and scrubbed herself at the end of the day, she never felt clean. She could never get it off her.

When the bombs hit a few months later, she barely had the capacity to feel horror anymore. There were girls to be attended to. So she turned off the radio describing the aftermath of the bombs and went back to emptying bedpans, changing poultices, and feeding ice chips to patients before falling exhausted into bed. She was asleep when the EMP bursts took out everything else.

All electronics were *gone*, just like that.

She woke up to darkness and a situation even more dire, though the day before she wouldn't have thought that was possible.

Two weeks later they were running low on everything—food, the most basic medicine and first aid supplies, and more importantly, water. As soon as they got news of the bombs, a few enterprising girls had filled as many bathtubs, buckets, and any other plastic container they could full of water. But they were quickly working through that supply and the taps did nothing but stutter when you turned them on.

To make matters worse, a mob of men had gathered around the bottom of the dormitory once they realized there was a group of healthy women inside.

Shay and the others knew there'd be no way to block the doors and windows to keep them out for long, so instead they'd worked to cut off access to the upper floors. Back when they'd had electricity, a girl had rigged a bump key for the elevator so they could use it for the manual override stop switch. They'd stopped it on the third floor to block the shaft.

Then they got as much furniture as they could and threw it down the two stairwells to create impassible blockades. As much as they were running out of, furniture was one thing they had in abundance. They filled the stairs up two stories high with chairs and bed frames and mattresses and end tables and any and everything they could throw down them.

And their defenses had held.

But for how long? They were basically living under siege conditions. Sooner or later, the food would run out. The water was an even more pressing matter.

Shay ran herself ragged trying to keep morale up but the situation grew more hopeless every hour. Several healthy women committed suicide by going up to the roof and jumping the five stories to the brick quad below.

Their only hope was for the National Guard to reach their town in time. Shay, never a person given to prayer, got on her knees every night and sometimes throughout the day.

The morning that they heard the noise of a plane circling overhead and then ran to the windows to watch the military cargo plane descending, they rejoiced. Their prayers had been answered!

The tanks came next and Shay had never known such immense relief in all her life.

The Army was there.

Everything would be okay.

She cried even though she was dehydrated from the water rationing. She didn't have to be strong anymore. She could sleep. Her hand went to her belly. She knew if she didn't start getting some regular sleep and nutrition, the baby would be in danger.

But they were safe now.

Later that afternoon, the Army men towed a fire truck over to the dorm and used the extended ladder to send an emissary up to them. He said their Colonel would like to speak with whoever was in charge.

All the girls unanimously nominated Shay. She'd managed a short nap but still felt like little better than death warmed over as she stepped out the window. She was terrified of heights, which seemed ridiculous after the ordeal of the past few months. But the soldier was kind and helped steady her. He was patient and talked her through it all the way down the ladder.

He assured her their first priority would be clearing a path up to the other women and Shay was glad, because she wasn't sure she could ever make that ladder trip again.

He beckoned her over to a car and she paused when she saw the purring engine. "How—?" she started to ask, but the soldier just smiled. "Army's got EMP-proof bases all over the US. Don't you worry your pretty little head. We'll get this country back up and running in no time."

Shay nodded as she stepped up into the passenger side.

The ride was a short one. Just over to the Administration building. Apparently the Colonel had set up his command base in the old dean's office.

Shay smiled as she walked up the steps, seeing soldiers in green fatigues standing sentry all along the streets. It was the first time in weeks she hadn't seen mobs roving everywhere. It looked like law and order was finally returning.

Her escort led her into the dean's office. She'd never been there before. It was an old, ornate building with ruby-red carpets and dark wood paneling.

The soldier knocked on the door marked DEAN and a voice called, "Come."

When the door opened, Shay was surprised at the man seated behind the large desk, shuffling through papers. He was much younger than she'd expected, for one. He didn't look a day over thirty-five, if even that. And he was handsome. She felt stupid for even noticing a thing like that during such a crisis, but she did anyway.

He continued glancing through the papers on his desk for several more moments before finally looking up and acknowledging her presence.

"Well hello there," he said with a smooth voice. "I understand you're to thank for stepping up and providing much needed leadership during this terrible time." He stood up and came around the desk. He was very tall, his chest broad.

He held out his hand.

"I'm honored to meet you. My name's Travis. Colonel Arnold Jason Travis. But I know that's a handful, so you can call me Jason."

CHAPTER TWELVE

SHAY

Shay and Charlie had been in Jacob's Well for almost three weeks and they were settling in... well, as much as they could.

Shay was having an easier time of it than Charlie, she thought. She spent her days working on her found object art sculptures. A term which baffled Charlie the more he watched her work the first week after they got to town.

"I don't understand. I thought you said you were making a *sculpture*," he said after hanging around and watching her bore tiny holes in several large chunks of black plastic she'd recovered and sanded down to the shapes she wanted. She usually worked at the kitchen table or on the covered deck out in the back yard in the mornings when it was still cool.

They were outside that day. There was a fresh breeze, the grass was green, and it was so tranquil, Shay kept getting distracted from what she was supposed to be doing.

Charlie looked absolutely baffled as he watched her thread the pieces of plastic together with fishing line to create a three-dimensional shape.

"But you aren't even using clay."

Shay laughed at that. "Sculptures don't have to be made out of clay."

"Okay, well I know some sculptures are made out of marble or granite—"

"No," she laughed again, tying off the fishing line, tugging at it with her teeth to make sure the knot was tight. "You're thinking about sculptures too literally. Or like antique sculptures like they used to make in the nineteenth and twentieth century."

Charlie looked at her skeptically.

She rolled her eyes. "Sculptures can still be made out of those materials, but trust me, this is also a sculpture."

After a whole week of him just standing around and watching her, she told him to go find a job.

He'd seemed surprised at the suggestion. "But what if something happens and I'm not here to protect you?"

"Like what?" she'd thrown her hands up. "Have you looked around? You saw the Security Squadron Command Center. They've got this place on lockdown."

"One of Audrey's husbands always stays with her."

That had her raising her eyebrows. "Since when do you want to emulate Audrey's husbands? Never thought I'd see the day. You and Nix made nice yet?"

He just glowered, not answering her.

That was when she put down the pieces of her sculpture-in-progress and walked over to him. She took his hands.

"Charlie."

He squeezed her hands back and immediately met her gaze. He was always doing that. It took her breath away each time. He was so open. So trusting.

He'd shaved his beard and it made his already expressive features even more so. He was handsome and kind and—

"What?" he asked when she didn't say anything for a long moment.

She had to swallow down a lump in her throat and force herself to smile. "You need to go get a job."

He frowned. "Are you trying to get rid of me?"

She'd smiled then—a real one. "Never." It was scary how much she meant it, too. She felt her smile dim. "But you need something else in your life. I can't be your everything. It's too much..." She shook her head and looked down. "I'm worried I'll..."

Break your heart.

Take your trusting nature and rip it to shreds.

Crush you like so many people crushed me.

"...that I'll let you down."

"Hey," he said softly, reaching to tip her chin back up so that she was looking him in the eye again. "That could never happen. Every day with you is a gift I never expected. You've already given me everything."

Oh God. Didn't he know that every word out of his sweet, gorgeous mouth just made it worse?

He stepped back, though, a gentle smile on his face. "But if it will make you feel better, I'll get a job. I heard Henry complaining that he couldn't get his pony express messages out on time because they were short on stable hands. I worked with horses back at my Uncle's. I rode when we used to go hunting and was pretty good with them. I'll see if I can't get some work there."

Shay wanted to reach for him even as she forced herself to push him away and nod. "That sounds good. You should go before someone else takes the job. Good ones like that don't stay open for long."

He'd nodded like he agreed but still didn't go apply until Gabriel got home a couple of hours later with the boys.

But that was just Charlie. He was never willing to take any risks when it came to her safety. He was so caring and considerate. He was the same in the bedroom each night.

A couple of weeks later and she still blushed as she got dressed, morning light streaming through the curtains. They'd all had a leisurely breakfast together this morning before everyone went off to work and now she was getting prepared for the day.

Charlie had gotten the job at the stables. Of course he did. Anyone who spent time with him was drawn to him. He made you feel like a better person just by being around him.

And the nights. Oh God, the nights.

Shay had never known sex like this before. She couldn't remember what it'd been like with her first boyfriend, Andrew. And beyond that, there'd never been sex without... well, *fear*.

Maybe in the very earliest days with Jason she hadn't been afraid. But all of it had been an illusion. She'd just survived what was basically a three-month long siege on her dorm, watching hundreds of girls die. She'd been so screwed up, she'd barely known up from down.

But Charlie and her other husbands... they were the perfect mixture of tender and rough, hard and soft. Well, mostly hard—lots of nice, hard bodies—she chuckled to herself as she pulled a yellow summer dress on over her head and combed her long blonde hair out.

She glanced in the mirror and then lifted her hands to her warm cheeks. She swore she'd never blushed more in her life than in the last three weeks. All day long, her mind was either on the night before or the night to come.

It was the last thing she'd expected.

She thought the sex would be... well, sort of a chore. Occasionally enjoyable, sure. She had needs like any woman.

But this insatiable and constant obsession she was forming for their bodies and their touch? No, that she had *not* seen coming.

She ran her hands down from her cheeks to her neck. Then she teased her fingers along her breasts, closing her eyes and sighing as she briefly pinched her nipples. Jonas had seemed obsessed with her nipples last night. Like he'd been determined to drive her to orgasm just through nipple-play alone.

He'd gotten her there, too. Well, Henry had started fucking her but she'd come literally within two thrusts, Jonas had gotten her that primed with his talented fingers. He said he wanted to introduce her to nipple clamps. Though that was never anything she'd ever thought she'd like, she found herself loving it the harder Jonas went at—

A knock sounded at the bedroom door. "Shay? You ready?" Charlie called. "Can I come in?"

She dropped her hands from her breasts, feeling her cheeks go even warmer. "Yes, come in," she said back. If it had been Rafe or Jonas, they would have just pushed the door open—they had no boundaries. It was their shared bedroom, after all. But the others tried to give her space. During the day anyway.

Charlie pushed the door open with a wide grin, immediately coming over to her and giving her a lingering kiss.

"Hello, wife," he said, pulling back, the boyish grin still on his face. "You ready?"

Shay blinked and fought the impulse to look away.

Right.

Today.

The task she had in front of her.

If she was honest, she knew she'd been up here distracting herself every way possible so she wouldn't have to think about what she was about to do.

"Yeah. Ready." Did Charlie notice the tightness to her voice?

If he did, he didn't let on. He just took her hand and together they went downstairs.

He grabbed the large cardboard box she'd carefully packed earlier and then together they walked down the block to Audrey's house. Every step they took made Shay's nerves string a little tighter.

Shay banged the knocker on Audrey's door.

"You look beautiful today, by the way." Charlie said it so easily and his voice was full of affection. "Did I tell you that yet?"

Shay squeezed her eyes shut. He had to stop. Didn't he know she could only take so much?

No. Of course he doesn't.

He was young and in I—

Her eyes shot open.

In *lust*.

He was *in lust*, that was all.

Shay expelled a huge breath of relief when Audrey opened the door. The last time she'd run into Charlie's sister, Sophia had been with her and had suggested they have a girls' day. So here she was. Charlie was just here as a delivery man

Audrey had volunteered her house and Shay had eagerly agreed. But now that she was actually here, her knees felt weak.

Was she actually doing this?

Shay forced a smile, a skill she was becoming disturbingly good at. "I come bearing gifts." She waved Charlie forward. He lifted the large box he was carrying, gesturing down at it. Audrey's eyes lit up.

"Charlie! And Shay, hi! Come in, come in." Audrey backed up and waved them inside. Shay knew Charlie and his sister spent time together every couple of days but Audrey still lit up like a Christmas tree whenever she saw him. It was endearing and spoke to what a good man Charlie was that his sister loved him so much.

"How you been, Sis?"

Nix was standing in the corner of the living room, arms crossed over his chest, and Charlie didn't even shoot him a death glare. He was clearly making an effort to be less confrontational.

Okay, well it was only a *quick* glowering look. Then Charlie turned back to his sister and started chatting with her even though he was still holding the box. It was big, but light.

It looked like they were the last to arrive. Sophia, Drea, and another woman Shay had never seen before were lounging in the living room chatting.

The woman was thin and even though she didn't look older than her early twenties, she had dark circles under her eyes. Her hair was cut really short in odd patches, like a blind man with a butcher's knife had given her a haircut.

Well, as Shay came further in the room, she saw it was more accurate to say that Drea and the woman were talking to each other.

"Okay, well look at this one." Drea twisted where she sat and lifted her shirt up slightly to reveal a long, thin scar. "Knife fight. Three on one. They might have gotten one good slice in but I took those fuckers out."

The other woman nodded. "Impressive, impressive." Then she grinned. "Still, I think I've got you beat." She was wearing loosely fitting jean shorts and she lifted the hem up to expose her thigh about two inches above her knee. There was an angry pink circular scar there.

"Gunshot. Some smugglers who thought they were gonna sell me to a damn brothel a few years back were bad sports about it when I escaped. Coward shot me as I was running away." Then she shook her head like she was disappointed in herself. "In all fairness, I was the dumbass who turned back to see if they were following me and that's when I got popped."

"Holy crap," Shay said as she walked further into the room. "I suddenly get the feeling I'm not badass enough to share the same air as you guys."

"Oh don't be silly," Sophia said when she noticed Shay. Then her eyes widened when she saw Charlie depositing the box on the coffee table and she clapped in excitement.

"Oh I love presents," Sophia exclaimed. "What's inside? Open it, Audrey. Hurry and open it."

"Don't you think it might be more appropriate to introduce Shay to Vanessa first?" Drea asked, looking Sophia's way like she could barely tolerate her over-the-top enthusiasm.

"Oh, of course," Sophia said, her eagerness only dimming the tiniest bit. And just for a moment, because the next second, she was bouncing over to Shay.

"Shay, this is Vanessa. Vanessa," Sophia gestured grandly at Shay, "this is Shay."

"Hi, good to meet you," Shay said.

Vanessa gave a little wave. "Hey. Guess we're past the formalities if you've already seen me comparing battle scars."

Shay smiled. The chick seemed cool.

Sophia looked at Shay. "Vanessa just got to town and had her own lottery a few days ago, isn't that wonderful? And she got the twins! Ross and Riodan, they were in my class here in the town school growing up. We all graduated together in May. They're great."

"Yeah," Vanessa said. "They're really great." She nodded, almost like she was surprised by the fact.

"I mean, I haven't exactly been around humans for a while, so I might be biased but everyone I've met here," she laughed self-deprecatingly and ran a hand over her mostly bald head. "Anyway, I've felt really welcome. It's been... yeah, well, I guess great's the best word for it."

Drea put a hand to Vanessa's back. "What I think Sophia *means* to emphasize in her introduction was the fact that Vanessa survived on her own for seven *years* in the wilderness. She's an example of strong female power that we could all do well to learn from."

But Shay was still stuck on one fact that Sophia had mentioned. She frowned, confused. "Wait, brothers? Isn't that, um, really unlikely? They pull numbers out of the lottery at random, don't they?"

"Oh there was all this drama," Sophia said, waving a hand. "The lottery box with all the names went missing at the last minute."

Vanessa winced, hand going to her head again. "Yeah... bad luck sorta follows me wherever I go."

Shay felt her eyebrows shoot up. "How does the *lottery box* go missing?"

"I know, right?" Sophia said, shaking her head. "So they had to scramble last minute to come up with a whole new system that would be fair, right there on the spot. Dad handled it great, of course."

Shay rolled her eyes internally. Sophia was such a daddy's girl.

"So they did it by groups. And Riodan and Ross were in the same group, so they both get to be her husbands, isn't that great?" Then Sophia stood up straighter, eyes darting to Shay and Charlie. "And afterwards Dad made sure to double check all the guys who got chosen were properly vetted," she reassured. "He was very careful."

"Are they identical twins?" Audrey asked.

Sophia nodded. "Yeah, but it's funny, they're nothing like each other. Looking at them, though, you'd never guess. Totally identical." Then Sophia leaned in, "Well I guess Vanessa's the only one who can confirm if they're *totally* identical, if you know what I mean."

"Annnnnnd I think that's my cue to leave," Charlie said.

"Oh, not before I open my present, my most favoritest brother in the world," Audrey laughed, hugging her brother and giving him a noisy smooch on the cheek.

"Ew, get off of me," Charlie said, pretending to push Audrey back.

Audrey just went up on her tiptoes again, lips puckered in an overexaggerated way. Charlie fended her off and instead, she went for his stomach, tickling him.

He let out a bark of laughter, then grabbed her by the waist, lifting her off her feet and making her squeal as he swung her around and tickled her at the same time.

"Uncle!" she cried, shrieking with laughter. "Uncle!"

He set her back on her feet, but not without going for her stomach one last time. She doubled over in laughter, shrieking again.

Shay stood frozen, watching them, her heart in her throat.

She didn't know that happiness could make you physically *hurt*.

But then, it wasn't just happiness, was it?

You're going to break this beautiful man.

She lifted a hand to her forehead, feeling faint.

"Uncle! I said Uncle," Audrey said, still giggling and gasping for breath. "I have to open my present. Besides, this is a girls' day. No boys allowed. You need to go away. You and Nix both."

"Okay, okay," Charlie said, holding his hands up. "White flag?"

Audrey nodded, grasping her stomach like she had a cramp, a wide smile still on her face. "White flag."

She finally moved and sat on the couch in front of the box. She pulled open the flaps on top and gasped. Nix immediately jumped forward but then Audrey reached inside. She stopped herself though, pulling her hands back at the last second. Her eyes lifted to Shay. "God, Shay. It's amazing. But I don't want to pull it out wrong and hurt it somehow."

Shay forced yet another smile she didn't feel. "It's sturdier than it looks." She leaned over and lifted out the three-dimensional eagle she'd created out of objects she'd found from the Scrapper Yard. Charlie pulled the box out of the way and Shay set the eagle on the table. She'd attached it to a thick, sturdy wooden base that she'd carved ornate decorations into using some of the power tools at Mateo's workshop— another of Audrey's husbands.

Appreciative noises sounded all around her. "And here, this wing attaches like this." Shay clicked the wing into place. Including wing-span, the whole sculpture was about four feet wide. It didn't fit in the box completely assembled, so she'd made the wing section detachable.

"Oh my God," Audrey said. "I mean, Charlie told me you were an artist, but I had no idea you were like, a *real* one." She leaned in and looked closer. "Are those wings really made out of... old spatulas?"

Shay smiled. "Yep. They have great flexibility if you just add a little heat. Plus, it was easy enough to find enough black ones so I could stick to a single-color story for each section of the bird."

"It's really beautiful," Vanessa said, her large brown eyes taking in every inch of the sculpture.

Their reactions were one of the reasons she'd always loved creating art in the first place. She loved taking the ordinary and creating something extraordinary out of it. She loved finding beauty in the mundane, even the ugly.

But she didn't feel pride as she looked down at the eagle she'd so meticulously crafted. She hadn't poured love into this piece.

And while she usually enjoyed people looking at her work from all angles, delighting in every minute, every second they took soaking up her creations, all she could think now was, *all right already, that's close enough. Nothing to see here. Back away.*

Because if they looked too closely, they might notice the thumbnail-sized listening device she'd installed right behind the crown of the eagle's head.

The one Colonel Travis—*Jason*—had instructed her to plant.

Because she was his spy.

CHAPTER THIRTEEN

GABRIEL

Gabriel would do anything for his children—*anything*.

Including entering that crazy marriage raffle so they could have a mother.

He'd always sworn to himself there'd never be another woman for him besides his wife, Letty. She was his soulmate. He figured a man like him was only lucky enough to get one of those in a lifetime.

But there were Alejandro and Timothy to think of. And they needed a mother. Timothy especially, though he'd be the last in the world to agree. That boy had too much stubborn in him. And he liked to think he was a man already even though he was just twelve.

Gabriel glanced out the back window of the kitchen, watching Alex and Timothy play chase. Shay was out there on the back deck, working on another of her sculptures. About fifteen minutes ago, Gabe had sent the boys out to play in the backyard. They were playing chase and shouting and laughing and generally making themselves hard to ignore.

It looked like Shay was still doing her damndest to anyway.

He sighed.

His plan seemed to be backfiring. He thought if he ever won the lottery, it would all be so simple. Get a mom for the boys. Be a big, happy family again.

But over three weeks in, Shay still hadn't taken to the boys like he'd hoped she would. She couldn't seem to even stand being in the same room as them. The couple times he'd tried to talk to her about it, she'd quickly excused herself and all but run away.

It was even more heartbreaking to watch her with Alex. He was just eight and he was the friendliest kid. He kept going up to her and chatting her ear off, but she'd only reply in monosyllables and then leave the room as fast as she could.

Through the window, Gabriel watched the boys run to the grove of trees near the left side of the yard, grabbing the branches and swinging like monkeys. They were good boys. In spite of everything, somehow they weren't too screwed up. Timothy still woke up with nightmares sometimes, but Alex had been too young during the worst of the Xterminate death riots. Tim, though. He'd been a wide-eyed four-and-a-half-year-old. Taking in things no grown man should ever have to see.

Gabriel lifted a hand to the glass as Tim helped his brother up into the tree. Gabriel smiled.

Tim was a good big brother. But there was an anger in him Gabriel didn't know what to do with. The older he grew, the more they butted heads. So Gabriel had thought, maybe if he could give him a maternal influence, someone he could talk to, confide in...

Besides, the odds had been stacked against him winning. He was in one of the lower draft tiers where the odds were lower.

But then his name had been called.

Gabriel's eyes moved from his sons to Shay. And the more he looked, the more he couldn't help his eyes traveling down her body.

She was a beautiful woman, there was no denying that. Truth was, he thought about her a lot more than he liked.

Especially after what happened last week.

He and the boys slept in the downstairs bedroom. But once in the middle of the night, he and Tim had both woken up at the same time and needed the restroom. Gabriel told Tim to take the downstairs one and he'd jogged up to the second floor.

He'd meant to go straight to the bathroom and then back down to bed. God's honest truth.

But he'd frozen in his tracks when he heard the muffled groans of passion. And he was drawn forward like a moth to a flame until he came to a stop in the hallway right outside the bedroom. And listened. There were men's voices. Well, *vocalizations*, he should say.

And then he'd heard her. Dear Lord.

Her little high-pitched feminine ecstatic gasps of pleasure.

His head went crazy imagining what was going on on the other side of the bedroom door. Was she taking two of them inside her at once? Did she like ass play? Or was she sucking one while the other entered her from behind?

He'd all but run back to the bathroom and shut the door behind him, breathing as hard as if he'd run a damn mile. And when he shoved his pants down, all thoughts of going to the bathroom were forgotten.

He replayed that gasp he'd heard and imagined scene after scene as he jerked himself to a hard, startling release.

It wasn't just that night, either. She was always walking around wearing these oversized t-shirts with tiny little shorts. It made it look like she wasn't wearing anything at all on the bottom. The t-shirts didn't help any either because her perky breasts still poked out like two gorgeous mountain slopes through the thin fabric. Half the time he could see the outline of her nipples. And he looked. Lord help him, he looked.

Then there were those *legs*.

Even now he couldn't help his eyes dropping to her legs as she bent over the huge sculpture of a rose she was creating.

Damn. The woman had legs for *days*.

Gabriel's breath got a little bit short just looking at her. Knowing that every night she was upstairs, wrapping those legs of hers around the other men in the house...

Gabriel shoved back from the window. He'd only put his name in the lottery for the boys, dammit. Not himself.

Letty was the only one he'd ever—

Letty would want you to be happy.

He pressed a hand to his temple. He didn't know if that voice was her whispering to him or just his little head trying to lead his big head around.

He'd go take a cold sponge bath. That would help.

Or are you just gonna go in the bathroom to jerk off to thoughts of those gorgeous legs wrapped around your waist?

Shit.

He stopped and breathed out hard. Maybe he should go out to play with the boys. Get his damn priorities straight again.

He'd just looked toward the back door when he saw a small shape fly out of the tree and land hard on the ground. Oh Jesus no.

"Alex!" he shouted, vaulting for the door.

As he threw it open, he saw Shay streaking across the yard ahead of him, pulling Alex into her lap. Gabriel was right on her heels, but when he got close, he slowed down. His first instinct was to yank Alex out of Shay's arms so he could make sure his boy was okay. But he stopped himself right at the last moment.

Shay was murmuring to Alex and he was responding. Thank the Lord, he was all right.

"Is he okay?" Tim sounded freaked out as he dropped out of the tree, landing deftly on his feet.

"All right sweetie," Shay said to Alex. "Follow my finger, can you do that for me?" She lifted her forefinger and moved it back and forth in front of Alex's face. His eyes tracked along perfectly.

"You're doing great," Shay cradled Alex in her arms. "You're so brave. It's okay to cry, honey. I know that had to hurt."

Alex's bottom lip had been trembling, and at her words, tears spilled down his cheeks. He turned his face toward her chest and sobbed.

"Oh, it's okay, sweetie," she cooed, clutching Alex to her and rocking him back and forth. She did it so naturally it was as if she'd been doing it all her life. "It's all right now. You just let it out. That's just fine. You're such a brave boy."

She held him to her so close and bent her head down, like she was breathing him in and reassuring herself he was real and safe at the same time. Gabriel knew because it was the same thing he'd done many times.

Suddenly Gabriel was the one fighting back tears. Did Alex really not think it was okay to cry even if he was hurt? Where had he learned that? And Shay... God, she was a natural. She was perfect. Everything he could have hoped for. Why had she been hiding this side of herself?

"Shh, you're okay now." She kept rocking Alex for a good five minutes before she glanced up, looking startled to find Gabriel and Timothy there.

And then her eyes widened. Like she was horrified. She looked down at Alex and her mouth dropped open. She pulled back abruptly from him. Alex blinked in confusion.

"Oh look, your dad's here now." She helped Alex stand and then stood herself. Alex grabbed her hand and she swallowed hard, then lifted the hand and tried to pass it off to Gabriel.

"I just remembered, I have to go," she mumbled.

But Alex didn't want to let go of her hand.

"I'm sorry, honey," she said. "I'm so glad you're feeling better." She leaned over and dropped a kiss to the top of his head at the same time as she peeled her hand away from his.

And then she started running—literally *running*—like she couldn't get away from them fast enough.

"Shay," Gabriel called. He looked at Timothy and Alex. "Stay here, boys." Then he started after Shay. "Shay. Wait!"

But he only got to the back door in time to hear the front one slam. "Dammit," he swore.

"What's up?" Jonas asked, standing by the kitchen counter, sandwich halfway to his mouth. He must have gotten home in the last few minutes.

Gabriel looked back at his boys, Timothy holding onto a still-shaken looking Alex as they came toward the house. "I have to stay with the boys. But can you go after Shay? She's upset."

To his credit, Jonas didn't ask anything else. He just dropped his sandwich and then took off for the front door.

"Is something wrong with new mommy?" asked Alex, concern knitting his small brow.

"Nothing for you to worry about." Gabriel kissed his son on the forehead. "Now why don't we all play pirates and robbers?"

"I'm the pirate king!" Alex shouted.

Timothy rolled his eyes but followed his brother out the door to find a stick that would make for a good sword.

With one last glance toward the front door, Gabriel followed his sons.

CHAPTER FOURTEEN

SHAY

It all sounded so simple when Jason first came to her and made his proposal. A proposal that was quickly followed by a threat.

Not just any threat, either. He went straight for the throat, threatening what she held most dear.

All she had to do was infiltrate Jacob's Well Township, he said.

Get married and become part of a clan.

Fuck them. She'd get a birth control shot before she left so she wouldn't have any of their bastards.

Get close to other clan women.

Make her ugly little art shit for all the important clans and plant bugs in them. She just needed to be Jason's eyes and ears.

Why did he need her? He already had spies in the camp. She knew he got regular reports of what happened in Jacob's Well. She was always mindful to listen and she heard things. So why did he want this extra level of intel?

She didn't ask.

She hadn't wanted to know.

But now that she was actually getting to know these people? Her husbands?

Her... *stepsons?*

She ran even harder and still it wasn't fast enough. She needed to run faster. Harder. At a more punishing pace. When she tripped on a pothole in the pavement and went sprawling, she welcomed the pain.

God, she deserved it.

She deserved it and so much more.

What the fuck was she doing?

She could be destroying people's *lives* by helping Jason. Not just destroying them.

Ending them.

She stumbled to her feet just long enough to run over to the bushes at the side of the road and throw up.

She'd seen what happened when Jason took over Central Texas East Territory. Not firsthand, but she'd heard enough about it because he was so proud of himself. He couldn't help bragging about it.

He didn't attack outright. Not like with guns and tanks. It was the same thing he was doing here. He got his men on the inside. And when they took over, to the outside world, it just looked like a coup from within the community.

But *she* knew. It was Jason's men who'd gone into the houses of the community leaders and slit their throats. Not just theirs, but all the men in their family, even the children. The women had been captured and brought to the Processing Facility. Then the assassins went after anyone in the community who Jason's spies had identified as a potential threat.

It was a bloodbath.

Jason had his puppets put in charge and there was barely a ripple in the surrounding territories. Unsurprising since on the south, Central Texas East was bordered by the Black Skulls MC territory and on the west, by Travis Territory. To the east, he set up a heavy patrol, which meant the only means of escape was to hazard the dead zone of nuclear fallout to the north, where Austin used to be.

Shocker, but it didn't seem anyone had taken that option, or if they had, they weren't talking. So news of the slaughter hadn't spread.

Now Jason was trying to do the same thing here.

And she was helping him.

She dropped her head into her hands, but then looked around her. God, she was just standing here like a wreck on the edge of the main road leading into town. Someone would see her soon. And she couldn't handle keeping up the façade of happy lottery bride right now.

She stood up and stumbled over to the side of the road. She was right by the quaint little rock bridge that led over the small tributary stream of the main river on the way into town.

Half stumbling, half sliding on her ass, she made her way down the steep embankment to the river.

She managed to stop herself right before she rolled into the water itself, but there were leaves and dirt all over her clothes. She ignored all of it, though, sitting up on her knees beside the gently moving water. The peaceful scene mocked her.

"You don't have a choice," she whispered to herself.

Her fate was sealed the day she walked into Jason's office.

She couldn't believe she'd ever seen him as a savior.

Closing her eyes, she was back in his office, that first day.

"I'm Colonel Arnold Jason Travis. But I know that's a handful, so you can call me Jason."

When he'd extended his hand, she'd shaken it so eagerly. "I'm Shay. You have no idea how good it is to see you. We were afraid for a while there that the government and the National Guard had forgotten about us."

Jason just smiled at her, calm and confident. He was a little young to be a colonel, but then, what did she really know about the Army or Army rank?

He was tall and broad-shouldered, with light brown hair and a face that was almost too angular to be strictly called handsome. But he definitely had a *presence* about him. She understood why men would follow him.

He asked her questions about the state of the women in the dorm and she told him everything they'd been through.

"So you're a nurse?"

She blushed under his intense gaze. "Oh. No. I was just taking my basic pre-med prerequisites and I did rotations as an orderly at the hospital sometimes." God, the hospital. It was just across the highway from the college. "Have you been there?" She felt stupid as soon as she'd asked the question. Of course his men would have gone there. "How is it?"

His face went grim. "It wasn't pretty. But my soldiers are getting things back in order. The women we rescue from the dorm will be taken there to be treated for any malnutrition or if they have other medical concerns."

Shay had to stop herself from putting a hand on her stomach. She felt the baby moving every day but still, she was constantly terrified that her limited diet was hurting her little sweet pea. She could at least get some prenatal vitamins at the hospital, or maybe from one of the local pharmacies if they hadn't all been completely raided.

The Army might be here and maybe that meant things could start getting back to normal—well, as normal as things could be with so many women dead—but she knew being pregnant could be seen as a liability.

Colonel Travis found her useful now. She'd do whatever she could to continue being useful.

Because being useful meant being protected.

And being protected meant her baby would be safe.

Even though having a baby was the last thing she'd have wanted even four months ago, now she couldn't imagine a future without her little sweet pea in it. Thoughts of holding her beautiful, precious baby had been the only thing that got her through the gruesome days of the past few months.

She wasn't even showing yet. And she'd lost weight since everything had started. That couldn't be good for the baby.

"Do you have any food?" she blurted. The soldiers with the fire truck had given her a bottle of water to drink but she was still starving.

Colonel Travis looked briefly surprised, but then he said, "Of course. Forgive me. I should have thought of that first. Here." He turned and unzipped a duffel bag on the floor. "Help yourself.'"

Shay felt her eyes widen as soon as she saw what was inside. Granola bars. Pop Tarts. Candy. Chips. It was like he'd emptied a vending machine into the bag. Hell, someone probably had. She didn't care. She dropped down and grabbed a granola bar, ripping the packaging and shoving half of it into her mouth.

Her mouth was still so dry. One water bottle hadn't been nearly enough.

"Water," she coughed out around the granola.

"Here."

Colonel Travis crouched down on his haunches and handed her another bottle of water, pausing to open it first.

She took it with a grateful nod, drinking a swig before downing the other half of the granola bar. Then she reached in the bag for another. And after it, another.

By the time she was done, her belly felt bloated and she was a little nauseous, but she didn't care. It was the first full meal she'd had in over two months.

"Thank you," she looked at Colonel Travis gratefully. "You have no idea how much I needed that."

Colonel Travis—*Jason*—was just watching her, his head slightly cocked to the side. "You've got a few crumbs. Just there." He reached forward and brushed his thumb over the outer edge of her lip.

And Shay didn't know if it was the intimacy of the touch, or the fact that he'd just fed her when she was all but starving—or if it was simply having someone take care of her after she'd had to take care of everyone else for so long—but she couldn't hold herself back.

She threw her arms around his neck. "Thank you. Thank you so much. You've saved us. You have no idea—"

He let her hug him and after a few moments, his arms came around her in return. She squeezed him with all her strength which, admittedly, wasn't much. But it felt so good to be held in his strong arms. He made her feel like everything would finally be all right. Like she could set down the heavy burden she'd been carrying for so long because he'd carry it for her.

When she pulled back, she wiped embarrassed tears from her eyes. "God, I'm sorry. Here you are just doing your job and I'm throwing myself at you."

"No, don't apologize," he said, his voice low. With a finger, he tilted her chin up so she was looking at him again. "You're a very beautiful woman, Shay."

Which should have been a giant fucking red flag. Who the hell said that to a girl who'd just been through what she had?

But then he went on. "The whole world's gone crazy. So many people gave up or gave into the madness of the riots and mobs. But you—" He shook his head, his face full of admiration. "You didn't. You fought and saved those women. You're extraordinary."

She dropped her eyes but again, he lifted her face back to his. And that was when she saw him leaning in, gaze on her lips.

And God help her, but she had wanted the kiss as much as he seemed to. She'd survived when hundreds of others had died. And then there was this charismatic, virile man, charging into town to save them all like the proverbial shining knight on a white horse.

Even the memory had her feeling like throwing up again.

Shay crawled the last couple of feet to the river's edge on her hands and knees, ignoring the mud she was getting all over her legs and shorts. She was sweaty and overheated from running. It was probably ninety-five degrees if not hotter. She dipped her hands into the cool water and splashed it on her face.

She couldn't believe she hadn't seen what a snake Jason was right from the beginning. For Christ's sake, he had her in his bed by the end of that first week.

She'd been so vulnerable and he'd taken every advantage.

She shook her head as water dripped from her face down her neck and onto her shirt. He'd put her in charge of settling the healthy women in apartments and acting as a liaison between them. She believed every line he fed her about how the US government was working on getting communications back up and that the military law and order he was establishing were just temporary.

Compared to the anarchy and mob mentality after D-Day, the constant military presence and curfews just seemed like common sense. They were only temporary, after all, she reasoned. Just until everything settled.

And Jason was such a good man.

Oh God. Bile rose in her throat again. How could she have ever believed that?

She cupped a handful of river water and lifted it to her mouth. She swished it around and then spit it out.

But Jason couldn't keep up the good guy façade for long.

It all came to a head when he realized she was pregnant.

She dropped her head, letting her hair fall into her face.

Maybe it would have all gone different if she hadn't tried to pass the baby off as his. But God, she thought she was in love. And when he first noticed her baby bump, he was so happy. And well, she didn't have the heart to tell him different.

Plus, and this was the stupidest of all, but she was so messed up after witnessing so much death and destruction, and then being saved by Jason—she *wanted* the baby to be Jason's so badly, part of her had begun to believe it *was* his. Yes, it was impossible and illogical. But she saw now she hadn't been in her right mind back then.

She squeezed her eyes shut.

Of course he realized she'd lied when she went into labor four months early. Or if he'd had any doubts, the healthy, eight-pound baby she gave birth to had erased them.

She'd started worrying when Jason didn't come to the hospital in the days after her baby boy was born.

He had to forgive her, she thought. She'd just explain it, and he'd forgive her. They loved each other.

But when she was finally ready to leave the hospital several days later, soldiers showed up at the door. They wouldn't answer any of her questions. She breathed out in relief when they took her to the house she'd been sharing with Jason.

She was sure once she introduced him to little baby Matthew, he'd fall in love with him just as much as she had.

But then the soldiers marched her downstairs to the full basement. She'd been even more confused when she saw that the room had been fitted out as a nursery. But why was there a twin mattress in the corner? She slept upstairs in the master bedroom with Jason. Had he hired some kind of live-in nanny?

She turned to ask the soldiers what was going on, but they were already headed back up the stairs. Matthew started crying and she clutched him to her chest as she ran toward the stairs. It was too late, though. The door at the top of the stairs had already slammed shut. She hurried up to the door anyway and tugged on it.

It was locked.

She didn't know how long she stood at the door banging, little Matthew wailing in her arms. There was never any answer from the other side and it never budged.

But about thirty minutes later, the downstairs television turned on.

That alone was shocking enough. It had been more than half a year since she'd seen a screen lit up. This must be more Army equipment that had survived the EMP. She rocked Matthew up and down as she walked back down toward the screen. His little face was red from crying.

She frowned when she saw a static image of the master bedroom upstairs. She sat down on the couch in front of the television and started nursing Matthew.

Then Jason walked onscreen.

He wasn't alone.

Shay didn't immediately recognize the woman. Not until Jason had her pinned up against the wall, hands above her head so he could peel her shirt off.

It was Brenda.

That *bitch*. She'd always done everything she could to get out of her duty rotation back in the dorm.

Shay could only watch in horrified shock as Jason finished stripping her and then bent her over the bed, spearing her with his cock.

That cock Shay had spent hours, entire days, worshipping.

Attached to the man she *loved*.

Betraying her only days after she'd given birth.

That day was just the first of Jason's cruelties, and by far the tamest.

He didn't let Shay out of the basement for six months.

She was treated to daily shows of him screwing Brenda or Amy or any one of a half dozen other girls.

The only contact she had with the outside world was when a

soldier brought food once a day. She tried to be smart by waiting at the top of the stairs, thinking she could ambush the soldier and escape.

But the soldier never came.

That was when she realized Jason must have cameras on her. The soldier only came when she was far away from the stairs, sitting on the couch in the small downstairs living room or in the bedroom. Then he'd drop the food on the small landing at the top of the stairs and quickly shut and lock the door behind him.

She told herself she hated Jason.

She told herself her love for him had never been real.

It had been an illusion, like the good man Jason had pretended to be. The man she'd loved had just been a fake she'd created in her head because she'd been so desperate after months elbow deep in the dead and dying.

But then, six months to the day of Matthew's birth, Jason himself appeared at the door.

And she'd barely stopped herself from running up the stairs to him. Some stupid small part of her still thought, *if he'd just let her explain*—

"Have you learned your lesson?" His voice was so cold it cut.

She approached the stairs. "Would you like to meet Matthew?"

His features morphed from indifference to scorn. "No, I don't give a fuck about meeting your bastard. Get up here." He snapped his fingers and pointed at his feet.

Shay's blood stirred. After locking her up for six months, he thought he could just come in and start ordering her around?

Matthew was napping in his crib so she *did* march up the stairs, but *only* so she could give Jason a piece of her mind out of earshot of her precious baby.

Jason just smirked when he saw her coming.

Oh, she was gonna enjoy wiping that smirk off his damn face.

When she got to the top of the stairs, she tried to push past him, but he grabbed her upper arms in a crushing grip. "Just where do you think you're going?"

She clenched her teeth. "Outside. I'm a little lacking in Vitamin D because someone locked me in a fucking basement."

Jason's eyes sparked at that. "Good to know you haven't lost your spirit. It would have been so boring if you had."

Boring? Son of a b—

"Your pussy better still be tight after pushing out that brat."

He pulled her through the door and into the living room even as she sputtered in fury. "You'll never know because I'll never let you near me again, you fucking—"

He ignored her and shoved his hand down the front of her flimsy leggings. She grabbed at his wrist but couldn't budge it.

"Come on, baby. If there was one thing we were always good at, it was this." Then he crashed his lips down on hers and pushed her up against the wall.

And damn him, *damn him*, but he was right. Sex with him was like nothing she'd ever experienced before. Andrew had been her first serious boyfriend and he hadn't known a clitoris from a collarbone. But Jason, oh God, Jason...

She hated how wet she grew around his fingers. What was *wrong* with her? Within minutes, he had her on the edge and she hated him for it. Hated him and loved him.

He was crazy. Maybe certifiably. Who the hell locked someone up in a basement for six months? And then slept with other women every night for all of that time, flaunting it in their lover's face?

A crazy person, that's who.

But being back in his arms, feeling the heat of him around her— God she'd *missed* him. She hated herself for it but she had.

So she kissed him back. But she used her teeth. She lifted his shirt up and dug her nails in. She hate-loved him.

And maybe that meant she was a little crazy too.

But when he spun and dropped her on the couch, yanking her leggings down, she helped him pull them off. Only moments later, he was impaling her with his cock.

He wrapped her ponytail around his fist the way he always loved to do and jerked her head back just far enough to look her in the eyes. "Tell me how much you missed me."

She glared at him. "Fuck you."

He just grinned maniacally and thrust even harder.

It was a quick, brutal fuck, and Shay came so hard white spots filled her vision.

She'd barely come down from it before Jason pulled out of her and stood up.

She blinked in confusion at his still full, hard cock, trying to catch her breath. "Did you—"

But he lifted a walkie-talkie before she could finish. "Come in now."

"Who are you talking to?"

Jason just smiled at her. It was a smile like she'd never seen on him before. Reaching down, he snatched her leggings and underwear off the floor, crumpling them in a ball and walking toward the kitchen. She scrambled up off the couch to follow him, suddenly feeling extremely naked. "Give me those back. Who's coming in?"

"That was just the appetizer, baby," Jason said as the back door opened and two people came in. Brenda and another man. "They're the main course."

Shay moved quickly behind the island in the kitchen to cover her naked lower half. Thank God she still had her top on.

But as soon as she had the thought, Jason pulled a knife from the block and approached her. Oh God, was he going to kill her? He really was crazy.

He grabbed her around the waist and she screamed.

"Help me hold her, Juan."

The other man came forward and grabbed her. She struggled even harder against the both of them, screaming her head off.

But when the men let her up, she realized Jason had only sliced down the back of her shirt. He yanked it down her arms where it fell in a useless puddle at her feet. She wasn't wearing a bra and she crossed her arms over her chest in a futile attempt to cover herself.

"She's beautiful," Juan said, running a hand down her back to her ass. She swatted at his hand and jumped away from him.

Jason laughed. "That she is."

"I don't know what you think is gonna happen here, buddy," Shay spat, "but it's not."

"Now darling, don't go being rude to our guests," Jason said. "I'm famous for my hospitality. And Juan here is one of my best lieutenants. *Mi casa es su casa.* Sharing my woman is one of the highest honors I can bestow."

"A true honor," Juan said, eyes locked on Shay's breasts. "And in return, I share my beautiful Brenda."

Brenda sidled up to Jason, running a hand down his chest and smiling coyly like the slut she was.

Shay held up her hands and backed away. Fine. She was *done* with this. They could have their fucked-up games. Jason wanted to keep her locked up down stairs? All right. She'd stay a hermit. She'd take care of her son and do her best to forget the name Arnold Jason Travis ever existed.

"Where do you think you're going?" Jason's voice cracked like a whip.

Shay stopped, everything in her wanting to scream at him that he was a fucking psycho and she was leaving this shitshow before it got any crazier. But she swallowed it down and responded, as calmly as she could, "I'm going back to my room."

"I don't think that's a good idea."

She was about to lose her shit and yell at him when he continued, "It sure would be a shame if anything happened to little Matthew," Jason said, cold stare locked on her. "That's his name, isn't it? Matthew?"

All the breath expelled from her lungs and in a single moment, her complicated feelings for the man in front of her sorted themselves out.

Hate.

If he was saying what she thought he was saying, the only emotion she had for him was hate.

"What are you saying?" she asked, barely able to choke the words out. She had to have it wrong. He couldn't really be—

Jason shrugged, nonchalant. "Just that accidents happen. Babies are so fragile." Again he leveled her with his cold stare.

Shay's entire body trembled. With fury. And fear. And hatred. But above all, with the desire to do whatever it took to keep her baby safe.

Because in that second, looking around, she realized that she was powerless. Jason had 'guards' stationed all around the perimeter of the house. Even without them, he could easily overpower her.

She had no chance against him.

Her voice shook as she responded after a long silence, terrified of saying the wrong thing. "They are fragile. W— What do you think is the best way to keep him safe?"

A smile curved Jason's lips. He liked seeing the fear in her eyes. She could tell. Who *was* this monster and how had she not seen it in him before? "Making my guests feel welcome would be a good start."

Shay's stomach sank as she looked back to Juan. He was still staring at her tits, a smug smile on his face.

Oh God. Oh God, how was she going to—

"Come to daddy," he said, reaching out for her.

And in spite of her absolute disgust with the idea, she forced herself to take several steps toward him. He wasn't bad looking. He was fit, medium height, and in any other situation she might have even found him attractive.

But right then, everything about him—from the way he looked at her to how he licked his bottom lip to the way he blatantly rubbed his hand over the tented front of his pants—totally repulsed her. She shuddered even as she stepped into his touch.

Jason grinned, obviously enjoying her discomfort. He grabbed Brenda and kissed her hard, his eyes on Shay the entire time.

Shay shook her head. What? Did he think he was making her jealous? After threatening her son, was he really egotistical enough to think she'd keep having feelings for him?

She looked away from him and focused on Juan. Jason wanted her to service his friend? Fine. She'd get this done as quickly as possible.

She ran her hand down her neck to her breasts, pinching her nipples and letting out a little gasp. Obviously fake, but it looked like it did the job for Juan judging by the way his eyes went dark. He reached for her again and she let herself be pulled into his arms.

It's just sex, she told herself. It was just her body. Not *her*.

So when Juan reached down and stuck his fingers inside her, she forced her body to relax. "Fuck, she's wet," Juan said, the excitement clear in his voice. "Bitch wants it. She wants it bad."

Shay licked her lips. "Yes. I want it. Fuck me. Please." She wracked her brain. What else did people say? Like, dirty talk? "Fuck me with your big cock."

Apparently that did the trick because Juan flipped her around so she was bent over the island in the middle of the kitchen.

"You sure I gotta wear a condom, man? Bitch is so hot. I wanna feel every inch of this cunt."

"Wear the fucking condom." Jason's voice was even colder than it had been earlier, if that was possible. Shay didn't look up at him. She closed her eyes. Just get through this. Then she could go back to her baby. She heard the rip of a wrapper and then felt a cock probing at her entrance. Where Jason had been only fifteen minutes before.

The thought made her want to cry. Which made her want to punch herself in the face. What, was she really going to cry over that monster?

Juan's cock kept bumping around her sex but not going in. Jesus, did he not know where it was? She reached down between her legs, cringing when she took hold of his shaft. He was much smaller than Jason.

"Ooo, yeah baby, that's right. Put me in."

She put him in.

He started pumping away so fast her eyes popped open. Jesus, did this guy think he was a jackrabbit? Did he think this was how women liked it?

Whatever. As long as he finished quick. She squeezed her eyes shut and held on to the edge of the island counter, ignoring the way it bit into her stomach every time he thrust.

But after another couple minutes, the pressure of his cock grew less and less until it barely felt like he was fucking her at all. She frowned.

Um. Seriously? Could the bastard not keep it up?

"She's just lying there," he said in a whining voice.

For fuck's sake.

If she wanted this over with, she was going to have to take care of it her damn self, wasn't she?

She pushed away from the counter and Juan moved with her, his pathetic cock slipping out. She glanced down at it. Dammit, he'd shrunk so much he was barely keeping the condom on. She reached down and grabbed his cock, giving it a few rubs up and down while she pulled him toward the living room. It immediately perked back up.

Spring wildflowers. She tried to think through all the different types. Anything other than thinking about the fact that she was literally leading some strange dude around by the cock. There were bluebonnets, obviously. Then Indian paintbrush. Pink primroses. Mustard—

They were finally to the living room and she pointed to the floor. "On your back," she ordered.

Apparently Juan was the kind of man who liked taking orders because he immediately laid down on the soft carpet. His cock was still only half-hard, though, so as Shay got to her knees and straddled him, she grasped her own breasts and pinched her nipples. Then she dropped one hand down her belly and circled her clit.

The groan she let out was genuine. She'd tried to fake orgasms before with her last boyfriend and he could always tell. If she was going to get this done, there was nothing for it but to go for broke.

So with one hand she fingered herself, and with the other, she stroked Juan. It did the trick. Only half a minute later, he was hard.

"You're so fuckin' hot, baby. Just like that. Shit. That feels so fucking good. Ride me, baby. Ride daddy good."

Ugh, could he just stop talking? That would make this whole thing go easier.

She grabbed his dick and lowered herself on top of it. Thankfully as soon as she started riding him, grinding down and swirling so that her clit got friction with every thrust, he did finally shut up. He just started making a series of groans, his features contorting and his face turning red.

But then he had to go and open his big mouth again.

"Tell me how big I am," he finally gasped, his hips thrusting awkwardly underneath hers. "How I'm better than any you've had before."

If it would get this over, sure. He was close, she could tell. She squeezed around him as tight as she could. "You're so fuckin' big." She ground her clit against him and let out a low groan. "Best I ever fucking had, baby."

And that was when Jason roared in fury and yanked her up and off of Juan. Shay barely had a second to get her wits about her before she realized Jason was holding a gun.

What the—

He aimed it straight at Juan's forehead.

Her scream was drowned out by the *BANG*.

Juan's face was frozen in shock, bullet hole right between his eyes. Blood pooled around him, soaking the carpet.

Brenda was screaming.

When Jason's furious eyes came to Shay, she fully expected him to turn the gun on her next. "Best you ever had?"

Shay's mouth dropped open. Her first impulse was to plead for her life. To say wait, he didn't understand. She was only doing what he'd ordered her to! On the threat of her baby son's life. That she found Juan disgusting!

All of which was true.

But she knew instinctively that the sociopathic maniac in front of her wouldn't hear any of it. All he would hear would be excuses.

And weakness.

So, fully naked, with blood spatter on her legs and torso, she just stood taller. Then she shrugged. She'd pretend to be like him. Maybe the only way to survive this nightmare was to play his game.

That spur of the moment decision would set the course for the rest of her life, a course she was still on to this very day. It meant she'd survived when so many that Jason found 'boring' had died.

For whatever reason, she'd managed the seemingly impossible. She'd continued to hold his interest. For nearly a decade now. Sometimes she wished she'd chosen differently that day. If only she'd fallen at his feet and groveled like so many others did, maybe then he would have put a bullet in her head too. She'd seen him do it enough times in the intervening years.

But one thing always stopped her.

Well, eventually, *two* things.

Matthew.

And his sister Nicole.

Nicole, who *was* Jason's child.

The two suns her life orbited around.

Because another thing that had happened that fateful night all those years ago? Jason realized he could make her do anything —*anything*—by threatening that which she held most dear.

Her children.

CHAPTER FIFTEEN

JONAS

Jonas had caught just a glimpse of Shay sprinting down the end of the long street and turning left. He'd immediately taken off after her. But it had been a few years since his track star days... okay, a decade. And being stoned all the time hadn't exactly *helped* his motivation to work out in the intervening years.

So it took him far longer than he would have liked to turn the same corner Shay had. And it was just in time to see her stumbling off the road into the woods by the old stone bridge.

What was she doing? Going down to the river?

When he *finally* got to the bridge, he looked down and searched the riverbank below.

He wouldn't have seen her if he hadn't really been looking. She was wearing a brown t-shirt, and with her tan skin she blended in with the bushes and scrub brush along the riverbank. She was crouched down, knees to her chest, right beside the river, staring at the water.

There was mud all over her legs and leaves in her hair.

Had she fallen on her way down?

STASIA BLACK — page 140

Jonas's chest went tight.

How could she be so reckless? What if something had happened to her? The embankment was so steep. She could have fallen and snapped her goddamned neck.

His jaw clenched as he marched around the side of the bridge and made his way down the same way she must have gone. He walked sideways, balancing carefully and *still* almost lost his footing several times.

And every time, his chest got tighter and tighter until it felt like a goddamned vice was squeezing all the breath out of his lungs.

What the fuck had she been *thinking*?

The moving river was loud enough that Shay only noticed him when he got close and stepped on a dry branch that snapped underfoot.

She looked back and her mouth dropped open a little, obviously surprised.

But she didn't say anything. She just went back to watching the river.

Jonas let out a long, slow breath.

He didn't know what to do with the mix of feelings swarming him.

He wanted to yell at her. He wanted a joint.

More than any of that though?

He wanted to take her over his goddamned knee.

The impulse was so strong he took a step back, startled. What the fuck? He hadn't thought about... not in years.

Yes, there had been a time—

Before Katherine. Before he'd been 'saved' or whatever. Before he'd become a Christian and decided to be a preacher. There was a six-month period where he'd... well, *experimented* with certain things.

He hadn't let himself think about that time in *years*. But standing here looking down at Shay, so obviously already in pain, all the old impulses came rushing back.

It had started off innocently enough.

He was in college and noticed all the porn he'd been drawn to lately had a similar theme. And his sometimes booty call, Marissa, liked it when he tied her up.

So one time, he took her to this club and... to call it an eye-opening experience would be an understatement.

Shit got crazy after that.

They went too far too fast.

He'd been killing himself with school. All that discipline and drive he'd had his whole life—he'd been pouring it into college with a vengeance, determined to graduate in two and a half years instead of four so he could start his law degree early. He was hell bent on becoming a hot shot defense attorney and making millions.

Notably his dad, the honorable Judge Bernard Gallagher, *hated* defense attorneys.

So he was studying and staying up crazy hours, living off Red Bull and cigarettes, barely eating—and it was like he just needed a goddamned release valve.

Which he found in taking a flogger to Marissa's ass. Or his belt. Or one time, his law textbook. He'd make her cry and then they'd fuck like animals on the floor of his dorm room.

Until one night when she brought a razor and begged him to cut her.

When he said no way, he wasn't going to *hurt* her, she asked, *"Why not? I thought you liked hurting me?"*

It freaked him the fuck out. Was that what she really thought?

It was just kinky sex. He didn't actually get off on hurting women. *Did he?*

He was so goddamned upset by the thought that he couldn't sleep all night after he asked Marissa to leave. The next morning, he showed up at church for the first time since he was a little kid.

And that, as they say, was all she wrote.

He committed his life to Jesus. Never looked back.

Of course, the never looking back part was easier to do when he was so stoned he couldn't even feel his own dick.

"Do you still believe in Hell?"

Her question caught him so off guard it took a second for it to register.

"Um," he blinked before gathering his wits and sitting down beside her on the muddy bank. He looked over at her but she just kept stubbornly staring out at the water.

"You were a preacher. So you believed in Hell, right? Like for bad people," she clarified, picking up a rock and toying with it before lobbing it in the river. "Do you think we'll all get what we deserve after we die?"

Jonas turned to look at her sharply. He had the feeling these weren't just idle questions. He'd spent enough years as a pastor to know when someone was beating around the bush.

After the catastrophe with Marissa, he'd made pastoral counsel his focus in Seminary. Never again did he want to be in a position where someone in front of him was in so much obvious pain and need and he had no idea what to do to help them.

"What's going on, Shay? Why'd you run out of the house like that?"

She didn't say anything for a long time. Then she just shrugged. "It's nice out here. Peaceful."

Avoidance. It was a classic defense mechanism.

He studied her more closely.

All right. She didn't want to face whatever it was that brought her out here head on? He could respect that.

After all, he'd spent eight years in a pot-induced haze rather than deal with his shit. He really wasn't in a position to judge.

At the same time, her putting herself in danger like she had was *not* acceptable.

So he decided to answer her first question.

"I used to believe in Hell. Right and wrong. It used to be so clear to me. There was good, and there was bad." He sliced a hand through the air. "The good people who believed in God and did good things? They got rewarded with eternal life."

He watched her closely as she swallowed hard. "And the others?"

It was his turn to shrug. "Well that was what was so nice about being so goddamned sure of myself all the time. It was all black and white." He followed her gaze and looked out at the flowing water. "People came to me with a problem and asked, *Pastor, what should I do?*"

"I always had an answer. I knew right from wrong. My dad was a judge and I'd grown up believing in justice as a very solid concept. The righteous were set free. The bad people were thrown in jail."

She was looking at him by now. He could feel her eyes on him but he didn't turn to meet her gaze.

"But then came Xterminate and D-day," she said.

He nodded. "Even before that, though. About a month before Xterminate, I found out my wife was cheating on me."

"You had a wife?"

He looked at her then, seeing the shock she didn't bother masking. He hadn't realized she didn't know. He wasn't intentionally keeping it a secret. It just wasn't something that came up often. He was used to everyone in town knowing all of his business. He'd lived here his whole life except for those few years of college in Dallas.

"What happened?"

He met her inquisitive green eyes. For the first time since he'd found her today, the despair he'd felt hanging around her seemed to have momentarily lifted.

So he barreled forward, as much as he hated to talk about Katherine. Who the fuck knew, maybe talking about it would help him too. He hadn't exactly been concerned with his own emotional health the last eight years.

He took a deep breath. "I brought her with me back here to this small town after my father died because..." he trailed off. Christ, he couldn't even really say why. If his dad had still been *alive* it would have made sense. But after he was gone?

He'd counseled enough people to know shit with parents usually ran deep but he'd never stopped to examine how his own dad's larger than life presence—whether he was actually there or not—had always influenced his life and behavior.

"Anyway," he dragged a hand through his hair, "Katherine was never happy here. Apparently she started up the affair with one of the deacons in my church just a few months after we moved in. Maybe to get back at me for dragging her away from Dallas and city life and everything she loved—"

Of course, at the time, he'd thought she'd loved *him* more than any of the rest of it. Wasn't that what marriage was supposed to be about?

Leaving everything else and cleaving to the person you married? Starting a *new* life, together? At least that's what he'd so naively thought when he'd stood in front of Katherine in her big white dress at the front of that church in Dallas with five hundred of their closest friends and family.

Yeah. He'd barely known anyone there. It had seemed like a big lotta hoopla for nothing. But whatever, Katherine had always dreamed of having what she called a 'fairytale wedding' so he went along with the endless tux fittings, the cake tastings, picking out the *perfect* card stock for the invitations, registering at five stores, picking out a china pattern, hiring the live band...

He shook his head. Ironic that the guy who thought weddings were bullshit ended up being the one performing them long after he left religion and all the rest of it behind.

Shit. A psychologist would have a field day with him.

He could *really* use a fucking joint. Anytime he ever thought of any of this shit, he lit up and forgot it all again. In fact, if it hadn't been for Shay, he'd be halfway through a damn bowl by now.

Instead, he took another deep breath and clenched and unclenched his jaw before going on. "So anyway, after living here and pastoring five years, I come home early from a pastor's retreat in Austin."

"I'm thinking I'll surprise Katherine, right? I got roses and everything." One of the speakers at the conference had talked about how important it was not to let the romance die and how wives were a Pastor's first and most important partner in their ministry.

So in spite of how cold and distant things had become with Katherine, he was determined to fix it. To do whatever it took to bring the old spark back.

At least until he had jogged up the stairs and saw Roger, the local CPA who did the church's taxes for Christ's sake, spanking Katherine before plowing her ass.

Jonas's mouth had fallen open in shock and his first thought had been, ridiculously: *she only lets me fuck her missionary*. Why the hell did he get to take her goddamned ass, a part of her Jonas had never even had? The one time he'd even tried exploring it with his finger she'd freaked the hell out and called him a pervert.

But Roger—fucking *Roger* got the whole kit and kaboodle?

"Three weeks later, she got the first boil."

Shay's hand went to her mouth. "Oh my God."

Jonas shrugged. "Don't think God had anything to do with it."

"Wait," she said, eyebrows scrunching. "Three weeks later? She stayed after you caught her with that Roger guy?"

"What was I gonna do? I was the town's favorite pastor. Think of the scandal." He huffed out a bitter laugh. "Plus there was the fact that he didn't have money for a hotel on a pastor's salary. Katherine certainly didn't have a job. She claimed Roger was going to leave his wife and they'd move into an apartment together. But then both she and Roger's wife got sick. Shit, you know how it was. Almost all the women got sick."

She nodded, looking down at her lap.

"So what happened then?"

Jonas shrugged.

"I took care of her until she died."

Shay's head came up at this, eyebrows lifting. "Even after...?" She shook her head. "I mean, did she regret it in the end? Betraying you?" Her eyes dropped again. "Did she apologize?" And quieter. "Did it matter at that point?"

Jonas shifted uncomfortably. Goddamn, he could really, *really* use a fucking joint.

"No."

"No she didn't apologize or no it didn't matter?"

He huffed out a quick breath. "Neither. She didn't apologize. And I doubt it would have mattered even if she had."

Shay pulled her knees up to her chest and wrapped her arms around them. "Why?" Her voice was small.

What did she mean, *why*?

"She'd lied to me for years. Years. I was always trying to do things to fix the distance between us. I read books. Brought her little gifts. Tried to surprise her by cleaning the kitchen while she was out getting her hair done. I'd set a candle-lit bath so she could relax after a day of committee meetings at the church."

He'd tried extending foreplay on the rare nights she did let him touch her, which was about once a month. And when she did, she'd only have it one way—ankles hiked over his shoulders, eyes squeezed shut, looking like she'd rather be *anywhere* other than underneath him.

"And then to find her bent over the kitchen table, him *spanking* her of all goddamn things and her moaning like it was the best she'd ever had—" Jonas stopped when he realized he was raising his voice.

He dragged a hand through his hair again. Shit. He still *really* had a chip on his shoulder about it all, didn't he?

Be honest. It was more like a giant, fucking gash. And he'd never dealt with any of it.

Repression. Classic coping mechanism.

Well shit.

Eight years it took him to diagnose himself. Some counselor *he* was.

"But you took care of her till she died anyway?"

He cringed at the look of admiration in her eyes. "I'm no saint." Time to clear up any confusion. "Outwardly, I continued being the perfect husband. I put on the poultices. I changed her bedding. Fed her broth and switched out her bedpans near the end."

He shook his head, one hand fisting as he remembered. "But I hated her the whole time. I hated her for what she'd done to me."

He thought Shay might pull away at his admission, but instead, her hand tugged her knee down from underneath her chin and when she relaxed it, he kept his hand on her thigh. He still couldn't look at her while he made the rest of his confession. "And she knew it. No matter how gently I bathed her or how patiently I spooned broth in her mouth. Her last months on earth were spent locked in a dying body and her only company was a man who would never forgive her."

Shay squeezed his hand. "Didn't the, um... her lover, try to see her?"

Jonas scoffed. "She kept asking for him. And finally, I swallowed my pride enough and went to him. But his own wife was sick. And he had his children to think of. The whole thing had only ever been a bit of fun to him. He'd never planned to actually leave his wife. None of it mattered in the end anyway. Katherine died and that was that."

Shay shook her head. "But you stayed with her."

"There wasn't anyone else to do it."

Shay squeezed his hand again. "Don't you see how remarkable that is? Plenty of people left their wives and sisters on the steps of the over-filled hospitals during the later stages of the disease. They couldn't cope. It was part of what made so many people go crazy. Staring their own cowardice in the face."

Jonas shrugged yet again. "I don't know. I probably just did it because I thought it was what 'good people' did. And I still considered myself good then. I thought I wouldn't carry any guilt if I did every-thing humanly possible to take care of her body. But in the end it was probably crueler to keep her locked up with me in that house. But they say everyone has a fatal flaw, right? Mine is that I can't forgive. I couldn't forgive my wife and I can't forgive God. I can't forgive, so I've done my damndest to forget."

He gave a half smile, but there was nothing humorous about it. Shay just nodded.

For a while, neither of them said anything.

Jonas took the time to breathe. Shit. He hadn't thought about all this in so long. He wasn't sure if talking about it made him feel better or worse. Talking about stuff was supposed to help, right? It was kind of the basic assumption for the entire field of psychology.

Then again, he'd counseled people for years and seen firsthand that shit often got worse before it got better.

Sometimes he fucking hated having the training he did. He didn't want to know that. He didn't want to know how messy it could get if he finally dug all this bullshit up from where he'd buried it.

He wanted to believe that now that he'd told Shay, finally talked about it to someone, that *boom*, he could dust his hands off. All done.

He really fucking wished it worked that way. And hated knowing that in most cases, it didn't.

"Why'd you say 'him *spanking* her of all things' like that? Why was it so much worse that he was spanking her?"

Well, shit.

"Oh, um." Jonas tugged at the collar of his t-shirt. "Just that, you know... um. Katherine was never that adventuresome in bed. I was always trying to get her to... anyway. But with him she was willing to let—"

"So you like that kind of thing? Spanking? Like, is that what you meant? Because you wished you could have been the one spanking her?"

Goddamn. Was she *trying* to fucking kill him?

"Like BSDM or whatever?"

"BDSM," he immediately corrected without thinking.

At the little triumph in her eyes, he wondered if she'd pronounced it wrong on purpose. He flexed his hand.

Oh she was playing with fire here.

"I've heard about it. Read about it in books."

Jonas almost choked. What kind of books had she been reading?

"What does it stand for? The letters in the acronym."

"Um," Jonas said, wishing he had a tall glass of water so he'd have an excuse not to answer until he could scramble to come up with something appropriate.

But she just kept staring expectantly at him. So finally he let out a breath. What the hell? Apparently today was sharing day.

"Some of the letters can stand for different things, but the basics are "Bondage, Discipline, Submission, and Masochism."

Her eyes perked up.

"Discipline. Does that mean like... as in, punishment?"

Ah, and now they were coming full circle. She'd started this entire conversation by asking about Hell. The ultimate place of punishment for sinners.

He softened his voice. "Do you feel like you need to be punished for something, Shay?"

He meant to follow up with some leading questions that would guide her to finally open up and tell him what was wrong.

What he didn't expect was for a determined, desperate excitement to glint in her eyes.

She reached out and gripped his hand so hard he bet he'd have little moon imprints from her fingernails later.

But it was her words that really made an impression on him. Especially his goddamned cock.

"Oh God, Jonas, yes. Please. Punish me."

Before he even fully thought through what he was doing, his hand was shooting out and grabbing her underneath her jaw.

At her sharp intake of breath and her expanding pupils, his cock hardened even more.

Yes.

Everything inside him roared the word.

He scraped his thumb across her bottom lip and felt the tremor that went through her entire body.

Holy fuck. Yes.

He wanted to shove her back against the riverbank, rip her jeans down, and impale her right there.

He wanted to bite her nipples until she screamed.

He wanted her to suck on his finger and then shove it up her ass while he—

"If I put my hand down your pants right now," he whispered through gritted teeth, "how wet would I find your cunt?"

She gasped again and sucked his thumb into her mouth. Her green eyes locked on him as she started bobbing and sucking on his thumb.

He jerked it out and stood up abruptly. Then he leaned down a hand for her. She took it and he pulled her to her feet as well. He wasn't gentle about it, either.

As soon as she was standing, he spun her around and smacked her on her impertinent little ass.

Fuuuuuuuuuuuck yes.

The sense of relief at finally giving in to his impulses was so overwhelming, he felt goddamned staggered by it.

It was what he'd wanted to do ever since he'd looked over the edge of the bridge and saw the danger she'd so carelessly put herself in.

He smacked her again, harder and she cried out.

It wasn't in pain, though.

At least, not only in pain.

Her little whimper had his cock hardening to fucking steel and he couldn't help making good on his earlier threat.

Holding her to his body with one arm, he yanked the button on her pants undone and shoved his hand down her underwear.

She was fucking drenched.

She squirmed against his hand. She wanted friction.

Her eyes were closed.

Fuck that.

"Open your eyes," he demanded, at the same time as he stuck his middle two fingers inside her sopping cunt.

Her eyes popped open, wild and dark as she continued gasping for air. He moved so that he was chest to chest with her, his fingers in her cunt directing her like a goddamned puppet. Then he reached around and smacked her ass again.

And again, he didn't hold back.

She arched her chest into his, head lolling to the side, never breaking eye contact with him.

He cradled her jaw roughly, thumb to her bottom lip.

And that's when he saw it. Beneath her desire, her desperation was as clear as day. It was a different desperation than Melissa had that night so long ago. Shay wasn't looking for someone to help her hurt herself to get relief from her demons.

No, Shay had the look of an animal caught in a trap. She wasn't giving into the demons chasing her like Melissa. She was terrified and fighting and hoping against hope for salvation from them.

And the last thing she needed was a man as fucked up as he was, just waking up to how much he himself had been repressing.

Goddammit.

He couldn't be what Shay needed right now.

He never thought he'd regret his years retreating from the world but shit, did he. The fact that he couldn't be Shay's white knight? Or even her dark one?

It gutted him.

And then he remembered. It was true, he might not be able to offer Shay the steady, loving guidance she needed right now. Not all by himself, anyway.

But he wasn't all by himself anymore, was he?

"Come with me." It was not a request and when he reached his arm out, Shay took it silently.

He didn't say a word the entire time he helped her back up the steep embankment to the road. Then, right before they made their way out of the woods onto the road, he stopped her.

He ran his hand down her throat and curved it around the back of her neck. Then he jerked her body to his.

"You are never to go down to the river and put yourself in such reckless danger again. Do you understand me?"

She blinked and at first, he thought she was going to object, but then she nodded.

"Good. Now. Your punishment's only begun, baby doll," he whispered darkly in her ear. Again, he felt her breath hitch and his cock pulsed so hard it was almost painful. Still, he kept his voice steady. "Follow me back to the house. And don't say a single word. Nod if you understand and promise to be a good girl."

He pulled back just in time to see her swallow hard and, trembling, give a shaky nod.

"Good girl," he said then he turned and started back for the road. He didn't look back once, but he heard the quiet footsteps behind him that said she was following obediently.

CHAPTER SIXTEEN

CHARLIE

Charlie had come downstairs after his sponge bath expecting to spend the rest of the late afternoon with Shay while she worked on the amazing rose sculpture she was creating for Sophia.

After a long morning and early afternoon at the stables, though, he didn't want to skip out on the bath. He even washed his hair, which was a bit of a feat with only a couple of buckets of water.

He couldn't believe how much had changed in just a month.

As much as he hated to admit it, Jacob's Well wasn't actually so bad. Audrey was right—not that he'd ever tell her that. It wasn't like what he'd first assumed. People in town were, well... nice. The other guys at the stable worked hard. And his sister really did seem genuinely happy.

He kept waiting for the dark underbelly of the town to show itself.

But... it never did.

Everywhere he looked, there were smiles on people's faces. They did their jobs, earned their local tokens to spend on food and at the shops in town, and went about their lives. If you didn't have enough tokens, you could still get a basic ration of food twice a day from the Food Pantry. So nobody starved.

It wasn't perfect. He'd explored a little while he knew Shay was safe at the house with one of the other clan guys. He'd seen some of the overcrowded apartments where men slept six or eight to a room. But according to the men themselves, that was just for the new arrivals. You could quickly work your way into better accommodations. Work hard and it paid off, that was what he heard over and over. The longer you were a citizen of the territory, the better the benefits.

All Charlie really cared about were his sister and Shay, though. And they were both undeniably happy. Well, his sister was anyway. Her only complaint was that she wasn't pregnant yet in spite of how hard she and her clan were apparently trying. Yeah, *that* had been an awkward conversation.

But with Shay he couldn't always tell.

She smiled often enough but her smiles didn't always reach her eyes. And he'd catch her staring off into the distance sometimes when she didn't think anyone was looking. Like she was thinking about something sad or someone she'd lost.

There was still so much about her he didn't know.

He pulled a shirt on over his head and toweled his hair off, then headed out of the bathroom, determined to try gently prodding her for answers again.

But she was nowhere to be found. There was only Gabe and the boys in the house. And after he'd asked about Shay, the littlest one, Alex, piped up, "New Mommy was sad because I fell out of the tree. Then she ran away."

Charlie jerked his gaze up to Gabriel. "What?"

"I thought I explained this. Mommy just needed to go for a walk, that was all. Why don't you go play with Tim? I need to talk to Uncle Charlie."

As soon as Alex ran off, Gabriel explained what had happened in the backyard while Charlie had been cleaning up.

"And you don't know where she went?" Charlie looked toward the front door. All his muscles were tense. He wanted to run after her. He wanted to call out the goddamned guard to find her and make sure she was all right.

Yet again, she'd needed him and he hadn't been there for her. "Goddammit, he swore."

"Jonas went after her," Gabe said, obviously trying to be reassuring. "I'm sure he found her."

Charlie ran a hand through his still-damp hair. "How long ago?" Damn, why had he spent the extra time washing his hair twice?

"About fifteen minutes."

Charlie swore, glancing toward the grandfather clock in the living room. He wanted to go looking for her, but what if he left and then she came home and he missed her?

So he paced back and forth in the living room, eyes on the clock until he thought the *tick, tick, tick* of the damn thing would drive him insane.

"That's it," he declared after another twenty minutes passed. To an empty room. Gabriel was out back preparing beans and rice over the cookstove. "I'm gonna go—"

But right then, the front door opened.

Jonas strode in, Shay on his heels, her head bowed, hands behind her back. What the hell was going on? Why did she look like a kid in trouble headed to the principal's office?

"Shay," Charlie started, heading toward her, but Jonas held a hand up.

"Don't. She's in the middle of a punishment."

What? He had to have fucking heard that wrong.

"Come again?" If Jonas was a smart man, he'd pick up on the steel edge to Charlie's words. He better start backpedaling, and fast, or else he was going to find his face rearranged.

But Jonas just looked at him calmly and over annunciated each word. "She's. Being. Punished."

"You son of a—" Charlie was about to take a swing at the man, former pastor or not, but Shay's head suddenly shot up. She jumped between Charlie and Jonas.

"No!" she said. "Charlie, no." Her eyes were almost wild. "Please." She grabbed the fist he lifted to punch Jonas and kissed his knuckles.

He'd never seen her eyes so pleading. "Please, Charlie, I need this. And if you care about me at all, then you'll let Jonas teach you so you can give me what I need, too."

Charlie felt his mouth drop open. What the *hell* was she talking about. But when he glanced to Jonas, he seemed to understand her words perfectly.

"Shh, that's a good girl," he said, combing his fingers through her hair from her temples down to the nape of her neck and drawing her close.

Charlie's first impulse was to scream at the manipulative fucker to get his hands off her. Here was the brainwashing bullshit he'd always suspected was going on in this town. It was playing out right in front of his eyes.

But Shay, God, her whole body went limp as she leaned into Jonas's touch. Every line of tension disappeared from her face and it was the first time, the *only* time, Charlie had seen her look truly... *peaceful*. Free from whatever burden she carried like an invisible lead weight on her shoulders everywhere she went.

Jonas walked to the back door and opened it. "Gabriel," his voice was sharp as a whip. When Gabriel jogged up, his voice was just as clipped. "Take the boys to Sophia's for the night. Then go get Henry and come back. Rafe's shift is almost over so he should be home soon on his own. Shay needs all of us tonight."

Gabriel didn't say a word of disagreement. He just went to call for the boys.

What the *fuck*? Was everybody under this bastard's spell?

Charlie turned back to Jonas, ready to call him out on his bullshit, only to find Jonas's steely glare locked on him.

"Come upstairs with us. You're important to Shay and she needs you now."

It was only Shay's pleading eyes that had Charlie biting his tongue.

Charlie told himself he didn't follow them up the stairs because Jonas ordered him to. He followed because no way was he going to let Shay be alone with that chameleon motherfucker. Some of the guys in the house were okay—mostly Gabriel and occasionally Rafe—but he didn't trust Jonas one goddamned bit.

Jonas led Shay straight to the master bedroom and once they were there, he immediately stripped her t-shirt off over her head. She lifted her arms to help him. When he reached for her jeans, she raised one leg and then the other.

Charlie stood and stared on with his hands fisted in frustration.

He hadn't said another word of protest as she climbed into bed and they took her night after night. It wasn't always all of them. But usually at least two and often more.

Himself included.

There were at least a few nights that she'd taken all four of them, one after the other. Gabe had stayed true to his word and always slept downstairs with the boys. Part of Charlie wished he could be as strong. Because being part of this always felt... *wrong*, somehow. Like they were taking advantage of her.

But then every night he'd find himself back in bed. And when she pleaded and gasped and begged, every night he gave in.

He told himself he was only doing what she wanted. She'd been right that first night. She should be the one with the choice. And if she chose... *this*, well then, who was he to judge?

But then why was she so distant all the time? Why did she seem so unhappy?

What if it was all some sort of act—her just performing the way she thought they wanted her to act? Yeah, she seemed to get off and orgasm, but that could be an act too.

Charlie's stomach only cramped with more worry as Jonas led Shay by the small of her back toward the bed. He laid her down in the center of it and then lifted one arm above her head. He was gentle at first, and then he roughly slammed it down against the mattress. Shay's breathing went from normal to quick little gasps.

Was she aroused?

Or afraid?

Shit. Charlie dragged his hand through his hair again.

All he'd wanted from the start was to protect her. And here he was, fucking up yet *again*. Just like he hadn't protected his own goddamned sister.

He'd known there'd been something off in the way their cousin

Rodney watched her when they'd been staying with their Uncle Dale. But Audrey said Charlie was being ridiculous, that Rodney was family. So Charlie had ignored that voice inside him and left her alone with Rodney. Then the bastard had attacked her.

So was he going to ignore that inner voice again? And let another woman he l— Another woman he *cared about* down?

Fuck that.

He strode forward, ready to shove Jonas out of the way and scoop Shay off the bed.

Right as he got within shoving distance, though, he heard Shay's whisper soft voice. "Will you put it in my ass? Will you make it hurt? Please?"

Charlie stalled only a few feet away from the bed, transfixed by the pleading look on Shay's face.

Jonas leaned over and ran a hand down the valley between her breasts to her stomach, stopping right before he got to her sex. Shay arched her back, obviously begging for more. But Jonas moved his hand away from her pussy—her glistening, wet pussy—and Charlie swallowed hard.

Because Shay didn't look like she was in any need of rescuing. In fact, she looked like she was exactly where she wanted to be.

"You want it to hurt, baby doll?" Jonas asked. He put his hands on her hips and squeezed. And then, in one quick motion, he flipped her so that she was face down on the mattress. "You want to be punished for your sins?"

"Yes," she cried out, her voice muffled by the mattress.

Fuckin' hell, Charlie's cock was getting hard. Just like it did every night in spite of his reservations.

With Shay naked and panting in front of him, though... nothing in the world could feel wrong.

She's only like this because they've brainwashed her into thinking it's what she wants—

But when?

Other than a few hours here and there, Charlie had been at Shay's side ever since they'd walked into camp. And she'd been enthusiastic about sleeping with all of them on their wedding night. That was on the second day and she definitely hadn't been out of his sight at that point.

So... what if there wasn't any brainwashing?

What if this was what Shay, and maybe his sister too, actually *wanted*. Okay, strike that. He shuddered. No thinking about his sister while he was staring at his gorgeous, naked wife *ever* again.

But then his thoughts stopped in their tracks.

His wife.

Had he ever really thought of Shay in those terms before?

As his *wife?*

Their wife?

If he let go of all the preconceptions he'd had growing up about marriage and lo— He swallowed. About *love*, and about what it meant to protect someone you loved, then maybe, just maybe...

Jonas raised his hand and slapped Shay's ass. So hard it left a mark.

"What are you—" Charlie lurched forward.

Fuck everything he'd just been thinking.

No. *Wrong.*

This bastard had just *hit* her.

Charlie grabbed Jonas by the arm and started yanking him away from Shay when she cried out, "Please! *Again!*"

Charlie froze and Jonas took advantage of his momentary shock.

"Feel her."

He grabbed Charlie's hand and jerked him forward. Charlie stumbled, pulled off balance by Jonas's force. But Jonas didn't stop. Not until he'd shoved Charlie's hand between Shay's legs.

Charlie started to object, but then he felt what Jonas meant for him to feel. Shay was wet. And not just a little bit. Charlie blinked and started to jerk his hand back but Jonas snatched his wrist, holding him in place.

"Keep touching her," he ordered.

Chest heaving, Charlie did as Jonas said. He kept his hand on her inner thigh that was slick with her juices.

And then Jonas slapped her ass again.

Both Charlie and Shay jolted at the blow. But whereas Charlie was ready to deck Jonas, Shay just wriggled closer to Charlie's hand.

His breath caught.

His thumb twitched the tiniest bit closer to her sex and her entire body shuddered. His eyes shot to Jonas and he just gave a knowing smirk.

"You like it when he touches you there, baby doll?" Jonas spanked her again.

Spanking. That was what he was really doing. Not slapping or hitting. He was spanking her.

At both the thought and the sight, Charlie's pants grew uncomfortably tight.

Shay let out a sweet little dissatisfied noise, wriggling on Charlie's hand again.

Jonas landed another *smack*.

"Stop moving. Your pleasure is not yours tonight. You don't get to say when or if you get to come. Only your masters do."

A small wheedling whine was Shay's only reply.

"Now you," Jonas said, nodding at Shay's round ass, pink from his attention.

Charlie felt his eyebrows lift. "What? I can't—"

"You can and you *will*." Jonas's glare was stern. "Because our wife needs it."

Holy shit. What alternate *Twilight Zone* version of his life had Charlie walked into that he was even thinking about doing this? Maybe Jonas had slipped him some edibles in his lunch stew and this was all a very vivid hallucination.

"Spank her," Jonas demanded. "She has to know that when she needs punishing, any of her husbands will be up for the job."

Punishing? Did they really have to use that word? She was a grown up and it wasn't like they were—

"Spank your wife," Jonas ordered with the tone of a drill soldier.

And Charlie swung his hand, palm down, and spanked Shay's ass.

He froze as soon as he made contact and then, realizing he still had his hand on her warm flesh, he jerked his hand back. He just hit her. He just hit Shay. He felt immediately sick with himself. Especially when he realized that his cock had gone stone hard.

"Now feel how wet you've made her."

Fuck this bastard.

Charlie's jaw went tense.

But then he remembered how wet she'd been after Jonas spanked her.

This is for Shay. You swore you'd do anything for her.

So Charlie reached down between her legs again. And sure enough, she seemed even wetter than before. Charlie teased his finger in her slickness up to her clitoris and she wriggled her ass toward him. Like she wanted more.

Goddammit. She *did* want to be spanked. He'd heard her with his own ears—she'd asked for it to hurt. He might not understand it but that didn't mean it wasn't valid for her to want. She'd even asked for...

Charlie slid the finger circling her clit down through her pussy lips, and then further back. All the way to the forbidden rosette between her gorgeous ass cheeks.

His breath stalled as he teased his index finger at the rim of her back hole. Then, before he could overthink it or stop himself, he pressed it inside.

Shay immediately bucked her hips and ass up so that his finger was buried up to the knuckle. Holy *shit*, did she know what she was doing to him?

He'd never even— Maybe in some of his dirtiest fantasies, the kind he would never admit to anyone, he'd thought about playing with a woman's ass. But now here he was, with his finger—

"Add another," Jonas said, running a hand down Shay's spine. She arched into it like a cat. "She can take it. Stretch her."

Shay let out a whimpering little groan and then looked over her shoulder at them. "You don't have to stretch me. Just put it in. It's okay if it hurts."

Jonas spanked her this time, while Charlie's finger was still in her ass.

"What did I tell you?" Jonas snapped. "Your pleasure is ours tonight. Not yours. Trust us to take care of you."

Shay turned her head back around and her forehead sank to the mattress.

Swallowing hard, Charlie put a second finger to the tiny puckered rosette of her ass and, working her hole back and forth with his fingers, finally got the tip of his second finger past her rim of muscles.

"You started without us."

Charlie glanced over to see Henry in the doorway, Rafe and Gabriel behind him.

Henry strode right in, Rafe on his heels. Gabriel stood frozen at the door. His eyes were locked on Shay's body, trailing up and down to where Charlie had his fingers in her ass.

"Get in here Gabriel," Jonas ordered. "Shay needs all of us tonight. That means you too."

Gabriel lifted a hand to the back of his neck, his tan skin going a shade red. "I don't know. Maybe I should just go back downstairs and —" He gestured toward the hallway behind him.

"Are you going to let her down when she needs you?" Jonas's voice brooked no argument, and though Gabriel looked tortured about it, his feet carried him forward instead of backwards.

Fucking hell, maybe *they* were the ones who'd been brainwashed and they didn't even know it.

But as Shay twisted and writhed underneath his fingers, goddamn, maybe being brainwashed wasn't the worst thing in the world.

Charlie worked his second finger in further and further, then leaned over and kissed Shay's pink ass where she'd been spanked. And then, when she squirmed against him, he couldn't help nipping her flesh with his teeth.

Her low groan went straight to his dick and he finger-fucked her a little bit harder, eliciting a shrill cry and a shudder. She was so fucking responsive.

"Everyone's here," Jonas said. "It's time. Up on your knees, baby doll."

Charlie didn't want to move his hand. He wanted to finger her for hours. He wanted to learn every contour of her body, inside and out.

"Henry, get the lube for Charlie. He's going to take sweet Shay's ass tonight."

Charlie's cock jerked in his jeans at Jonas's words. He removed his fingers only when Shay started to crawl off the bed.

Jonas didn't let her get far. He swept her up in his arms as soon as she got to the edge.

"Charlie, sit on the couch. Lube up and get ready to take our angel."

Charlie both wanted to object and to do exactly what Jonas said. Take her ass. Fuckin' hell, he couldn't imagine anything hotter in the whole goddamned universe.

But was it the right thing to do for Shay?

His brow knit in concentration as he sat on the couch and Henry handed him a small jar of lube.

He held it, frozen in indecision. Should he or shouldn't he?

But when he glanced Shay's direction, he found her eyes locked on him and the lube in his hand. She was gnawing on her bottom lip, the way she did when she was turned on.

Like every step down this rabbit hole, her desire was the deciding factor. He yanked his pants down and then off. And with one last big breath, he took the plunge, lubing up his rock-hard cock and sitting down on the couch as she approached.

Jonas paused right as he got to the couch, eyes going to Shay. "You want off this rollercoaster, you say red. Do you understand?"

Shay nodded.

"What do you say if you want things to stop?"

"Red," she repeated.

He nodded, leaning in and taking her lips in a slow, lingering kiss. When they pulled apart, he dropped his forehead to hers. "Now, baby doll," he said a long moment later, finally pulling back and looking her in the eye, "it's time to tell us your secrets."

Shay's eyes suddenly went wide as saucers but Jonas was too busy to see. Jonas positioned her on Charlie's lap, chest to chest. Charlie's hands immediately went to cup her perfect breasts.

Holy fuck, he'd never tire of holding them. Squeezing them. Staring at the way those gorgeous little nipples of hers went so hard when he ghosted his thumbs right across the very tips—

She gasped and arched toward him even as Jonas helped position her feet on the very edge of the couch, knees up, to either side of Charlie's body.

"Come help me hold her," Jonas called to the others in the room. "We're all part of this."

Henry and Rafe immediately came on either side of Jonas, each of them helping to hold Shay steady by an elbow. Jonas grabbed her waist and then suddenly, Shay was reaching down to poise the tip of Charlie's cock at the puckered little hole his fingers had been playing with earlier.

Were they serious? Just like this? He was just supposed to fuck her in the ass now? With no more preamble? They were just going to—

"Holy fuck," Charlie swore as the head of his cock slipped through Shay's ring of muscles with a little pop.

He heard all of her breath hiss out and her ass clenched around him. He grabbed her waist from behind, his hands right below Jonas's.

"Shh, that's right baby doll," Jonas said. "Relax. Let it happen. Let him fuck that dirty little ass of yours."

She sank all the way down and fuckin' *hell*. Charlie never thought— The grip was so tight, he— And holy shit, when she squeezed like that around him, he was gonna—

"Now up and down. I want you to feel every inch of his cock, gorgeous."

Charlie moved his hips down at the same time everyone holding on to Shay helped lift her off of him. And holy fuck did the friction feel good. He'd never look at sex the same after this. It was so good, so fuckin' good. Every moment of every day from here on out would be taken up with thoughts of how glorious Shay's ass felt gloving his cock.

Shay sank down again and when she was next lifted up, Charlie swatted her ass, which got her to clench on him so fucking good he thought he might die. He spanked her again, this time on the other ass cheek.

Her ass was everything. Charlie stared down, mesmerized at his cock disappearing into her body. Not the normal hole. Jesus fuck, he'd never seen anything as hot in his entire life as Shay's ass taking his cock. He wasn't small either. He might not be as big as Rafe, but he was a good eight inches.

He dragged Shay back down until his balls were flush up her ass. Holy fuck, he was so fucking *deep*. So deep in her.

He dragged her toward him, ignoring the others who had a hold of her, and kissed her deep. "You feel me, sweetheart?" he asked, dragging his mouth from her lips to her ear. "You feel me so deep inside you? Fucking your ass so deep?"

He wrapped one arm like a bar around her back and pulled his hips back before shoving in deep again.

She cried out and it only made Charlie want to fuck her harder, deeper.

"You feel me there, sweetheart?" he growled. "You like it hard like this?"

"Yes," she cried, her voice hoarse. "Yes, I need it. Please. More. Harder. I need it."

Her words flipped a switch. He thought it had been good before, but having her beg like that? It drove him fucking insane.

He wanted to stay in her ass all night. All week. A hundred years. But it was too much. The way she shuddered around him, watching his cock disappear in her ass, smelling her arousal, even listening to the other guys who were so close swearing and reaching forward to pinch her nipples or rub at her clit—he fucking lost it.

With a roar, he squeezed her as tight as he could to him and he fucked her ass furiously, emptying his balls into her ass.

He'd barely caught his breath and sank his sweat-slicked forehead against Shay's back when Rafe sat down on the couch beside him and slapped his thighs.

"I've been dreaming of that ass," Rafe said. "My turn now."

CHAPTER SEVENTEEN

GABRIEL

What was he doing here? He should *not* be here?

Yet he couldn't tear his eyes away as Shay was passed from one man's cock only to be deposited on another's.

And not just for normal sex, either. They flipped Shay around so that Shay's back was to Rafe's chest, her feet on his thighs as she lifted herself up just enough so that—

Gabriel swallowed as sweat broke out on his brow.

They were taking her *ass*.

Gabriel couldn't help dropping a hand to his cock. He palmed himself through his jeans. And then immediately jerked his hand back.

Shit. He should have stayed with the boys. What was he thinking, coming back here? He hadn't had any illusions about what Jonas meant when he said to take the boys to Audrey's. That Shay needed *all* of her husbands tonight.

He should leave. Now. Right now. Back up. Turn around. Go down the stairs and take a long, hard jog to get his body back under control.

So.

Why.

Didn't.

He.

Leave?

He just kept standing there. Blinking and thinking—that guy Rafe's cock was bigger than the first she'd taken. Even if Charlie's had stretched her, Rafe's was still going to be a challenge.

And as Henry and Jonas helped to line her up so that she hovered right on the tip and helped her sink down on it, he saw the moment Shay realized it, too.

Her eyes popped wide open.

And her gaze collided with Gabriel's.

All the breath expelled from his lungs in one great *whoosh*.

She bit her bottom lip, her face strained in what looked like concentration but could also have been pain as she was lowered, inch by inch, on Rafe's huge dick.

Jonas looked over his shoulder at Gabriel, obviously following Shay's line of sight. And then Jonas waved him over. "Don't just stand there. We all have a part to play."

And no matter how much the logical part of Gabriel's brain screamed at him to turn and run like Joseph in the Bible did when he was tempted, his feet took him further in the room. Until he was so close he could smell Shay's arousal.

"Eat her out," Jonas demanded, eyes on Gabriel. "But don't let her come." He put a hand on Gabriel's shoulder to urge him down but Gabriel shrugged it off and glared back.

He'd known the preacher for a few years now and while at first he hadn't respected the stoner, he'd seen him settle dispute after dispute that would have stymied any other man. So Jonas had his respect. But that didn't mean the man had the right to start ordering him around.

One glance down at Shay's glistening pussy, though... She'd spread her legs wide, leaning back against Rafe and exposing every inch of her drenched cleft to Gabriel. She was so damn wet. And while she'd obviously gotten hot while Charlie had taken her, she hadn't come.

Rafe was still lowering her slowly onto his huge shaft. She wasn't even fully seated yet. She needed to relax if she was going to take him all the way, which by the look on her face, she was determined to do.

This isn't why you signed up for the lottery. You were only supposed to be in this for the boys. Not to get your dick wet.

But seeing to her pleasure wasn't wetting his dick. And an orgasm might help her relax and accommodate Rafe. It was really only *her* he was thinking of...

Gabriel dropped to his knees in front of the couch, between both her legs and Rafe's. From this close, her smell was overwhelming. *Dios mio.* He hadn't smelled a woman like this since Letty.

Letty's face swam in the forefront of his mind. Her breasts. Her sweet pink pussy. All the times he'd reach for her in the middle of the night or right after he woke up in the morning, spooning and pressing his erection against her ass. How she'd either giggle and turn in his arms or swat at his shoulder before pulling away and saying, *What are you thinking, there are so many things to do today. Get up! Get up!*

He thought if he was ever in this position again, he'd be awash in shame—that he'd feel like he was betraying Letty.

But it had been almost eight years. And while Shay's smell reminded him of Letty because Letty was the only other woman he'd ever been with, Gabriel found that, after the initial stomach clench that always came when he thought about Letty, he was back in the moment. With Shay. With her gorgeous, weeping cunt.

Still, his hands trembled as he lifted them to her inner thighs that were splayed over Rafe's. Rafe for his part was still moving slow. He'd gotten Shay almost all the way seated on his cock, and then, hands under her ass, was lifting her up again.

And Gabriel couldn't stand it anymore. There was only so much a man could take.

He dove in. It wasn't a tentative or gentle exploration. No. Screw that. He wanted a face-full of pussy and that's what he took. He smothered himself with her, elongating his tongue and thrusting it up her soaked entrance. Then he flattened his tongue out and licked up her slit, bottom to top.

And the way she reacted when he got to her clit? Her whole body trembled like he was an earthquake shaking the foundation of her very being.

He was a *god*. Her god. Her entire universe was narrowed down to the cock in her ass and the tiny bud of flesh he sucked into his mouth.

How could he have forgotten this feeling? *Dios mio*. He let go of her clit with a little pop and then dove in again, licking all around her pussy. She was so sweet, so, so sweet. He could eat her forever. She'd be his last meal and he'd die a happy, happy man.

Hearing her whimpers turn to a high-pitched wail as her body began to shake in earnest? It was like touching heaven. He was going to come without even touching himself. She was that hot.

But then, right before her wail could reach a crescendo, hands dropped to Gabriel's shoulders and yanked him back from the sweetest pussy on God's green earth.

Shay cried out in dismay and Gabriel was ready to lay down with whoever the hell had interrupted his angel before he took her over the cliff to ecstasy.

But then he heard Jonas's commanding voice. "Tell us what you've been hiding, and we'll let you come."

Gabriel's eyes shot to Shay and her features, moments ago strained with pleasure, were now transformed. Jonas's words scared her.

"You're going to tell us before this night is over," Jonas said darkly. "You're going to tell me why you asked to be punished. We are your husbands and you will not keep secrets from us."

Gabriel breathed out hard, not sure if he wanted to punch Jonas or shake Shay to get her to talk. He knew she had secrets. Something in her past tormented her. And she'd come to Jonas and *asked* him to punish her? What was that about? He hadn't missed the way that Shay's eyes dropped and she'd brought her arms up around her chest defensively.

She put them back down to brace against Rafe's thighs but there was definitely something there.

Jonas chuckled darkly. "You're gonna be stubborn, baby doll? Is that how you're going to play this?" Jonas stepped up right in front of her face. "Because I promise you, we'll wear out your every hole before this night is through if that's what it takes to break down your barriers.

Now open up." He tapped underneath her chin. "Bad girls who don't tell the truth get their faces fucked."

Shay's eyes flashed at that. And she promptly dropped her mouth open. Like it was a challenge.

Jonas wasn't slow to respond, either. He had his pants unbuttoned and shoved them down around his ass in record time. Then he held Shay's jaw and lifted his cock to her mouth.

And he did exactly what he promised—he fucked her face. Mercilessly. Relentlessly. He held her head in place and pumped his hips back and forth.

Jonas wasn't small, either. A fact Gabriel bet Shay was beginning to regret right about now. Especially since Jonas wasn't shy about shoving himself to the back of Shay's throat and then down it. At least that's what it looked like, his cock disappeared so far in her mouth.

"Why do you need to be punished?" Jonas asked, only slightly out of breath as he continued fucking her mouth.

Rafe had picked up his pace too.

Shay's body jolted every time Rafe dragged her down his length. She choked more than once on Jonas, but he wouldn't let up.

Jonas pulled back after shoving in especially deep. A line of spittle connected her mouth to his cock and her lips were red and puffy from the blowjob.

"Why do you need to be punished, Shay? Tell us now."

But Shay just pursed her lips. "I just do."

Jonas's face darkened. "Wrong answer. Fuck her ass harder, Rafe." Then he lifted his cock back to her mouth. For a second it looked like she might resist him, but when he slapped her lips and cheek with the head of his cock, she opened.

And it was such a glorious sight, Gabriel couldn't help unbuttoning his pants and pulling out his own cock. *Dios mio.* He was going to hell. He'd promised God that if God gave him a wife, Gabriel would treat her only as an honored mother to his two boys. He'd vowed to God— to *God*—that he would stay celibate.

But as he stroked his cock up and down as he had so often to thoughts of Shay, he knew that after tonight, it would be impossible to keep up the farce of thinking of her platonically. She wasn't his friend or his sister or any of the other bullshit he'd been trying to spin for himself over the past month.

She was a hot, gorgeous sexual being, and he'd never been more attracted to anyone in his entire life. Maybe not even Letty.

He forced away the last thought as he dropped back to his knees and maneuvered himself between Jonas's legs and the couch where he could get back to Shay's pussy.

Rafe was holding her stationary but moving underneath her with quick, jerking movements that made his balls slap against the bottom of her ass.

Gabriel shoved her legs upwards and was just able to squeeze in between them to start lapping at her sweet cunt again.

He held onto her with one hand and grabbed his own shaft with the other. He was still *technically* keeping his vow of celibacy if he didn't actually penetrate her, right?

He thrust his tongue in and out of her channel in the imitation of fucking and dragged the skin around his shaft up and down, squeezing and twisting every time he came to the head.

Dios mio, he was gonna die. Her smell. Her taste, the way her clit hardened and swelled when he sucked on her and grazed the edge of his teeth along—

Oh fuck, oh fuck, oh fuck, *oh*—

Jonas dragged Gabriel backwards from her pussy again right as ropes of cum shot out of Gabriel's cock in the most powerful orgasm he'd had in years.

He slumped to the carpet, still heaving as he stroked his cock one last time and even more cum dribbled out the top and down over his hand.

He could only watch through half slit eyes as Jonas withdrew from her mouth and gently pushed her sweat-slicked hair back behind one ear. "We can keep this up all night, beautiful. Tell us what we need to know. There's no place for secrets in this marriage. Why did you think you needed to be punished?"

Tears spilled down Shay's cheeks and Gabriel's chest felt ripped in two at the sight. But when she opened her mouth, he thought she might finally give. She might finally tell them about the ghosts that haunted her days and nights.

Because, second only to his children, Gabriel would do anything for this woman who'd quickly come to mean more to him than he'd ever meant for her to.

CHAPTER EIGHTEEN

JONAS

Her tears were so beautiful. Jonas wanted to taste them. So he did. He bent down and kissed away the tears on one cheek and then the other, his tongue coming out to savor her salt on his lips.

"Tell us, baby doll," he murmured, moving his mouth to her ear. "Tell us why you need to be punished. We'll make it better." He dropped a hand down her body to tease at her swollen sex. She pressed against him but he withdrew. She was on the edge of climax. So close, he knew, that even a few seconds of friction would probably send her over.

He lifted his hands and pinched one nipple. Hard.

She cried out and when her gaze lifted to his, it was a glare.

Jonas wanted to chuckle. God, she was perfect. Even when he'd dabbled in BDSM back in the day, he'd never found any woman to be so full of contradictions. Submissive one moment and then rebellious the next.

Shay wanted to pour out her secrets. Jonas had spent enough time giving pastoral counsel—what was in many ways the Protestant equivalent of the Catholic confession—to know when someone was itching to confess their sins.

But while she wanted to tell everything, for some reason, there was an equal or more overwhelming force inside her that was keeping her from freeing herself of her burdens.

And it was tearing her apart.

"I wish I'd gone deeper into the woods so you'd never found me this afternoon," she spat. "And you're wrong. You aren't the one in control of my pleasure. *I* am. This was fun and all but you can go and fuck off now."

Then she dropped a hand like she was going to get herself off.

Oh no she didn't.

"Henry," Jonas snapped, grabbing Shay's right hand by the wrist and pinning it down by her side. "Charlie."

Jonas glanced over at Charlie, having no clue if he'd actually comply. If a clan was like a pack, he was claiming alpha tonight. Problem was, there were several others in the clan who were alphas in their own right.

And that was fine. As long as they followed his lead when it mattered most—when it came to doing what was best for Shay.

This was not a fucking democracy.

So Jonas expected another challenge from Charlie. But to his surprise, Charlie just took hold of Shay's other arm.

"Shay, please," he pleaded. "I think Jonas is right. You need to talk to us. We can protect you. I promise, we'll—"

Shay's head whipped toward him. "You can't promise anything. You men walk around thinking you can make things happen—*poof*—just because you say so. Well that's not the way the world actually works. You have no fucking clue—"

Now she was just starting to piss Jonas off. If she was getting so defensive that she was lashing out at all of them like this, it meant they were hitting a nerve. Getting closer. It also meant she was just going to keep throwing up more walls to try to keep them out.

But if there was one thing Jonas knew, it was how to commit to a plan of action. He hadn't finished four years of seminary in three or become one of the New Republic's top hash growers because he was bad at setting goals and meeting them.

And it felt like he'd never had a more pressing goal than this. He'd get to the bottom of whatever Shay was hiding even if he had to hand-cuff her to the bed and keep her as their sex slave for weeks.

Jonas moved to the couch to the right of Rafe and Shay, still holding her hand. She struggled against his hold and he cupped her face. "Would you like to mention any particular color, baby doll?"

She paused, all her struggles ceasing for the briefest moment. Jonas met her gaze and could only hope he was communicating all the things he couldn't say. *Come on, baby. Don't give up on us yet.*

The truth was, no matter how much he commanded her or claimed mastery over her body, Shay was the one who ultimately had all the power here. One word uttered from her lips and it all stopped.

But when she dropped her eyes and shook her head just the tiniest bit, so slightly that Jonas would have missed it if his attention hadn't been zeroed in on her every tic and twitch. Satisfaction roared through his chest. She didn't say *red*.

Which meant he'd been right—deep down, she *did* want their help. She wanted to tell them everything. Her heart was theirs. Now they just had to break down her intellectual barriers. And the way to the heart and soul was through the body. To prove that she could trust them when they were all stripped down to their most basic, raw selves. If she could trust them here, then tomorrow, back in the real world, theirs would be an unbreakable bond.

"Henry," Jonas said, "take our wife's pussy. Bad girls get all their holes fucked until they tell what secrets they're keeping."

Shay's eyes widened as Henry stepped up, his pants already at his ankles. He stepped out of them and finished unbuttoning his shirt before tossing it to the side.

Henry had been surprisingly quiet during the whole session. Usually he was one to fight for dominance too, but for whatever reason, tonight he'd been apparently happy for Jonas to lead.

"You have never looked more beautiful," Henry whispered as he pushed her knees up and then ran his hands down the backs of her legs all the way to her pussy. "Our beautiful, sexy wife."

Shay bit her lip, and Jonas had watched her enough to know it was in anticipation, not fear. Because while this was *punishment*, it was equally about pleasure. Jonas knew of others who'd lived the Dominant/Submissive lifestyle who operated by much harsher laws of obedience and punishment, but that had never appealed to Jonas.

He had no need to become Shay's absolute God. No, instead he'd rather use pleasure and pain together as a means of breaking down barriers and in this case, of giving Shay the freedom to let them take on whatever burdens were weighing her down so badly.

"Destroy that pussy, Henry."

Henry didn't look at him once or even acknowledge him. No, his eyes were locked on Shay, ping-ponging up and down from her face, to her breasts, to her sex.

He dragged his cock up and down the lips of her pussy, circling her clit with the tip of his cock. Twin expressions of ecstasy took over both their faces.

"She doesn't get to come until we say so," Jonas reminded him with a harsh clip.

This, finally, earned Jonas a glare from Henry. Jonas just lifted one smirking eyebrow toward the other man. Henry only shook his head and focused his attention back in on Shay as he began to breach her. Henry was a similar size to Charlie—big but not huge like Rafe or as thick around as Jonas's own girth. Whereas Charlie's shaft was straight as an arrow, Henry's was slightly crooked. Would that make it easier or harder for him to bring their wife pleasure? Or was it simply something different, which made it novel in its own right.

Either way, as soon as Henry impaled her with his cock—and he did not go slowly or gently, Shay's eyes shot open. Rafe had just pulled her down deep on him and she cried out.

"So full. I don't know if I can—"

"You can," Henry whispered through gritted teeth. "You can take us both. Relax, lovely. Let us in."

"Do you love it?" Jonas got up, leaning one knee on the couch. "I bet you love it, don't you, baby doll?" he whispered in her ear. "You're stuffed so full of cock. The pressure on your G-spot has got to be insane." He held up a hand for Henry to stop and again, Henry followed direction without balking.

"You're so close, baby."

Shay dropped her eyes closed as Jonas caressed her face, running his thumb over her swollen bottom lip. Then he leaned in and kissed her. Not just any kiss, either. It was a kiss that said, *you're mine*. It was a kiss that said, *stop fighting and give me all your burdens*. And it said, *you're so damn hot all I want to do is fuck your brains out*.

Okay so that last one might have been unintentional but damn, she was so hot. For a moment he got lost in his purpose because she kissed him just as hungrily in return.

Then she pulled back and looked at him with those huge, green eyes of hers. "May I please come, sir?"

She asked it so prettily.

And it was a crock of shit.

Utter fucking bullshit.

She was trying to direct things again. Making a show of being submissive all the while thinking she could lead them around by their dicks.

Jonas didn't break her gaze as he said, "Change of plans."

Only when he saw the uncertainty enter her eyes did he look away, up to Henry. "Back up. You can have her mouth. Let her taste herself on your cock."

Henry seemed only too happy to comply. Shay on the other hand went tense all over. Jonas watched her, waiting to see if she'd say red.

As Jonas stood up and then he and Henry exchanged positions, Jonas watched Shay more carefully than ever. As Henry positioned his cock at her lips, Jonas reached down and caressed her cheek. "Snap if you need us to slow down or stop. Your mouth will be too full to say anything."

Shay blinked rapidly but nodded.

"Out loud. Tell me you understand."

"I understand." There was a slight tremor in her words but other-wise, her voice was strong. And, Jonas noted with some satisfaction, she wasn't yelling at them anymore. Some part of her was edging closer to surrender.

Now to take her all the way there.

His hand still on her face, Jonas urged her to open up and allow Henry in. Henry groaned as her lips closed around the head of his dick and her cheeks hollowed with suction.

Just the sight had Jonas's cock going steel.

And they'd come to it, finally.

Jonas pulled his shaft out of his pants and stroked himself roughly, staring straight at Shay's pretty pink pussy. Meanwhile, Shay's eyes were locked on his thick cock even while Henry held the back of her head and slowly fucked her mouth.

They both knew that every time Jonas fucked her it was a tight fit. What he lacked in length, he made up for in girth. And now, for him to enter her while her ass was already so stuffed full of Rafe?

"The only way you get through this is by giving in, baby doll. Give it all up to us."

He lifted one leg up on the couch and leaned in, rubbing the fat head of his cock up and down her dripping pussy.

She shuddered and Henry let out a sharp, pleasured curse. She must have started sucking more fervently or even bit down a little in response to Jonas stimulating her. She shouldn't be right on the edge of climax anymore, but she was still probably close enough.

He circled her clit with his head and *Jesus*, her flesh was so soft, so wet.

"You ready to be punished, baby?"

The only response he got was the rapid lift and drop of her chest, those perfect breasts heaving. Charlie played with her nipples. Gentler than Jonas would have, but it was the stimulation that was important.

Jonas lined himself up at her entrance.

He could have eased himself in. Let her accommodate his girth with Rafe in her ass, inch by slow inch.

Yes, he could have done that.

But she needed punishing. She wanted it, and frankly, he wanted to give it to her for lying by omission.

So when he sank his cock into the hot depths of her pussy, he shoved in relentlessly, thrusting hard until he was buried to the root.

Shay cried out around Henry's cock.

Her whole body had gone tense, her sex clenching like a vise around him as if she was trying to force him out even as he pushed in.

He watched her hand. It was limp, not even poised to attempt snapping.

So he pulled back the slightest bit and then drove in again. She cried out and clenched even tighter, though Jonas wouldn't have thought that was fucking possible. She was clenching so hard that, combined with the already tight fit of her sex with Rafe's shaft buried up her ass, it was almost painful. The best pain Jonas had ever experienced in his entire fucking life.

"Surrender," Jonas growled, pulling back and then ramming in again, so quickly that the sound of his balls slapping her ass echoed in the room. "It's the only way."

Her brows were drawn so tightly together and she choked around Henry's cock. Henry had apparently gotten fully on board with the program, because he wasn't taking it easy on her, either. He fucked the inside of her cheek with one thrust, then a few light bobs, then down her throat. Spittle dripped down the edges of her mouth. There was nothing pretty or ladylike about what they were doing to her.

This was stripped down.

Raw.

Fucking.

Bulldozing those walls she'd tried to erect around herself.

Tearing her down so she could rebuild stronger, more solid, and more secure. With them at her side. Her *side*, as equals. The bedroom was the only place he'd ask to be called Master. Because this woman, this gorgeous woman was so damn strong. He had no idea what she'd survived to get here tonight, so alive and perfect underneath them. But he thanked everything in the universe that she was. And now she needed to know she didn't have to fight alone anymore. She had a family now.

So he fucked her without mercy.

He stretched her pussy to its limits and then fucked her harder to push her beyond anything she'd taken before.

And for a long time, Jonas couldn't tell how long, time had almost lost its meaning in the sweaty haze of sex and lust and longing and *Shay*, but he was so in tune with her body, he witnessed the moment.

He had dropped a hand between them, toying with her clitoris every so often, bringing her to the brink and then pulling back, careful to fuck her at an angle that provided no friction to the place she needed most.

And then it came—the beautiful, holy moment when she surrendered.

There were no words. No explicit signals.

But her entire body relaxed and went liquid. She yielded her every hole to them. She gave over her entire body. And where the body goes, the soul will follow.

His beautiful, beautiful baby doll.

Jonas wanted to shout her praise from the rooftops. He wanted to scream it from the mountains.

He'd been doing mostly shallow lunges, but now he sank the deepest he had since his first thrust, aiming for her G-spot.

At the same time, he dropped a hand between them to stroke her engorged bud.

She went off in seconds.

"Come on her chest, Henry," Jonas ordered. He didn't want her having to gag on a cock through her orgasm. He just wanted her to feel every moment of the sensations they were ripping from her body.

The moment Henry pulled his cock out, Charlie maneuvered his body to kiss Shay, cupping her limp head in his hands as she cried her release. It was awkward with all of them bent over her, but Charlie didn't seem to care, and neither did Shay who shuddered and screamed and arched and then shuddered some more.

Jonas kept fucking her through it, amazed when it just kept going. Ten seconds. Fifteen. She was still coming. Wave after wave seemed to hit her. It was the most magnificent thing he'd ever fucking seen.

Hold it. Jesus fucking Christ, hold it in.

The bottom of Jonas's spine lit up and he knew he was about two seconds away from losing it. But, no, dammit, he had to see this through.

Rafe seemed to be having the same problem, because a long, almost pained grunt came from behind Shay as they fucked her in tandem—in, out, in, out, and then—

Jonas couldn't take it anymore. He sank to the root and held himself there. Even the tiniest bit of friction could send him over at this point. When Rafe pulled out and pushed back in one last time, Jonas thought that was it. His balls drew up and he felt his own orgasm start to quake through his body.

It was only by harkening back to his long years of discipline that he was able to force it back. He gritted his teeth and squeezed his eyes shut against the glorious site of Shay's cum-covered tits. Apparently Henry had let go too.

But there was too much at stake. Too much at fucking stake.

Jonas pulled out of Shay and, before she was even done shuddering from her orgasm, he stood up and drew her into his arms.

Jonas only spared the briefest glance to Rafe, who was sitting on the couch with his head leaned back, his mouth dropped open and eyebrows up in astonishment like his world had just been blown a-fucking-part.

Henry sat on the couch beside him with a similar expression. Meanwhile, Gabriel and Charlie were right on Jonas's heels, following as he took Shay and deposited her in the center of the bed.

Jonas immediately crawled over her and sank back inside her. The few moments of not being gloved by the world's most perfect pussy had helped his sanity a little bit, but he felt his balls draw up just as tight the second her hot flesh closed around him again.

But he had a fucking mission. She'd surrendered and he was taking the goddamned spoils before she decided to close back up again.

He braced one hand beside her head and with the other, he teased at her clit again. She gasped and her eyes flew wide. Within two strokes, her features were contorting again—almost as if she'd never finished her marathon orgasm on the couch and she was just picking up where she'd left off.

"Good, that's right, baby doll," Jonas murmured. "You let yourself go for us."

Charlie crawled onto the bed and cleaned Henry's cum off her chest with a damp towel he must have run and gotten from the bathroom. As soon as she was cleaned up, he dropped his head to suckle one of her nipples. She arched into Charlie and her features contorted even more, a high-pitched keening noise coming from her throat as they took her higher and higher.

Jonas fucked her slow and they continued pleasuring her until her breathing grew more regular, her legs only spasming briefly.

Then Jonas moved so that he hovered over her completely, elbows braced on either side of her face.

"Now tell us, baby. What is it you've been hiding? What has you feeling so ashamed?"

She bit her lip and looked down. Which was ridiculous, because Jonas was so close, he took up her entire field of vision. Down, up, left, right, it was only more *him*. Or Charlie or Gabriel who'd climbed on the bed on either side of him.

It was time to face the music. If she tried to backtrack, so help him God, he'd—

A tear trickled down her left cheek and it was like a knife to Jonas's kidneys. His first impulse was to back away. Tell her it was okay, everything was fine. She didn't have to tell them anything, he'd just hold her all night.

But that was the coward's way out. It wasn't what would help Shay. To set a bone, sometimes you had to break it. So even if it tore him apart, he'd see this through.

"Tell me," he demanded. "Tell me now."

Her eyes flashed up to him and for the first time all night, they weren't full of defiance. She looked... like she felt helpless.

"Oh baby." He leaned down and kissed down her temple, over to her cheek, again tasting her tears. "Just tell me, baby. You're not alone anymore. You don't have to carry this alone."

When he pulled back, it was to see her swallowing. And when she raised her eyes again, there was something new there. Trust? Or at least a willingness to take a chance on him? On them?

"In Travisville, I wasn't just a maid," she said. She lifted her legs up and wrapped them around Jonas's waist like she needed something solid to anchor herself to. He didn't expect the swell of emotion the action gave him. He continued moving inside her, inching so slowly in and out it was more like a caressing internal touch than sex at all. Another means of grounding her.

"What did you do there, baby?" Jonas asked, starting his slow thrust inward again.

She bit her lip, but finally answered. "There was a powerful man there. He took me as his woman. And I— He forced me to do terrible things sometimes. And I did them. Because I was..." she trailed off and more tears cascaded down her cheeks. She hiccupped for breath and Charlie was right there, caressing her hair back from her face and whispering, "Shhh, shhh, sweetheart, you're doing so good. You're perfect. You're doing so good."

Jonas noticed Henry had come up behind Charlie, a concerned expression on his face as he watched their wife in such distress.

Shay took another gulp of breath and then continued, her voice wobbly. "I was pregnant when the bombs dropped. This man took me in. And when the baby came..." Her eyes squeezed shut briefly before she went on. "He wasn't happy the baby wasn't his. H— He didn't treat me well. But he kept me and my son. And eventually I had another baby. Nicole. Nicky for short. Matthew and Nicky. Matthew and Nicky," she repeated before dissolving into sobs.

Gabriel leaned in and Jonas lifted up some so he could embrace Shay. He whispered to her in Spanish. Jonas wasn't sure if Shay spoke Spanish or could understand him, but she seemed soothed by it all the same.

After several minutes, she was calm enough to continue, hiccupping every few moments. Henry handed her a handkerchief to wipe her eyes and nose.

Jonas's heart was already torn in two because there was no way this story had a happy ending.

"The man didn't treat me well. But it was when he hit Matthew and threatened Nicky..." She hiccupped. "That was when I knew I had to get them out of there. So I made a plan to escape. I'd get us out. All three of us."

She shook her head, the tears pouring out of her eyes indiscriminately now. "We didn't even make it past the first checkpoint. I'd hidden us in the back of a supply truck. But there were some red ants,

I don't know if they were on the vegetables that were in the truck or if we carried them in our clothes. But one of the ants bit little Nicky and she started wailing loud enough to wake the dead. We were dragged out and— and—" She squeezed her eyes shut again, her face contorting.

"That was when he branded me. And Matthew and Nicky— He— They—" She broke down sobbing, unable to keep talking.

"Where are they now?" Gabriel asked, grasping her hand and pulling it to his lips, a deep furrow of concern between his eyebrows.

"Gone," she whispered hoarsely, scrubbing at her eyes with her palm. "They're *gone*. And it's all my fault. All of this, it's *my fault*. The things I did. I was just trying to protect them, but I've done terrible things."

Jonas could only shake his head and hold her to him. Oh Lord, he'd never expected something like this. The first part, yes. He knew there was no way she'd been just a maid. Sexual subjugation or even slavery, that he'd been prepared for. But children? She'd lost her *children*?

How could they— There was no way to make that better. To heal that wound. Jonas had never felt more helpless in his life.

"Please," Shay whispered, and Jonas dragged his eyes back to hers. She shook her head like she was pleading with him but he didn't know for what.

Her pained confession had shrunk his cockstand when moments earlier he would have sworn nothing could. But when he moved his hips to pull his half-hard cock out of her, she only clenched her legs around his waist even tighter.

And again, that one word, "Please," so deep and growled like it was dragged from the depths of her being.

Oh *Shay*. He knew his pity would do her no good, even though it went so much deeper. It wasn't what she needed. And he'd sworn to himself that tonight was all about *her* needs, not his.

So no matter that he felt out of his depth, he would take his cues from her. And they'd just wrenched one of her deepest, darkest truths from her. There was no turning back now.

So instead of pulling away, Jonas pushed back in.

It wasn't difficult to get hard again. One look at her beautiful breasts, her tearstained face and the way she was laid out so vulnerable and perfect before him—his cock was stiff in fifteen seconds.

Every one of her husbands laid hands on her while Jonas fu— No. He cut the thought short. This wasn't fucking.

For the first time since the early months of his first marriage, Jonas was making love.

Shay tipped her head back and her hands went out, bracing herself on Gabriel's arm on one side, and Charlie's on the other. Henry slid in between Charlie and the headboard, stroking Shay's hair. Rafe came up behind Jonas to caress her legs.

Altogether, as one, they made love, hearts breaking and mending and then breaking again at the thought of everything Shay had been through.

For the first time in years, Jonas found himself praying. *God, please heal the unhealable. Let her find peace here with us.* He knew they'd never be able to fill the hole her children had left behind. His Shay would always be incomplete and it was a sadness she'd live with their entire lives. But if she'd just let them love her through it—

Love.

The thought hit him like a sledgehammer in the face.

He loved her. But it was too soon. He couldn't— He knew he wanted to help her and he—

But as she clenched around him and he looked into her green, fathomless eyes, he couldn't deny the truth.

He loved his wife.

It was only luck that he'd been grinding against Shay with each thrust and she came again at that moment, clenching around him as her shudders began.

Because he absolutely lost it. There was no holding back after he realized he loved her. He clutched her to him as he emptied inside her once, twice, and a third spurt as he came so hard it felt like his body was exploding into a supernova and being swallowed up by hers.

He slumped to the side, carrying her with him. He couldn't bear to lose contact with her. Couldn't lose her. Ever.

It only went to show, he might have been the dominant tonight, but in the end it was Shay who'd mastered all of them completely.

CHAPTER NINETEEN

SHAY

The sun beat down on Shay's head the next day as she walked through the narrow lanes between the heaps of garbage in the Scrapper Yard.

It was so hot. And not just because of the intense Texas sun. Last night had been... She shook her head as she pulled her hair up into a ponytail, feeling the sore muscles in her arms as she lifted them. God, *every part* of her was sore. Which only served as more of a reminder of the night she knew she'd never forget.

All day it had been replaying on an endless loop in her head. Every moment... every touch... She trailed her fingers along her collarbone.

When Jonas had entered her at the end, she didn't think she could take it. He was too much. She was too small and they were too much. It was all just... *too much*.

She'd thought she could keep them out. Keep them out of her heart even as she let them fill her body.

She took a shaky breath as her eyes skimmed over the piles of junk.

Then she swallowed hard as she glanced behind her, seeing Rafe right on her heels. Her ass cheeks clenched even at the sight of him.

He'd been inside the most secret part of her for so long last night. Splitting her wide open with his... her eyes dropped to the camo cargo pants he was wearing.

"You keep starin' and I'm gonna have to give you something to look at, honey."

Shay's gaze jerked back up to his face. From the dark look in his eyes, he was remembering last night in just as much detail as she was.

She turned away from him and hurried down the little path, lifting a hand to her cheek and taking several deep breaths.

She couldn't believe she was acting like such a schoolgirl right now. She wanted to laugh at the ludicrousness of the situation.

Lives might dangle in the balance and all she could think about was the amazing sex she'd had last night.

And just like that, all the worries that had momentarily subsided came flooding back in.

She didn't know the particulars of Jason's plan—he only revealed the part you *needed* to know to accomplish what he wanted of you— but she knew he'd wanted Jacob's Well Township for years, even back when she lived with him and the kids in his sprawling mansion on the hill.

At the time he'd been too busy defending and establishing his own borders and setting up steady supply chains. But the past few years the crackdowns had largely put a stop to the looters and road bandits who attacked supply caravans.

Which meant Jason had the resources to devote to expanding what he considered *his empire*. It wasn't just about the land or the Jacob's Well spring, either. He'd talked about the Commander a few times, when he was especially drunk.

It was personal between them somehow. When Jason drank, he got so slurred it was hard to understand him, but he'd definitely talked about Commander Wolford by name—except he'd called him Eric. It was only through context clues she'd realized Eric was the Commander of Jacob's Well.

Jason ranted about how Eric betrayed him. About how Jason gave up everything for Eric. Even got kicked out of the *Army* for him. *"Annnnn how ya thannnk me, huh? You betray me, you sonnabitch!"*

He'd shouted it so loud Shay had scrambled back and run out of the room for fear he'd take out his rage on her like he often did.

And now here she was.

Caught in the middle of two impossible choices.

Her kids—or all the people she was starting to care about here in Jacob's Well? Including her two new stepsons.

She'd be a monster no matter which she chose.

But she had made a decision. After last night... there was no going back.

She couldn't work for Jason anymore.

That was the decision she'd come to as she poured out her partial truths to her husbands.

She knew they thought that when she'd said her children were *gone*, she'd meant they were dead. A shudder went through her body even at the thought.

But it would have been too obvious a leap to her real purpose here if she'd let them know her kids were still alive.

She'd *wanted* to tell them everything.

She'd wanted to *so badly*.

She almost had.

But then she remembered something, and it had stopped her from blurting out the complete truth.

Jason was paranoid. He almost always had a Plan B.

Arranging for two spies in the same small group so that they could watch and report on each other was just the sort of thing Jason would do.

It was one of the reasons she'd been so adamant about having Charlie as one of her five. With him she knew there'd be *one* person she knew wouldn't have a hidden agenda. Someone she could trust completely.

But she could come up with a scenario where even *Charlie* was the spy. Jason could twist anyone and Charlie could have easily been *posing* as a prisoner back in Travisville to throw Shay off.

Shay doubted Charlie would be tempted by riches or position, but what if Jason had some way to get to Audrey? Charlie would do anything to protect her. Who knew what combination of manipulation, torture, or threats Jason might have used to get Charlie to work for him?

She could imagine far less creative motives for all the others. Henry was ambitious. He made no secret of the fact that he liked the finer things in life. Was Jacob's Well too tame a playground for a man of his drive and determination?

Then there was Jonas, *Lord*. She shook her head. He was so change-able. Sometimes she wondered if she knew him at all. Was he the stern dominant he could be in the bedroom, or the care-nothing stoner he'd hidden behind for years? Could a man who could change personas on the flip of a dime ever be completely trusted? Still, he had such an authenticity to him... or was that the greatest ruse of all and she was being the world's biggest idiot to rule him out?

With Rafe it was impossible to tell because he always adopted that devil may care attitude everywhere except the bedroom. But under-neath it all, sometimes, she thought she detected an... anger at life because of what had happened to him. Shay knew just how good Jason was at flaming men's anger and directing it for his own purposes.

And Gabriel? Well, he'd do anything for those boys. It was easy to imagine Jason using the same threat he had on Shay herself. If Jason had some way of getting at the boys and threatening them, what wouldn't Gabriel do to keep them safe?

All of which left her... stuck. She wanted to do the right thing. She just didn't know what the hell that was in this circumstance.

Jason already had so many other agents working in Jacob's Well, not that she knew who they were. But evidence of them was abundant.

For example—Jason knew a delegation would be going to visit the President's Palace in Fort Worth—something that according to Sophia hadn't been planned until last week.

But Jason had known over a month ago.

And Jason knew she'd be asked to bring a sculpture to give to the President. When Shay gave Sophia her rose sculpture, a local newspa-perman had been there and taken a picture. Apparently, this paper had circulated to the capitol where notice had been taken of a *promising new young artist*.

The whole thing smacked of Jason's interference, especially when she was then commissioned to make a sculpture of the President's bust. Because Jason had given her a two-piece black device slightly larger than her hand and ordered her to install it inside said sculpture.

Shay shuddered to think how deep his spy network went in Jacob's Well. Not to mention how difficult it would be to do what she now had to.

Because there was only one way out of this if she wanted to keep her soul intact and still protect her own children.

She had to play both sides.

She'd continue to work for Jason—or at least *look like* she was working for him. Just long enough to get her kids back. Then they'd escape for real.

If only she could talk to *someone*. Even Audrey or Vanessa. She'd grown close to the two women over the past month. And Audrey's husband Nix was the head of the Security Squadron. He'd helped bring down another of Jason's spies just a few months ago.

But what if that was just a ruse because the man had already exposed himself? And anyway, Audrey and Nix and their whole clan was out of town for a couple more weeks until the trip to Fort Worth. Apparently they'd decided to finally take their honeymoon.

Which was sweet and romantic... and left Shay back at square one.

She had to figure out for herself who she could trust and who she couldn't.

All the while knowing that every day she didn't speak up was one day closer to bringing all the people she was coming to care a great deal for in terrible danger.

But she had at least until the trip to the President's Palace. If Jason wanted her to plant that device, he wouldn't move on Jacob's Well before she'd had the chance. That was three weeks from now.

Three weeks to figure out which of her husbands was also working for Jason. Without tipping them off.

Hence asking Rafe to join her today as she hunted for materials for President Goddard's portrait sculpture. She planned to spend one on one time with each of her husbands to see if she could get one of them to slip up and reveal something to prove they were working for Jason.

She squinted in the sunlight as she crouched down to run her hands over a snapped off side mirror from a car. She was playing with shadow and reflection in the sculpture and this would be perfect.

Her whole clan would be going as part of the delegation, along with Clan Hale and the Commander and Sophia. Shay would have to work non-stop to finish the sculpture in time. She had the rough outline of President Goddard's face and most of the shadowing blocked out so far, but she still had all the contour and detail work to do.

"You wanna add that to the bag, babe?" Rafe asked, his big body blocking out the sun and shading her as effectively as an umbrella.

Shay turned to look up at him. He was just a dark shadow against the bright blue sky.

"Yes, please," she smiled at Rafe and handed him the broken off side mirror. He turned it around in his hands, eyebrows lifted.

"So you can really make something, like, arty, outta all this shit?" He dropped the mirror into the large canvas bag.

"Careful!"

"Oh, sorry." Then he grinned at her. "Am I not treating the garbage with enough care?"

She rolled her eyes and smacked him on the arm. "It's the mirror I want, jerk. It's lasted this long without getting broken. If only it can survive *you*."

"All right, all right. I'll treat the bag of shit like it's precious cargo."

"You're a charmer, aren't you?"

He shot her another panty-melting grin and she turned away, fanning herself and trying to pretend it was because of the hot day.

Surely it wasn't *Rafe*. He was so... charming.

But Jason had been charming, too.

In the beginning.

And she'd only known Rafe, what, a little more than four weeks?

Anyone could pretend to be a good guy for a month.

Shay had been around Jason long enough to know what he looked for in his agents. Ambition, but not too much. After all, Jason only wanted people working for him that he could control. No one who would actually challenge him for power. Ruthlessness and self-centeredness were plusses. Either that or desperation. Jason was always happy to capitalize on desperation. Like Shay's desperation to have her children back.

After they were caught trying to escape, Jason *had* threatened their lives. And more.

It wasn't only her who'd been branded that night the guards dragged her and the children back in front of him.

At least he'd had little Nicole taken right back out again.

But Matthew, oh God, Matthew...

"You think you can run from me?" Jason jerked her chin up roughly, and then, with his other hand, he slapped her hard.

Pain exploded through her face but what was worse was hearing Matthew scream and knowing he was so afraid.

And knowing he had reason to be. God, please don't let him hurt my son. Please don't let him hurt my son.

"You can never leave me, you little whore. You wanna know why?"

Jason jerked her head up by her ponytail, pressing his other thumb into the lip he'd just split open. She couldn't help the whimper of pain in spite of promising herself she'd be strong for Matthew.

She nodded piteously, praying for Jason's rage to work its way out quickly. And all on her. But as mad as she'd seen him in all their years together, it was nothing to the insane gleam in his eyes tonight.

"I said do you wanna know why?" he shouted.

"W-why?" she finally managed to get out, the coppery taste of blood thick on her tongue.

Jason leaned down until his face was only an inch away from hers. Then he screamed at the top of his lungs, "Because you're fucking mine! I fucking own you!"

And then he called in the blacksmith who held a red-hot branding iron.

She'd only been able to watch on and scream uselessly as the big man pressed the *T* brand into the soft flesh of Matthew's back.

By the time the man came to her, yes, the brand hurt like pain she never knew, but worse was knowing her baby had just suffered the same.

She swore to herself then and there, as the screams of her baby boy echoed in her skull, never to underestimate Jason again or do *anything* that could endanger her children.

She'd obeyed every order, done every task, enthusiastically fulfilled every one of Jason's whims after that day.

Still, he'd banished her from the mansion. It had been a year and a half since she'd laid eyes on either of her children.

She only got updates through one of the maids she'd been friendly with while she'd still lived there, so she knew they were safe—well, as safe as they could be living under the same roof as that monster.

But when Jason had come to her promising he'd reunite her with her kids—and more importantly, threatening Matthew's life if she *didn't* do what he said—what choice did she have?

There's always a choice.

Well, she was making one now. She refused to be Jason's puppet anymore. She'd find a way to get Matt and Nicky back without sacrificing a whole town.

So. Back to the task at hand.

She studied Rafe surreptitiously as she picked through the old junk.

Ambition. Desperation. She ticked them off in her head. What else did Jason look for in his agents?

Well, he did prefer men who weren't as smart as he was. Again, it was part of the control thing.

So where did Rafe fall in that metric?

Frankly, Shay didn't know. She had a feeling his flirty and fun side was as much a mask as her fake smiles.

What was going on in that handsome head of his behind the facade? She was determined to find out.

"Tell me about yourself," she said as they walked down a narrow path between towering piles of junk. "I barely know anything about you."

He squinted at her in the bright sunshine. "What do you want to know, babe?"

"Well, where do you come from?"

"Here and there." He shrugged.

She rolled her eyes. And the winner for the most indecisive answers of all time goes to... "Okay, but where did you grow up?"

Another shrug. Was it just her imagination, or did he seem more closed off than normal? "What's it matter? I'm here now."

"What's it matter?" she scoffed in disbelief. "Our pasts make us who we are."

Then she took a breath. All right. Maybe she should share first if she was going to ask such personal things of him. "Take my mom for instance. All growing up she couldn't have given less of a shit about me. She was always way more interested in whatever loser of the month was taking up her time and attention." Shay looked out at the manmade hills of junk all around them. "I always swore I'd be nothing like her when I grew up."

She'd never let *her* life revolve around a man, she'd told herself so self-righteously.

Ha. Hahahaha. Good one, universe.

"No one wants to be like their folks," Rafe said. "That's just how it is, ain't it?"

Shay cocked her head sideways. "I hope not. I don't think Gabriel's boys will feel that way."

Rafe nodded, giving yet another shrug. "Huh. Maybe not."

"So what were yours like? Your parents?"

Rafe just kept walking for several moments, not saying anything, then he stopped and grabbed Shay around the waist. "Look, babe, I don't do this stuff."

Shay stopped with him, frowning. "What stuff?"

"This." He waved a hand between them. "This small talk shit. I'm a simple guy. There's two things I was put on this earth for. Flying fighter jets," he leaned in close, his lips brushing against her ear, "*and fucking*. Seeing as I got my arm blown off and am no good for flying planes or fighting any more, I'm happy to focus on my second talent."

With that, he pulled her several steps forward around the corner to a culvert of the junkyard where large appliances were stacked haphazardly on all sides except the one they'd come through. He flipped her around, eliciting a little *oof* of surprise out of her before he pushed her chest down across the stovetop of an old oven. Then he bent over her and again, his breath was scorching on her ear.

"You were so damn hot for it last night. Hottest chick I ever seen. If I rip your panties down right now, how wet you gonna be?"

Shay's eyes all but rolled back in her head. It was wrong to get so turned on by his crude words and manner. Or was it?

She made no move to stop him as he unbuttoned her jeans and jerked them roughly down her thighs. Next went her underwear and then his thick fingers probed at her sex.

"Fuck," he hissed. "I was right. You're already drenched. You been thinking about me fucking you the whole time we been out here? Or you get this wet in these last couple minutes?"

He moved his pelvis against her and she could feel his hard length through his jeans, pressing against her ass. Which only made a fresh round of wetness gush. Embarrassment heated her face, but Rafe only pushed his fingers in and out of her slick sex more quickly.

"Taste how much you want it." He slipped his fingers out of her pussy and the next thing she knew, he was shoving them in her mouth.

Where was the relaxed, easy going Rafe who joked around the dining room table and winked while he stole an extra ladleful of stew?

Him shoving his fingers in her mouth like that, so forceful, almost brutal—

It was wrong.

Wrong.

She bit down on his fingers and he pulled them out. But she'd only done it so she could whisper breathily, "Fuck me. Fuck me hard."

She didn't know why she liked it this way. Considering all that had happened to her, it was probably really messed up that she did. But his hand on her back, the growl of his words... God, she couldn't get him inside her fast enough.

She was wearing a spaghetti strap shirt that was easy to push down her shoulders. She continued tugging on it until it was pooled at her waist. Feeling the sun beat down on her exposed breasts was just another reminder of how wrong it was to ask what she was asking. They were exposed. The appliances only closed them in on three sides. Anyone passing them by would be able to clearly see her lily-white ass and breasts, and now she was asking him to—

He kicked her legs further apart and then—

"Oh," she couldn't help a brief cry as he thrust inside her pussy from behind. Then his hand clapped over her mouth and he pushed her chest down over the stovetop.

She felt three seconds away from coming. The unexpectedly sharp rise of pleasure took her breath away. It was *so* good. His cock, oh shit, oh shit, it was— He was—

She lifted her ass back against him with his every thrust so he could go as deep as possible.

"Fuck, you love that don't you?" he grumbled, hand still over her mouth. "You love taking my huge cock in every fucking hole. You'd be howling and letting the whole goddamned yard know how much you loved it if I let you, wouldn't you?"

He pulled his hips back and then jackhammered back in again and Shay had to bite the inside of her cheek against the pleasure lighting up her core. Oh God, he was hitting that spot, punching it with every thrust.

It was *so* good.

And so... familiar?

She'd been fucked like this before, except even more brutally.

Guess you don't hate it so much if you're coming. You must like being my whore, you're so wet for it.

She squeezed her eyes shut.

No. It wasn't Jason behind her.

It was *Rafe*.

Her *husband*. This was pleasure she didn't have to be ashamed of, not mixed with hate. Rafe swiveled his hips and fucked her harder. She clenched her teeth against the pleasure as it spiked from her core, tightening around the cock spearing her.

"Goddamn, babe," Rafe growled.

But then he gathered the hair of her ponytail and tugged her head back.

And in a second, the sunshine was gone.

Rafe was gone.

The Scrapper Yard was gone.

It was her and Jason back in their house in Travisville and he was slamming her facedown on the kitchen counter.

He yanked her head backwards by her ponytail even while he shoved her chest down to the counter and threw her skirt up. Then he fucked her, hard, the whole time calling her all sorts of names.

"Fucking whore!" he shouted, shoving his cock in before she was even wet. "You're just a bitch in heat, aren't you? I saw those fuck-me eyes you were giving my lieutenants at the dinner table. It make you feel like a real hot bitch to have all my men panting after you?"

And no matter how much she cried that *no, no, she only had eyes for him, that she never wanted anyone else*, it never made a difference.

Just stay still.

Don't make him any angrier.

He'll be done soon.

Just don't fight. Whatever you do, don't fight. He's too strong. He's too strong.

In and out he went, and as he did, her own pleasure rose too. Oh God, how could she? She hated him. Why would her body—

See, you did *want it. He was right.*

"No!"

"Shay? Shay! Holy shit, *SHAY!*"

Shay blinked. She wasn't in the kitchen with Jason.

It wasn't Jason behind her.

It was Rafe.

She shoved back against him.

And he *moved*. He didn't keep holding her down. Didn't keep fucking her.

She spun around in shock, blinking for several long moments. She lifted a hand to her forehead. God. She'd had vivid flashbacks in her dreams, but never during the day like this. What the fuck?

She stumbled sideways and dropped a hand to her stomach.

Oh shit.

She fell to her knees and emptied her stomach to the side of the old stove.

CHAPTER TWENTY

RAFE

"Shit. Shay?" Rafe stepped close and reached out a hand for her elbow. The second he made contact, she flinched and jerked away.

Fuck. Was she afraid of him? He shoved himself back in his pants.

But the next second, she swung toward him and glared. "He'll kill you if I tell him you touched me like that. You know that, don't you?"

What?

She was staring at him like she was watching for some reaction to his words.

Shit. This was bad. "Shay? Do you have your water bottle?" She didn't answer. "Fuck."

It had to be ninety-five degrees out here. She could have heat-stroke. He ran his hands over his head before looking around them.

Then he stepped close again, hands up so she'd feel safe.

"Come on, babe. Follow me, okay?" Jonas's grow yard wasn't far. Just down the block. He'd know what to do.

Shay watched him warily for another long second before finally nodding, her whole body sagging.

He held out his one good arm and she sank against his. And she didn't flinch when he touched her to pull her shirt and jeans back up.

Thank Christ. The sense of relief that washed through him was so immense he had to take a breath. But Jesus, she felt so tiny against his side.

What the hell had he been thinking, fucking her out here in the ninety-degree heat? He hadn't been thinking, at least not with his big head.

She was just so gorgeous and she'd been flashing that gorgeous ass of hers every time she bent over to examine some little scrap of junk.

Still, it was no fucking excuse.

Or was he just trying to prove to himself how goddamned useless he was at this too—the one thing he was supposed to still be good at?

You're just fucking kidding yourself. You should have died when that land-mine went off on the eastern front.

He gritted his teeth against the thoughts and stopped the first Scrapper he saw. "Water," he demanded.

The man in the blue overalls took one look at Shay by his side and fumbled with the water flask at his belt. He held it out, which was a good thing, because Rafe was about to yank it out of his damn hand. Well, Rafe would have if he had a spare hand.

As it was, he kept his one good arm in place, supporting Shay as she stood. She took the water bottle for herself and took a long drink. She only emptied half the flask.

"More," Rafe ordered. "And do you have any gum?" He knew it was a tall order. Gum was hoarded almost as much as cigarettes. But lo and behold, the man produced a pack of Big Red.

Rafe pulled one of the last pieces out as Shay shook her head. "I don't want to drink all his—"

"More," Rafe growled again. Rafe leveled the man and he immediately started waving his hands.

"I don't mind. Drink it all. And take another stick for the road." He held out another stick of gum.

At least his size could still intimidate people. Even if he was fucking useless in a gun fight. Or most fist fights. He even had to teach himself how to eat with a goddamn fork again. Cause naturally it couldn't have been his left hand that got blown to bits. Nope, it was his dominant hand. And he was left trying to learn how to wipe his own shits with his clumsy non-dominant fucking hand, much less retrain himself in knife and gun play. He could practice his old combat drills two hours a day for the rest of his life and never get back to his old skill and speed.

Now here was this gorgeous woman and of course he was fucking letting her down, too.

As soon as she drank down the rest of the flask, Rafe hurried her forward. He needed to get her to one of the other clan men. Someone whole who could actually help her. Someone who wouldn't make her cry and freak out when they fucked her.

Yeah, he hadn't missed the fucking *tears* in her eyes when she panicked and told him to stop.

There was a separate lottery pool for wounded veterans. He'd thought—what the hell? He never thought he'd win. But they all did it, cause... he didn't know. Hope or some shit?

Otherwise it was hard as fuck not to take his old pistol and put a bullet through his damn temple.

After The Fall when almost all the planes got fucked by the EMP and there was no more Air Force to speak of, he'd joined up with the Elite Guard and trained his ass off, becoming the New Republic's version of a Navy Seal. The baddest of badasses.

When everyone else was running away from a fight, they were charging toward it. He'd spent years honing his skills as a killing machine. He proudly fought in President Goddard's army, but after two tours and six years, he'd rotated out and settled in Jacob's Well.

He only made it four months before reupping. Civilian life just wasn't for him, he'd thought. Too boring.

He was a fucking idiot. Taking life for granted. Now he was forced to forever be a civilian. He thought, he didn't know, maybe he could get married. Pop out a couple of kids.

But he couldn't even do that right. And what the fuck else was the point of a one-armed fighter pilot?

"Here," he said, unwrapping the stick of gum and handing it to Shay. She took it and popped it in her mouth, then they started walking. Her little body solid against his made his hammering heart slow slightly, but only slightly.

She'd looked so fucking scared when he'd finally realized she wasn't with him anymore when they were having sex. It had just been a couple seconds—she was with him, she was with him, and then suddenly she wasn't. The thought that he might have put that look on her face—Jesus, it was a wonder he hadn't joined her in upchucking his lunch.

"Jonas," he called out as soon as they came onto the shaded lot where weed grew like... well, weeds.

It was close to the river so it was the one place in town where the trees actually grew taller than a shrubby ten to fifteen feet and provided actual shade.

Rafe saw Jonas sit up from his slouch in a lawn chair by the small, maroon shed. He stood and immediately started striding straight toward them.

Thank Christ.

"What'ssss goin' on? Somethin' wrong?"

Jonas's glassy eyes moved from Shay to Rafe. But they did it slow.

Son of a bitch. Was he—

"Are you high right now?" Shay asked the question that was on the tip of Rafe's tongue.

She pulled out from under his arm and stood up ramrod straight. Rafe felt one eyebrow shoot up. She looked *pissed*.

Jonas blinked and tried to stand up straighter too. All it did was make him wobble slightly. Damn, looked like Rafe might not be the only fuck up today.

"After last night, you really thought coming here and getting baked off your ass was the best thing to—" Shay broke off with a high-pitched scoff. "You didn't even think that I might need—"

She heaved out a huge breath, nostrils flaring as she glared Jonas down.

Jonas lifted his hands, the fact that he was in hot water obviously finally sinking into his pot-addled brain.

"You wanna get outta here?" Rafe asked her, but she held up a hand sharply.

"This is bullshit," she said. "I thought you were a *man*." Rafe stepped back but thank Christ, the barb was aimed at Jonas.

Jonas took a step toward Shay, his own nostrils flaring but Rafe moved in between him and Shay. He thought weed was supposed to chill people the fuck out.

"Get out of my way. It seems like our baby doll here is forgetting exactly who she belongs to."

Aw hell no, he didn't. Shay's eyes widened like she wanted to stab Jonas's eyes out and roast them over an open fire.

"I. Belong. To. Myself," she said through gritted teeth. Then she looked to Rafe. She only gave him two words, but it was enough to get her point across. And he'd never been happier to follow an order in his life.

"Hold him," she said.

Rafe grabbed Jonas with his good arm and swept his legs, taking him down easily and pinning him to the ground.

So Jonas could do nothing but struggle feebly while Shay walked around the rows of plants to a metal barrel. Rafe couldn't see what was inside it from his vantage point, but whatever it was, it sure got a reaction out of Jonas. Especially when Shay pulled something out of her pocket.

"Shay. Don't. Shay," Jonas said in a warning voice, suddenly sounding a lot more sober. "Don't you dare, baby doll."

But Shay just turned their way. A match. That's what she was holding. She lit it against the side of the barrel. And then she gave a wicked fucking smile that had Rafe's dick hard in seconds as she lifted the match over the barrel and then dropped it in.

On some level, Rafe realized what she was doing in that brief moment before she dropped the match. But it wasn't until the flame whooshed up that he fully contemplated all the ramifications.

"Shay!" he yelled, letting go of Jonas and jumping to his feet, hurrying over to where Shay stood, coughing and backing away. Because after the initial flame, smoke now poured out the top of the barrel. Right into Shay's face.

Aw shit.

Rafe took a deep breath and lifted his shirt to cover his face as he went in and grabbed Shay around the waist before pulling her out from the cloud of smoke.

As soon as he got her back across the small side yard, she was giggling her ass off.

For fuck's sake.

It was always out of the frying pan and into the fire with this one.

Rafe looked down at her and grinned, shaking his head.

She kept blinking and swiping at her eyes with her fists, like she couldn't manage much more coordination than that.

Fuck, she was cute.

Never thought he'd see the day a chick had him whipped. And certainly never thought he'd be so damn happy about it.

CHAPTER TWENTY-ONE

JONAS

What the fuck was Jonas gonna do with his baby doll? He didn't know what had Rafe bringing her here like he had. The first instant he'd seen them, her limp against Rafe's side, he'd known something was wrong and he'd almost lost his shit.

But then she'd gotten so full of piss and vinegar when she realized he'd been smoking.

Yeah, maybe he shouldn't have toked up when he got to work today. It was just old habit and damn, last night... He had to get his mind off it somehow if he didn't want to walk around with a giant stiffy all day.

A problem which should have been immediately solved on seeing the shipment he was supposed to send out to East Texas go up in smoke.

But after he ran over and threw a bucket of water on the barrel— from the side opposite the smoke was billowing out—and hurried back out before taking a full breath of the smoke, all he could do was stare at Shay.

She was giggling and grasping for Rafe's arm like he'd just told her the funniest joke she'd ever heard in her whole damn life.

Jonas looked at Rafe over her head and the guy just grinned and shrugged.

Son of a—

Jonas strode over to both of them, biting the inside of his cheek and doing his best to keep his temper back as he looked down at Shay. "You're in big trouble, baby doll."

Shay froze and blinked up at him, her eyes glassy. "You mean..." she trailed off. "You're going to... *punish* me?" Then she started cracking up, slapping at Rafe's chest.

Jonas rolled his eyes. He'd only taken a couple hits off a small joint and any buzz he had was quickly wearing off. He wanted to both kiss and spank Shay. Not necessarily in that order.

She was fucking beautiful. He'd never seen her so carefree or smile like that. It looked good on her. Great, actually.

Then suddenly she spun on him and had her finger pointed in his face, her features hard. "No one owns me." She turned back to Rafe, so quickly her ponytail smacked Jonas in the face. "And no pulling my hair when you fuck me."

Then she turned back to Jonas, spitting out her gum on the ground and pulling her tank top off as she did.

"What the—"

"Shay!" Jonas said, grabbing her hands before she could yank it off over her head and looking around. It was lunchtime so his field hands weren't around, but there were guards on the perimeter of the property at all times.

Shay bounced up and down. "But I wanna fuck," she whined. "I'm so hornyyyyyyy."

Fuck. Him.

Jonas and Rafe exchanged another look over Shay's head. Rafe just shrugged again like, hey, what are you gonna do?

Jonas rolled his eyes again.

"Baby doll, come on. Let's get you back home. Then maybe you can lay down for a nice nap."

But she struggled against his hold when he tried to guide her out of the yard.

"Stop it!" she yelled, jerking away from his hold. He let go as soon as he was sure she was steady on her feet.

He didn't understand what was going on. He'd never seen her in such a volatile mood. Maybe it was the pot, but she'd gone from obviously upset to pissed even before she lit his stash. And Rafe looked just as clueless as he was.

He'd only dabbled in BDSM before converting to Christianity and then marrying Katherine... maybe he'd done it wrong last night. He'd just been going from instinct and the basic principles he remembered from back in the day.

At their most stripped down, all power exchanges were about... *trust*.

He frowned down at Shay.

What had happened between last night and this afternoon? What did she mean about the pulling her hair thing? Obviously something had happened between her and Rafe. But then she'd been clinging to his side when they came in the yard, so—

All the sudden, Shay flung herself against Jonas, knocking him back against the shed.

And then she reached back a hand for Rafe.

Jonas could have easily moved out from under where she pressed her body against his. But something was obviously going on. And for the moment, he decided to watch and take his cues from Shay.

She tugged Rafe until he was flush against her back and then she squeezed her eyes shut, snuggling closer against Jonas, sandwiched between them. She lifted a hand behind her to hold Rafe by the back of his neck. Like they were grinding on a dance floor, but she just stood there, all three of them unmoving.

A furrow grew between Rafe's eyebrows as he skimmed a hand down Shay's exposed side.

She let out the sexiest groan as she dropped her head back against Rafe's chest.

"My husbands," she whispered, eyes still shut. "This is what my husbands feel like."

Jonas frowned, sensing something much deeper was going on underneath the surface. "That's right, gorgeous," he whispered, slipping a hand down to her hip and just holding her. Wanting to anchor her to them like she seemed to need.

She breathed out like she was letting go of a hundred years of tension and stress. Fuck but Jonas wished he knew what was going through her head at that moment. She'd bared herself to them last night. But she'd still held plenty back.

Like what life had been like before she lost the children. And who the children's father was.

But when she lifted her head and smiled at Jonas, it was so goddamn sweet it about split him down the center. When she lifted up on her tiptoes to whisper in his ear, "Make love to your wife," he couldn't help wrapping an arm around her waist and dragging her up against him.

"Hey," Rafe said from behind them and Shay giggled, turning to him. "Don't worry. I meant you too."

"That's not what I—" He huffed out a breath. "I'm not sure that's the best idea at the moment. Just a little bit ago— And you're—"

Shay's features darkened and she flipped around in the small space between them so that her chest was to Rafe's. "I'm high on *weed*," she giggled. "I feel all floaty. But my body is still *mine*." She went up on tiptoes again and whispered into Rafe's ear, but not so quietly Jonas couldn't hear. "And it wants to fuck *yours*."

Then she ran her hand down Rafe's stomach and it disappeared into his pants.

"Fuck woman," Rafe hissed. "You don't play fair."

She reached up and grabbed Rafe's hand and placed it on her shoulder. Then she dragged it downward to her breast. As soon as he made contact with where she wanted, she cried out and arched into him. At the same time thrusting her ass against Jonas's hard-on.

Goddammit. Little vixen was going to get what she wanted, after all.

Jonas only had one brief moment of reflection to realize—maybe that was the point. Maybe in this moment, she needed things on her terms. Her way.

The next moment he was too busy shoving open the door to the shed and dragging Shay through it, Rafe following like his hand was superglued to her breast.

There were a couple of high windows in the shed but it was still dim inside. It was enough to see Shay yanking her shirt over her head again.

Rafe moved his hands back. He was obviously still not sure if this was okay. But the way Jonas figured it, while her decision making might be impaired by the weed, she still seemed to know what she wanted. And they'd been together as recently as last night.

So when she threw her arms around Jonas's neck and started making out with him, he went with it.

"Touch me," she gasped between kisses. "I'm already so close. I swear I'll go off if you just touch me."

Fuck. Him.

Jonas glanced back to Rafe. "You heard her. Fucking touch her."

Rafe shot him a glare, but it only lasted a moment. Because the next second he smoothed Shay's hair out of her face and kissed the back of her shoulder over to her neck. And then he reached around to her waist. Jonas felt Rafe's hand sneak between their bodies and backed up slightly.

He knew the instant Rafe made contact because Shay's hands flew up, one hand burying in Jonas's, the other in Rafe's.

She dug her nails in too.

Which made Jonas so fucking hard.

He grabbed her cheeks and kissed her more forcefully, teasing his teeth along her tongue.

She gasped and arched and then, holy shit, she was coming. She cried against Jonas's mouth and he kissed her, swallowing her moans and her air and everything that was Shay.

"Aw fuck," she whimpered. "Fuck. Fuck. Fuck. It just keeps going. Oh God. It's so good. And it just keeps *going*."

Her pelvis kept thrusting against Rafe's hand like she couldn't get enough. From the way her body kept shuddering, she really was having some mega-orgasm. Fucking hottest thing Jonas had ever seen. He'd heard that pot could increase women's orgasms but he'd never had any first hand proof—

"It's still— oh, *Goooooooooooooood*! I need the fullness. Please, one of you. Fuck me." Her hand clenched in Jonas's hair so hard he wondered if he'd have a bald patch tomorrow. But he didn't fucking care.

He shoved his cargo shorts down and when he reached for Shay's pants, found that Rafe already had them down. Shay was just kicking them off her feet as Jonas freed his cock. He didn't waste any time hiking her leg up and around his hip and then—

Jesus *Christ*, there was the promised land.

He sank into her dripping pussy and could have fucking died right there on the goddamned spot and been a happy fucking man. Shay's pussy. Songs should be written about this pussy. Empires fought over it. Lives lost.

But it was theirs.

She was theirs.

Then he remembered her vehement words. Her body was her own.

Fine. Her body could be her own.

As long as his was hers too.

"I'm yours," he swore as he pulled out and thrust in again. "My body is yours." He clutched her close, lifting her up off the floor as she wrapped her other leg around his waist. Rafe helped support her from behind, cocooning her between them.

"Every part of my existence is fucking yours," he growled, kissing down from her throat to her breast and sucking her nipple into his mouth.

And she just kept squealing and writhing on him as she apparently continued riding the mother of all orgasms.

CHAPTER TWENTY-TWO

HENRY

When Rafe came to Henry's office saying that Shay needed him, the last thing he expected to find when he ran upstairs was Jonas's face buried in her pussy.

He'd rushed over here thinking something was seriously wrong. Had they *really* come and interrupted his business dealings just for a midafternoon booty call? Did they have any idea how important his job was? He'd been in the middle of a meeting with the Trade Secretary from Central Texas North discussing a major deal to import several tanker trucks full of natural gas.

"Thank God," Jonas said, lifting up from Shay's engorged flesh.

She just murmured unhappily and reached down for Jonas's head, urging him back down to her sex.

"Tag in," Jonas said, eyes going to Henry. "Please. I can barely feel my tongue anymore."

What the hell was going on here? It was no secret there was no love lost between him and Jonas. They tolerated each other and played fair in the bedroom because of Shay but the man had never gone out of his way to give up a turn with her.

"Henry," Shay moaned, her voice full of need as he came closer to the bed. She sat up and reached for his shirt. Her fingers clenched in the Italian fabric. "I need it deep. So deep," she groaned, running her hand down her chest and roughly squeezing her breast.

Henry frowned. Something didn't look quite right.

"Shay, are you oka—?"

"She's high as a kite," Jonas said, moving off the bed and flopping backwards on the couch by the window. He wiped his sweaty brow with his forearm.

"What?" Henry spun to glare at Jonas.

"Hey, it wasn't even my fault," Jonas said, then he paused. "Okay, well it *mostly* wasn't my fault. It was an accident. But anyway," he gestured toward the bed. "Cannabis turns her on like a house on fire. Rafe and I have been fucking her for hours. She just keeps coming and coming and *coming*. I don't even know if they're separate orgasms or just little spikes in one long giant one."

Henry's eyes shot back to the bed where Shay squirmed, her own hand dropping between her legs. Watching her slip her fingers inside her slick pussy had him hard within seconds.

"Charlie was out on a ride somewhere with the horses and Gabriel, well you know him. I doubt he'd be up for giving her what she needs. So you're up to bat. If we stop she gets all frantic, just saying how bad she needs to come and how she needs it deep."

"*Deep*," Shay echoed. "Henry, fuck me deep."

Well, when she put it like that...

Henry felt like he ought to stand and chastise Jonas more for letting their wife get into this state—but his cock was hurting from how tight his slacks were getting and well, who was he to deny his gorgeous wife when she needed him?

He yanked off his pants and in no time, was climbing between her legs.

She immediately reached down to grab his ass and guide him inside her.

She moaned and he swore because *good Lord*, even though he'd made love to her as recently as last night, he'd swear it got better and better every damn time.

"Deeper. Oh God, Henry," Shay keened desperately, eyes closed and chest arched. "Deeper. I need you to touch that place so deep. In my center. Get to my center."

With her blonde hair splayed all around her on the mattress and her breasts arched toward the ceiling like that, she looked like a wild sex goddess. There was a slight sheen of sweat glistening all over her skin and she was gripping the sheets so hard her knuckles were white.

"Shay," Henry groaned, shifting so that he covered her body with his. He braced one hand beside her head and with the other reached down to grab her ass so he could seat himself even more deeply inside of her.

She let out a little satisfied grunt as he slipped in that last half inch. Henry leaned down and sucked on her breast. He knew she liked it hard, so he drew it into his mouth with relentless suction, nipping with his teeth at the end.

She squealed and her hips thrust artlessly against his. It was like she was so desperate for release she couldn't manage to pace herself even if it might bring her pleasure sooner.

That was all right. Henry would see to her pleasure. As he lifted his head and looked Shay in the eyes, he felt the strange spike of emotion hit his chest like it sometimes did when he was with her. He'd never felt anything like it before. Never in his life.

And it made him want to bring her pleasure more than anything in the world.

Because everything else—his job, the waiting Central Texas North Trade Secretary, the natural gas deal, all the things he worked so hard for—they all fell away under the spell of her green eyes and her perfect body wrapped around his.

With his hand under her ass, he lifted her to the perfect angle so that, not only did he hit the spot deep inside her she'd been begging for, but his pubic bone also dragged against her clit with every thrust.

He bowed his head into her chest. He couldn't handle those eyes.

He was forty years old for God's sake. It was too late to change who he was. To change the entire focus of what he wanted.

Shay was only supposed to be an ornament in his life. Not to become his whole reason for being.

It was insane. Nonsensical.

So why did this moment making love to his wife feel more significant than all the money, privilege, and achievements that he'd fought so hard for?

In spite of himself he lifted his head and locked gazes with her again. Her glittering green eyes were full of lust and need and lov—

Everything in him rejected the possibility even as Shay clenched and wrapped her arms around his neck, crying out his name. "*Henry.*"

His name on her lips sent one of the most powerful orgasms he'd ever experienced ripping through him.

He thrust and felt her body spasming around him even as he emptied his essence deep inside her. Then he pulled back and plunged in again, deeper still.

And when he had no more, he wrapped his arms around her and pulled her to him so tight there wasn't a breath of space between them. She was still quaking as he whispered roughly in her ear:

"What are you doing to me?"

"Loving you," she whispered back.

Henry jerked away in shock from her but her body had gone slack, eyes dropping closed. Within moments, she was asleep.

CHAPTER TWENTY-THREE

SHAY

"All right boys, where did we leave off last time?" Gabriel asked his boys as they sat down on either side of him on the couch in the living room.

Shay paused where she was cleaning up in the kitchen after dinner to watch them. In the couple weeks since The Great Smokeout as the guys had come to jokingly call it—something Shay would be mortified about forever—she'd determined two things.

One, she'd never go anywhere near marijuana again with a ten-foot pole. Because while she'd come harder and longer than she'd thought humanly possible, she hated feeling out of control like that.

And two, she still had no idea which of her husbands, if any, were working for Jason.

So far, she'd spent one on one time with Charlie, Jonas, Rafe, and Henry, probing to see if they were sensitive on any of the weak spots she thought Jason might exploit.

First she'd spent time with Henry. Maybe because she thought she'd told him... But no, she'd been so high and out of it. She couldn't have really told him she *loved* him.

Her face and neck flushed even thinking about it. He wasn't acting any different around her than normal and surely he would be if she'd *actually* said it, so... That part was just a vivid dream.

But then, how come she could remember the rest of her time with him so clearly? The way he'd clung to her, the urgency in the way he'd—

Shay shook her head. Anyway, she went to his office last week and found him smoking a Cuban cigar while wheeling and dealing over a video call with a trade outpost near San Angelo. He shared his office with the town's Communications and Surveillance Department and he could request to borrow a laptop with access to the new internet whenever he needed.

As Trade Secretary, there wasn't much Henry couldn't get his hands on if he wanted it. What could Jason offer him that he couldn't get for himself? Or was she missing something obvious?

So then she moved on to the others. She felt fairly confident Charlie wasn't the mole. Because he was, well, Charlie.

She even thought about telling Charlie the truth. But what would be telling him do, other than maybe make her feel better? She remembered what he'd been like when they first got to town. He'd been so angry and ready to fly off the handle. What if she told him and then he did something foolish and reckless that put all of them in danger?

No, she couldn't. She just couldn't.

She needed a plan.

And to have a plan, she needed to decide who else she could trust.

She needed to do it fast, too. Their trip to the capitol was just a week away now. And when the device Jason had instructed her to plant in the President's sculpture didn't do... well, whatever it was meant to do, he'd realize she wasn't working for him anymore. She'd have a very narrow window to go get her kids back, and for that, she'd need her clan.

But her so-called investigations hadn't turned up much of anything.

Well, at least until earlier today.

Her eyes flicked back to Gabriel.

Ever since that night when Jonas brought her home for punishing and Gabriel had touched her for the first time, Gabriel had worked almost every day, sun up to sun down. Even his days off.

At first she thought he was doing it to avoid her, but Jonas said those were the kind of hours Gabriel used to work. The aberration had been the few weeks after their wedding when he took days off each week and came home early on others.

So maybe none of them were a mole for Jason and she'd just been overreacting about the whole thing.

She'd clung to that thought for a couple of days.

And then she'd gone back to hunting for clues. She searched their belongings on the few occasions everyone was out of the house.

She left no stone unturned. No drawer unruffled through. No pocket unturned out.

She checked every floorboard to see if any were loose. She unscrewed every heating vent to look behind them.

Nothing.

At least until she got to Gabriel's room earlier today.

"The one about the fire men!" Alex cried, bouncing up and down on the seat cushion beside his dad. "Read it again, read it again."

Tim huffed out a breath. "This is lame. Can't we just go to bed already?"

"Ay, what would your grandmama in heaven say if I didn't teach you your Bible lessons?" Gabriel made the sign of the cross. "Just because we don't have a preacher in town anymore is no excuse for you not to grow up knowing the scriptures."

Tim expelled a dramatic, drawn-out sigh and dropped his head against the back of the couch, face to the ceiling.

Gabriel ignored him and opened the big black Bible he always kept in the center of the coffee table.

Shay listened as Gabriel read about a king who put up a giant gold statue of a god and ordered everyone to worship it. When three men refused because they worshipped the Jewish-Christian God, the king had them thrown in the furnace. He even had the furnace heated seven times hotter than normal.

But they didn't burn. The three men walked through the fire and as everyone looked on, a fourth figure appeared, walking with them.

Shay felt the little hairs on her arms stand on end as she listened. Her mom always partied hard on Saturday nights with whatever loser was currently occupying her attention, so making it to church on Sunday mornings had never exactly been a priority.

"That's the angel!" Alex said. "The angel is walking with them and protecting them from the fire!"

Gabriel nodded and smiled, running a hand through his younger son's hair. "That's right. The angel protected them."

Then he kept reading, "So then King Nebuchadnezzar approached the opening of the blazing furnace and shouted, 'Shadrach, Meshach and Abednego, servants of the Most High God, come out! Come here!'"

"So Shadrach, Meshach and Abednego came out of the fire. The prefects, governors and royal advisers crowded around them. They saw that the fire had not harmed their bodies, nor was a hair of their heads singed; their robes were not scorched, and there was no smell of fire on them."

Alex started clapping and Tim just banged his head against the back of the couch as his dad finished out the story.

"At least Timothy sees through it."

Shay jumped at Jonas's voice and looked over to see he'd come up beside her. She hadn't even heard him come in from the backyard where he'd been cleaning out the ashes from the cookstove after dinner.

"What do you mean?" Shay whispered, not wanting to disturb the scene in the other room.

Jonas scoffed. "That bullshit. What does Gabriel think he's teaching them? That they can walk through fire? All that's going to get them is third degree burns. Because miracles don't exist."

Shay turned away from the living room to stare at him. "Well maybe when you're a kid, you're supposed to believe they do."

But he just shook his head at her. "Why? So when you grow up you can be even more pissed because the people you trusted lied to you your whole life? That just makes it ten times worse." He looked away from her, his jaw working. "Believe me."

Shay breathed out, looking back to the living room where Gabriel was giving each of the boys a long goodnight hug.

She both loved and hated watching their goodnight rituals. It reminded her of her nights with Matthew and Nicky. Sometimes she couldn't handle being in the same room.

"Come on," Gabriel said, standing up. "Time for bed."

"Just one more story," Alex said, a whine entering his voice.

"Boys who want to be tucked in better get moving. Now."

Alex's shoulders dropped but the next second he'd hopped up off the couch. "Last one to the room's a rotten egg!"

Tim had continued looking bored out of his skull for Bible story time, but all of the sudden he shot to his feet and raced after his brother.

"You're a rotten egg!" he yelled, grabbing Alex by the shoulders at the last moment and slipping in the room in front of him.

"No fair. Dad. Dad, did you see that? He cheated!"

Gabriel shook his head. "Boys. How many times have I told you not to run in the house?" He looked exhausted as he crossed the room to deal with them. Alex and Tim just started arguing with each other about who was right. Which quickly devolved into a wrestling match.

"Boys!" Gabriel said sharply, but they ignored him. Gabriel hurried across the room and pulled them off each other, hauling them into their bedroom. As soon as he shut the door behind him, their voices cut off.

Okay, time to get Gabriel alone as soon as he got the boys settled.

She slid out from underneath Jonas's arm. "Didn't you say you were going to go check on your harvest or whatever after dinner?"

He pulled back, one eyebrow lifted. "You trying to get rid of me, gorgeous?"

She felt herself blushing. "No. I just—" There was no way to explain why she wanted the alone time with Gabriel. She waved a hand. "I—"

"You're cute when you're flustered."

He pulled her close and landed a kiss on her forehead. Then his grip around her tightened and his lips moved to her lips. He kissed her deep, the bright, citrusy flavor of the orange he had for dessert sweet on his tongue.

When he pulled back, she was more than a little breathless.

"I should be back in about an hour. Try not to fall asleep before I get home."

She licked her lips and nodded. "I'm suddenly feeling very awake."

He grinned and her heart did a little skip. He gave her hip a squeeze and then he was off, heading for the front door.

God, how did she still feel like a schoolgirl in the middle of all the stress she was under? These men had her so addled.

She tilted her head as she watched Jonas go. The saying *sad to see you go but happy to watch you leave* popped in her head.

Because damn but that man had a fine ass.

She let out a little sigh as the door shut behind him. She picked up the plates she washed and was about to put them back in the cabinet when Gabriel came out of his and the boys' room.

It was all quiet inside now. He'd obviously settled them down.

He was such a good father.

There was no way he could be Jason's spy, no matter what she'd found. There had to be some other explanation for it.

Then she frowned. It was *because* she was a good mother that Jason had been able to so easily get her to work for him.

What if he was somehow doing the same to Gabriel?

She set down the plates and walked out to the living room. "Hey. Can we talk?"

"Sure. What's up?"

Shay glanced behind him at the door he'd just closed.

"Maybe in the back yard. Or upstairs in the bedroom."

Gabriel's eyes widened. "The backyard sounds good."

He still rarely joined her and the others in bed. What was holding him back? He'd come in the room a couple more times since the first, but he always stood by the wall and masturbated without ever touching her.

Could he not bear the intimacy of sex with her because he was keeping a big secret? Like the fact that he was working for Jason?

...Or—she swallowed as another horrible possibility struck her—or was it because he knew exactly how jealous Jason could get? Did he know that if he ever stuck his dick anywhere near her and Jason found out, Jason might—

The thought made Shay sick but she still pasted a smile on her face and held out a hand toward the kitchen and the back door. "After you."

Gabriel cracked a smile. "I think that's supposed to be my line." But he passed in front of her, going to the back door and holding it open for her.

The sun was just setting but the air was still so hot that when you breathed in, it felt like you were being smothered in a blanket from the inside out. Summer was really settling in now.

Shay sat down on one of the lounge chairs that they kept a towel slung over so it wouldn't burn your ass.

"Hold that thought," Gabriel said, lifting a finger and then jogging back into the house. A couple minutes later he came out with two big glasses of water.

Shay's heart melted a little. He was always so conscientious like this. Thinking of the little things.

He handed her one of the cups and sat down in the lounge chair beside her. He smiled at her and then looked out at the sunset. He didn't say anything, just looked happy to be there sitting with her. She'd noticed this about him. He was never in a rush to fill the silences like Charlie or crack a joke like Rafe. He had a calmness to him she envied.

Could he really sit there looking so peaceful if he was secretly working for Jason? She frowned. He was a good man. A religious man. Surely if he was working for the enemy he'd feel conflicted about it.

Or would a man so devoted to his sons have made peace with the sacrifices he was forced to make if he felt his sons were in danger?

Her mind went back to what she'd found earlier when she'd searched his room. His had been the final one she'd looked in. Frankly, along with Charlie, he was the last she'd suspected.

Turned out she should have looked there first.

She almost hadn't found it, either. Under his pillow there was a framed picture of a woman who looked like Alex. Obviously his mother. Gabriel's wife. What had happened to her? Xterminate most likely.

Shay had almost stopped right there. It hurt to see how obviously he still loved her. Which was ridiculous. Of course he should still love the mother of his children.

And Shay hadn't gotten married so she could fall in love.

She'd gotten married so she could betray an entire town and serve them up on a platter to Colonel Arnold Jason Travis.

If she was going to put a stop to it, she had to put aside hurt feelings and continue. Leave no stone unturned.

So then she'd lifted up Gabriel's mattress and searched underneath. At first there was nothing. But when she kept reaching?

There, in the center of the mattress, she felt something. Her heart sank as she pulled out the small notebook and started flipping through it.

It was a detailed accounting of crop rotations, what was planted when, and the locations and amounts of ration stockpiles around town. Along with detailed drawings of the irrigation system.

All extremely valuable intel Jason would need when he took over.

Her stomach dropped the more pages she flipped. It was all in Gabriel's handwriting, too. He'd made all these notes. Some pages were filled with math calculations in addition to notes, stuff Shay couldn't follow at all. Gabriel obviously had a lot more potential than just as a day laborer.

Was that Jason's angle in with him? Had he promised Gabriel a position as director of architectural operations in the territory or something?

Or was it like Jason had done with her—both threaten and promise?

Both would fit with Gabriel's central goal of helping his kids have the best life possible. If he had a better job, he could give them more. And keep them safe from whatever Jason might have threatened.

Shay turned to Gabriel as he took a long drink of water.

"Why'd you put your name in the lottery, Gabriel?"

He looked over at her, surprised. "For my boys," he said. "I told you."

She stared at him. He was the sort of man you looked at and just thought, *masculine*. His hair was so thick and dark and he always had a five o'clock shadow growing in by the time he got home from work, even though he shaved meticulously every morning.

"You work hard for them. Jonas told me that before we got married, you used to work seven days a week trying to give them all the best in life."

He nodded, gaze going back out to the orange and purple sunset. "I want them to have all the things I never had growing up. My parents came here from Mexico determined to make a better life for our family. I'm determined to do the same thing."

Shay frowned. "But if your parents spent their whole lives trying to give you a better life than *they* had, and *you* spend your whole life trying to give your sons a better one than *you* had, well... when do any of you get to actually enjoy life while it's happening?"

"Well that's not—" He broke off. "They're all that—"

"Matter?" she asked softly, completing his sentence. "What about you? Don't *you* matter?"

He paused, blinking. "I mean, I do, I guess. But they come first. Always."

Shay nodded. She understood it, the way he was thinking. After all, it was how she'd justified so many of the things she'd done.

Marry five strangers?

If it was for Matt and Nicky, fine.

Plant bugs in people's houses, all right, she'd do that too.

Help Jason take over an entire territory, even knowing the terrible, terrible things that would happen in the process?

Shay looked back out at the sunset. The purple-blue was overtaking the orange as the sun dipped below the horizon line.

"So you'd do anything for them?"

"Anything." His answer was immediate.

She glanced his way. "Eat a scorpion?"

He chuckled. "Yes."

"Jump off a cliff?"

"Yes."

"Kill somebody?"

There was a moment's hesitation and he looked disturbed by her question, his eyebrows furrowing. But he didn't blow her off. Finally, he nodded. "If it meant saving Alex or Tim's life, then..." he swallowed. "Yes. I'd do whatever it took to keep them safe."

Whatever it took.

Shay swallowed, looking down at the dried-up grass of the lawn. Grass in Texas never stayed green. Before The Fall, some of it was green, but only because people had extensive sprinkler systems. It was hard enough to keep the crops irrigated with river and spring water, and that only worked because of some clever engineering.

But she was just stalling now. Anything to avoid the matter head on.

She took a deep breath as she looked over and found him watching her. Their gazes locked. "But if you did that, if you killed someone for them. And they found out about it..." she trailed off, not knowing how to put what she was trying to say. "Well, wouldn't that sort of ruin their lives? Them knowing you'd sacrificed your morals for them?"

"Especially since they're little mirrors of us. The biggest impact we have on them isn't what we tell them, it's what we show them. The way we live our lives."

This time when she looked back at Gabriel, it was to study him for any little tell. A tic in his eye. The slightest twitch of his mouth.

Anything that would give her the tiniest hint that her words resonated with him in a significant, possibly Jason-related way.

She got nothing. Just that slight crease in his brow.

"What are you getting at with this, Shay? Do you think me working so much is fucking them up or something?"

He didn't sound mad but he was definitely more than a little on the defensive side. Was his question a deflection?

How else could she find out what she wanted to know without just coming out and asking?

Would you go as far as feeding information to the enemy? Will you be reporting back about this very conversation?

Shay knew she should keep pushing. Maybe if she told him she'd found the notebook? That she just came across it accidently while she was cleaning?

Yeah, you lifted his mattress up and shoved your arm all the way underneath to the armpit... accidently. While you were dusting.

Because that was believable.

If Gabriel *was* working for Jason and she tipped him off, what would happen then? What would Jason do if he thought she was poking her nose where she shouldn't?

"If I get even a whiff of you blowing off this mission or fucking it up..." Jason said, and that was when Jason had motioned the bastard holding Matthew to nick his throat with the knife.

"Forget about it," Shay said, standing up abruptly. She hadn't thought this all the way through. She could all too easily fuck everything up.

She'd regroup and figure out another approach.

"Shay? What the hell?" Gabriel stood up too. When she tried to move around him to go back in the house he got in her way.

She stopped short, looking up at him.

"Why did you really bring me out here to talk, Shay?"

His brown eyes were intense as he looked down at her, his face shadowed in the dim light of the setting sun.

She searched his eyes. "Why won't you sleep with me?" she blurted.

He let out a quick breath and took a small step back. Like he was afraid of her.

Her? Or Jason?

The thought pissed her the fuck off.

"Wow," Shay said. "You can't even bear to be too close to me, can you?" She closed the small gap between them, laying her hands on his warm chest. "Why is that, Gabriel? Do you not find me attractive?"

Gabriel barely seemed to breathe as she slid her hand down from his chest to his stomach. And then lower.

His entire body jerked when she made contact with his cock through his jeans and her eyes widened in surprise. She thought she'd have to rub him a little bit but he was already fully hard, cock straining against the denim.

But yet again, he pulled back. When she looked up, he was shaking his head. "You don't understand. I made a promise."

Shay's mouth dropped open.

"To who?" *To Jason?*

Gabriel took another step away from her, hands up. "God."

"God?" Shay felt her eyebrows shoot to her hairline.

He nodded fervently. "I promised him if he would just give the boys a mama, I'd spend the rest of my life obedient and celibate."

Shay crossed her arms over her chest. He had to be kidding. Everyone made rash promises to God when they wanted something. No one ever took them seriously afterwards.

No, her Jason hypothesis was much more likely.

And screw that. Screw Jason and screw Gabriel if he was working for Jason.

She kept eye contact with Gabriel as she reached down and took the hem of her dress in her hands. Then, without another word, she lifted it up and over her head.

By the time she was free of the cotton fabric, there was just enough light left to see the dumbstruck expression on Gabriel's face.

She undid her bra next, letting it fall down her arms and drop to the ground at her feet. Then her panties until she was standing completely naked right as twilight fell.

Gabriel shook his head even as she stepped closer. And when she reached for the arm hanging limply at his side, he only stared at her hand as she grasped his wrist.

His hand stayed mostly limp but he did lift it when she urged him to. And when she pulled it so that his palm curved around her breast, he squeezed like it was an instinctual response.

A long, low breath hissed out through his teeth. "*Te deseo,*" he whispered under his breath. "*Quiero besar todas las partes de tu cuerpo.*"

Shay's brows furrowed. "What does that mean?"

But he just shook his head, his thumb skimming ever so gently over the tip of her nipple.

Now it was Shay's turn to gasp.

She'd ripped all her clothes off to make a point. Or something. She'd been pissed, anyway. And looking for control, if she was honest.

Was it fucked up that the way she kept doing that was to flaunt her sexuality. Yes, of course it was. But the more Gabriel flicked her nipple, the more all her fury was finding a very different focus.

The need that rose up inside her like a sudden wave caught her completely by surprise.

Friction. She needed friction.

She hiked one leg up and wrapped it around Gabriel's hip, grinding her center up against his hardness.

And when he sat back down on the reclining lounge chair, she was only too happy to follow him.

She climbed over him and ripped his shirt open, not caring that the buttons went flying. It was even hotter, in fact.

She just had to get at his skin. Had to touch his skin. The skin she knew would be burning for her.

When she slid her hand down his chest to the inside of his jeans, he was whispering in Spanish again, but this time it sounded like he was cursing.

He had his hands clenched on the side rails of the lawn chair but when she looked up at him, she saw his eyes were focused on everything she was doing as she lowered her head, kissing down the path her hand had just taken.

His stomach was hard and muscled, and she felt him suck in a sharp breath when she licked the trail of hair leading down from his belly button into the top of his jeans.

When she yanked the button loose, he let out another string of Spanish. This time Shay could make out two words, repeated over and over. *Dios mio, Dios mio, Dios mio*.

But when she got her hands in his boxers and pulled out his ramrod stiff cock?

He fell completely silent.

The only sounds were the crickets, the wind, and Gabriel's heaving breath as she jacked his shaft up and down several times while teasing her tongue along the small slit at the tip.

She decided to stop torturing him, though, and give them what they both wanted.

She popped his crown in her mouth and felt his whole body go tense. God it was intoxicating to have so much control over a man. To know that in this moment, his very existence balanced on the flick of her tongue or the twitch of her hand.

But then his hand dropped to her head. She wasn't wearing her hair in a ponytail today, thank God. And even so, Gabriel wasn't trying to pull her hair.

He just stroked her hair gently.

Like he treasured her as she gave him this gift.

Which just made all her feelings about ten thousand times more complex. She'd brought him out here because she thought he was working for Jason.

So how had she ended up with his cock in her mouth?

And if he was working for Jason, why was he touching her so tenderly?

Gabriel's hips twitched restlessly and Shay realized she hadn't moved in who knew how many seconds. She smiled around his cock. He wasn't demanding about it—he might not even realize he was impatiently shifting for friction. Still, it was nice to know he was as much a man as any other.

She increased her suction even as she dropped a hand down to her own sex. There was something about blow jobs that had always turned her on.

And Gabriel finally giving into her like this? It was hot as hell.

She was on the edge in moments, groaning her pleasure around Gabriel's cock, knowing the vibration would drive him even crazier.

Her orgasm was quick and sharp. They came so fast these days, it was insane. She didn't know if she was entering her sexual peak or if it was just being surrounded by these five, powerful, sexual men who were never stingy in the bedroom.

Gabriel swore in a mixture of English and Spanish and when she looked up through her lashes, mouth full of his cock, she found his feverish eyes still locked on her.

She didn't stop circling her clitoris. She was greedy. She wanted another one. He must have seen it too, because he finally slumped back against the recliner, chest pumping with each heaving breath, cock straining fuller than ever in her mouth.

The sight of him so close to losing it had her on the edge within seconds. She cried out her second orgasm. It was longer, and harder, and so fucking *good*.

His hips started pumping then. He was on the verge.

But no.

She'd started this with a plan.

Well, sort of.

Driving him crazy had been the general intent.

But she'd also done it to see if he was Jason's man.

If he was and he was smart, he'd never fuck her.

So she climbed up his body, her mouth letting go of his cock with a loud *pop*. Right before she could position her pussy over his straining cock, though, he crawled backwards, half falling off the damn lawn recliner in his determination to get away from her.

Shay sat back on her heels at the foot of the recliner.

Oh God.

He was running. He was literally about to run away from her.

She wrapped her arms around herself but then he stopped and bowed his head.

He came back and bent down on the ground in front of her. He grasped her face in his hands and in the moonlight, she could see the mix of struggle and devastation and lust on his face.

"*Mi cielito.*" He pressed his forehead to hers. "You have to know I want to make love to you more than anything in this world."

"Then why don't you?" Shay hated the way her voice cracked as she asked the question.

He shook his head, forehead still to hers. "Please understand. I made a promise." Then he let out a sad laugh. "I don't know anymore. I'm asking you to understand when maybe I don't understand myself."

He pulled his forehead back from hers, looking her in the eyes and still cupping her face. "All I know is that you are the greatest gift that's ever been given. To my boys and to me. What if I break my promise to God and he takes you away?"

Shay's heart felt squeezed by a vice.

Oh God.

If he wasn't working for Jason? If this man before her was genuine? If all the emotion in his eyes was true, was for *her*?

She wrapped her arms around his neck and drew him close.

And felt his erection poking her in the stomach. She laughed and pulled back. Gabriel was covering his face with his hands but she pulled them down.

"Stop," she said, still laughing, but then she grew serious. "Okay, so if I respect your decision not to sleep together. Can I still do something about..." She gestured downwards.

When he didn't say anything one way or another, seeming stuck in indecision, Shay dropped her hand between them and grasped his shaft.

"Come here," she said, gesturing for him to sit on the lounger beside her.

He did and they both turned sideways. He held her to his chest, one hand toying with her breast and plucking her nipple as she stroked him to release.

He held her to him for long moments afterwards, whispering, "*Mi cielito, Mi cielito*," and then finally, so softly she barely heard it, "*Mi vida.*"

CHAPTER TWENTY-FOUR

SHAY

One more week of watching the guys and trying out all sorts of small little tests, and she still had no clue if any of them were a mole or not.

Maybe none of them were and she was just being paranoid for nothing.

After all, if Jason sent her in as a spy, it had to mean he was a little desperate, right? Why put her in if he already had an inside man?

So she was Plan A and that was it. No Plan B. Or Plan B was someone completely unrelated to her clan. That was reasonable, wasn't it? Wasn't it?

God, it was enough to drive her crazy.

And every day—and night—she spent with her husbands, not telling them what was going on felt more and more like betrayal.

And today the whole clan was leaving as part of the big delegation to the capitol in Fort Worth.

She'd finished her sculpture just yesterday. It was a large five-foot-tall portrait of President Goddard created out of tons of old computer processors, reflective metals, and mirrors. She'd built it about ten inches deep. The perfect width to hide the black device Jason had given her to mount at the heart of the sculpture. Everything that went in or out of the Palace was x-rayed, but since basically her whole sculpture was metal, it wouldn't much matter. The box was perfectly hidden.

And hid it she had, exactly as Jason had instructed.

But—and this was a big but—she'd only installed *part* of it.

Shay had spent days staring at the device trying to determine what to do with it. It wasn't just a small bug like he'd given her for the other houses. Which she supposed she could understand. The president's apartments would be far more extensive. It had to be a parabolic microphone of some kind. Maybe a thermal imaging camera? Or even a device that could be used to attack their wireless network from within? From everything Henry had said of the capitol, they had the most advanced computers that had survived the EMPs.

Or hell, maybe it was all of those things and then some—it was sure big enough to be. The main part of the device was five inches long by about two deep.

The second piece? Well, that was where things got interesting. It was slim, maybe only a quarter of an inch thick and as long as her thumb. When she held it near the first piece, it synced along the bottom of it like a magnet. For just a second when they first locked together, it made a sort of low-pitched *humming* noise.

Shay had immediately detached them again and looked around the bathroom like someone might have heard—which was ridiculous because it had been no louder than a whisper. She'd locked the door and no one was home except for Gabriel. But he was with the boys downstairs.

Carefully, she clicked them together again and the humming noise came back. Shay froze, staring down at the device in her hands...

But nothing else happened. The hum died off and she was left with the heavy black box in her hand.

Whatever it was, she was almost sure the secondary attachment was a battery of some kind.

Which was why she ran downstairs and got her miniature screwdriver kit that Audrey's husband, Mateo, had let her borrow for working on her sculptures.

She'd created the shadows on the President's face out of tons of little fiberoptic photonic chips from old phones and laptop boards and she'd needed the miniature screwdrivers to open the cases without damaging the chips.

When she came back upstairs, she'd locked the door again, thrown open the curtains, and gotten to work on the battery. It had come apart without much effort and the insides looked like... she hadn't known exactly what she was looking at—well, besides a thin black rectangle glued to a silicon motherboard along with a couple of wires.

She frowned. Why hadn't she ever taken at least one computer engineering course somewhere along the way? All she knew how to do was rip things apart and pull out the pretty, shiny bits.

But really, she just needed it *not* to work, so how hard could that be?

She cut the wires and then used a normal sized screwdriver to pry off what she thought was the battery itself.

After jamming her thumb with the screwdriver a couple times when the battery case slipped, she finally got the damn thing to pop off.

"Shit," she swore, sucking on the thumb she'd sliced with the front of the screwdriver as she fit the outer case of the battery back together, minus its innards.

She winced when she saw a long scratch along the underside from one of her mishaps with the screwdriver. But fuck it. It was going to have to be good enough. She'd use some sharpie to try to color the scratch back in.

When she held the casing back to the first piece, it no longer clicked in place on its own. Not surprising. But that was fine. She'd just superglue the damn thing on.

All she needed was for it to look right in case any of Jason's other agents checked to see if she'd done what he'd asked.

But obviously, eventually he'd figure out it wasn't doing whatever he was putting it in place to do.

Which meant Shay was out of time.

And that scared the shit out of her.

She forced her eyes shut as she finished folding a shirt and adding it to the overnight bag she'd be taking with her.

No more stalling. She had to decide who to trust and tell someone everything.

Now. Today or tomorrow.

On the trip.

Shay looked at herself in the mirror and tucked a long strand of blond hair behind her ear. As she did, she thought about Vanessa.

Poor girl. To have been alone out in the wilderness for so long...

Oh God—she watched her own eyes widen in the mirror as the realization struck—oh *God*, she was such an idiot.

Vanessa.

Of course!

Shay stumbled, she backed up from the mirror so fast.

But God, it was so obvious. Vanessa had come to town, what, only a couple weeks after Shay herself? Where exactly had Audrey said she'd been picked up? Shay squeezed the bridge of her nose and paced as she tried to remember. Wasn't it something about a Scrapper team finding her in the neutral zone between Central Texas South and *Travisville*?

Shay remembered thinking how lucky the girl had been that it was Central South men that had found her instead of Travisville thugs.

And then there was that confusion with the lottery box... It could have been a way to arrange for all her husbands to be Travis's spies, too. Or at least some of them.

Shay stopped pacing.

If that bitch was working for Travis, Shay would get to the bottom of it.

Right now.

She was supposed to be packing for their trip to the capitol—they were leaving today, in fifteen minutes, in fact—but she had to know.

Shay hurried out of the master bedroom and then down the stairs. She heard one of her clansmen call her name as she rushed through the living room toward the front door, Henry, she thought, but she just called over her shoulder, "Be right back!" before slamming the door behind her.

Then, before any of them could come after her, she sprinted down the road toward Vanessa's house. Almost all the clans lived in the same little historic neighborhood close to town, so Shay only had to go down the block and around the corner before she came to the pretty little ranch style house where Vanessa and her clan lived.

"Bitch better be home," Shay whispered under her breath. She forgot what Vanessa did as a day job. Without Audrey here, she hadn't hung out with her much. Audrey had gotten home a few days ago but Shay had gotten wrapped up in her own shit and just hadn't made an effort to—

But, no, screw feeling guilty! Vanessa was most likely the one working for Jason!

Shay pounded on the front door with her fist.

No answer.

Shay huffed out a furious breath through her nose and pounded again.

Still nothing.

She was just raising her fist again when the door opened.

To a red-faced Vanessa swiping repeatedly at her eyes with her forearm like she was angry at herself for being caught crying.

"Oh. Hi," Vanessa mumbled. "Sorry." Her lip quivered as she turned her face away and took another swipe at her eyes. "Allergies."

The fiery interrogation that had been on the tip of Shay's tongue only moments earlier suddenly sputtered out. What could make badass Vanessa *cry*?

"What's wrong?" Shay stepped into the house without being invited and went to Vanessa, wrapping an arm around her. For a second Vanessa went stiff as a board, but then she softened and turned into Shay's chest.

She was so tiny and birdlike that Shay could feel her bones as she held her. Damn, were they not feeding this woman? It had been a couple months and still she could hardly weigh more than a hundred pounds.

"It's nothing," Vanessa said, waving a hand as she pulled away from Shay.

"Bullshit," Shay said, tugging Vanessa into the living room and sitting down on the couch beside her. Was it Jason? Did he have Vanessa in a similar bind as he had Shay?

"Fine, you're right." Vanessa pretended to glare at her, then gave a wan smile before dropping her head into her hands and running them through her inch and a half long hair.

"It's just..." She lifted her head and looked out the window. "I really want this to work." She laughed humorlessly and swallowed. "The guys, the marriage, the whole thing." She shook her head. "I never had anything like this in my whole life, but it's all I ever wanted."

Shay felt her eyebrows rise. "A bunch of husbands?"

Vanessa rolled her eyes and swatted Shay on the shoulder. "No, dumbass." She looked away again like she was embarrassed to admit it out loud: "Family."

"My folks..." Vanessa waved a hand, "Anyway, I've been on my own for a long time. I thought it would finally be different. And some days I think I'm pulling it off. But others..." she shook her head. "It turns out that after the apocalypse when guys outnumber women twelve to one, no matter how hard I work, how much I try," she shrugged helplessly, "it still might not be enough."

Shay scooted closer to Vanessa, hating the hopelessness she heard in her voice. "Enough for what, honey?"

Vanessa's voice was toneless as she replied, "Enough to make them love me."

All right, where the fuck were Vanessa's husbands? Because Shay was about to introduce them to her fist. How dare they make Vanessa feel like this? What the *hell* was wrong with them?

But just as Shay was about to tell Vanessa what a load of crap it was that they were making her feel this way, the little alarm on the watch Henry had given her went off.

"Shit," Shay swore, looking down at it.

Vanessa stood up, putting on a fake smile. "It's fine. I'll be fine." She waved a hand. "I'm just being hormonal. You know." She did a fake little laugh. "That time of the month."

Shay's heart hurt for her friend. Yes, her *friend*.

God, was she really this desperate? Looking for conspiracy theories everywhere because she couldn't stand the thought of one of her husband's being the mole?

Vanessa was just a girl trying to make her way in life after being dealt a shit hand, and here Shay had been about to accuse her of betraying them all.

Look in a mirror much?

Shay winced even as she said, "I'm so sorry, honey," and leaned in to give Vanessa a quick hug. Then she pulled back, holding Vanessa's hands. "But I promise, we'll figure this out. Audrey and I'll be back from Fort Worth in a few days. We'll figure it out."

Vanessa gave what was obviously a pacifying smile.

Shay wished she could stay and convince her of it, but her watch beeped again. Dammit. The caravan was leaving for Fort Worth in five minutes and she still hadn't finished packing her bag.

"See you soon, hon."

She gave Vanessa a quick kiss on the cheek and then she was sprinting back to her own house.

Where she was back at square one.

Back to her own husbands as the best suspects.

But this trip had to be her last test. She'd watch each of her husbands every move while they were at the President's Palace. And if she still didn't see anything suspicious, well... it was time.

Time to tell them.

Everything.

CHAPTER TWENTY-FIVE

HENRY

Henry was glad he wasn't driving the large van as their entourage drove into Fort Worth. Because watching Shay's face as they entered the city was priceless.

Her mouth dropped open and stayed open, from the time they first came in sight of the city lights to the time they were driving through the downtown streets.

He understood. It was a lot to take in at first. But watching her excitement made something break loose and then expand in his chest like a balloon being filled with helium.

So this was what pride felt like.

He'd arranged this trip. He was giving this to her. And if he had his way, he'd give her so, so much more. He'd give her everything she deserved.

"I don't understand," she finally whispered, eyes widening even further as they slowed to a stop and pulled into the underground parking lot for the towering Omni Hotel.

Lights lit up the hundred or more floors of the structure. Not candles either.

Henry grinned at Shay. "Oh, did I forget to mention that the President has restored power to the Fort Worth grid?"

She all but choked. "No. No, you did not happen to mention that." She smacked him on the shoulder, all her attention on him now. "How?"

He grinned, basking in her confused excitement. "All the wind farms in this part of the state. When the wind is up, it is enough to power the grid to the city. President Goddard had all the power stations that were blown on D-Day repaired around the Fort Worth grid and *voilà*." He gestured around them, pushing open the door when the van pulled in front of the hotel, holding out a hand for Shay.

The van with Clan Hale pulled in behind them and Sophia, the Commander, and that outspoken woman, Drea, were just getting out of the car in front of them.

Shay stepped out of the van and then hurried to the edge of the covered drive, ignoring the line of armed guards who went on alert at the sudden movement.

"Shay," Henry called, along with Rafe and Charlie.

She stopped at the line of shrubs before heading into the street, mouth dropping open again as she looked around. While some of the downtown buildings were completely dark, there were a fair number that were just as lit up as the Omni. "It's incredible," she whispered.

Charlie's eyes narrowed as he followed her gaze. "It's a waste. If they repaired the grid here, why haven't they repaired it further south and shared the power?"

Henry could have punched the bastard for ruining Shay's moment. If he were prone to such brutish methods, that was.

But still, he was tempted, because Shay's obvious awe dimmed as she turned to Charlie. "Oh. I didn't even think of that."

"If you'll all please come this way," said a man in a suit with a clipboard, eyeing all of them nervously. "There's an extensive security screening and the sooner we get through with it, the sooner you can get to dinner. The president hates to be kept waiting for his dinner."

Henry barely stopped himself from rolling his eyes. He just bet. He'd only visited with Goddard a few times in the past five years, and each time the man's waistline had expanded exponentially.

The President Goddard of today was a far cry from the hard-nosed General who'd had the command and respect of enough Army and Marine battalions to declare himself president and unite the country after D-Day.

But that was the way of politics, right? Ideals rarely stood the test of time against unlimited money and power.

"Come on, lovely," Henry said, putting his hand to the small of Shay's back. "I want to show you our rooms."

Each clan had one of the premiere suites for their stay, second only to the President's penthouse apartments.

Sophia came bounding up to Shay and grabbed her hands. "It's so exciting, isn't it?"

Shay smiled and held onto Sophia while Sophia did a little bouncing dance up and down. She only stilled, the smile dying on her face when she looked over Shay's shoulder and saw Henry standing there.

"Oh. Hi."

"Hello, Sophia. How was the ride?"

"Fine. Just fine." She tried for a smile but ended up just looking miserable as she gave Shay's hands one last squeeze before spinning and going back to her dad.

Shay turned back to Henry, a furrow growing between her brows. But Henry just pulled her close and kissed her temple before urging her up the stairs and into the hotel.

The security screening was intensive.

Just short of a damn cavity search.

Every bag was sifted through and they were patted down. And up. And down again. At least they had a female guard to pat down the women, but still.

"Is this really necessary?" Charlie asked in exasperation as one of the guards felt up the inner seam of his pants.

Henry tried to shake his head at him but it was too late.

The guards passed a look between them and Charlie was pulled out of the group and taken to a back room where Henry knew he'd be required to strip completely, bend over, and well, spread 'em.

President Goddard was nothing if not thorough when it came to his safety.

He had reason to be. There had been no less than *seven* attempts on his life, two in the past year alone.

He was notoriously paranoid because of it. He had tasters try all of his food before he ate a morsel, was rarely seen in public, and conducted almost all his business right here at the Omni where he could control the environment.

Henry could respect the man's dedication to safety even if the thought of it made Henry chafe. While he was all for success, he never wanted it at such a high cost. He was happy to stick to working off to the side of greater men, arranging side deals and taking care of the details that really made empires run. While enjoying his freedom and all the perks of the job, naturally.

He looked across the lobby to where Shay and Sophia were talking and laughing. Especially if he could share some of those perks with Shay.

He was still smiling as the guard handed him back his briefcase and bag.

He wanted to show Shay the time of her life tonight. Because while the President was a paranoid shut-in, he also settled for nothing less than the best when it came to food and drink.

And after the cornmeal and bean mush that was their main staple broken up by the occasional bit of meat or vegetables, Henry was certainly ready for some fine dining.

And wine. God, he'd kill for a perfect glass of Chablis. Which he just happened to know was the President's favorite, since he was always on the lookout for a case everywhere he went trading. He also just happened to have brought two cases that he'd saved up especially for this occasion.

He got them a few months ago for a couple pounds of Jonas's lousiest bud. The dumb fucks who traded it didn't realize the priceless gem they had on their hands. Apparently they'd opened a bottle, decided it tasted like 'goat piss' to use their colorful colloquialism, and brought it to the San Angelo black market. He shook his head at the memory. The lack of culture in their foundling little country truly boggled the mind.

But tonight, Henry would show Shay all that was possible.

CHAPTER TWENTY-SIX

RAFE

Rafe tugged at the collar of the stiff button up shirt Henry had insisted he wear. He didn't see the point. It wasn't like the President was fucking royalty or anything.

They were all sitting around the biggest table Rafe had ever seen in his whole goddamn life—his clan, Clan Hale, the Commander, his daughter, Drea, and a bunch of other people he didn't recognize.

A waiter came around pouring wine into champagne glasses with stems so skinny Rafe was sure it would snap under his grip if he even looked at the damn thing too hard.

Why couldn't they have some beer anyway? This bastard was supposed to be the richest guy in Texas, right? So couldn't he have at least taken drink orders. Who the fuck liked fucking *wine*?

"I would like to make a toast," Henry said, lifting the wine glass with his fingers around the tiny ass stem. "To our president. Who fashioned this great country out of chaos and gave us a legacy worth defending."

Rafe switched his attention to the fat man at the head of the long table. He smiled and lifted his glass, clutching it the globe in his ham fist. "To me," he chuckled, and the three women on either side of him giggled and raised their glasses.

Rafe glared and didn't touch his glass.

He'd always respected President Goddard. Or General Goddard, as he'd always thought of the man, like most of his fellow Elite Guard did.

Rafe had only seen General Goddard a few times when he was stationed at Fort Worth before The Fall, but he'd been intimidating. The General had been in his late forties at the time. Iron gray hair. Stern demeanor. Always barking orders. He was infamously tough and exacting, but he was famous for always looking out for his troops. Or so the rumors went. Rumors that became legend and then a rallying cry after The Fall.

Just went to show how fucking green Rafe had been at the time. Cause it was hard to imagine this motherfucker as anything other than a little bitch.

He was fat, red-faced, and his three so-called *girlfriends* he had hanging all over him were so obviously just short of paid whores it was fucking embarrassing.

Rafe glanced across the table to Shay.

She looked just as uncomfortable as Rafe felt.

Which just pissed him off.

Why the hell hadn't Henry warned them this was what they'd be walking into? But when Rafe looked over to Henry, he was just smiling like nothing was the matter?

Was this the kind of shit he did on a regular basis? Hobnob or whatever the hell you called this, with fat, entitled pricks who wouldn't know hard work if it punched them in the face?

"So, sir, one of the reasons you asked us here was so we could talk about the possibility of expanding the marriage lottery policy on a wider basis. Here we have two clans, Clan Hale, headed by our illustrious Security Squadron Captain, Phoenix Hale over there. Give us a wave, Phoenix."

Nix glowered, looking as amused as Rafe felt, and inched his hand up from the table briefly before dropping it again.

"And Clan Cole," Henry continued, again either oblivious to the tension in the room or pretending to be, "which I have the honor of heading. Every time a lovely young lady joins Central Texas South, a lottery is held to determine what lucky lads will win her hand in marriage."

President Goddard scoffed, downing his glass of wine and either not realizing that some had spilled out the side of his mouth onto the white of his tux shirt or simply not caring. He slammed the wine glass so hard on the table Rafe was surprised the damn thing didn't shatter.

"See now, what I'd find interesting was if it was a lottery for five women to one man." He broke out in a fit of wheezing laughter and his three girlfriends tittered along with him. "Am I right?" he waved to the rest of the table.

Only Henry chuckled along with him.

"Yes, sir. Well, that would be something. But since the world's short on women these days, really the other way does make more sense."

The president waved his hand. "I don't know. I like to reward industriousness. I think Fort Worth's system might work just fine for the time be."

"And what system is that?" Drea asked. Then, obviously speaking through gritted teeth, she added, "Sir."

The president cocked his head sideways at her. "Well aren't you a pretty thing? I've always had a soft spot for blondes." He winked at Drea and his girlfriends, two of whom were blonde, giggled.

Aw shit. Rafe didn't know Drea that well, but even he could see the steam coming out of her ears.

She took a deep breath in and out before responding tightly. "So. You were saying. Your policy here? For women?"

"Oh that." Goddard waved a hand. "It's simple really. Men who are industrious and provide goods and services that benefit the city and the government are rewarded."

Drea's nostrils flared. "And— The women—" Every word sounded like it was being choked out. She took another deep breath. "They're the rewards?"

The president was busy waving the waiter over for more wine and only seemed to be halfway paying attention to Drea. He waved a hand again. "Something like that. It's in their interest, too. Who wouldn't want to be with the wealthiest men in town? It's good for everyone."

He took another long swig of wine before clapping as a line of waiters brought out plates piled high with food.

"Oh look, our feast begins."

"So the women don't get any choice," Drea said, all but talking over the President. "They're just assigned to some man. Because he's rich."

"Drea," the Commander said in a low tone. "I'm sure we don't want to—"

"Okay..." She took a breath, obviously trying to get herself under control. "Well, I came here for another matter. I'd like to ask your permission to head a mission to rescue the women being held against their will at what was previously Nomansland island." Drea never moved her hawkish gaze from the President, even though he was full on frowning at her now, clearly displeased.

Aw damn. Rafe wasn't big on diplomacy and shit, but even he could see this was going nowhere fast.

The Commander started to wave his hand again but Drea just plowed on. "The women are being held in inhospitable conditions, being repeatedly raped until they're sold off as slaves. If they survive long enough, that is."

President Goddard continued frowning, though now he was looking around, accepting the plate of food his waiter handed him and shoving it in front of the one non-blonde girlfriend. Then he settled his napkin in his lap. He took another gulp of wine and waved for another refill. He was basically doing anything to avoid even glancing Drea's way.

"It wouldn't take many resources. Central Texas South's Security Squadron would be more than enough. If we just had one mid-size plane, we could easily overwhelm Bautista's defenses and—"

"Enough!" Goddard roared, finally looking at Drea. "I'm trying to enjoy a meal here."

Drea blinked, obviously stunned by the outburst.

"Drea," the Commander warned in a low tone. "Don't. You promised—"

"Women are being *raped*. Right now," Drea hissed, throwing down her napkin. "While you enjoy your fucking wine and antipasto."

"Drea," the Commander snapped, pushing his chair back.

But it was too late.

President Goddard snapped his fingers and just like that, guards materialized from where they'd been stationed in the corners of the room.

"I will not be talked to like that in my own home."

The guards converged on Drea's chair and were dragging her up and backwards.

"Drea!" Sophia yelped before her dad put a warning hand on her forearm and shook his head. She looked like she was going to ignore him and run after her friend but something in his look must have stopped her because, though her jaw went hard, she stayed seated and stared down at the steak and mashed potatoes on her plate.

Rafe's eyes shifted to Shay. Shit. He hoped she wasn't thinking of doing anything reckless either.

But while her eyes were wide and her knuckles were white as she clutched her fork and knife, she didn't so much as make a peep.

Rafe didn't miss the way her hands shook as she lifted them to try to cut her steak.

Charlie reached over and murmured, "Here, let me." She looked at him gratefully and dropped her hands to her lap while he cut her steak.

And Rafe glared at Henry, only somewhat gratified to see that he too looked taken aback by what had just happened. Henry's eyes were locked on Shay, which again, made Rafe feel less like punching the bastard.

"Well, at least the one good thing about there being less women around is that there's less bitching to deal with, am I right?" the President chuckled.

Only his girlfriends laughed with him. He was too busy grabbing his plate from the girlfriend who was his taster to notice, though. As he cut off a large hunk of steak and shoved it into his mouth, he looked toward the Commander. "So, Eric. it really has been too long since I've seen you. And little Sophie. Not so little anymore." He laughed and grabbed his napkin to wipe sloppily at his mouth, missing some gravy that had dripped down his chin. "I'm so glad you brought her like I asked."

Asked. More like ordered, Rafe bet. Looking at how tense the Commander was, he couldn't imagine there was any way he'd have brought Sophia here voluntarily. As a lowly Scrapper, Rafe didn't have much to do with the Commander of a whole territory, but everyone knew the Commander worshipped the ground his daughter walked on.

One time a guy new to town whistled at her when she was walking down the street and the next day, the guy was thrown out of town on his ass, face black and blue.

Nobody fucked with the Commander's daughter.

But if the President tried something? Rafe's hand slid under the table to his belt out of habit. But of course his knife wasn't there. All their weapons had been removed downstairs.

"I thought your own daughter might be here. Sophia's always wanted to meet her."

Goddard's face darkened. "Abigail is...Well, she just doesn't under-stand that a man of my position is entitled to certain," he let out an annoyed huff and then smiled and grabbed one of his girlfriend's hands, "rewards for my long years of service."

He grinned lasciviously at one of the blondes and Rafe was almost put off his steak. Almost.

Goddard gave a long chuckle, waving a fork in the Commander's direction. "I still think about our last stand at Texarkana, you know. You and your battalion saved my ass. I'm not too proud to admit it."

"I was happy to serve, sir," the Commander said.

"Those Southern Alliance bastards thought they could take us with those cannons but they didn't know we had that huge fucking stock-pile of RPGs or that almost all the Oklahoma boys had defected to our side."

He laughed a wheezing laugh as he shoved a huge bite of steak in his mouth. Then he turned to his girlfriends. "You shoulda seen the way those chickens ran. They were exploding left and right. Boom!" he made an explosion motion with his hands, bits of food flying out of his mouth as he continued speaking. "*Boom!*"

The Commander pushed his plate slightly away from him, setting his silverware down. "It was certainly a bloody day."

"I know," Goddard said, sawing into his steak that had been cooked so rare, red pooled all over the plate.

Rafe had to keep his gaze steadfastly away from the repulsive president in order to get his own steak down. It was hard to imagine that man had ever known a day of discipline in his whole damn life.

Still, he couldn't help glancing over his shoulder in the direction they'd taken Drea and, if he wasn't imagining things, thought he caught the Commander doing the same. This shit was fucked.

"When do I get my present? I've heard so much about this new famous artist from Jacob's Well. Finding the next great artist of the new era is just what the country needs. We've got to prove to the common folk that we're just as sophisticated as the old US of A, and nothing says sophistication like the arts. Am I right, my beauties?" He looked to the fawning girls and they simpered in agreement.

Rafe was glad his usual expression was one of bored disinterest because he couldn't have pretended to smile for this fucktard even if a knife was to his throat.

"Tomorrow, sir," Henry said, smiling wide and rubbing a hand in circles on Shay's back. Rafe couldn't tell if she was comforted by the gesture or if it strung her even tighter. "We thought it might make for an excellent PR moment, you standing by the unveiling of your portrait."

Rafe ignored Henry as he prattled on about what good press it would be. To him, one thing had become very clear during this lunch. He'd heard mumblings about the President's lavish habits but hadn't wanted to believe it. Unfortunately, this visit was only confirming everything he'd heard.

It was time for a new president.

The question was: what was he going to do about it?

CHAPTER TWENTY-SEVEN

ERIC 'THE COMMANDER' WOLFORD

"I can't believe you just sat there smiling while that— that *man*—" Sophia broke off with a frustrated expulsion of breath. "And after those gorillas dragged Drea out, how *could* you—"

Eric shook his head at his daughter as they strode away from the hotel down the sidewalk. He'd suggested the walk because he knew Sophia would have just this kind of reaction and there was no way to know who would be listening. President Goddard was paranoid enough to have every room in the place bugged, but *especially* the suites for visiting dignitaries.

"I should never have brought you," Eric muttered under his breath. "You or Drea."

Sophia let out another outraged noise, stopping in her tracks but Eric took her elbow and propelled her forward again. "Keep walking."

She must have heard the seriousness in his tone because she obeyed. Good girl. If there was one thing he could say for his daughter, it was that as much as he'd always tried to shelter her, she wasn't as naïve as he wished she could be.

All he'd ever wanted was for her to have a safe, normal childhood. Or as normal as possible considering the world had ended. At least the world as they'd known it. Every decision he'd made for the past eight years, every step he'd taken—they'd all been for her.

And still, he made so many mistakes.

Including bringing her on this trip.

He shook his head at himself. They walked a block in silence and then he risked what he hoped looked like a casual glance over his shoulder.

Two of the Palace Guards were following about twenty feet behind them. That was to be expected. What worried Eric was whoever he *couldn't* see.

Still, out here in the open on the well-lit street—something that was still so strange he found himself constantly looking around at the novelty of it—they should be relatively safe.

"They have so much energy they waste it on streetlights," Sophia murmured, looking around. She looked half in awe and half appalled.

Eric's chest went tight as she echoed his thoughts. His beautiful daughter. God, she slayed him. She was so much like him. Too much. Stubborn. Determined. When she decided she wanted something, God help anyone who got in her way.

In other ways, though, she was all Pamela. Her mother had been beautiful and good. Too good for him, that was for damn sure.

"What are you going to do about Drea?" Sophia asked, blue eyes blinking over to him.

Eric shook his head again. That was his Sophia. So blind in her trust of him. She thought he could fix anything. Do anything. No mountain too high, no bridge too far. That was his little girl.

He let out a long sigh. "President Goddard is very different from the General Goddard I once knew. He was a good man once. But power..." He trailed off, then continued in a lower voice. "You remember that quote from your civics lesson in seventh grade I made you memorize—*power corrupts and absolute power corrupts absolutely?*"

She frowned but nodded.

"There was a reason I wanted you to focus on that lesson. It's important in the world we live in now more than ever." He was quiet a moment as he shook his head, thinking about the scene back at the hotel. "Power. It's changed the James Goddard I knew."

The furrow between Sophia's brows only grew deeper. "But you have power. It hasn't changed you."

Eric laughed and put an arm around her shoulder, pulling her close and planting a kiss on the side of her head as they continued walking. *Never change*, he wanted to say. At the same time—no, he knew these were things she needed to understand. She needed armor against the world. She needed to know the way things *really* worked.

"Jacob's Well is a different kettle of fish than all this, honey." He gestured around them at the lit-up buildings that towered on both sides of the street. "And so is being the President of a whole country. I'm just the governor of a small territory."

Sophia shook her head. "You might not have absolute power, but you said *power corrupts*. Any power. But you have power and it hasn't corrupted you at all. All you want to do is help people. It's why you've made Central Texas South such a safe place. And you take care of all the women. You have power and you're still a good man."

He dropped his arm and looked at her as they walked. She was so beautiful with her long auburn hair and those inquisitive blue eyes. The light scattering of freckles across her nose still reminded him of the little girl she'd been even as he could see the woman she was becoming. How could he tell her that he was just as bad as the President in some ways? Everything he'd ever done since being dishonorably discharged from the Army eight and a half years ago was absolutely for selfish, personal gain.

It was just that the things he wanted weren't money or fancy wine and food. They were safety and happiness. Namely, his daughter's safety and happiness.

And he would sacrifice anything, do *anything*—double deal, double-cross, and double down if it meant providing his and Pamela's daughter the life she deserved. If only he could give her all the things he'd failed to provide his family with when he should have been with them instead of fighting in pointless wars halfway around the world for almost all of Sophia's youngest years. He'd spend the rest of his life paying penance for his many, many failures. And that was fine with him. He didn't matter. Only Sophia did.

"You're nothing like that horrible man back there," Sophia continued vehemently, her cheeks going pink in her anger. "Drea was right to stand up to him."

Ice trickled through Eric's veins at her words and he froze, dragging her to a stop with him. "What Drea did tonight was *foolish*."

Sophia flinched at his harsh words, but he didn't soften his tone. "We might not like James Goddard the man, but as President Goddard, he built a cohesive country out of the chaos after the bombs dropped. More importantly, he commands the largest army of all the territories and that simple fact holds warring factions in check."

Eric lifted a hand to his daughter's cheek. "Listen to me, honey. He doesn't have to be a good man to be a great man."

But Sophia just kept shaking her head and when she backed away from his touch, she looked betrayed. "So you'll abandon Drea? Just like that?"

The disappointment in her eyes stung, Eric couldn't lie. He'd always known this day would come. Honestly, he was surprised it had taken this long—the day when he fell off his pedestal in his daughter's eyes. The day he stopped being her hero. It was inevitable.

But her welfare had been the one guiding star in every decision since he vowed to do right by Pamela and their daughter as he stood over Pamela's grave. And it led him now. What was best for Sophia?

Certainly not picking a fight with the President of the Republic. No matter how much he increasingly disagreed with the man's personal choices and public policy decisions.

He wouldn't have brought her if President Goddard hadn't insisted on meeting the daughter Eric had bragged about for years. And of course he'd assumed Goddard's own daughter Abigail would be there too.

But it had been another damn mistake on his part. As for letting Drea come along... Jesus, she'd just made such a nuisance of herself, demanding to have an audience with the President to plead the case for sending a rescue mission to Nomansland. And look how that had turned out.

Eric pulled Sophia into his arms. For several moments, she was stiff as a board against his chest. But he just kept holding her. His sweet, precious little girl. When had she gone and grown up on him? Her nineteenth birthday was only a couple of months away.

He'd overheard her talking excitedly about her own lottery. He was more than tempted to move the lottery age to twenty before then. Especially with the infiltration of Travis's spies in Jacob's Well. And that mess with the lottery box disappearing for the newest girl. Yes it had been found quickly but it only exposed another of the many weaknesses of the system. And as far as Travis's spy network, their investigations had turned up *nada* so far.

Jeffries had mysteriously ended up dead before they could interrogate him. There had only been fifteen minutes between the time his betrayal was revealed in the town square and the time Eric got to the Security Squadron for the interrogation. Only to find Jeffries dead on the ground, his throat slit. He'd told everyone it had happened in the crush of the crowd, when they'd realized what Jeffries had done and turned on him.

But in reality, Eric knew it had to be one of Travis's other spies. It killed Eric knowing that it could be any one of the men he surrounded himself with every day. It was hell questioning the loyalty of everyone and anyone. Constantly being on guard against overheard conversations. Watching what information you fed to who, trying to catch people in a lie to ferret out moles... It had all taken its toll on him, he wouldn't lie. He'd been the Commander of Jacob's Well for eight years, but sometimes it felt like twice that. On the bad days, it felt like a century.

He squeezed Sophia even more tightly. He hadn't protected her this long just to throw her to the wolves at the last moment.

She finally gave in, relaxing against him and squeezing him back. "What are we gonna do, Daddy?"

He breathed out in relief even as she broke his damn heart. She was still his little girl. He wasn't ready for the day she outgrew him. He wasn't sure he ever would be.

"We'll give it a few days, sweetheart. The president is paranoid. Not without reason. He'd lived through multiple assassination attempts. Drea confronting him like that in his personal meeting place was the worst thing she could have done."

"But she was just trying to—"

"I know," he cut off her objection, smoothing a hand down the back of her hair just like he used to do when she was little. "I know, honey. He'll calm down in a few days." *After he sobers up*, he added silently.

"I'll petition him to release her as a favor to me." It would mean owing the man a marker. If that wasn't enough to get Drea free, he could always offer free water rights to the well for a year.

"One way or another," Eric continued, "we'll get her back. I never leave a man behind. Or a woman."

"Oh Daddy!" Sophia repeated, but this time her voice was full of her usual hero worship.

Eric sighed and held onto his daughter even tighter. Looked like he'd stay on his pedestal for one more day after all.

He could only hope the day he fell—and he had no doubt that he would fall—she'd eventually find it in her heart to forgive his many sins.

CHAPTER TWENTY-EIGHT

HENRY

Henry woke up in the middle of the night only to find Shay wasn't in the bed beside him. When they'd turned in, she'd been tucked between him and Charlie, but now only an indentation on her pillow marked where she had been.

After everything that had happened at dinner, they'd all been pretty demoralized and headed to bed early. Shay understandably hadn't been in the mood for anything other than sleep and he knew she had things on her mind she wasn't sharing. More than just worrying about Drea.

Nothing about this trip was going the way Henry wanted. They were in *the* most luxurious, fully functional hotel in the whole of the Republic of Texas and it was being completely wasted. He'd wanted to show Shay the world, to wine and dine her...

If only that fat, paranoid fuck hadn't ruined everything.

Henry's mouth soured as he rolled out of bed. Neither Charlie or Gabriel asleep beside him stirred. Rafe had left after dinner to go catch up with some of his air force buddies who still lived in town. Guess he wasn't back yet.

Henry pulled the bedroom door shut behind him as he went hunting around the suite for Shay.

She wasn't in the living room area or the little kitchenette. But then he noticed the sliding glass door to the patio was open.

He walked out and saw her dressed in a long, flowing silk night-gown, standing against the balustrade.

God she was beautiful. Like had happened before when he looked at her, her beauty struck him so hard his heart seemed to stop in his chest. The longer he knew her, the more beautiful she got.

He must have made some noise because she looked over her shoulder at him.

"Couldn't sleep either?" he asked, trying to keep it light. She looked... forlorn, maybe that was the word for it. Anxious and sad in some deep way. He never pressed. But he'd noticed her mood grow more and more distant lately and it concerned him.

She gave a small shrug, then looked back out at the view of the lit-up city. "It's beautiful, isn't it?"

"The most beautiful thing I have ever seen."

He wasn't talking about the city. His eyes stayed locked firmly on her. Her neck sloped so perfectly to the most gorgeous pair of breasts on God's green earth. Her nipples were hard little pebbles underneath the thin silk fabric. Was it from the cool breeze or because she felt his stare?

His cock stirred at the sight.

When she next looked his way, she quickly averted her gaze, lowering her head.

Henry joined her, leaning his elbows on the ledge, forearm grazing hers. Good Lord, just the merest touch of her skin had all his nerve endings firing. How did she *do* that?

He didn't say anything for long minutes, hoping that maybe out here, just the two of them, she'd feel like she could finally open up to him.

But the time just passed and he could tell she was content for it to continue that way. It was another thing he'd never experienced with a woman before. That just their *presence* was enough. To be with another person and not have to fill the space with chatter. Not to have to spend every second worrying about impressing or one-upping or thinking about how to finagle your next promotion...

Shay was peaceful.

Henry hadn't had peaceful in a very, very long time.

If ever.

Finally, maybe five minutes later, it was him who broke the silence. "It's mind-blowing to come here and have everything be just like it was. Like the last ten years never even happened."

Shay scoffed. "Except for the fact there's barely any women. And apparently the ones that are here are given out like Christmas bonuses to the rich."

Henry winced. "I am so very sorry about Goddard. He gets worse every year." The man was a pig but tonight's display had really been beyond the pale. Henry turned so he was looking straight at Shay. And again she took his breath away.

Would it ever get old? This constantly being stunned by her?

And again, he had the thought—in all his years, out of all the many things he'd strived for and achieved, none of them had felt like this. None of it compared to being with Shay.

None of it compared to wanting her and being wanted in return.

It didn't seem to be a passing thing, either. Not just lust or the excitement of a new attraction.

The past two months had opened up parts of him... God, he hadn't even thought he'd had the capacity for— And then she came and—

"To tell the truth though," he said, eyes still locked on her, "the world outside Jacob's Well could be falling apart and I would not care. Because I have you. And you are everything."

Even as he said the words, he knew they were true.

Shay looked down again like his words embarrassed or even upset her. It was a look she'd been getting a lot lately whenever anyone in the clan complimented her. Enough beating around the bush. It was time to get to the bottom of it.

He took her hand and pulled her away from the ledge. She came where he led, a small crease between her brows.

"What are you—*oh!*" she exclaimed as he pushed her up against the glass of the hotel window.

"For a long time, that was all I could think about." He waved a hand behind him at the city even as he pressed his pelvis into hers. Even the brief moments of friction had him hardening almost to his full length.

Shay let out a small moan and her hips thrust restlessly against him.

God she was always so hot for it. Even with the five of them to satisfy her, she kept them on their toes. She was the most magnificent thing he'd ever—

"What do you mean? You wanted to come live here?"

He shrugged, pulled back into the moment by her question. "I wanted what this city represents. I wanted to be wealthy. Powerful. I wanted to be at the center of everything. To live some place where I could be an important man." He laughed self-deprecatingly as he leaned in to nibble on her ear. "I wanted to be a big fish in a big pond."

Shay hissed out a quick breath and arched into him. "And now? Has that changed?"

He pulled back and met her eyes. There was enough ambient light from the city and the full moon to make out her features. Her beauty really was fucking breathtaking. But it was more than that. He'd known beautiful women before. And after five minutes of talking to them, they grated on his nerves so much he could barely stand their faces anymore.

But Shay. Every day he spent in her company only made him want to spend *more* time with her.

His whole life, nothing came before his work and his relentless ambition. *Nothing.*

"Everything's changed," he whispered, running his hand down from her temple to the V of her collarbone and then down to her chest, right above her breasts. Over her heart. "You changed everything." He couldn't help his brow furrowing as he said it, though.

"You don't look exactly happy about it."

He huffed out a laugh. "I just..." He dropped his forehead to hers. "I had this picture of my life, okay? I was wealthy and respected and had all the things I never did growing up." He shook his head and then nuzzled his nose with hers. Then he drew his lips ever so slowly back to her other ear and nibbled a moment before quietly whispering another truth. One he'd never told anyone.

He shut his eyes as he confessed it. "Sometimes I think I can never wash the stink of that trailer park off me, no matter how much success I earn."

"Henry." She wrapped her arms around his neck and buried her fingers in his hair, pulling him tight against her.

"And I know how superficial that sounds. And just stupid. Like if I got enough material things, it could make up for all I didn't have as a kid. It's pathetic, really." He dropped his face to bury it between her neck and shoulder.

"Henry," she tried again, but again, he just shook his head and went on. "But still, I had this barometer of what success meant. Good job. Good house. Okay," he smiled down at her. "The best job and the best house." His smile dropped and his eyes went intense. "And the most beautiful wife that anyone ever had. *Ever.*"

Shay started to wave off his comment but he took both her hands in his.

"What I never expected or even thought to want was a wife like you. Someone as smart as she is beautiful. Someone who would make all that other shit pale in comparison to the way you make me feel every day."

Shay swallowed hard and looked like she was suddenly fighting tears. But now that he'd started, Henry had to get the rest of it out.

"What I didn't know to want, because I'd never really had it, was family. But Shay, you've given me that. You've shown me what it feels like to be important to someone. What it feels like to..." This time it was him swallowing. But then he stood up straighter as he squeezed her hands. "You've shown me what it feels like to love someone. I love you, Shay. And it changes everything."

Tears spilled down her cheeks.

"Don't cry, beautiful," he whispered, cupping her cheeks and wiping away her tears with his thumbs. "Never cry. I'm going to give you the world. Just you wait." Then he dropped his head. But just before his lips made contact with hers, she whispered urgently, "Stop! I have to tell you something."

He paused, then pulled back at the distress on her face. "What? What is it?"

"I haven't been completely honest with you."

She took a deep breath.

"It all started the day the tanks rolled into town..."

CHAPTER TWENTY-NINE

SHAY

"Holy shit, Shay."

He looked away from her, out at the dark night. Her whole body went tense, waiting for him to pull away. Waiting for him to call her a hundred names, to slam the door on her and go tell the other guys what a traitor she was.

But the next second he was pulling her into his arms, his hand at the back of her head holding her tight against his chest. "You've been carrying this alone all this time. It must have been hell."

Her arms flew around his waist as relief washed through her body. He wasn't rejecting her. Oh thank God, he wasn't rejecting her. Or leaving her.

Still, when he pulled back, the old fear resurfaced and she went tense, preparing for the worst.

"Have you told anyone else?"

She shook her head.

"Okay," he said, nodding, his face knit in concentration. He took her hands and looked around like he was afraid there might be cameras or something. Then he pulled her close again. "I haven't said anything because I never wanted to worry you, but the Commander's known for a while that there's a faction working against him in the Township. There's a small council of us the Commander trusts absolutely who knows. We've been investigating it."

Shay's eyebrows shot up. "What have you found?"

He huffed out in frustration. "A lot of dead ends. We narrow down one spy and arrest them quietly, but they don't have any information about Travis's larger agenda."

Shay felt her shoulders sink. Of course. She could have told him that much. "That's how he operates. In cells. No one knowing what the other is doing except for a few key players."

Henry nodded. "That is what we figured. Has anyone contacted you since you have been in Jacob's Well?"

Shay shook her head. "No. Jas—Travis gave me all the equipment I was supposed to plant before I left Travisville. But Henry, I think he'll attack soon. I know he wants Jacob's Well. We have to do something. You said you're on the council. So you can talk to the Commander. Let him know that an attack is imminent. Maybe even talk to President Goddard—"

But Henry was already shaking his head. "You saw that man last night. He only cares about the bottom line and Travis is a supposedly 'loyal' supplier of goods that Goddard relies on. More than that, Goddard is terrified of him. Travis has the second largest army in the Republic so unless we have proof, Goddard will not do a thing."

"But Travis told me to plant the device in the sculpture I'm supposed to present to the President tomorrow. Surely that—"

"Will only get you arrested," Henry finished sharply. "No. And you saw what he did to Drea. Do you want to end up in a jail cell beside her? We will not speak a word of this to that man. He is completely unpredictable and I do not trust him."

Shay let out a frustrated sigh. He was right. Of course he was right. "But the Commander. You can tell him."

Henry nodded. "Yes. And the sooner the better. I will go see if he is up now, in fact."

Shay let out a huge breath of relief. Oh thank God.

"But Shay," Henry said, taking her hands and glancing back at the hotel room, "You were right to be cautious. We still do not know who we can trust."

Shay swallowed the lump in her throat as she followed his gaze. "But surely they can't be— I mean, we know them. Just a little bit ago you were talking about family and how it's—"

But Henry just kept vehemently shaking his head. "There is a reason there are only four people on the security council. The Commander barely trusts anyone and we all swore a vow of secrecy. The consequences are too dire to risk any leaks."

Shay nodded. She hated keeping up the deception, but Henry was right. And if the Commander knew, that meant the town could start fortifying its defenses. They'd be prepared and on the lookout for whatever Jason sent their way.

"Okay." Henry looked around one last time. The furrow in his brow deepened. "I hate to leave you here."

"Go," she urged. "I'll be fine."

He still looked indecisive.

"Go," she said again. "Look, worst case scenario, one of them is a mole." She could barely even get the words out, the thought was so terrible. She barreled on. "But the rest aren't. And you know you can trust them to protect me."

Henry stood still for another long moment, eyes going back and forth from the sliding hotel room door to Shay.

"All right. Fine. But promise me you'll stay awake and alert until I get back?" He cupped her face in his hands. "You're my life now, Shay. I couldn't bear it if anything happened to you. Do you understand me?"

She nodded, again swallowing back emotion. "You be careful too."

He nodded and planted a swift kiss on her lips before pushing the sliding door aside and disappearing through the curtains.

Shay wrapped her arms around herself and raised her eyes to the dark sky, praying to the God that Jonas could never forgive to please, please keep them all safe.

CHAPTER THIRTY

SHAY

Shay must have been dozing on the patio chaise lounge because the next thing she knew, lights were flooding the suite. As she blinked awake, Audrey shook her shoulder and urged her back inside.

"Something's happening," Audrey whispered. "I don't know what's going on, but Nix, Graham, and Clark have been in with the Commander for half an hour and they sent Henry to bring me and the rest of my clan here."

Shay rubbed at her eyes as she hurried to her feet and all but tripped following Audrey back inside. She shut the sliding door behind her and searched the faces of her clan and half of Audrey's, along with Sophia.

Rafe was the only one from her clan not there. He'd left after dinner to go spend time with some of his old Air Force and Elite Guard buddies who still lived in Fort Worth.

"What?" Shay asked, gaze locking on Henry. His features were tight. It was bad news.

Oh God, had the Commander totally flipped out when Henry told her what she'd done? Was he under orders to arrest her?

Her eyes darted around. If that was the case, where was Nix? Wouldn't the chief security officer be the one to do the arresting?

Or maybe Henry had argued to have the responsibility himself because he wanted to make it easier on her?

Her mouth went desert dry.

She deserved whatever punishment they came up with, as long as they came up with some way to go rescue her kids. Oh God, Matthew, they had to find a way to sneak in and get Matt—

"Travis's troops have Jacob's Well surrounded," Henry said grimly.

Shay's hand shot to her mouth as Sophia gasped, "No!"

"Graham hasn't had direct access to the satellite feeds since he's been here. He's had to rely on intelligence from his backup." Henry's eyes drifted to Shay. "Who was apparently working as a spy for Travis."

Gabriel was immediately moving, shoving clothes in a backpack and then throwing it on the floor. "I have to go. My boys!"

Henry nodded. "The President is lending a battalion. It's outright insurrection against the rule of law. Nix and Clark will be heading back with them to Jacob's Well and I'm sure you can go along. They'll be heading out within the hour, though, so hurry. Here, take this." He handed Gabriel a keycard. "They're meeting in Conference Room C, fourth floor."

Gabriel nodded and went for the door. Then, before he could yank it open, he paused, spun on his heel, and ran back until he was standing in front of Shay. He cupped her face in his hands and looked her straight in the eye.

"I love you."

Shay choked, the tears she'd been managing to hold back spilling. Oh God. She'd been so wrong about him. Whatever that notebook was, it couldn't have been for Jason. Gabriel would *never* put his boys in danger like this. "Don't you dare say that to me. Not because you think you might not— Not right now."

His face went soft. "But it's true."

He leaned in and placed the gentlest kiss on her lips. If she hadn't been gone before she was after that.

"Go protect our boys," she blubbered before throwing her arms around him. And inside, there was a voice screaming, *hypocrite! Hypocrite! You could have stopped this but you didn't!*

Or at least made sure they were so much better prepared. All it would have taken was a word...

Gabriel nodded and then pulled away. He kissed her forehead and then hurried out of the room.

Charlie came over to her and looked ready to pull her into his arms, but she held a hand out to stop him.

At the other side of the room, Mateo had Audrey held to his chest. Danny was at her back, his arms draped around her from behind.

Shay wanted to bury herself in her own clan's arms like that more than anything in the world. But how could she after she'd betrayed them all?

She'd waited too long.

Her intentions didn't matter at this point. All that mattered were the facts.

"H-how many troops?" Shay finally managed to stutter out. "How many of Travis's troops are there?

Henry came close and when he ran his hands down from her shoulders to her elbows, she let him.

He knew, at least. He knew and he was still looking at her like he—

Like he—

"I love you, too," he whispered and she collapsed into his arms. He still loved her. Even after she'd told.

When she felt Charlie's warmth behind her, she didn't push him away. And then Jonas closed in on her right.

She didn't reach for anyone but Henry, though. He knew and he still loved her. She squeezed her eyes shut. She could only pray the others would be as understanding.

Though even as she had the thought, she realized how self-centered it was. Jacob's Well was in danger because *she'd* been too afraid to speak up until it was too late—and now all she could think about was if her husbands would still want her after learning what she'd done.

People would *die*.

She squeezed her eyes shut and nestled her head into Henry's shoulder, trying to block out the night and all its realities. Tomorrow. Tomorrow she'd let it all in and deal with it.

But one last night, she'd soak in the comfort of their embrace as they surrounded her on all sides.

————

Henry came and went throughout the night, but after several hours of no updates other than to say the Battalion had departed for Fort Worth, Shay dozed on one of the living room couches with her legs over Charlie's lap and her head in Jonas's lap.

They were all exhausted by the time dawn broke over the Fort Worth skyline. Shay squinted and turned onto her side, burying her face against Jonas's thigh. He stroked her hair and she sank into the touch.

Maybe it wouldn't have made any difference if she'd warned them about Jason... Didn't she know firsthand just how useless it was to stand against him? He crushed anyone and everyone who stood in his way.

Which was even more evidence for why she *should* have told someone right away. The Commander. Why hadn't she gone straight to the Commander? Stupid. She was so fucking *stupid*.

Or had she not told anyone not because she couldn't trust them, but because deep down, in her heart of hearts, she'd been too afraid to act against Jason?

He said he'd kill Matthew if she did anything against his orders.

And if she'd told the Commander and somehow it got back to Jason...

So was that the truth of it? She valued one boy's life over an entire town's?

She squeezed her eyes shut harder.

"Did you hear that?"

Shay lifted her head and blinked against the morning sun at Sophia's voice.

"What?" Audrey asked.

Sophia had stood up from a lounge chair across a wide coffee table and was looking toward the door. After a long moment of silence she shook her head. "Nothing, I guess. I just thought I heard something."

She sat back down, still frowning.

Shay sank against Jonas. But right as his fingers began to stroke through her hair, an ear-splitting alarm rang throughout the hotel suite. She jumped and sat up as did everyone else who'd been dozing around the room.

The next second, someone started pounding on their hotel door.

Jonas, Charlie, and Henry jumped to their feet, along with most everybody else in the room.

"It's Eric," shouted a muffled voice.

Shay frowned. Who was—?

"The Commander," the voice clarified, barely audible over the wail of the alarm.

Jonas and Mateo hurried to the door.

"Careful, it could be a trap," Charlie hissed, running after them.

But they were already swinging the door open. And it *was* just the Commander. He swept into the room, shoving the door shut behind him.

"Move out," he barked. "Now. Leave everything behind. There's no time. They're coming."

"W-what?" Sophia stammered as her father grabbed her by the arm and hauled her toward the door. "Who's coming? What's going on?"

"Let's go," Charlie said, hurrying back to Shay and urging her toward the door as well.

Shay didn't need to be told twice. Something had happened. Something big and something bad. That was enough for her. She slid her feet into her sneakers and followed Charlie.

Audrey and her two clansmen already had the door open again and were heading through.

"But Dad," Sophia said, trying to stop as her dad all but dragged her out the door. "What's—"

"No time," was all he said.

She huffed as the Commander led them down the long hallway to the stairway. Shay looked left and right before following them into the stairwell. The way the Commander was acting, she expected armed troops or something. Her heartbeat was racing a mile a minute and she grabbed the railing to keep her balance.

Was the capitol under *attack*?

It was the only reason she could think of for the alarm.

But who would be attacking? Had the Southern States' Alliance regrouped somehow and she hadn't heard about it?

The sound of all their running footsteps became a roaring echo in the concrete stairwell. No one said anything, they all just hurried down the stairs, floor by floor, all fifteen stories.

"Daddy, stop." Sophia planted her feet once they got to the underground parking level even though the Commander was again trying to literally haul her out the door. "Tell us what's going on."

The Commander let out a frustrated noise, then obviously decided the quickest way to get her moving was to explain. "President Goddard's been assassinated. They're blaming it on us. Now come *on*."

What? But that didn't make any sense.

"That's ridiculous!" Sophia said.

"Not when it's Shay's sculpture that exploded and killed him."

CHAPTER THIRTY-ONE

JONAS

"Oh God." Shay's face went suddenly pale and Jonas was just about to reach for her when she whispered, "But I didn't—" She blinked in horrified confusion. "I mean, I took it out."

She took it—

What?

WHAT?

Everyone's head swung in her direction and she looked back and forth like she just realized she'd spoken out loud.

"It, it was just supposed to be, I don't know, a parabolic microphone or something." She waved a hand. "But it doesn't matter because I took it out! There was a battery. Or something." Her eyes searched the wall. "If it was a bomb then maybe that part was a phone to detonate it." Her gaze shot back to them. "But I took it out! You have to believe me. I buried the battery back in Jacob's Well!"

"What the fuck are you talking about?" Jonas asked at the same time Charlie let out an anguished, "*Shay*, how could you?"

"I didn't—"

"There's no time for this," the Commander said with a sharp swipe of his hand. "Move out," he ordered again, yanking the door to the garage open and taking Sophia's arm to pull her along after him.

Henry did the same with Shay but for a long second Jonas couldn't move.

Who was she working for?

Christ, did it matter? She'd lied. It had all been a lie.

And he'd fallen for it.

Again.

Just like with Kathleen.

So why did it feel a thousand times worse?

Maybe there was an explanation. Maybe it wasn't as bad as he was thinking and he was just jumping to conclusions?

Memories of Katherine's tearful pleas flashed through his mind.

We didn't mean for it to happen. But you were working all the time and—

I was busy ministering to people. I always invited you to come along to the soup kitchen and when I preached Wednesday nights at the—

That was your thing, not mine.

You knew what you were getting when you married me. You knew what life you were signing up for.

I was twenty years old! I had no clue what the real world was like.

What a crock. You started up with Roger just a few months after we were married. You never even gave us a chance.

Well I'm sorry. I'm sorry some of us are human and can't live up to your perfect standards.

I never asked for perfection. Just fidelity. *Which you promised when you accepted my fucking ring on your finger.*

You're impossible! Don't I deserve some happiness too?

All this while Jonas's feet moved mechanically. They were hurrying across the garage. Piling into the two vans they'd brought.

Rafe stuck his head out of one. "Damn, thought ya'll would never get here. Jump in."

He held open the passenger door and gestured for Shay to take it.

Jonas aimed for the other van.

He couldn't stand the sight of her right now.

Charlie, of course, followed Shay. Not only that, but Jonas saw him making sure her seatbelt was buckled.

Fucking Charlie. Jonas shook his head.

What a sucker. She'd made fools of them all and there he was, signing up for more.

He was like a golden retriever. Loyal. But sometimes, dumb as a bag of goddamned rocks.

Jonas climbed in the very back seat of the other van.

The Commander was at the wheel, Sophie in the front seat beside him. Then Audrey was in the middle seat with Danny and Mateo on either side of her.

Jonas ignored the twinge he got in his chest thinking of how just last night, he'd had that. Of how perfectly Shay's body fit against him when he pulled her to his chest. Her head notched right underneath his chin and her hair had felt so angel soft between his fingers as he combed through it while she fell asleep and—

Who was the sucker again?

Jonas slammed the door shut, his jaw working.

Oh she was good, Jonas would give her that.

And he'd thought he was so in command of her in the bedroom. He thought he'd cracked her wide open to bare the deepest part of herself. That they'd *connected* on some deep almost spiritual plane.

He laughed humorlessly.

"Hold on!" the Commander called over his shoulder as the van burst through the flimsy barrier of the plastic parking gate.

A couple of the others cried out but Jonas just stared out the window. In the light of the early morning, his face was reflected in the glass.

And looking into his own eyes, he knew it wasn't Charlie who was the fool. After everything he'd been through, he'd *still* been on a spiritual quest in his time with Shay. A different kind, sure.

But some part of him, a big part, had kept on believing there was more to life than the physical animal.

All this time and he was still looking for significance.

Meaning.

As if, if it was possible to connect so deeply to another person, then it proved... Well, he didn't fucking know. It proved there was some goddamn point to it all? That he mattered? That any of it fucking *mattered?*

The van jostled everyone as the Commander pulled a sharp right turn. Mechanically, Jonas reached for the hand rest to steady himself.

He should be afraid right now.

But even as he thought it, it was like he was outside himself looking down at the situation. Nothing mattered, so who fucking cared?

His hand went for his pocket, but it was empty.

Of fucking course.

He would *kill* for a joint. Or maybe a whole bowl. Or two. Or you know, ten. He wouldn't mind disappearing for a whole week. A month of drifting in the haze. Not being able to feel his body.

To let the world turn and turn and turn.

Without him.

That sounded just about perfect to him right now.

They pulled another sharp turn. And another.

Jonas let his eyes fall closed.

Not here.

He wasn't here.

He'd pretend he wasn't in his body even without the weed. He'd had enough practice at it. He was floating above the van. Above this city. Above the whole damn earth. Looking down from the clouds.

They were all little ants, scurrying around. Sure their little lives were so important.

How God must be laughing. If he ever existed.

Maybe the nihilists were right and God was dead. After he built the world like a complex machine, he saw how they were all fucking it up and threw his hands up, like, *a'ight, I'm out!*

Maybe he'd had moved on to some other universe to start over.

So they might as well just give up too and forget about their useless fucking existences and—

The van came to a sudden stop and Jonas's head smacked into the back of the seat in front of him.

Son of a bitch!

Jonas rubbed his forehead. Shit. Well, while he was stuck in this earthly body, it would probably help if he wore his seatbelt.

But before he could even reach for it, he realized the van had stopped because they'd reached their destination.

He followed Audrey and her clan out of the van.

And regretted it as soon as he did, because before he'd even gotten a foot fully on the pavement, Shay was grabbing his hand.

"Please, you have to let me explain."

Jonas jerked his hand back but Shay was looking around to everyone now.

"It was Jason. Travis, I mean. My two children. Nicole and Matthew. He didn't kill them after we attempted to escape the first time. But he branded Matthew like he did me. And he took them away from me. Nicole is his daughter but Matthew—"

Jonas took a step back. She'd *been* with fucking *Travis? Been with,* been with? Had a *kid* with him?

"I was pregnant when Travis came to San— When he came to the town where I was going to college. It was horrible before he came. The looting and riots. The women—those of us that were left were barely hanging on and when he came with his troops." She shrugged, crocodile tears running down her cheeks. "I didn't realize what he was until it was too late. Far, far too late."

"How old is Nicole?" Jonas asked, jaw so tense he felt like his teeth were going to crack.

Shay looked confused by his question. "She's six."

"So that means you stayed with him for years even after you realized *what he was?*" He emphasized the words she'd used to describe Travis.

Shay swiped at her eyes. "You don't just leave a man like Jason. And I told you, when I tried, he caught us."

"Which explains why you're working for him now... how?" Jonas asked, hands out.

"I'm not working for him!" she exclaimed, then took a huge breath. "But I was. I stopped, though."

Jonas scoffed. "Like we believe that."

"It's true," she said, glaring at him with tears again glittering. "He took my kids away and threatened that if I ever stepped out of line, he'd kill Matthew. So I did what he said, cooked, cleaned..." Her eyes dropped. "Came when he called. And," her eyes shot to Charlie, "when he told me to take food to a new prisoner, I didn't think anything of it."

"But then he pulled me aside and said he had a mission for me. He brought Matthew in the room with us." One tear spilled down her cheek. "It was the first time I'd seen my boy in a year and a half. He'd grown so much but he was still my little boy. A man held a knife to his throat. He even nicked him and drew blood. I shouted that I'd do anything—anything—as long as he didn't hurt my boy."

Shay's chest heaved as she took a deep gulp of breath.

Henry moved beside her and rubbed her back. "It's okay. We're here for you."

Charlie took her other side, clasping her hand.

But Jonas stood stock still and stared Shay down. "So your boy lives but all the people in Jacob's Well die for him instead? Including your stepsons?"

"No!" Shay cried. "I changed my mind. I stopped working for him. I took down all the listening devices I'd installed in my sculptures." Her eyes went to Sophia and then Audrey. "I'm so sorry. And I'm so sorry I didn't tell anyone earlier about Travis's plans for Jacob's Well. I didn't know who I could trust. But it's no excuse. If I could have warned someone..." Her voice broke.

"You tried," Henry said. He pulled Shay even tighter to his side. "She told me everything last night before any of this started."

Then she looked back to Jonas. "But I swear, I *swear*, I thought I'd taken out the battery from the device Travis gave me to plant in the President's portrait. I thought that would stop it from working. And I never thought it was—"

"And you didn't think to tell anyone, hey, one of the most powerful governors in the country told me to plant a bomb in the President's apartment?"

"It didn't look like a bomb!" she said. "I had no idea, I swear."

"See," Jonas said, "You keep swearing. But that doesn't really mean shit coming from a habitual liar."

"Hey," Henry said, taking a step toward Jonas.

Jonas laughed and took a step of his own until their chests were all but touching. "Oh you wanna fight me? Let's go. You're what, a buck eighty? If you've had your morning latte? Pretty sure I can take you."

"Oh and you're such a big man," Henry said, narrowing his eyes. "Cause you were a track star and everybody's golden boy. You had a big fucking silver spoon shoved up your ass your whole life and then you wanna whine about how *hard* things are for you when you never knew a real day's work in your whole damn *life*."

"*Enough*," the Commander said forcefully, his voice brooking no argument. "What's done is *done*. We're in danger every second we stay in this city. All we can do is move forward."

"So what do we do?" Sophia asked. "Where do we go from here?"

"Take the vans. Get out of town. Clark," he looked to one of Audrey's husbands who worked with Henry, "you have a safehouse on the outskirts of town, right?"

Clark nodded.

"Good. Don't tell me where. Just get everyone there and sit tight until you hear word from Jacob's Well."

"Where are you going?" Sophia asked. "And why don't you want him to tell you where it is?"

"Sweetheart." The Commander moved to her and took her face in his hands, pulling her close and kissing her forehead. "I have to go back for Drea."

Sophia threw her arms around him, nodding into his chest. But then she pulled back. "I'll go with you. I can help you. I can—"

But he was already firmly shaking his head no.

"But—"

"No. Sweetie, you know me." He looked at her through lifted brows. "You know I'd never, ever willingly put you in danger like that."

Sophia huffed but then closed her eyes and gave a small nod.

The Commander kissed her forehead again and looked like he was about to walk away when Shay spoke up.

"Wait."

The Commander turned back around.

"I need a car. Or truck. Or motorcycle. Anything. Do you know where I can get one?"

"What—?" Henry and Charlie started at the same time but Shay spun on them.

"Travis never stays behind when he sends his troops out. It's a point of pride with him. With all his soldiers at—" She swallowed and looked down, but only briefly before lifting her gaze to the Commander and standing strong. "I've seen him mobilize his troops twice before, and each time, he leaves a skeleton crew behind in Travisville. Right now is my best chance to get my kids out. He won't be there and almost all his artillery will be out of town. I have to try."

"Do it," the Commander said, his hard gaze softening the tiniest bit. "I understand just how much a person will sacrifice for their child."

"But Shay," Henry started. "You can't—"

Shay spun and interrupted him. "I can and I will."

Henry held out a hand to her. "I was going to say, you can't go alone. I'm coming with you."

Charlie and Rafe stepped up too.

"It kills me that you didn't think you could trust me," Charlie said. "But I believe you. I know you." His eyes searched hers. "I trust you."

Jonas just barely held back his sarcastic scoff.

And then there was Rafe, holding out a hand to Shay. "He threatened your son's life. When it comes to family, we're blind to everything else."

"So where exactly were you again while everything was going down?" Jonas asked, taking a step closer to the happy huddle. "Let's say Shay's not lying, *for once*," he slid hard eyes her direction, "and she did disarm whatever device she put in the President's portrait. Who did?" He glared Rafe's direction.

"You got something to say, you just come out and say it, *mijo*," Rafe said, going to toe to toe with Jonas.

"Fine," Jonas said. "Maybe you're working for Travis too. And if you go with Shay now, you'll just turn on her as soon as you cross into Travis Territory."

"Big words from the coward staying behind, not standing up for his woman." He looked to Charlie, Henry, and Shay. "C'mon, let's get outta here."

"Not so fast. I'm coming too."

Shay's face shot toward him, hope in her eyes. Or what looked like hope. Christ, she was such an actress.

And if she wasn't? a tiny voice at the back of his head asked. *What if she* was *telling the truth?*

It still didn't change the fact that she'd lied to them. Straight to their faces, for months. Or that she'd put everyone in town in danger. Women, other people's children.

Either way, he couldn't afford to let her out of his sight.

He looked around, eyes pausing on Rafe.

He couldn't let any of them out of his sight.

If he'd learned anything in this fucking useless life of his, it was that you should always expect the worst of people. A lesson he thought he'd learned already, but obviously not.

Charlie glared at him. "If you come, are you going to be a problem?"

Jonas held up his hands and pasted on his most flippant smile. "Who, me?"

"Henry, you're resourceful. Can you get a spare set of wheels?"

Henry just lifted one eyebrow. "Why use wheels when we can fly? You were in the Air Force, right Rafe? You think you can still fly? Because I might have a little something stowed away for a rainy day."

Rafe's face lit up like he was a kid and a decade of Christmases had just been given to him at once. "Yes, sir."

CHAPTER THIRTY-TWO

CHARLIE

Charlie didn't like it. Any of it.

He didn't like being up in a tiny commuter plane with a retrofitted engine that Henry had just happened to have stashed away for what he called a 'rainy day.' Henry never would give a straight answer as to where he'd gotten it from. Much less when it had last been up in the air or been given a thorough inspection.

Charlie didn't like the fact that Shay had lied to them. He could understand her not trusting the others.

But him?

He'd thought of them as a team. Yeah, he'd eventually accepted the other guys in as part of their family, but at the core, it was always him and Shay.

Apparently she had never felt the same.

It hurt. Which was stupid.

That bastard Travis had threatened her *children*.

Her children who were alive after all.

He looked over at Shay who sat in the seat beside him, her eyes closed. She wasn't sleeping though. He could tell by the way her hand clenched the side rest between them.

He could understand. Turbulence had been shaking the plane for the last half-hour and even he'd been tempted to give the barf bag a go a few times.

He reached down and pried her hand off the arm rest and interlaced his fingers with hers. The look of gratitude reminded him of why he was here instead of heading to the safehouse with the others.

Yes, she'd lied.

Yes, there were consequences to those lies.

But the simple truth was, he'd stand beside her no matter what.

And not just because of the vows he made that night of their wedding, though he did take those seriously. When he'd vowed to stay by her side in good times and in bad, he meant it. Come what may, he'd committed his path in life to walk beside hers.

But what had him immediately taking her side back there when she confessed?

He loved her.

It was as simple as that.

He loved her.

He had for a long time. Maybe as far back as when she used to bring him meals in his cell.

It didn't matter that he now knew she'd been doing it on Travis's orders. She'd needed him as a believable entrance to Jacob's Well.

It would have been much harder buying the story of a woman all on her own showing up at the border of Jacob's Well. There would have been more questions. But with Charlie by her side, with his sister already established in the town, no one even batted an eye about the woman with him. Other than to be excited when she was so agreeable to the marriage raffle.

She used him.

She used all of them.

But it had changed... hadn't it?

He squeezed Shay's hand and her eyes flashed gratefully as she clasped his back.

Yes, it had changed for her.

He didn't know if she *loved him*, loved him, but she had feelings for him. For all of them. For now, that was enough. After they saved her children, she'd finally be free to explore those feelings without a sword hanging over her head.

If the Commander would let her back in to Jacob's Well, that was.

And if there *was* even a Jacob's Well to go back to once Travis got through with it. Henry didn't have any updates about what was going on in Jacob's Well when Charlie had last asked him.

Then again, it wasn't like back in the day of cell phones. Henry had a sat phone, sure, but he couldn't just use it to check in every half hour. Battery life on those things was precious, so they were used as sparingly as possible.

The door from the cockpit opened and Henry came out. Speak of the devil.

"We're almost there. Everyone get ready."

Shay's hand clenched Charlie's tighter and he gave her a reassuring squeeze. It felt like they'd barely been in the air and now they were landing. He swallowed hard and sat up straighter. If he acted confident, then maybe he'd start to feel it, right?

All he knew was there was no fucking way he'd let Shay down like he had his sister, time and time again.

If he had his way, she'd have gone to the safehouse with the others and not gotten within a hundred miles of Travisville.

But Shay was stubborn. She had that in common with his sister.

And when it came to her children, it was more than obvious there was almost nothing she wouldn't do.

Henry came and sat down on the seat across the aisle from them. Jonas was all the way in the back. Charlie had ignored the asshole the whole flight.

Charlie's ears popped as they started descending. Shay squeezed her eyes shut.

Charlie looked out at the window, watching the greenish brown fields dissected occasionally by a road. The seconds ticked by and the ground grew closer and closer.

But his stomach really leapt into his throat when he realized Rafe was aiming for one of those tiny ass roads as a makeshift runway.

Holy shit, no way.

No way Rafe was going for that one.

It was a narrow two-lane country road that looked barely big enough for two cars to pass each other.

What the fuck was that maniac thinkin—

SHIT.

The wheels bumped down, bounced, then they were briefly airborne before they touched down again.

Shay let out a little shriek but didn't open her eyes. Charlie shoved the arm rest between them up and pulled her into him, shielding her with his body.

Not that it would do anything if the whole damn plane crashed and they ended up a giant fireball of burning metal and—

Another bounce. *Jesus.*

Charlie's eyes widened and the little breath he had left in his lungs went out in one giant whoosh.

The runway. Road. Whatever.

It wasn't empty.

Up ahead there was a tangle of cars, like people had been fleeing but then a wreck or a barricade had congested everything.

Jesus *Christ.* They were gonna die.

Charlie squeezed his eyes shut too and held on to Shay as tight as he could. If there was anyway his body could shield hers then maybe—

The squeak of tires burning rubber shrieked so loudly around them Charlie wanted to clamp his hands over his ears. But nothing in the world could make him let go of Shay. So he kept his eyes shut and prayed and held Shay and—

The noise finally stopped.

And—

The plane... Had it... stopped moving?

Charlie hesitantly blinked one eye open.

Right in time to see Rafe jump up from the cockpit with a loud *whoop.*

"Did you see that? Did you *see* that? There had to be less than two-thousand feet of runway. And I stopped this bird with at least ten feet to spare. Damn, I still got it." He started to do a dance in the tiny aisle like football players used to do in the end zone when they made a touchdown.

Charlie's eyes went back to the window and holy *shit*. They were so close to the barricade blocking the street Charlie would swear the nose of the goddamned plane was all but touching it.

Shay laughed a tremulous laugh and pulled away from Charlie.

He immediately wanted to yank her right back. And never let her go. Ever.

"Okay," she said, her voice shaky. "Where to now?"

Was she serious? They'd just survived a death defying landing and she was all gung ho to hurry into the next life and death situation?

Because while Charlie might not have seen much of Travisville, he'd heard enough rumors when he and Audrey lived with Uncle Dale and seen enough when he was prisoner here and briefly during their escape to know that Arnold Jason Travis was an evil fucking bastard.

One he and Shay had both been lucky to survive the first time.

But he wasn't here.

And her children were on the line.

So he took a deep breath and undid his seatbelt, then Shay's.

"Everybody solid on the plan?" He looked around and everyone nodded, even Jonas.

Charlie took Shay's hand. "Let's go save your kids."

CHAPTER THIRTY-THREE

SHAY

"Are you sure you're okay with this?" Charlie asked Shay as Rafe spread dirt on her face and shirt. She pulled her hair out of her ponytail and shook it out.

"I'll be fine," she said, squeezing his hand again.

He huffed out a breath. "I'm supposed to be the one reassuring *you*."

She smiled even though, truth be told, her insides were churning at the thought of voluntarily walking back in to Travisville.

It had been hell on earth for most of her adult life. And everything in her experience told her that what they were about to attempt would fail.

No one who stood up against Jason came out the other side.

He was too strong. Too ruthless. He had too many allies who were just as brutal as he was. Somehow, he'd just assassinated the President.

If the sculpture had exploded and it wasn't her who'd planted the bomb, it had to be someone else who knew she was supposed to plant it.

Jason and his damn Plan Bs.

But she only had to think about Matthew and Nicole and her resolve came back. She was *so close* to having them in her arms again. So close.

She wouldn't turn back.

She'd failed them as a mother too many times.

"We'll be right behind you," Charlie said. "I won't fail you. I promise."

"Yeah, babe," Rafe said, leaning in for a quick kiss in spite of the grime he'd just spread all over her face. He looked far too cheerful considering the fact that they were about to walk into an enemy encampment. "We got this."

Then he stepped back, examining her critically. "Lookin' good. You have the—"

Shay nodded, touching her back pocket just to double check it was there.

"And you know how to use it?"

Shay nodded again, looking down at herself.

Rafe had ripped her t-shirt and rubbed dirt and grime all over it and her jean shorts. It was important for their purposes that she was noticeably female. "No, wait. Your hair looks too clean."

After closing her eyes and letting him rub dirt in her hair as well, he finally pronounced her ready for real.

Jonas brushed past her as the guys headed off the road and Shay's heart clenched. He hadn't said a word to her since they'd left Fort Worth.

She reached a hand to stop Jonas and he turned back. "Please. I'm sorry. I wanted to tell you. So many times."

He shook his head, disdain clear on his face. Then he leaned in and she'd never seen his eyes that hard before. "I know what betrayal feels like and this, baby doll, this is it."

She flinched at his use of her pet name said so hatefully.

She shook her head slowly. Because *screw him*. He didn't have children and he hadn't even *tried* to understand.

When he turned to go again, her arm shot out to grab his elbow and she continued through clenched teeth. "Do you think I didn't second guess myself every day? Do you think I didn't fall in love with Alex and Tim? I would have done anything to avoid Jacob's Well being attacked."

He sneered cruelly. "Anything except tell someone Travis was coming."

She let go of his elbow and took several steps back.

She laughed humorously. "I guess I shouldn't be surprised. You warned me, right? Your fatal flaw? You don't have the capacity for forgiveness."

She turned away, if only so he wouldn't see how well his last barb had landed. *Anything except tell someone Travis was coming.*

Maybe it was foolish to expect Jonas to forgive her when she wasn't sure she'd ever forgive herself.

She kicked off her shoes and started the long trek down the road. It was time to forget all that and focus. Worrying about what was happening in Jacob's Well would only distract her when she needed all her concentration in the here and now.

The barest movement in the woods off to her right assured her that her clan was following with her, but she'd never felt more exposed.

It was still mid-morning and there were no clouds in the big blue sky to shield her from the Texas sun.

At least the pavement wasn't as molten hot as it would get later on in the afternoon. She'd kept her socks on, but even through them, she felt the heat of the asphalt on her soles.

After about fifteen minutes of walking, a neighborhood came into view, and beyond it, the university buildings up on the hill.

A familiar sight even if she hadn't seen it from this angle since before The Fall.

More importantly, though, she saw the guard station in the center of the road up ahead. She dropped her shoulders and let her left leg drag a little as she approached.

The road was empty other than the guard building, and behind it, a small pick-up truck.

Both guards stood up and came outside the guard station to wait for her.

But, she noted, neither of them reached for the radios on their hips. Well, most likely only one of them had a radio. There were only so many short-wave radios to go around and Jason liked to spread resources as thin as possible.

If one of the guys had approached, the guards would have radioed first thing. That was why it had to be her. She let her hair fall forward over her face and smiled.

But as soon as she got closer, she arranged her features and cried out, "Oh thank God!" She staggered forward like she was at the last of her strength. "I thought I'd never find civilization again." She coughed and then grabbed her throat, gasping the last bit. "A man. There was a man. He had me, but I got away. Please, you have to help hide me from him. I'll do anything. Just hide me."

She stumbled the last bit until she was right in front of the two guards.

They were wearing the green military fatigues Jason had all his soldiers don, but unlike his elite forces, these two men were obviously out of shape. Well, one of them was, the other was just really young.

They were the kind who'd be left behind when all the other more able-bodied men went off to war.

The older one had a pot-belly that threatened to bust the buttons on his shirt. He stepped forward after exchanging a glance with the young, swarthy-faced one.

"You'll do anything, eh?"

Even though the lascivious look in his eyes made Shay's skin crawl, she just kept nodding guilelessly.

He took several longer than necessary moments looking her up and down. Shay caught movement out of her periphery but forced her eyes to stay on the guard in front of her.

He smirked at her, eyes locked on her chest as he reached for the short-wave radio at his belt. "Let me just let some folks know that you're here and then we'll take you into the town proper. We'll make sure you get looked after *real* good."

That was when Shay struck.

She jerked the taser out of her back pocket and shot it right into the chest of the man before his hand could even get to the walkie.

His entire body began to shake and he dropped backwards to the ground, stiff as a board.

"Hey!" the younger one shrieked, reaching awkwardly for the billy club at his waist. He didn't even have a chance, though, because less than a second later, Rafe was standing behind him, a wickedly sharp knife at his throat.

"You know, I wasn't so sure about this whole left-handed thing at first, but it turns out practicing a couple hours a day for three years straight will really do a lot for coordination." A disturbing smile crossed Rafe's face. "And it's been far too many years since I got to spill the blood of coward scum. A man gets an itch after a while, ya know?" He scraped the edge of the knife down the man's cheek like he was giving him a shave before lining the blade back up at his jugular.

The kid immediately froze, his hands lifted in surrender. "I-I won't. Please, mister. I ain't d-done nothing to 'er. You can have 'er back."

"Well, how generous of you," Jonas said sarcastically, coming up behind Rafe.

Rafe narrowed his eyes, only glancing over for the briefest moment at Jonas before moving his knife and dropping an arm around the guard's throat.

"Wait," Shay said. "What are you—"

Rafe just looked at her coolly over the man's head as he choked the life out of him and Shay's skin went cold.

"No one can know we're here."

"You don't have to kill him," Shay hissed.

Rafe just gave a shrug, his bicep flexing even more as he applied more pressure. Shay took an involuntary step right as he went limp in Rafe's grip. Rafe let go and he dropped to the ground.

Shay gasped but Rafe just said, "What? He's not dead."

"I'll tie him up," Henry said, grabbing his arms and pulling him into the guard station. Wordlessly, Jonas and Rafe each grabbed the arm of the larger man and did the same. Shay looked up and down the road. She didn't see anyone else. That was good, right?

Security cameras were a thing of the past, thank God. At least outside the President's Palace anyway.

Even though it was hot, Shay rubbed her arms up and down.

Charlie and Rafe came out of the guard building, Charlie holding up a pair of keys and smiling. "Look what I found."

It took longer for Jonas and Henry to make it out, and when they did, they were wearing the guards' uniforms. The pants on Jonas were so short they looked like capris, only coming up to mid-calf. But he'd be in the truck most the time, so it shouldn't be a problem. Right?

Shay put a hand to her chest like she could somehow slow down her speeding heartbeat.

Charlie jumped up into the back of the pickup and held a hand down to Shay while Henry and Jonas climbed up into the cab. Rafe joined Shay and Charlie in the back of the truck, all three of them laying down flat.

Rafe unfolded a tarp they'd brought to cover the three of them. He and Charlie settled it so that it laid flat over them, holding the edges down.

Only moments later, the roar of the engine turning over cut through the quiet of the morning. Shay's heart beat so loud it rivaled the engine. She was in between Rafe and Charlie and she grabbed onto Rafe's pocket since his good arm was in use holding the tarp. Charlie clasped her other hand as they began the bumpy drive up the road that led by campus and then wound around town up into the hill country.

Jason had claimed the wealthiest property in the entire area as his own soon after arriving and rechristening the town Travisville. It was a mansion high up on a hill with a spectacular view of the hill country.

He owned—or well, had commandeered—all the property for miles around as his own. So if they could just skirt the town without any trouble, then they'd be golden.

A big *if.*

Shay felt the *bump bump* pause *bump bump* that meant they'd just crossed the railroad track. She gulped. The railroad track was right next to the old college football stadium. They were in town now.

Jason had converted the stadium into a huge tent city for his soldiers. She didn't know how big his army was now. He'd first come into town with five thousand men but in the eight years since he'd been here it had grown to fifteen.

How many were still in town?

Surely he would have taken almost all of them to Jacob's Well, right?

Then she squeezed her eyes shut. Was she really hoping he'd taken more soldiers to Jacob's Well just so they had a better chance of getting to Jason's house and her children undetected?

She knew when she accepted Jason's offer, it was as good as selling her soul to the devil. But he had a knife to Matthew's throat, what else could she have done?

Something else.

Anything else.

A smarter woman would have figured a way out of it. All that time wasted, when in the end, none of her husbands had been in league with Jason at all.

Stupid. *Stup*—

Wait. Why were they slowing down? It wasn't like there were traffic laws to obey anymore. There were barely any vehicles on the road.

Shay held her breath as the truck slowed even more and turned her head the slightest bit to look at Charlie.

His eyes were just as wide and alert as she imagined hers were.

Slower.

Slower.

Finally, they rolled to a stop.

Then she heard voices.

Shay couldn't hear perfectly, but she got enough. Someone was asking what they were hauling. Where they were going.

And then Henry's strong, confident voice answered in return. The back window of the truck was open so she could hear him better than the other man.

"We got reassigned while the boss is gone. It's like a ghost town around here, huh? All hands on deck."

The other voice said something Shay couldn't make out.

"Yeah, I hear ya," Henry said, laughing. "All right. Stay outta the sun. Looks like we're gonna be roastin' today."

The voice responded and Henry laughed again, then clapped his hand on the side of the truck before pulling forward again.

Only after they were going at a good clip did Shay relax, letting out a huge breath of relief.

"Holy shit," Charlie whispered.

"Yeah," Shay said with a shaky laugh. She turned her head to look at Rafe. He didn't say anything, but she looked down and saw he was palming a huge knife in the same hand he was using to hold the tarp down.

Her eyes popped wide open again before she decided, you know what? How about she just kept them shut for the rest of the ride?

One Mississippi, two Mississippi, three Mississippi, four— She counted to sixty. Then did it again, over and over again. How long did it take to drive up to Jason's? Five minutes? Ten? How fast were they going?

God this was torturous. The waiting before they got there and she could finally hold Matt and Nic—

The truck slowed down again and her entire body went rigid. Shit. They'd gotten off easy with that last stop. They hadn't even tried to check the back of the truck. No way they'd get that lucky a second time.

Shay only barely stifled her shriek when the tarp was ripped back.

"Shhh," Henry said, his head suddenly appearing in the too bright sunshine. "We're here."

Shay blinked, covering her eyes as she sat up. They'd stopped on an empty stretch of road. The mansion was about a quarter mile's walk up ahead.

"Jesus, I almost sliced your face off," Rafe muttered.

Henry stepped back once he saw Rafe's knife and Jonas chuckled. "Aw, pretty boy's face might have been ruined. Tragedy of tragedies."

"Do you always have to be obnoxious?"

"The answer to that is obviously *yes*," Jonas quipped back.

"Quiet, all of you," Rafe snapped, keen eyes looking up and down the road. "Move out."

Henry just lifted his chin and shook his head at Jonas. Then he held out a hand to Shay. "Let's go."

Shay took his hand and Charlie moved to her other side, a hand at her back, eyes moving left and right, as alert as Rafe.

He was so laid back most of the time she forgot that he'd lived a whole life before she met him.

They moved into the woods and approached from around back of the house. No one else said a word and Shay tried to walk as quietly as she could but every branch that cracked underfoot sounded as loud as a gunshot in her ears.

Yes security would hopefully be less than usual, but there was no way Jason would leave his house completely unguarded.

Especially with the children there. He might not care if Matthew lived or died, but Nicole he had a certain fatherly pride for. It helped that she had a lot of his features, something Shay had thanked God for more than once over the years. No matter how many times Jason had lost his temper with Shay and beat her and Matthew, he'd never laid a hand on Nicole.

Finally the woods stopped and there was a brief clearing before the fence line that marked the back of the property.

Rafe pulled out a pair of binoculars and looked through one of the warped slats in the wooden fence.

"All right, it's like you said," he whispered. "I see one guard patrolling the west side of the house. And Jesus, does that pool actually have water in it?"

Shay didn't bother responding. Jason had the roof covered in the biggest and best solar panels. Wasting energy on things like a pool pump meant nothing to him.

"Okay," Shay breathed out. "If he hasn't changed anything, then there'll be another guard on the other side of the house."

Rafe gave one sharp nod, then he and Charlie went right up to the fence and propped their knees against it for Shay to use as stepping stools. She used them to climb up and boost herself over the sturdy wooden fence.

As soon as her head popped over the top of the fence, the barking started up.

"Hurry," Jonas whispered.

She bit back her annoyance as she pulled her body up and hiked one leg over the fence. Did he think she was moving anything other than her fastest? For Christ's sake.

She ignored the dark blurs streaking across the back lawn toward her. Okay, she had one leg over.

Now the other.

Almost.

Almooooooooost.

There.

She dropped to the manicured lawn just as the two Dobermans reached her and leapt.

"Who's a good boy?" she asked, giving Tito a good scratch behind his ears as he climbed all over her, almost knocking her off her feet.

"Oh I'm sorry, Killer, are you feeling neglected?" Shay turned to the other dog and rubbed underneath his chin. Killer immediately flipped on his back and exposed his belly for her to scratch.

Shay gave him a good belly rub, careful to keep her voice relaxed and easy. "You boys haven't changed at all, have you. You're still such big softies."

She continued showering attention on the dogs while the others came over the fence. Killer only flipped off his back and went into his attack stance once, growling and showing all his very sharp teeth at Rafe.

"Killer," Shay admonished sharply. "*No*. These are friends."

Killer whined and turned to her, nuzzling at her hand like he hated her displeasure. "It's all right, boy," she said more softly. "That's a good boy. You're still mama's good boy. Here." She pulled out homemade beef jerky from a little pouch they'd brought with them and fed him some.

Not to be left out when it came to treats, Tito was immediately trying to nose Killer out of the way.

She briefly looked up and met Rafe's gaze. He nodded and then he and Charlie were off, running swiftly across the lawn.

Shay kept cooing to the dogs and scratching them while Rafe went and... did what Rafe did. Even one armed, she suspected the man was far more lethal than anyone had a right to be. Probably better if she never knew the details.

"All right, all right," Shay said, keeping her voice light and pulling more jerky out. "There's enough for everyone."

———

Ten minutes later, they were in the house. It was just as cold and forbidding as she remembered. A huge central staircase led to the second story, with banisters branching out to both sides. To the left, another staircase led up to the third floor. There were rooms up there that sat empty for years. It had always been way too much house for the four of them, but Jason demanded the best.

A quick search of the first floor revealed an empty house. Rafe went to head up stairs, but Shay grabbed his arm and pointed to the door that led down to the basement.

To the apartment she and the children had always shared.

Charlie was ahead of them and reached for the door handle.

It didn't budge. It was locked.

Locked from the outside.

Were Matthew and Nicky down there? Had Jason locked them and whoever their nanny was in while he went off to fight? It would certainly be in character.

"Open it," Shay whispered, hating the thought of them down there, afraid and confused by their father's whims and rages.

Charlie nodded and pulled out a Leatherman, quickly going to work on the door. While the house was flooded with light from the mid-morning sun, Shay pulled the candle and lighter out of her back pocket and lit it, then shoved the lighter back in her pocket.

She hoped Travis hadn't been cruel enough to lock them down there without any source of light... but he'd done it before.

It wasn't that the house didn't have electricity, because yeah, the solar panels. There was energy to spare. It was just another means of psychological warfare for him.

She remembered endless hours in the dark, clutching Nicole and Matthew to her side. She'd tried to make a game of learning to guess what things were by using all their other senses than sight.

"What do you think this is, baby?"

"A ow-ange!" little Nicole squealed.

"Okay, what about this one?"

"It's a— It's a— Um... What do you think, Matty?"

And then Matthew's confident voice in the dark, always so sure and strong even though he was still just a boy. "It's a deck of cards, silly. Can't you smell the old paper smell?"

The lock finally clicked and Shay all but barreled down the door in her eagerness to push it open and rush down the stairs.

"Wait," Rafe called but Shay had waited long enough.

The basement was dark. Pitch black except for her candle. Jason was such a fucking bastard. Cutting the lights while he was gone on his military victory was just plain spiteful.

"Matt?" she called. "Matty? Nicole? Honey? It's Mommy."

She swung the candle around as she hurried across the living room. Everything was so familiar.

Travis hadn't changed a thing since she'd left two years ago. There was still the overstuffed tan couch with those horrible orange throw pillows. The knitted afgan blanket with the cows on it crumpled and hanging haphazardly off one side, like Nicky had just been curled up on it while Matt read to her for an hour each morning.

"Matt?" She hurried through the small kitchenette. There was a bowl of half-eaten cereal on the counter. With milk still in it.

Oh God, where were they? Did something— Had Travis—

"Shay, wait—" Charlie called from behind her.

"Matty?" Her voice was on the edge of hysterical as she shoved open the door to the bedroom where they all used to sleep.

And breathed out a huge breath of relief.

Because her two little angels were right there. Asleep in their beds. She couldn't help her cry of relief.

It happened sometimes during the dark days. They'd lose track of day and night and sleep on and off at odd hours.

The room looked the exact same as always. Shay held up her candle. The mural she'd painted on the wall of a window looking out on a bright meadow hadn't been covered over. She'd hung gauzy curtains to complete the illusion and they were still up too.

How many hours had she and the kids spent in front of that painting, daydreaming about the life they'd one day have outside this prison?

Now they could start that new life.

Shay hurried over to the closest bed. "Matt. Nicky. Guys, wake up."

She went closer to Matt's bed and reached for his shoulder to shake him.

"Matt—"

She screeched as soon as her hand made contact.

Because it wasn't a warm little boy's shoulder.

It was a pillow.

She ripped back the blanket and saw what she'd first mistaken for her son was just artfully arranged pillows.

"Shay," called Charlie and Rafe. They were just outside the bedroom. Any second they'd come in.

But Shay was frozen.

Because suddenly the room was flooded with blinding light. And right beside her, Jason himself stepped out of the closet with a gun trained on her.

"Run," she screamed. "It's a trap!

CHAPTER THIRTY-FOUR

SHAY

The room flooded with light and to her horror, Shay saw that it wasn't just Travis.

Four guards stood up from where they must have been crouching at the same time as her clansmen barreled into the room—

"No!" she cried, uselessly holding up the candle when she saw that everyone in the room was pointing a gun at one another.

Oh God, oh God, oh God, what had she done?

Jason won. Always.

Good didn't triumph over evil.

Life wasn't a fucking fairytale. In the real world, the strongest, most devious, evil motherfuckers won.

She'd known. She'd known there was no point standing up against him. What had she *done*? Now they'd *all* die.

Everyone she loved. Because of her.

Oh *God*.

"Drop it," Travis demanded.

"Like hell," Rafe said, moving his gun from pointing at a guard to directly at Travis's head.

Then all of the sudden, Travis moved, jerking Shay in front of him like a shield. She screamed and fought his hold. At least until she felt the cold barrel of a gun against her temple.

"Well hello there, baby," Travis growled into her ear. She went stiff with revulsion at his voice and the feel of him behind her. He ground the tip of the gun into her skin until she cried out again. "Fancy finding you here. I thought I ordered you to plant my little boxes and not to say a word of our arrangement.

"So imagine my disappointment when a birdy told me you were doing the exact *opposite* of my instructions. And to think, I actually believed you when you said you'd learned your lesson last time."

He grabbed her shoulder, digging his thumb painfully into the spot where he'd branded her.

She gritted her teeth, determined not to give him the satisfaction of another reaction.

"Where are the kids?" she asked.

He laughed. "I'm standing here with a gun at your head and you think you get to be the one asking questions? You're a faithless *bitch*. I'm not telling you anything!"

He looped his arm around her neck and squeezed, cutting off her air supply. She turned and twisted, her free hand going to his arm.

But it was no use.

"Colonel Travis!" Henry yelled. "Let's be reasonable. We can all walk out of here."

Henry held up his hands and then slowly, carefully, lowered his gun to the floor.

No. He couldn't give up!

"What are you doing?" Shay gasped with the little breath she had left. And even as she said it, she realized she believed it. They couldn't give up.

It didn't matter if Travis was always destined to win. If the weak never had any chance against the strong.

Some things were worth fighting for, even if it meant fighting to the end. The bitter, bitter end.

Shay ignored the tear that dropped down her cheek.

"Go! Find— the— kids." She could barely get the words out, Travis's grip was so tight. Black spots started dotting her vision, but she fought them. She wrestled against Travis's arm enough to say, "I don't care if he kills me. Find them—"

"Stop it, Shay," Charlie snapped, gun moving back and forth between several guards. It looked surprisingly natural in his hands. "We're not going anywhere without you."

"You have to," Shay rasped. "Just promise. Promise you'll save them."

"Enough of this melodramatic bullshit," Travis said, tightening his grip. It was only when he did that Shay realized he hadn't really been holding her with real killing intent before.

Oh God.

It was really happening now.

She was going to die.

She felt her grip around the candle loosening as her strength ebbed.

And then her eyes widened.

The candle!

Why hadn't she thought of—

"Enough," Henry shouted, taking a step forward. "Arnold, *enough*. Put the gun down. We had a deal."

CHAPTER THIRTY-FIVE

HENRY

Dammit, it wasn't supposed to happen like this.

Shay was never supposed to know.

But Travis was obviously a fucking lunatic. Henry should have known making a deal with him would bite him in the goddamned ass.

But at the time, when Travis had first approached him last year while he was on a diplomatic trade mission to West Texas, he'd dangled everything Henry had ever wanted in front of him.

A wife—and not just any wife, but the most beautiful wife Henry had ever seen.

Luxuries beyond anything that could be bartered for by traditional means.

No more democratic allocation of resources like Commander Wolford so stubbornly insisted on in Jacob's Well.

Shouldn't the new world be a meritocracy? Men should enjoy what they *earned*. What they deserved.

Henry had worked hard his entire life for the American dream. Only there was no more America. But there was Texas.

And Henry had been around long enough to know that it was men like Travis who would be writing the future history books.

So what was he doing hitching his wagon to a backwards thinker like Commander Wolford when here Arnold Travis was, offering him a place in the new world?

It had all made so much sense at the time.

"What are you talking about?" Shay asked in a raw, shaky voice. That meant Travis wasn't cutting off her air supply. Thank God.

Henry breathed out, his entire body shaking.

Okay. Okay. He could still salvage this. It had all gone tits up but he could fix it. He'd been in worse spots before.

It was time for damage control.

"Baby, it's not what you think," Henry said.

"You're not working for him?" she asked, eyes full of hurt and hope. Hope that he'd tell her he wasn't working for Travis.

"Just listen a second. It's not like that. I'm just trying to give us the best future, okay? We have to think about this long term. For all of us. You, me, the kids—"

"What about everyone in Jacob's Well—?" she cried, her voice breaking. "What about our stepsons?"

"No, no," Henry shook his head rapidly. She wasn't hearing him. She just needed to *listen*. "They're fine. Everyone in Jacob's Well is fine."

"How can you say that?" Tears rolled down her cheeks and more than anything he wanted to go over, shove that fucking bastard off her, and gather her in his arms.

"I swear, they're all safe," he pleaded for her to understand. "You know me. You know I love the boys. I'd never hurt them. They aren't the target. Travis's troops moved right past Jacob's Well. They didn't fight anyone there. Baby, please, you have to believe me."

She just kept shaking her head, more tears running down her cheeks.

He looked to Travis to confirm everything he was saying but the bastard just sat there with a smug smile like he was enjoying the show.

Henry's jaw hardened but then he looked back to Shay and his chest felt scooped out by how miserable she looked.

"I swear I'm telling the truth. He never wanted Jacob's Well. He wants the capitol. That's why he assassinated President Goddard. That's where the troops were really headed. He was just using Jacob's Well as a diversion to draw some of the troops away from Fort Worth and to get everyone's attention off—"

"You—" Shay gasped. "It was you who replaced the battery in my sculpture. Or cell phone. You made it so it could detonate."

Henry swallowed, looking down briefly. Yes, he had replaced the receiver. And he'd had a hell of a time getting it past security too. But none of that mattered now.

He straightened, standing tall and looking her in the eye. "You saw what a despicable human being President Goddard was first hand. No one will miss that man."

"You *killed* him," Shay whispered. "You killed a man."

But Henry just shook his head. This was bullshit. Why wasn't she even trying to understand? "I did what needed to be done so I could give you and our family the life you deserve. Don't you want to give your children the best of everything. All the things you didn't have when you were growing up?"

When she just kept looking at him, those damn tears still flowing, he pressed even harder. "You were almost as poor as I was. More than any of them," he gestured around them without taking his eyes off her, "you should understand what it's like. But we can have it all, don't you see? The whole world will be at our feet!"

"Henry," she shook her head, horror and... was that *pity*, in her eyes? Pity, from her? He stumbled back a step. It hurt worse than a blow would have.

No, no, she just didn't understand. He had to make her listen. If she would just—

"Henry," she whispered again, devastation clear in her voice. "Didn't you see the brand on my back? He'll never let me go."

Wait. What?

He paused, brow furrowing. He'd expected more accusations or tears, but—

"She's right, you know."

STASIA BLACK

Henry's eyes lifted to Travis just in time to see him move the gun from Shay's temple to aim it at him.

Then there was a noise that made his ears hurt.

Something knocked him backwards off his feet and then his chest was on fire.

What the fuck had just—

He looked down.

Red blossomed on his white shirt.

Wait—

No, this was—

Wrong, this was wro—

He looked up for Shay but she wasn't there.

Instead there was fire. Curtains. The curtains were on fire. Why were there curtains in a basement? Screaming. *Bang. Bang.*

Shay.

Where was she?

His picture of his life. Shay standing beside him. So beautiful. So proud. His.

Why wasn't she beside him?

This wasn't how it was supposed to—

Why was it so cold?

He couldn't feel his—

Shay.

Why didn't she come?

SHAY, he screamed.

Shay.

The picture. They both had gray hair. They were surrounded by grandchildren. So proud. She was still beautiful. It was the light inside her that made her beautiful. She made him warm when everything was cold. He never knew how cold life was until he met her.

Until she made it warm.

Shay.

Please come. Come and make me warm again. Please.

It was so cold.

Colder than he'd ever been.

Colder than the closet when Mama made him hide. Don't lock me in with no blankets, Mama! Please, I just want to be warm.

Mama?

Shay?

Please.

CHAPTER THIRTY-SIX

SHAY

Five Minutes Earlier

Shay knew Travis would kill Henry.

She knew the second she realized what Henry had done. That he'd been Travis's Plan B all along.

For one, Henry kept calling her his *wife*, which would have been enough all on its own to set Travis off—though Travis occasionally liked to humiliate her by letting his friends fuck her, he was insanely jealous. As soon as his friends left, he usually took out his jealous rages on her and sometimes, if the 'friend' was unlucky, on them too.

But even without that, Henry was too ambitious. Too intelligent.

Except when it counted.

God, Henry, *why?* She thought of their last night together. Of how tenderly he held her. His kisses that made her melt. The fervent way he'd always made love to her.

And she wept.

There was no way Henry was making it out of this room alive.

She *wept*.

And kept asking Henry question after question, even knowing as she did it that it would egg Travis on.

"Henry," she whispered, her heart breaking. "Didn't you see the brand on my back? He'll never let me go."

Henry paused, looking momentarily confused.

She cried even more even as she braced herself. Travis's grip around her neck had loosened more and more as she and Henry talked. He always did love gloating when he bested someone. If ever someone loved pouring salt on an open wound, it was Arnold Jason Travis.

"She's right, you know."

The second the gun swung away from her temple, she threw the candle behind her toward the curtain. It was a flimsy organza and within seconds, *whoosh*, the entire thing was aflame.

She heard the gunshot but she didn't look.

Couldn't look.

She took advantage of the momentary confusion to twist and knee Jason in the groin.

"*Ooof*," he coughed, doubling over.

She grabbed his gun out of his loose grip, each of her movements executed just like she'd been envisioning over and over in her head throughout the last five minutes while she talked to Henry.

After all, when a man's clutching his balls, the last thing he's thinking about is holding tight to his gun.

She aimed the gun at Jason's head. "Where are they?" she shouted.

It was chaos all around her. There'd been more gunshots than just Jason's and out of her periphery, she could see men fighting. Jason's guards and her clan. But she couldn't spare a second's attention. More of the room was catching fire by the second and the smoke was only making everything more insane.

"If I tell you, you'll just shoot me," he yelled back. "Not much incentive."

"Shay," Charlie came up beside her, coughing. "We have to get out of here!"

"Where are the children?" she screamed.

And then she moved the gun, aimed for Jason's kneecap, and pulled the trigger.

He screamed and lunged for her. "You fucking bitch!"

Charlie pulled her back and Jason collapsed on the ground, his face mottled with fury as he pushed himself up with his hands and yelled, "Stand down!"

The scuffles around them stopped but still, Shay didn't take her eye off Jason for one goddamned second. Even though she could see Henry on the ground right beside him. Unmoving, his shirt that used to be white now completely red.

There was so much blood, Jason's hands were slipping in it.

Oh *God*. She forced her shaking hand steady and swallowed back the tears.

Later.

She'd mourn Henry properly *later*.

"Get me up the goddamned stairs," Jason yelled to his men.

"No," Shay said, aiming the gun back at Jason's head again. "Tell me where the children are."

"Go ahead, bitch," he snarled, spit flying from his mouth. "Then we all die."

What? What did that mean?

"Are they in the house?" Her stomach dropped through her feet.

Oh God. What if they were in the house? She'd just assumed that since this had been a trap and Jason had known there'd be guns involved, he'd have sent the children somewhere safe.

But if he hadn't and they were in the house?

The house she'd just set on *fire*?

She handed the gun to Charlie. She didn't know if he still had his or not. "Keep this on him and don't look away from him for a second!"

Charlie nodded and then she shouted, "Out of the way," to her husbands. "Out of the way!" She spared the briefest glance for Jason's guards—at least the two that were still left standing, both of them who had their hands up in surrender—before yelling. "What are you waiting for? Get him up the goddamned stairs!"

She ran out of the room, pausing in the kitchen to look in the cabinets and living room. Okay, with the lights on, she could see, the kids definitely weren't down here. But smoke bellowed out of the bedroom so thick, it was already hard to see down here.

She ran for the stairs, taking them two at a time.

Jonas was right behind her and together they ran from room to room.

"Matthew!" Shay shouted. "Nicky! Nicky baby, can you hear me?" Why the fuck was the house so big. Nobody needed a house with seventeen fucking bedrooms, two game rooms, a home theater, a mini goddamned ballroom—

She ran back into the front room where Jason was standing, but only because his two guards were holding him up on either side. Charlie stood several feet away, gun trained right between Jason's eyes.

"Rafe's looking upstairs," Charlie said as soon as he saw her.

Black smoke billowed out from the door to the basement and when she'd gone to one of the back bedrooms, she'd seen flames licking up the outside of the house. There was a small side of the basement where the soil had eroded over the years so that it was above ground. Enough for the fire to get through, apparently.

She grabbed the gun from Charlie. "Where the fuck are my children?" she screamed in Jason's face.

Jason just laughed.

Fucking *laughed*.

For the briefest moment, Shay could only stare openmouthed. "Nicole is your daughter too."

Jason shrugged. "I can knock a chick up any time I want. Watching you squirm is worth it."

Shay dropped the gun, barely even bothering to aim before pulling the trigger again.

"Fucking whore bitch fuck cunt!" he screamed at the top of his lungs.

She moved the gun back toward him and shook her head.

"And to think," she huffed. "For years I cowered in fear of you. You're a fucking coward. Your power was just a lie." She shook her head as she realized the truth. "You only had the power I gave you. All of us crouching in fear."

She leaned in. "Well I'm not afraid anymore." She put the barrel of the gun to *his* forehead.

He saw that she meant it. That he could be seconds away from his own life ending. For a man like Jason, it was a shocking revelation.

And for the first time in her life, she saw what it looked like when Arnold Jason Travis was afraid. His eyes had gone wide and there was sweat on his forehead. The vein in his neck pulsed rapidly and each breath was a short, panting gasp.

Shay's voice was colder than the Arctic when she demanded, "So tell me where my children are before I blow your goddamned brains out."

"Th-they're upstairs," Jason stammered.

"Where?" she demanded.

"I-in the attic." Then, blinking as if he just realized what he'd admitted, he took a deep breath and closed his eyes.

When he opened them and some of the steel she recognized was back, she tightened her grip on the gun.

He tried for a cocky smile, but it was tremulous at best. "Or the second master bedroom. Or maybe I locked them in the gaming room closet." He laughed and it sounded maniacal. "With all this blood loss, it's hard to fucking remember. Guess you better check them all before the smoke inhalation gets to the poor kiddies."

Shay's jaw hardened and she wanted to pull the trigger more than almost anything in the world.

Almost anything.

She wanted her kids safe and sound more.

"Watch him," she shouted to Jonas, handing off the gun to him this time.

"Come on," she grabbed Charlie's hand and together they ran for the central staircase that led to the second story.

"Do you think they're any of the places he said?"

"The attic."

There was a second there, brief as it was, where Jason had been scared. Right before he'd put back on his armor of bullshit, he'd been scared. And he'd told the truth. She was mostly sure he'd been telling the truth.

Not sure enough to end him just in case he was lying and the kids weren't anywhere in the house after all. But pretty sure.

Shay ran up those goddamned stairs faster than she had ever moved in her life. Once she reached the second floor, she dashed down to the end of the hallway where she yanked on a hanging string. A rectangle of ceiling dropped down, revealing a retractable wooden staircase that unfolded. The second the bottom of it touched the ground, she scrambled up the stairs.

"Matthew!" she shouted. "Nicky! Can you hear me?"

"Mom?"

Oh thank God. A jolt of relief spiked through her at hearing Matt's voice. His head appeared at the top of the rectangular opening in the ceiling overhead when she was just a few rungs up.

"Matthew!" Shay said, almost crying with relief. "Get your sister. We need to leave. Now!"

Matthew's head swung away and when he looked back, his eyebrows were furrowed apologetically. "We heard noises. She got scared and went to hide in our special place."

Shay hurried even faster up the ladder. "Where's that, honey?" She tried to keep her voice calm so she wouldn't scare him but she knew every second they wasted, the fire was spreading.

"Out there." He pointed somewhere behind him as she finally got to the top of the ladder and pulled herself over the edge, up onto the plywood platform that made up the floor of the attic. She dragged Matthew into her arms.

He was real. This wasn't a dream. She really had her boy back in her arms.

"Oh thank God." She kissed the side of his head. "So where's Nicky?"

Shay looked around and didn't see her daughter anywhere. The attic was unfinished. It was just meant for storage. There wasn't even plywood flooring everywhere, just around the opening here. Further back, the beams and insulation were totally exposed.

When Matthew pointed again, Shay was terrified he meant Nicky was hiding somewhere back in the recesses of the attic where there wasn't any flooring.

But then she realized it was much, much worse.

"She's out there," he said, pointing to the crow's nest window on the other side of the attic. "We go out on the roof sometimes when Dad's in one of his really bad moods. We look up at the stars and I tell her stories. I said I'd stay in here to stand sentry in case anyone tried to come for us. I told her I'd protect her."

"And you did a great job," Charlie's deep voice said from behind Shay. She hadn't even seen him follow her up the ladder. "But now you need to run downstairs and get out of the house where it's safe."

Matthew's brow crumpled in confusion and he looked back to Shay. She nodded fervently. "This is Charlie. You can trust him. He's a good man. And there's a fire honey, so I need you to go out to the yard where it's safe."

Matthew looked at Charlie distrustfully. Understandable since the only men he'd met in his short life had mostly been violent assholes.

"Go," Shay urged, giving him one more quick squeeze. "We'll get your sister and be right behind you."

Charlie moved out of the way so Matthew could get to the ladder but Matthew didn't move.

"Matt," Shay said, using her mom voice. "Go."

But Matt just stood up taller. "It's my job to look after Nicky."

Shay couldn't stand here and argue with him. She looked to Charlie. "Get him downstairs," she said, then turned and headed for the window. After a few steps, she was forced to straddle her feet and walk on the beams. She moved as quickly as she could anyway.

The window was still open and right before she got to it, she heard a scream.

A girlish, high-pitched scream.

"Nicky!"

Shay ran the last few feet on the beams to the window, shoving her head out.

Oh God.

Her heart stopped. Literally stopped for a moment, she was sure.

Because out there, huddled in the corner between the sloping A-line roof and the flatter roof of the extended deck, was Nicky.

And behind her flames licked up toward the sky.

Shay screamed, "Nicky!!!"

But Nicky either couldn't hear her or she was too terrified to move or respond. How on earth had the fire moved so quickly? She was supposed to have more time. There was supposed to be more time.

"Wait, honey! Mama's coming!"

But right as she went to lift her leg over the low ledge, hands dropped on her shoulder and drew her back.

"Wait, what—?" she screeched, half-expecting to see Jason. But it was Charlie. "What are you doing?" she screamed at him. "I have to go save my daughter."

But the resolute look on Charlie's face didn't change. He dragged Shay behind him and then he was climbing over the ledge and out onto the roof.

"Get our boy to safety," Charlie said, only looking briefly over his shoulder. "And tell him I'll bring his sister down safe. I swear it."

And then Shay could do nothing but watch as he bounded across the roof to where Nicky sat wailing with her knees to her chest.

"Mom!" Matthew exclaimed, coming up beside her at the window. "I have to go with him to get Nicky. I promised I'd keep her safe and—"

When he started to climb out the window too, Shay wrapped her arm around his waist to stop him. "He'll bring her down safe." And even as she echoed Charlie's words, she knew they were true.

She knew she and Matthew needed to get moving. She watched as Charlie scooped Nicole up into his arms. Everything was going to be fine. She knew Charlie wouldn't let anything happen to her little girl.

Still, she lingered. Charlie would bring Nicky back and then they could all go down togeth—

BOOM.

An explosion rocked the building.

Shay was knocked backward. She stumbled off the beams she'd been standing on, landing right between two slats in the pink insulation... and kept on going. She shrieked as her foot broke through the ceiling below.

"Mom!"

Her legs were wrenched painfully wide as the foot that went

through kept going—all the way until she was thigh deep through the ceiling of the floor below. Just one leg, though.

Maybe if it had been both, she could have broken cleanly through and landed on the floor below. As it was, her legs were winched in a painful, awkward splits.

"Mom," Matthew called again. "Are you okay." And then, after a short pause, more frantically. "Mom! The fire!"

That got Shay's attention and she pulled herself out of her momentary pain stupor. Bracing her elbows on two of the attic slats, she tried to haul herself up. And barely budged an inch.

Goddammit!

"What do you see?" she asked, hoping she didn't sound as frantic as she felt.

"There's fire everywhere, Mom," Matthew said, sounding more terrified than she'd ever heard him. And she'd been there with him the night he got branded right beside her.

"It's going to be okay, Matt. I swear. It's all going to be okay."

She bit back tears at what she was afraid were empty promises. She braced her elbows and forearms on the attic beams and this time when she lifted her body, she gritted her teeth and thought of her daughter and the man she loved out on a burning building.

She'd stood up to Jason tonight. She was *so* close to getting her children to safety. She was *not* going to let her leg getting stuck in some goddamned sheetrock stop her now.

She pushed down with all her might on her forearms, yanking her torso and leg upwards at the same time.

At first, nothing.

And then, *finally,* her leg came unwedged from the ceiling and she hauled herself up onto the slats.

Nicky. *Nicky and Charlie.*

It was all she could think as she crawled along the slats toward Matthew at the window, ignoring the stinging itch all over her hands and legs from the fiberglass insulation.

Oh God.

She lost the little remaining breath in her lungs when she looked out the shattered window. Almost the whole roof was covered in flames. In another few moments, the window would be blocked almost completely.

Charlie stood with Nicky in his arms right on the edge of the roof, looking around him in all directions.

He was facing the fire and took a step back, almost losing his footing and toppling off the roof.

"Charlie!" Shay screamed, reaching her hand out toward them before jerking it back because of the heat.

Oh God, no. She couldn't watch her husband and baby die. Surely God hadn't let them get this far only for—

"Mom," Matthew said, pulling on her arm.

"Not now," she shushed him

Charlie looked behind him and down at what had to be the twenty-five-foot drop to the ground below. The fire was coming at them from all sides.

"Charlie," Shay screamed again, knowing even as she did it that it was useless, that he probably couldn't hear her through the winds and whipping firestorm.

Then Charlie pulled Nicky close to his ear. He must have whispered something because Nicky gave a small nod.

"Mom!" Matthew shouted, "look."

Shay turned her head and saw what had him so upset. On the attic wall opposite them, the fire had come through. Actual flames licked up the pitched wooden ceiling.

They had to go.

Now.

Shay turned back to the window. Maybe Charlie could—

"No!" she screamed.

Because Charlie and Nicky weren't at the edge of the roof anymore. There was only fire.

They were gone.

CHAPTER THIRTY-SEVEN

CHARLIE

Five Minutes Earlier

"Wait, honey!" Shay yelled as she and Charlie looked out the window at her daughter huddled in the corner of the roof. "Mama's coming!"

No, no, no. No fucking way.

Shay lifted one leg like she was gonna step out the window but Charlie dropped his hands on her shoulders. She was nuts if she thought he was letting her out on that roof while the damn house was on fire.

"Wait, what—?" she shrieked, turning around. "What are you doing?" Her features were contorted with panic. "I have to go save my daughter."

Yes. That little girl out there did need help. She'd die if they didn't get to her soon.

But he'd vowed to protect Shay no matter what. That vow extended to her daughter.

For once in his life, he was not going to fail the people he loved.

For once in his life, he was going to live up to his promises.

He pulled Shay behind him and then lifted his leg, climbing out the window. He only spared one look back for Matthew. The boy reminded him so much of himself when he was that age.

"Get our boy out," Charlie said to Shay. "And tell him I'll bring his sister down safe. I swear it."

Then he hauled himself the rest of the way out of the window and ran across the roof to where the little girl was huddled.

Even though the fire was still just on the other side of the house, the heat from it was already intense. Charlie held up an arm over his head as he got closer to her.

She was tiny, all curled up with her knees against her chest and arms over her eyes. She couldn't be much more than six years old, if even that.

"Nicky," Charlie called out when he finally got to her. He dropped to a crouch and grabbed her up.

She screamed and kicked out at him.

"Whoa," he said, stumbling a step back and wrapping an arm around her little waist to make sure he kept hold of her. "I'm with your mom. Look, she's at the window. I'm with your mom," he repeated.

Her thrashing stopped for a moment. He barely heard her words above the fire. "Mama?" But then she screamed. "Mama!"

"We're here to take you to a good place," Charlie said. "But we have to go now, okay?"

The girl looked up at him for the first time.

And Charlie thought her mom had done a number on him.

But the second Nicky's big, sweet green eyes blinked up at him, he knew he was a goner. He'd protect this little girl to the ends of the earth and beyond. Nothing bad or dark would ever touch her life again. It would be his life's mission.

And when she gave a hesitant nod, placing her trust in him, it felt like one of the greatest gifts he'd ever received.

He didn't stop to ponder it though. He got his ass moving.

Right as he turned back for the window, though—

BOOM!

The entire roof shook, knocking Charlie off his feet. Even as he fell backwards, though, he cradled Nicky to his chest, making himself a shield around her. He landed on his ass and it *hurt*.

"Are you okay?" he asked the little girl frantically.

She was sobbing but she clung to his neck and he thought she nodded.

Charlie got to his feet in spite of feeling dazed by the fall.

And that was when he saw that, oh *shit*, the fire was everywhere now. There was a solid wall of flames between them and the attic window.

Maybe if they—

But even as he took a step toward it, the flames jumped even higher. Charlie looked around him, moving back quickly when he saw how fast the fire was moving.

The fire just kept coming, though.

Until he ran out of roof.

There was fire on all sides and Charlie's stomach flipped inside out as the precious little girl in his arms clung tighter than ever.

No.

No. No. *No.*

Not again.

He couldn't fail again. Not now when it counted most.

She was just a little girl. *Please God.*

But God didn't answer.

And when he took another step backward—

Oh *FUCK*!

They teetered on the edge of the roof and he managed to counterbalance just in time so they didn't.

What the fuck? He almost just killed them. Because the fire wasn't enough on its own, he had to help it along by falling two stories to the concrete of the patio around the pool, was that it?

He looked down and his stomach bottomed out seeing just how far it was they'd have fallen.

And then his eyes widened.

The pool.

No. He immediately rejected the thought.

It was too far.

Way too far. They'd never make it.

"Too hot!" shrieked Nicky in his ear. "It's coming at me!" She buried her head in his chest like if she couldn't see it then it wasn't real.

Charlie looked over his shoulder and gulped.

The fire was coming closer. And not just inch by inch. It'd be on them any second.

It wasn't a choice. Not really.

"Hold onto me tighter than you ever have. Wrap your legs around my waist, okay. No matter what happens, you just keep holding on. Okay? Let me know you hear me."

Nicky pulled her head out from his chest just long enough to nod, eyes still squeezed shut.

There was no time for indecision.

Charlie moved back the small amount of clearance he had on the roof, just about four feet. Then he ran and then jumped as hard as he could, praying the whole time for a miracle.

CHAPTER THIRTY-EIGHT

JONAS

Five Minutes Earlier

Jonas stood with his gun trained on Travis but all he could think about was Shay upstairs. Would the kids be one of the places Travis said, or had all of it been lies and they weren't even in the house?

And Jesus Christ, when the bastard had the gun to Shay's head, he realized how close he'd been to losing everything. And his last words to her had been so hateful and angry and—

"So, you get stuck with babysitting, huh?" Travis said, somehow laughing even though the only way he was staying upright was the two guards holding him up on either side. "She always was fickle with her favors. Guess you're not in the inner circle, huh?"

Jonas glared at him. "Shut up."

"Oh, touched a sore spot, did I?"

"No, but if you keep talking, I might not be able to help myself from shooting you."

Travis laughed again. Jonas didn't get what was so fucking funny.

"You're the preacher, aren't you?" Travis coughed. Smoke from the basement was slowly seeping out of the closed door and filling the room.

Where was Shay?

"I heard all about you. Henry had plenty to say in his reports."

Jonas's jaw flexed. He couldn't think about Henry right now, not if he was going to keep his cool.

But Travis just gave a quick nod of his head and the two guards holding him took a step backwards. Toward the front door.

"Preacher turned pot farmer. Quite a one-eighty there. But Henry also said he didn't think you'd changed as much as you thought you had."

The guards took another step toward the door.

"Hey," Jonas said sharply, bringing up his other hand to help brace the gun. "Stop! You take another step and I'll shoot."

"Here's the thing." Travis just shook his head. "I don't think you will. I think, underneath, you're still a preacher after all. And preachers don't kill people."

Travis smiled an evil, smug fucking smile. And then he nodded to his guards and they took yet another step toward the door.

Jonas had never fired a gun in his life but he'd been sure as soon as Charlie handed him the weapon he could if he had to. Because Travis was evil. In a chaotic world of gray, here was something that was black and white.

Arnold Travis was an evil man.

Jonas had heard the stories of his ruthlessness during the war. And he'd heard rumors of the things that went on here in Travis Territory. While usually he might not put much stock in rumors, everything he'd witnessed today only confirmed his opinion of the man.

So why, when the guards took yet *another* step toward the door, did his finger hesitate on the trigger.

"It really is a shame about the oil furnace," Travis said even as Jonas took several steps to cover the distance Travis's guards had opened up between them.

"What?" Jonas barked, holding the gun even straighter.

"You know," Travis said conversationally. "The oil furnace? On the far side of the basement from the bedroom." Travis shrugged. "I can't imagine it's going to be a good combination when the fire reaches it."

"You're bluffing," Jonas snapped.

"Am I?" Travis asked, still with that know-it-all-smirk.

Jonas raised the gun even higher. "What about your daughter? You'll just leave her here to die? Or were you lying all along and she's not even here?"

"I'll have others," Travis said, then he looked to his guards and barked, "Go! Now."

"Stop!" Jonas yelled.

They didn't stop. They ran for the door.

Shoot.

Shoot them!

His finger hovered over the trigger. Touched it.

They got to the door. One of the guards opened it.

Fucking shoot them! They're escaping.

And then they were gone through the door, slamming it behind them.

"Godfuckingdammit!" Jonas yelled. He ran forward.

He couldn't let Travis get away. He'd fucking *branded* Shay. *And her son.* Jonas shook his head in disbelief at himself, clutching the gun as he jerked the door open. What the fuck was wrong with him? Why hadn't he pulled the trigger?

"Hey, has Shay come back d—" Jonas's head swung toward the stairs at Rafe's voice. "Where the fuck is—?"

He never finished the sentence though. Right as Rafe got to the bottom of the stairs, the floor underneath the couches at the far side of the living room collapsed with an ear-splitting explosion that rocked the entire house.

Jonas was knocked into the doorframe by the force of it. When he finally grabbed onto the door and dragged himself back to his feet, he had to hold an arm up against the heat. When he finally turned around, his heart leapt into his throat.

Oh Lord.

The fire. It was everywhere.

Shay.

She was out of time. They were all out of time.

He had to get her out. Now.

But when he looked toward the stairs, he saw Rafe lying unmoving on the floor. Fire raced across the carpet toward him.

"Shit," Jonas yelled, dropping the gun and running toward Rafe. He got to him right before the fire did.

"Rafe!" But he was unconscious. Jonas grabbed him underneath the armpits and dragged him backwards.

Fuck. Jesus. Fuck!

Waves of blistering heat.

Hot. So hot. Like he'd imagined hell.

The stairs were carpeted. They'd catch fire.

Shay was still upstairs.

But he couldn't just leave Rafe here. It had only been a minute or two but the far side of the room where the floor collapsed was already an inferno. He had to get Rafe out first.

Jonas coughed and yanked Rafe with all his might.

He kept on pulling until he had Rafe ten feet out the door. Then he dropped him and started running right back in.

"Jonas! Where's Shay?"

Jonas spun to see Charlie running around the side of the house.

Why the fuck was he drenched like he'd just dunked himself in a baptismal tank? And there was a little girl clinging to his neck—

Jonas's breath caught. Shay's little girl.

"Shay's still inside," Jonas yelled as Charlie ran closer.

Charlie's eyes widened in horror as he looked through the still open front doors at the raging fire inside.

He peeled the girl off his neck. "I have to go get your Mommy," he said as he deposited her on the ground by Rafe, who was coughing now and sitting up.

"No!" she shrieked, running after Charlie when he started for the house. "Don't leave."

Rafe caught her in his arms while Charlie ran through the door. "Whoa there, honey."

"You got her?" Jonas asked Rafe.

He nodded. "Go."

Jonas barely waited for the word to get out of his mouth before he ran after Charlie. He sucked in one huge breath before he entered.

Oh Jesus.

The stairs were on fire. The carpet had lit up like fucking kindling.

And Shay was at the top with her son. She'd taken her shirt off and had it over his face but Jonas could see her hopeless expression even through the thick smoke.

Charlie was waving his arms at her and she nodded at him, her features going hard with determination. Then she lifted her son up and over the curved banister.

Oh shit, was she going to—

Charlie positioned himself underneath her. Jonas had only a second to run up beside him as Shay let go of her son.

Jesus! Oh fuck, she really was—

Jonas lifted his arms beside Charlie right as—

The boy hit them and the impact knocked them all down. But a second later, Charlie was on his feet, helping the boy up and shoving him toward Jonas.

"Go!" Charlie shouted, looking back up toward Shay.

The boy was coughing hard but otherwise looked fine. Nothing broken from the fall. Thank God. Jonas hiked him up in his arms and ran for the door.

He barely felt the kid's weight. All he could see was the rectangle of sunlight—the doorway out of Hell. And even as he ran toward it, he kept picturing Shay trapped upstairs.

He burst out the front door and on to the lawn, depositing the boy beside Rafe and his sister. Then he spun on his heel and headed back for the house and Shay.

Except right before he got to the door, a flaming chunk of ceiling crashed down in front of the entryway.

"No!" he shouted, instinctively raising an arm to shield himself.

He dropped it the next second, running as close as he dared to see if Charlie was even still standing.

And what he saw was an image that would stay with him for the rest of his life.

Charlie was running up the stairs.

Through the flames.

Through the flames.

Jonas's heart stopped. Literally stopped, he would have sworn.

Shay ran to Charlie at the top of the stairs and it was like it had been choreographed. Like they were dancers.

He swept her up, one arm under her back and the other underneath her legs, at the same time he pivoted and started down the stairs.

Again. Through. The. Flames.

Like Shadrack, Meshack, and Abendigo.

It was a fucking miracle.

But whereas time had seemed to slow to an otherworldly pace while the whole thing happened, suddenly Charlie was back at the bottom of the stairs again and everything sped back up. Way the hell back up.

The door. The front door was blocked. Shay was finally downstairs but what were they going to—

But Charlie's momentum didn't once slow. He just kept running. Straight toward the large bay window off to the left of the door. The floor was marble there so the flames hadn't completely covered it yet.

Jonas felt his eyes widen and he held out an arm as Charlie barreled forward.

Right at the last second, Charlie turned and hurled himself back first towards the window. He and Shay crashed through in an explosion of smoke and glass and fire.

CHAPTER THIRTY-NINE

SHAY

"But he'll be okay?" Shay asked Dr. Kapoor, hovering over where Charlie was laid out on the exam table in the clinic.

Her voice was hoarse from all the smoke she'd inhaled and right after she asked the question, Gabriel urged her to put her oxygen mask back on. She did, but only so she could focus on Dr. Kapoor's answer.

The last few hours had been some of the worst in her life.

Gabriel settled his arm back around her. Rafe stood on her other side with Nicky asleep in his arms and Jonas hovered at her back. Matthew had been attached at her hip until he'd finally gotten too tired and fallen asleep on a clinic cot they'd set up at the other side of the room, an oxygen mask secured over his face too.

"His boots protected his feet from the worst of it," Dr. Kapoor said, standing on the other side of Charlie's bed. "But his legs..." the doctor shook his head. "He has second degree burns on his thighs and third degree burns on parts of his calves, especially his left leg."

Shay looked down at Charlie's legs that were wrapped in gauze and felt the millionth tear roll down her cheek today.

She'd been ready to die up there. As soon as she got Matthew to safety, it didn't matter.

All she'd ever wanted was for her children to be safe. She'd always been willing to sacrifice her life.

But then Charlie was running up the stairs—*through the fire* —for her.

She thought he was an angel.

She thought he'd died in the fire on the roof and come back as an angel sent from God to rescue Matthew. And then her.

She shook her head as she looked down at Charlie. Amazing, astonishing, *foolish* man. The doctor had sedated him, thank God. After he had thrown himself through the window, shielding her the whole time, he started screaming in pain.

They'd rolled around on the ground some after going through the window, so they weren't on fire. At first she thought it was glass in his back causing him so much pain. It took her and Jonas and Rafe far too long to figure out it was his jeans.

She wouldn't understand fully until later. He'd jumped into the pool —that's how he'd gotten off the roof with Nicky.

So he was drenched when he'd run into the house. That had been both a good and bad thing. The wet clothes meant he didn't catch fire when he ran up the stairs for Shay. But water conducted heat even better than air. It turned the water in his jeans to steam and it started cooking him while—

She shuddered just thinking about it.

He'd started screaming about his legs and finally they'd pulled his steaming jeans off. His legs were already red and blistering and oh God, it was so horrible.

Jonas and Rafe hefted him in the back of the truck and they raced back to where they'd left the plane... but it was gone.

Shay suspected Jason himself had taken it. Henry had obviously tipped him off that they were coming and he'd no doubt been watching for their arrival. Maybe Jason was the reason Henry had even had access to such a fancy plane in the first place. It might have been part of their plan all along—for Henry to get the plane to Jason so he could fly it back to Fort Worth.

Anyway, there was no choice but to drive the two hours back to Jacob's Well, Charlie crying out in pain every time they hit a bump or pothole until finally, mercifully, he'd passed out.

When they'd gotten home, the town was surrounded by soldiers, but not Jason's. They were the troops President Goddard had sent from the capitol before he was assassinated. Sent to guard against an attack that never came. Meanwhile reports came in that Jason's forces were overwhelming the capitol and that he was hours away from taking it over completely.

"But yes," Dr. Kapoor continued, "with the proper medical attention and penicillin tea in case of any infection, there's a good chance of recovery."

"A good *chance*?" Shay looked toward the doctor sharply. "What does that mean?"

The doctor sighed. "Some of his burns have gone completely through the epidermis all the way through to the tissue underneath. I can't say it won't be a painful process of recovery. And he'll have scars for the rest of his life."

"He'll wear them with honor," Rafe said from beside her but Shay just shook her head repeatedly back and forth.

"I don't give a shit about any of that," Shay said, running her hands through Charlie's unkempt hair. "I'm already honored more than words can say just to be his wife." Then she turned to look at Rafe and Jonas. "Yours too."

She couldn't stop her tears. It felt like she'd been crying for hours. Days. Just when she didn't think she had any tears left, still more came.

After everything that happened with Jason, Henry, and then Charlie, and then finally having Nicky and Matthew back in her arms—God it was just too much for one day.

And it wasn't over. She knew that in the back of her mind but literally could not handle thinking about it. So for the moment, she was pushing all thoughts of Jason and what was happening at the capitol aside.

"Come on," Gabriel said quietly. "You're exhausted. You need to rest. All of you."

Shay shook her head. She had to stay with Charlie. She had to—

"What good are you to him if he wakes up just to find you looking dead on your feet?" Gabriel said softly. "You know he'd be upset and worried about you."

Shay sighed and sank against Gabriel. God, she hated it, but he was right. She was dead on her feet. After dropping her head to his chest, she couldn't imagine lifting it. Ever again. In fact, now that she thought about it, every part of her body felt like it was strapped with hundred-pound weights.

When the guys led her to a cot beside Matthew's to lay down, she was asleep within moments.

CHAPTER FORTY

GABRIEL

Nix and Audrey sat at the dining room table, the morning after they'd gotten back from the Travisville mission. Audrey and the rest of her clan had made their way back to Jacob's Well once they realized it wasn't Travis's true target.

Gabriel looked around at the tired, worried faces of his own clan. Minus Charlie, who was resting in bed in the downstairs bedroom.

And of course, Henry.

Gabriel felt the familiar waves of fury and grief even at the thought of him. How could he have done that to them. To Shay?

"Other than small skirmishes," Nix said, commanding all their attention, "Colonel Travis has taken over the capitol. He's pretending he's the President now."

Rafe scoffed, shoving back from the table and standing up. "It's more than pretending. How do you think Goddard became president? There wasn't a fucking vote. He had control of the biggest army at the time. Now Travis does. How many troops does he have now? Fifty thousand?" He looked to Nix. "Sixty?"

"Sixty-five."

"Shit," Rafe said, dragging his hand through his hair.

"It's only a matter of time before he comes back for Central Texas South and Jacob's Well," Shay said.

Gabriel swallowed.

All of them had been thinking it. She just had the balls to say it out loud.

"And after what we did to him—after what *I* did to him..." She shook her head and looked around the table. "None of us will be safe when he does."

Gabriel noticed Jonas's hand shaking as he reached to take a sip of water from his glass. Damn, this whole thing had them on edge.

"I'm surprised he hasn't already sent planes," Nix said. "Most of the bombers not taken out by the EMP were destroyed in the War for Independence against the Southern States Alliance. But there were still a few left."

Shay gasped and Gabriel reached for her hand.

"Graham's been watching the satellite feed," Audrey hurried to say, "and he hasn't seen any movement of their air force."

"Yet," Nix said grimly. "We don't know what's stopped or delayed them. But Travis will be eager to fix whatever the problem is, especially with ten thousand of General Preston's Elite Guard on the loose in our territory."

"Elite Guard?" Shay asked. "Is that different from the regular Army?"

Rafe huffed. "Are they diff—" He shook his head. "One Elite Guard is worth *five* normal soldiers. They're the New Republic's version of Navy Seals. The toughest of the tough."

Fat lot of good that did *them*, Gabriel thought. "But now they're just making us more of a target"

Nix nodded. "That's why they're decamping to the hills as we speak."

"And us?" Jonas asked, eyes on Shay. "How do we stay safe?"

"We run," Shay said, looking around at all of them, eyes finally settling on Nix. "It's the only way."

Again, Nix just nodded. He'd already decided on a course of action before even coming over, Gabriel could tell. This was an announcement, not a discussion.

But Gabriel didn't see any other way. "Where?" he asked. There was no point beating around the bush. He had no doubt Nix had already worked that part out, too.

Nix nodded to Audrey and she pulled out a map from a knapsack she had slung across her chest. She laid it out on the dining room table and they all poured over it.

"Well, we have several different options. Scrapper teams have scouted all of our territory and most of Central Texas North." He pointed out the territories on the map. "So no doubt that's where Travis will expect us to go."

Rafe's brow was knit in concentration. "What if we went here?" He pointed to the oval area highlighted in orange around and to the northwest of Austin."

"Are you crazy?" Jonas said. "That's the fallout zone. We'd get radiation poisoning."

But Rafe was shaking his head. "It's been eight years. The bomb was an air-burst bomb so it was only the top ground soil that was affected. Think about it. People moved back to Nagasaki and Hiroshima a few years after the bombs. We had to read up on this shit at the Air Force Academy. After eight years, most of Austin should be safe now."

"Should," Nix said with a dark glare. "I'm not willing to gamble my wife's life on a should."

Rafe looked like he was about to open his mouth again but Nix cut him off.

"Or my baby's."

Gabriel felt his eyes widen as he looked down to Audrey's stomach.

"Oh my gosh," Shay exclaimed, a hand going to her mouth. "Audrey, it finally happened."

Audrey smiled, but it was wobbly. "I wish I was bringing them into a more peaceful world."

Rafe nodded but continued. "I guess that makes sense for you guys, but that doesn't mean our clan can't—"

"Rafe," Shay said, putting a hand on his arm.

Rafe stopped, looking over at her. "What?"

"We're in the same situation."

Good Lord. Was she saying—

Rafe's eyebrows furrowed. "What do you—?"

"You're pregnant?" Gabriel choked, shoving his chair back and running around the table before falling to his knees at her feet. He kissed her stomach and then bowed his head against it. "But I thought — Didn't you say you took a birth control shot before you ever came?"

When he finally looked up at Shay, she seemed stunned. "Y-yes, but it must have been over ten years old and who knew where Jason got it from. It could have just been saline solution for all we knew."

Then she whispered, "But I don't understand, Gabriel." A pained look crossed her face. "You know you can't be the father."

But Gabriel just shook his head. "I'll be a father in all the ways that matter." He grinned at her. They were going to have a baby!

He got to his feet and pulled her with him until he had her gathered in his arms, then he spun her in a circle. "We're having a baby!"

She giggled and shrieked and Gabriel had never heard a more wonderful sound in the world. Rafe had gotten up too and he hugged Shay while she was still in Gabriel's arms. Jonas just sat at the table looking pale and a little shell-shocked.

Gabriel almost laughed. Everyone reacted differently to the news of impending fatherhood, he guessed.

Gabriel kissed Shay on the forehead and vowed right then and there that no matter what terrible shit was happening in the world around them and no matter how difficult the months in front of them would be, he would do everything possible to cherish and pamper his beautiful, precious wife.

And then, still holding her close, Gabriel turned back to Nix. "So where are we going?"

Nix moved his finger on the map from Jacob's Well down south and west.

"But that's—" Jonas sputtered, finally looking like he'd started breathing again.

"It's San Antonio Territory."

Rafe just stared at Nix like he was crazy. "But we got good intel that said San Antonio was taken over by the Black Skulls. Who just happen to be Colonel Travis's closest allies. And you want us to go over the border into their territory?"

"Exactly. While they're busy trying to root us out in Central Texas South and North—"

"We'll be hiding right under their noses," Shay finished for Nix.

He nodded. "Exactly."

"But where?" Rafe asked. "That far south isn't even still in the hill country? It's just flat. Where could we hide that Travis wouldn't see us with sat imaging?"

Nix just got a big smile at that—which to be honest, with his giant face scar, looked more menacing than anything else.

"We got a lead on a place. Audrey, why don't you tell them. You've been there before."

All eyes turned to Audrey. "Well," she said, clearing her throat. "You remember field trips? In school? Did any of ya'll ever take one to Natural Bridge Caverns?"

———

The next night they loaded up several vans—their clan, Nix's, and several others Nix thought Travis would target if and when he came to town—and headed south.

Other clan families planned to evacuate as well, but no one other than Nix knew where to.

The plan was to wait it out until they had a better plan. Travis had to have a weak spot. They just needed to find it. And drum up support for their cause in the meantime.

They drove several hours south on back roads and unloaded when they got to the neutral zone between Central Texas South and San Antonio Territory, then their drivers hauled ass back to Jacob's Well so they wouldn't be leaving any vehicles behind as a giant red flag of where they'd gone.

The next part of the trip—five miles—had to be made on foot, at night. This had been hardest on the kids, but Matthew and Tim had been great, making a game of it for their younger siblings. They hid out and slept during the day, sticking to paths Nix was familiar with from his Scrapper days.

They spent several days that way, slowly and carefully moving their way toward the caves. They'd finally gotten there in the dead of night about a week ago.

Charlie and Rafe met them at the cave. That was the riskiest part of the entire plan. Rafe had posed as a smuggler from Hell's Hollow. He'd been driving an ancient white van right down I-35 straight into San Antonio with Charlie in the back.

Along with a shit-ton of Jonas's best bud.

When he was stopped at the border by three night highway patrolmen, Rafe said he had a special delivery for Bautista himself—the head of the Black Skulls MC.

One of the patrolman had lazily drawn his weapon on Rafe, but he had no idea he was dealing with a former Airman turned New Republic Elite Guard.

Even one-handed, Rafe was able to disarm the guard, taser him, and shot the other two at the back of the van full of tranqs from a gun he'd borrowed from Nix.

Then he unloaded a fair quantity of the marijuana, figuring the patrolmen would be less likely to kick up a fuss and notify everyone in the damn territory if they suddenly found themselves with a fortune in green leaf. After all, if they never told anyone about the mysterious stranger in the white van, then they never had to declare or relinquish all that weed.

After all, what harm could it be to just let one man into the territory?

Since then, they'd all been settling in at the cave. It was the biggest cave in Texas with over two hundred caverns, some of which were huge.

And when Gabriel said huge, he meant *huge*.

They were there for over an hour before they discovered a small band of malnourished and road-weary people already hiding there. They were happy to welcome the clans when they realized they were willing to share their food and medicine. Audrey immediately took charge of distributing rations.

They were just finishing up their dinner in one of the bigger caverns they'd turned into a communal space. Candles had been arranged in a circle and people from different clans lounged and chatted as they finished up their rations of cornbread and jerky.

"You wanna come and play?" Alex popped up in front of Nicky. "Yesterday me and Tim found a room as big as a football field!"

Gabriel paused, watching surreptitiously to see how Shay's little girl would respond. She and her brother had stuck together like glue to each other and their mom ever since they'd been reunited.

Alex and Tim kept inviting them to play or go exploring with them. Gabriel always chaperoned and he'd seen more stalactites and stalagmites over the past week than he'd ever needed to in a lifetime. But after the stress of the journey, he was happy to give the boys something else to focus on.

Though Nicky always said no and clutched tighter to Matthew's side, the last few days she'd watched Alex and Tim play like she really *wished* she could go along. She was a good little soldier, though, so she stayed by her brother and mom's side.

As always, when Alex asked, Nicky's eyes immediately sought out her brother's. Matthew shifted where he was sitting, looking to the dark recesses of the cave, then back at Nicky, then to his mom.

Shay nodded encouragingly but then looked toward Gabriel. "As long as Gabe doesn't mind taking you."

But Rafe spoke up before Gabriel could. "Why don't I take you guys this time? I keep hearing about this giant football stadium room but I gotta see it to believe it. I think you guys might just be BSing me."

"What's BSing?" Alex asked and Gabriel smacked Rafe on the back of the head.

"Um," Rafe said as he stood up. "Bull shoeing."

Alex nodded, whispering to himself, "*Bullshoeing, bullshoeing.*"

Gabriel put a hand over his eyes and Shay laughed. "Have fun guys. Make sure to take a couple flashlights with extra batteries and some candles too. And stick to the rooms with a handrail so you know you can find your way back."

Rafe made a face at her. "Yes, mother," he said in a high-pitched voice and she smacked his shins.

Matthew stood up and held out a hand for his sister. She popped to her feet and started bouncing up and down. "Slagmites, slagmites, slagmites!"

"It's *stalag*mites," Matthew corrected gently. "Stalag."

"Slag."

"*Sta*lag."

"Slag. That's what I'm *saying*." She lifted her arms up in exasperation and it was so cute, Gabriel about died.

He looked over at Shay and saw a misty-eyed smile on her face, too. Then he glanced down at her stomach.

Would the baby be a boy or a girl?

Gabriel was secretly hoping for another girl. He'd always wanted to have a big family. And his beautiful Shay was giving him that. She was making all his dreams come true.

Now if he could just give her a world where their children could grow up safely. He'd always wanted to give his boys the best future they could possibly have.

Now he'd just settle for any future at all.

Please, God. Please, please keep my family safe. And please take that monster, Colonel Travis, down to hell where he belongs.

Amen.

Gabriel quickly made the sign of the cross as Rafe gathered the supplies for their exploration. Shay helped Audrey clean up from their meal and stack the dishes that would be taken to one of the deeper caverns where a well had been dug down to hit the aquifer below the cave. Each clan was assigned a week's worth of water duty and thankfully, they weren't on this week.

"Let's go check on Charlie," Shay said, once she'd handed off the dishes. She looked to Gabriel and Jonas.

Jonas nodded and stood up, not saying anything.

That was nothing new. He barely said a word these days. Not since the Travisville mission. It had pissed Gabriel off at first, thinking that Jonas was still mad at Shay for lying to them. But when Gabriel confronted Jonas about it their second day in at the caves, he'd looked shocked that Gabriel could think that.

"Of course not," Jonas said. "That monster had her *children.*"

Shay grabbed one of the large candles from the center of the circle and took the lead, heading down the now familiar passageway through the caverns.

Before The Fall, the cave had been a longtime tourist attraction, so in a lot of places there were hand rails and clear walkways—at least in the outer chambers. None of them had explored the deeper recesses, though apparently the caverns went on for over two miles.

Gabriel held his candle up, looking around at the waxy looking stalactites that dripped from the ceilings and down the limestone walls. It was cool down here, almost cold at times. You'd never believe it was nearing a hundred degrees just a couple hundred feet straight up above their heads.

Shay was quiet as they walked, which meant that Jonas and Gabriel were quiet too. If Rafe were here, he'd probably be cracking jokes, but he wasn't. And without him, it was even more glaringly obvious that their five had become four, and with one of those four injured, they had become three.

Now Jonas was so withdrawn, well, it was hard not to feel lonely. Gabriel had wanted a family but he'd never expected it to be like this. So complicated. So messy.

Then again, maybe that was what real family was all about. And Gabriel wouldn't trade his in for the world.

They finally rounded the corner to their clan cavern. It was spacious. If there was one thing the caves weren't lacking in, it was space.

They'd hung curtains up on strings looped around the thickest stalagmites by the entrance to the cavern, so there was a modicum of privacy. Shay pushed back the curtain and entered first.

What?

"Charlie," she cried.

CHAPTER FORTY-ONE

JONAS

Shit. Jonas ran into their clan cavern right after Shay when they saw Charlie slumped over, half off the cot, half on it.

"Baby," Shay said, cupping his face in her hands after Jonas helped her roll Charlie back on his cot. "What were you doing?"

He was conscious at least, so that was good. But he was also breathing hard and clenching his teeth in a way that made it clear he was in pain.

"You... weren't... here." Each word was forced through his teeth and she reached down to grab his hand. He seemed to relax at her touch but only marginally.

"Have to... protect... you."

What did he think he was gonna be able to do in this state? Hobble in front of a bullet? He could barely make it to the sanitation bucket and back without help.

"Hey pal, we got her for the next few weeks, okay?" Jonas said, leaning over to grab something from his pack and then coming back to

Charlie. Jonas might not be good for much, but this he could give. "Take a big bite of this, okay?"

Charlie made a face. "Don't like...the way... it tastes."

"Well we ran out of morphine and even the doctor says this is the next best thing." Jonas didn't have the patience for proper bedside manner. Charlie was in pain. This would stop it. End of fucking story. "I'll drag his ass back down here again if that's what it'll take."

"Please," Shay said, "eat it. For me?" She scratched her fingers through Charlie's hair and then caressed down his face. His eyes closed at her touch and Jonas could tell that even though he was in immense pain, her touch comforted and distracted him.

Charlie nodded just the tiniest bit and opened his mouth.

Jonas handed the oat bar to Shay and she broke off a piece, popping it in Charlie's mouth.

"How long before it starts taking effect?" Shay whispered to Jonas as she pulled back from Charlie.

"Sometimes up to two hours. With the dose I gave him, though, and considering what a lightweight he is, it could be as soon as thirty to forty-five minutes."

"And in the meantime?"

"Well, lighting up a joint would get it done faster, but—"

"No smoking," Charlie growled. "Our wife is pregnant."

"We could send her out into the other cavern and—"

"Not gonna send—*ohhhh*," Charlie groaned suddenly, except this time it didn't sound like he was in pain.

Jonas's eyes snapped down to find Shay's hand disappearing down into the front of Charlie's towel. He couldn't even put on boxers, the skin on his legs was so fucked at the moment.

But from the reaction Shay was getting, the fire had clearly not gotten to one important part of his anatomy.

"Then we'll just have to find another way to distract you," Shay said.

Charlie closed his eyes and pressed his head back to the cot as Shay lifted the towel to reveal his hard cock.

Jonas looked away.

He should leave.

Instead, he glanced back.

Shay's hair fell across Charlie's stomach as she leaned over, careful not to touch any part of Charlie except to lick the slit of his dick with her tongue.

Fuck.

Jonas went hard in ten seconds flat.

Why the fuck was he still standing here watching this? He didn't deserve to be here.

He blinked and finally took a step back. He was about to turn and run from the goddamned room but his shoes must have made some sort of noise because Shay stood up straight and spun to look at him.

"Where are you going?"

Her bright green eyes looked almost hurt.

Jonas swallowed. "I— Um, I just—" He dropped his head and let out a deep breath before finally looking back up at her.

"You look like you're all set here. There are some chores that need to be done out in the main cave so I'll—"

But Shay's eyes just flashed. "Don't you dare move another inch. Tell me why the hell you keep running away from me. It's like you can't even stand to be in the same room as me since we got back from Travisville."

"Of course I can't!" Jonas snapped.

Shay's mouth had dropped open in a wide O and Gabriel looked like he wanted to slug Jonas. Jonas really, really wished he would. Jesus, he deserved it. And so much more.

"Talk to me," Shay pleaded.

Jonas threw his hands up in the air. "And say what?"

"Say what you feel. Say what's going on in that head of yours. What's going on in your heart?"

Jonas scoffed, grabbing his hair with both hands, shaking his head. "My *heart*? Who the fuck gives a shit about my heart? Why aren't you yelling at me? Screaming at me?"

"For what?" Shay said, throwing her arms up.

"He let Travis... get away," Charlie said from the bed and Jonas held out a hand like, *ding, ding, ding, we have a winner*.

Jonas knew everyone in camp was thinking it. It was almost a relief for someone to finally fucking say it out loud.

"That wasn't your fault," Shay exclaimed.

Jonas laughed. "Are you kidding? I was standing there holding a gun on him. And then he just started backing up because he knew I wouldn't shoot him. *I* didn't even know, but *he* knew. And the bastard was right."

Jonas huffed out a merciless laugh, taking a step back toward the cavern's exit. "How many thousands of people will die because I couldn't pull the damn trigger? Because I choked when it mattered most?"

He shook his head. "I shouldn't have even come with you. I deserve whatever Travis would have done to me if he found me in Jacob's Well."

In a streak, Shay was across the cavern. Then her hand was flying.

Nothing could have surprised Jonas more than her slap. It wasn't hard. She hadn't put her whole weight behind it, but it was a startling sting.

"Now you listen to me," she said, face tilted down and eyes up. "You are never going to talk such fucking nonsense again. Do you hear me?"

Jonas just stood, frozen.

"I said, *do you fucking hear me?*" She shouted the last five words and Jonas was quickly nodding.

"Good. Now get your ass over here, on your knees." She walked back to the side of Charlie's cot and pointed at the floor.

Jonas went. She was using his own tactics against him, but right now, he would grovel at her feet if she asked. He'd lick her boots if he thought it would make her happy. He'd spend the rest of his life as her servant and still it would never, ever make up for what he'd done. Or *not* done.

Shay pulled her cotton t-shirt off over her head and unclasped her bra. Her gorgeous breasts bounced a little as she freed them and Jonas's hard on was back to full mast.

You don't deserve this. You don't deserve her or to be happy when—

"Help me with my pants," she ordered, eyes on him as she unbuttoned them and slid them partially down her hips.

Everything in Jonas screamed at him to put a stop to this. To tell her that no. He couldn't. She was too pure and good and he was—

"Now," she snapped and Jonas let his eyes fall closed even as he reached up to drag the denim down over her hips, his thumbs caressing her soft, soft skin as he went.

From his position on his knees, he could smell her arousal.

Jesus, just how wet was she? Jonas inhaled her and stroked himself, then immediately felt wracked by guilt and yanked his hand away. Why should he get to sit here and fuck his woman when other people would be dying soon, if not already, at Travis's hand?

"Gabriel, you come here too."

Gabriel approached reluctantly. It was obvious Shay was in a mood. She was not to be fucked with.

"Take your pants off and fuck me."

Gabriel's chest heaved at her command.

"What the fuck are we? Are we a bonded clan or just some people who hang out together sometimes?" She looked down at Jonas, then back to Gabriel, then to Charlie. "Because fuck that. Our entire lives have been upended time after time in the last eight and a half years. We survived," her eyebrows bunched. "But at times, it's broken us. Each of us."

She made eye contact with them again, one at a time. "The only way we get through this is as a clan that's bonded tighter than ever. Which is why I want us to reconsummate our commitment. This time with no secrets. No bullshit. Just our love. I already talked to Rafe about it and he agrees."

She kicked off her jeans, standing before them completely and gloriously naked, obviously unashamed. "Now it's time for you to make your decision." She looked to Gabriel. "I know you loved your wife and I would never try to take her place. But I can be a good wife to you. I hope you'll let me into a different corner of your heart someday. Because I love you."

"Oh *mi alma*, my soul, you have already captured me completely," Gabriel's words came out in a rush. "I was just so afraid. It seemed impossible to me that God could give me and the children so much—I didn't dare ask for more." He shook his head. "But you were right that day when you asked what kind of example I was setting for them. If I don't show them I'm living my life to the fullest, how will they learn anything but to kill themselves with work at the expense of everything else?"

"You're a good father," Shay said, reaching a hand out to him. He walked forward to take it and Jonas felt the sinkhole in his stomach open even wider.

Here was a man truly deserving of Shay.

Unlike *him*.

But right when he started to get up off the floor, all the softness left Shay's face.

"Where do you think you're going?"

Jonas bowed his head, settling back on his knees even as conflict warred in his chest.

He was not this man.

He was not the one on his knees taking orders.

But the man he'd been was a coward who couldn't step up and do what needed doing in the moment, so what good was he?

Maybe this is who he should have been all along. Meek. Obsequious. Obedient.

Maybe then when Charlie had put a gun in his hand and told him to pull the trigger, he would have been able to do it.

Shay moved in front of him, facing the cot, her cunt right at his face. He took a sharp breath in and her scent overwhelmed him. With each of his senses, he took in her arousal. The pretty pink lips of her pussy glistened and with every breath in, he took more of her aroma into his lungs.

He couldn't stop himself from reaching up to part her slick folds and then to lick upwards in one slurping pass of his tongue.

Her flavor burst along his taste buds and he was instantly ravenous for more.

Especially when he heard her low-pitched breathy moan—the one that meant she was trying to be quiet about her pleasure and only *barely* managing it. Somehow Jonas always found that even hotter than when she screamed it to the rafters.

He had to adjust his head to the side when she bent over at the waist. It took Jonas a second to figure out—

Ohhhhh. The muffled groans were a dead giveaway. She was sucking Charlie's cock again.

Fuck.

Jonas reached up and grabbed hold of her hips. His gorgeous baby doll wasn't wasting any time, was she?

How quickly would Charlie pop off? The pain might keep the orgasm off for a while. Or the blow job might be such a good distraction from it that he came in minutes.

Either way, Jonas couldn't afford to waste a minute of glorious access to Shay's delicious pussy. He licked and speared his tongue inside her and then suckled on her clit.

It was while he was sucking mercilessly on her clit that he heard her say, "Now!"

And a few moments later, he felt Shay's body jerk forward. Like...

Jonas pulled back just far enough to see Gabriel's cock disappearing into Shay's pussy. Gabriel was taking her from behind and Shay's frantic groans around Charlie's cock increased in volume.

If she didn't quiet soon, everyone in the whole damn cave system would know what they were up to.

Not that Jonas minded.

Most of the men who'd come with them were part of their own clans, but there were a handful of unbonded men who'd come from the Security Squadron and though Nix trusted them, that meant nothing to Jonas. It had been his second in command who'd turned out to be Travis's spy last year.

Yeah, and you were no better at spotting Henry—

But Shay's frantic cries of pleasure were soon tuning out any other thought.

She was coming. Her pussy quaked and spurted her sweet juices into his mouth. Jonas lapped them all up.

Fuck. She was his favorite meal. Always would be.

She shuffled backwards from the cot, and when Jonas looked up, it was to see her licking her lips and swiping at her chin with her forearm. She was a swallower. So fucking hot. She was the sexiest damn thing he'd ever seen in his whole goddamned life.

"Love you," Charlie said, reaching out a hand for her. She took it, lifting it to her lips. She was smiling so wide that tears glistened in her eyes.

"You're my hero." She leaned down and kissed him on the lips. "My miracle. You walked through fire for me. My protector."

Jonas watched the peace that settled over Charlie's face at her words.

And he was so fucking jealous he could barely stand to be in his own skin.

Jonas got to his feet and was about to try heading out again—they'd all fucked like Shay wanted, so she could count that box checked.

But Shay's hand flew out to block him, eyes dark when he looked over at her. "Now tell Gabriel how you want him to fuck me. I'd like it if you do it at the same time, but I leave the details up to you."

She took a step back to put herself on display, then lipped the tip of her finger, circling her own nipple like the goddamned vixen she was.

"What are you—" Jonas tried to object. "I'm not going to—"

"Oh yes you are," Shay said, teasing the same finger down her stomach all the way to her sex. She gasped and arched her back as she rubbed her finger over her clitoris. "I want a G-spot orgasm, and you two are just the ones to give it to me."

Jonas's eyes shot to Gabriel but he held up his hands like, *hey man, this is on you.*

Then Shay spun where she stood on the blanket they'd laid out on the cave floor as a makeshift rug.

She looked over her shoulder at Jonas, ass out. Her bottom was positively luscious in the flickering candlelight.

"Who do you think should take my ass, Jonas? You? Or do you want Gabriel to fuck me there while you plow my cunt? I'm not sure I could take you back there." Her eyes flicked down to Jonas's erection that he'd freed while he ate her out. "You're so thick." She bit her bottom lip while she said it, and when her eyes came back to his, he'd swear she was all but salivating. "But if you think I should try to take it, I will."

Her words set a fire blazing in Jonas's chest.

His baby doll was toying with him and it both pissed him the fuck off and turned him the hell on. He wanted to march over to where she was standing and bend her over his knee. He wanted to turn that pale, milky white ass of hers pink with his hand print.

And, as if she could read his thoughts, she leaned over and grabbed hold of the bottom of the cot, her ass on display like the Thanksgiving turkey. Bent over as far as she was, Jonas could even see her pussy. The candle light glinted off the moisture drenching her.

When he didn't move—because Jesus, he could barely breathe—Shay shifted slightly so she could look around her shoulder at him.

And what he saw in her face fucking slayed him.

"Baby, I think the reason you couldn't pull the trigger was because you're a good man, not a coward. And the thought of taking the life of another human being, even one as worthless and evil as Arnold Jason Travis—" she shook her head "—was too abhorrent to the kind of man *you* are. A good man."

Jonas started to say something but she held up a hand to stop him.

"And even if that wasn't why you couldn't shoot him, I don't have your fatal flaw, Jonas. I'm capable of forgiveness. The question is, can you be a real man and accept it?"

Jonas's eyes fell shut at her words. They hit him like a tsunami crashing over his soul. Because goddamn, just like always, she'd seen straight to the heart of it, hadn't she? She'd seen what a hypocrite he was. He'd been a nasty, cold bastard to her when her mistakes came to light.

People aren't perfect, she'd once said. *They make mistakes. If you can't ever forgive them, how will you ever let anyone close to you?*

But Jesus Christ, it was like he'd lived as if *he* thought he was perfect. Judging everyone else around him so harshly. Decades after he'd rejected his father's path, he'd still been just like him—passing judgement on everyone he met. The world failed him? Fine, he'd withdraw from society. Shay made a mistake? He wouldn't even hear her out. She was all but dead to him.

Who the *fuck* did he think he was? Jesus?

Probably not even Jesus could live up to the impossible standards Jonas had set.

"Shay," he said, his throat so raw her name came out half-croaked. "I'm so sor—"

"I forgive you," she cut him off, eyes full of compassion. But then she smiled and a wicked gleam entered her eye. "If you really want to make it up to me, though, you and Gabriel can fuck me so hard I'll feel it into next goddamned week."

Heat flared through Jonas's skin and his cock jumped. "Oh baby doll." He rubbed his hands together. "Be careful what you wish for."

And then he stalked like a predator over toward the woman who'd turned his life upside down more times than he could count—and who just now had, yet again, saved him.

EPILOGUE

Meanwhile, Right After President Goddard Was Assassinated...

Compared to all the other places Drea had been imprisoned, the President's personal detention center was pretty nice, all things considered.

It was in the basement of the Omni. He had to have had it build special—a series of ten cells, bars and all. Smaller than you'd find in say a local county jail, but then, these were obviously just meant to hold one person apiece.

Because that wasn't creepy. That the President of the Republic kept his own little jail-slash-torture chamber in the bottom of what was essentially the capitol building.

"Ya know, like you do," Drea whispered under her breath, working her way down the bars, testing each one for weaknesses again. "Not abnormal at all."

The bars were steel, she was pretty sure. So bending them and trying to slip through wasn't an option. And the joints and pegs were on the opposite side of the door so she couldn't jimmy those loose. But maybe if she—

"You sure are pretty."

Drea didn't give the guard the satisfaction of a reaction. He was middle-aged, had hair that was more gray than brown, and a potbelly that hung so far over his belt she imagined it had been half a decade since he'd been able to see his toes.

Drea stood stock still.

"And with all that pretty blonde hair. I bet you could make a fella feel reaaaaaal good."

Drea breathed out a sharp breath.

Don't lose your temper. Don't lose your temper.

Use *all* the tools at your disposal.

Even if it makes you want to gag on your own dreadlocks.

She slowly crossed her arms across her stomach in a way that propped her boob up and out. She rubbed her arms up and down.

"Say, it sure is chilly in here," she said, face slightly downturned so that she was only looking the guard through her eyelashes. "Do you think I could borrow your jacket?" She bit her lip and continued blinking up at him. "I promise I'll be good."

Shit, she was laying it on too thick, wasn't she? He'd see right through her act and—

"Well, I could always warm you up."

Or not.

She smiled and dipped her head. "If it wouldn't be too much trouble, I mean. I know all you men here at the capitol have such important jobs. Working for the *President* and all."

"Aw he wouldn't mind me seeing to the comfort of a prisoner. The New Republic is all about treating people humanely after all."

"Oh my gosh," Drea said, jumping up and down and clapping her hands—she was just purely channeling Sophia now.

Jesus, never thought she'd see the day. She might only be eight years older than the nineteen-year-old, but it felt like five decades separated them.

The guard was just eating this shit up, though.

Men were so fucking easy.

She'd shake her head if she weren't so busy keeping to her act.

That's right, buddy. Reach for those keys.

She fought to keep her eyes on his face while his hand went to the keyring at his belt.

He lifted a warning finger. "Step back now. Don't give me any trouble or you'll regret it." His hand went to the retractable billy club on his belt.

"Oh no, sir," Drea simpered. "I would never. If I could just have a friend in this cold place, it would mean everything to me. I'll do anything just to have someone on my side helping me. I'll pay you back however you want."

He grinned lasciviously. "However I want, huh?"

Drea nodded over and over, feeling like a bobblehead. She backed up against the far wall right beside the twin bed, hands up where he could see them.

He reached down and readjusted himself right before sliding the door open.

Patience.

Not yet.

He stepped inside the cell.

Not yet.

Smile. Look innocent and harmless.

She giggled and ducked her head as he shrugged out of his guard's jacket halfway across the room.

NOW.

She struck while his arms were still half-caught in the jacket, yanking and twisting it to trap his arms at the same time she swept his legs with a low kick.

Dad would be so proud.

Right as the guard hit the floor she was on him, yanking the billy club off his belt. Because the other thing Dad taught her?

Hit first and ask questions later.

It was something of a family mantra.

In one swift downward motion, Drea had the billy club extended and she went to work.

The guard was a screamer, so she went for the throat first. One swift hit to his larynx had him grasping his throat and choking.

She *tut tut tutted* at him for being dumb enough to expose himself like that. Because obviously her next hit was going to be to his scrotum.

That was just female self-defense 101.

She struck a few other of the best impact points to make sure he was disabled. One hard blow to the solar plexus, then, when he curled in on himself, a couple of strikes to the kidneys from the back.

He gasped for air and—was he crying?

She shook her head at him. Pathetic.

Let it never be said that she ever behaved like one of those clichéd blondes from old horror movies who always celebrated too early without double checking that the monster was really dead. Drea always made sure that her was enemy *down*.

She raised the club one last time and put all her weight behind a hit to his knee.

Then she reached and grabbed his keys off the floor from where the guard had dropped them, then she hurried out of the cell and locked it behind her.

Only to find the door to the stairs was being pushed open.

Shit.

Of course there were probably cameras on the cells. Someone had seen. The question was how many they'd sent down to subdue her.

Screw it. She'd come this far.

She raised the billy club and ran at the door, knowing surprise was her best weapon.

"Drea?"

Wait, what?

"*Eric?*"

She was running so fast she couldn't stop herself in time and she collided with him. He wrapped his arms around her and together they rammed into the door, knocking it shut.

For a second it was just the two of them, breathing hard, him looking down at her. Wow, his eyes were really *blue* blue weren't they?

Wait, wait, wait.

Record scratch. Back the fuck up.

She hated Eric, *The Commander*, Wolford.

Okay, maybe *hate* was a strong word. But she strongly disliked him. He was a chauvinist pig who'd come up with the most ridiculous, degrading system of treating the women in his territory. Giving them out as fucking lottery prizes, for Christ's sake. She'd had to lie and say she was a lesbian else he was gonna try to force that shit on her.

And he refused to help her go back to the Gulf Texas island where he'd found her to rescue the other hundred women who she'd once been a leader to. Until a fucking man came and made them all prisoners.

Drea jerked away from Eric. "What are you doing here?"

He raised his arms in an *isn't it obvious?* motion. "Rescuing you."

Drea huffed out a laugh and then waved back at the guard on the floor of her cell behind her. "Thanks but I can rescue myself just fine." She pushed the billy club back into its retracted position and shoved as much of it as she could in her pocket.

Eric crossed his arms and leaned against the wall. "You got out of your cell, but how exactly were you planning to get out of the city in the middle of a coup?"

Wait, what? She couldn't have heard that right.

"A what?"

"A coup."

"I know what a goddamned coup is." Drea narrowed her eyes. "What makes you say one is happening here?"

"Oh you didn't hear? President Goddard was just assassinated. About..." He looked down at his watch. "Twenty-eight minutes ago."

Drea felt her eyebrows all but hit her hairline. Shit.

"Even better, they think it was someone from our group. I'm surprised your pretty head is still attached to your neck."

Despite herself, Drea's hand lifted to her throat. As soon as she realized what she was doing, she dropped her hand and glared at Eric.

"And why do they think that?"

He waved a hand to brush her off. "Shay's sculpture *may* have exploded and either someone in her clan or Vanessa's is most likely working for Arnold. Colonel Travis I mean."

Drea coughed in disbelief. "And you're so calm about this... *why?*

"Well, it's all finally happening now, isn't it? I've been waiting for the shit to hit the fan for a long time and," he held out his arms. "Shit, meet fan. Now come on. I know where the President keeps his private helicopter."

"Why didn't you fucking open with that?" Drea growled, pushing past Eric

"You're a very complex girl to rescue."

Drea pulled the billy club out of her pocket. "Call me a girl one more time."

Eric lifted his hands in a surrender gesture. "I apologize. You're a very complex woman."

"And I rescued myself, remember?"

"Ah, but I'm the one with the helicopter, remember?"

———

"You were saying?" Drea put a hand on her hip as they looked out the window of the door that led out to the President's private helicopter pad.

The helicopter pad currently swarmed by soldiers wearing black and gray fatigues.

"Shit," Eric swore. "Those are Travis's soldiers. I thought they were at Jacob's—" Then he shook his head. "It doesn't matter."

He took Drea's elbow and started pulling her back toward the stairs of the four-story parking garage that was a block away from the Omni.

Drea jerked out of his grasp. "Okay, we tried it your way. Now it's my turn." She strode in front of Eric and started down the stairs.

As she did, she realized this had been her problem all along.

She wasn't the kind of woman who waited for other people to help her get shit done. No, she blazed ahead and did it herself.

Why the hell had she even come to Fort Worth pandering to that asshole of a President in the first place. She should know—you wanted shit done, you did it *yourself*.

Well, lesson learned. How much time had she already wasted? She was going back to Nomansland to rescue her people today. Fuck everyone else.

"What do you— You don't even know this— Have you even been to Fort Worth before?"

She didn't answer him until they got to the first floor of the garage before turning to face him. "No. But I know how to hotwire one of those." She pointed to the Harley she'd seen on the way in. In fact, there was a whole bunch of them lined up. She smiled sweetly and tilted her head at Eric. "Now, you don't mind riding bitch, do you?"

Eric's face darkened as he glowered at her. "I hate motorcycles," he muttered. But he did start walking in the direction of the Harley.

She had the thing hotwired within three minutes and she handed a helmet to Eric. "Safety first."

He took the helmet but stared down at the growling motorcycle as she slung her leg over it. "You realize this is most likely a Black Skulls motorcycle."

Drea just grinned. "Where do you think I learned how to hotwire a hog? 4H?"

Seeing how Eric's eyes went saucer-wide almost made the whole shitty day worth it. She patted the seat behind her.

"Climb on."

He shook his head like he was rethinking his decision to ever come back for her in the first place. But he put the helmet on and climbed on behind her.

And if she noticed how good it felt having his strong arms around her waist? Well, that was just her damn hormones talking.

She turned her head to the side, not looking all the way back at him. "Hold on tight. I'm not gonna take it slow, and if you fall off, it's your own damn fault."

Eric's only response was anxious swearing.

Drea laughed and closed the face visor on her helmet before pulling out of the garage. He'd be in for a surprise when he realized they weren't heading for Jacob's Well. Having the purr of a big twin engine between her legs felt far better than she'd like to admit.

And as she rode south, the morning sun to her left, she thought, *aw, this might even be fun.*

———

Continue reading to enjoy an extended preview of Theirs to Wed the next book in the Marriage Raffle Series

CHAPTER 1

LOGAN

"Piss off." Logan Washington shook his head at his supervisor, Phoenix ("Nix") Hale, as he drove the ancient four-by-four truck on the dirt road that cut through a field. He and Nix had worked side-by-side as part of the town's elite Security Squad ever since Logan arrived eight years ago from Austin (or what was left of it).

"I feel for you, Ghost. I do," Nix went on.

Logan glanced over, and his jaw went tight at the concerned expression that puckered the scar on Nix's face. They called Logan "Ghost" for a reason. With the exception of work, he kept to himself. It was better that way. For everyone. He forced his attention back to the road without acknowledging Nix's attempt at empathy. It didn't suit him.

The truck jumped as they hit a rut, and Finn swore from the back seat. "Take it a easy. There's no padding on these damn jump seats. You keep jolting me around like this and my balls are gonna be black and blue tomorrow."

Logan ignored him. Finn had been complaining for the last hour and the drive was only three hours long. It was early May, and they were out on a Scrapper run in the westernmost edge of Central Texas North. Closer to the border with Trader's Territory and West Texas Territory than Logan preferred.

Those bastards could be ruthless, especially if you ran into scavengers from Hell's Hollow, one of the most prominent townships and trading posts in Trad Territory.

Most of the best shit had already been scavenged right after the bombs fell eight years ago, but Graham, one of Nix's clan mates, always watched the satellite feeds. He swore the recent flooding had washed a biplane out into a clearing near here.

Since their own township, Jacob's Well, was one of the few places that had access to such technology after the EMP attacks, they had a good shot at being the first to reach the site. It was doubtful the whole plane would be worth hauling back, but if they were lucky, they could strip it for parts and start heading home before nightfall.

This all sounded good to Logan. Between Finn's complaining and Nix's constant hassling, he already had a headache the size of the New fucking Republic of Texas.

"Another woman could come to town any day now," Nix said, continuing to push the issue. "You should have put your name in for the girl who got here last week. When's it gonna be? At least put your name in next time. What's the harm?"

Logan didn't respond. He didn't see the point in answering stupid questions. He didn't put his name in the lottery box because he wasn't looking for a bride, or a clan for that matter; he was looking to be left alone. Nix was smart, so why was this so hard for him to understand?

"Well I'm sure never gonna miss a chance to put *my* name in," Finn piped up again from the back seat. "I haven't missed one since I turned eighteen, but I'm in the fifth tier so my odds are shit. But damn, Ghost," he punched Logan on the arm, and Logan glared at him in the rearview mirror. "You're in the first tier. I'd kill for odds like that. They've got to be like what, one in thirty?"

Again, Logan didn't answer, and the tension at his temples stabbed at him like red hot pokers. *Another good reason not to put your name in the box.*

Fuckin' Finn kept rambling. "But in a couple months...when I get that promotion you promised me, it'll mean moving up to the fourth tier. Just you watch. I'm gonna be married by the time I'm twenty-one and have me a litter of kids before I'm thirty."

Logan rolled his eyes but when he glanced over toward the passenger seat, Nix was staring intently back at him.

Logan returned his focus to the road. Okay, so calling it a road was generous. At this point it was more field than road—but every so often he'd make out ruts from where the road used to be, which told him he was still on track.

"Your woman..." Nix's voice was quiet. "Man, she's gone. You can't mourn her forever."

"Can't I?" Logan asked, and he meant it. He was thirty-eight. He and Jenny had been high school sweethearts. He'd been married to her for twelve years and now widowed for eight. But some nights he woke up just as raw as the day he realized he'd lost her. Some wounds were so deep, time didn't do shit to heal them.

Jenny. What he'd give just to see her again. He'd even take one of their knock-down, drag-out fights. He'd give his right nut just to hear her calling him names. "Logan, you stubborn ass!"

It didn't make sense that God would take someone whom the world so clearly needed. Whom *he* clearly needed. She had an IQ that was through the roof, curious, inventive, and so damn beautiful. Tall. Pale gray eyes that could always see right into the heart of him.

No, he had no interest in getting married again. And *no* interest in disrespecting his wife's memory with some stranger shoved in his life by a goddamn lottery. Not to mention, sharing a new wedding bed with four other men...? *Damn.* He knew the world was different and all, but some shit he'd just never understand.

Nix chuckled as if he could read Logan's thoughts. "I know. I thought the same thing, but it can work. Look at what I have with Audrey and my clan."

"Your wife is exceptional. No doubt, man," Logan said. "Jenny was, too. But what if something happened to Audrey..."

A low growl rumbled out of Nix's chest.

"Easy, asshole. But you just made my point. If something happened to Audrey, you think you'd jump into bed with the next woman who stumbled into town?"

"No," Nix growled, obviously upset at even the thought of it. Then he huffed out a loud exhale. "But you're hardly *jumping.* It's been eight damn years. A man shouldn't be alone that long. It's not natural."

"I like being alone."

"You'd like having your balls sucked more," Finn said, his head popping up between Nix and Logan.

"Jesus," Logan said, and he ran his hand through his hair.

"Like you know anything about it," Nix shot back at Finn.

"Well I'm *gonna.* Just you wait. Fourth tier. I'm telling ya, this is my year."

"If it's going to be anyone's year, it's going to be Logan's," Nix said.

Logan fought the pressure building in his chest. He knew from experience that Nix wouldn't let this go. His badgering had gotten worse and worse lately. It was time to shut it down once and for all.

"Fine."

"Fine?" Nix asked, blinking in surprise. "You mean it? You're finally gonna put your name in the box?"

"Yeah. I'll finally put a name in the box." He'd do it, too. As soon as a new woman came to town, he'd make a big show of it—bring Nix with him and get that ugly fucker off his back once and for all.

But Logan would never be writing his own name on a ballot. He'd already come up with an alias. *John Steinbeck*. He'd read his ancient copy of *The Grapes of Wrath* so many times the pages were barely legible. What could he say? Reading about the Depression cheered him up.

"Wow, just think if both our names were to get called," Finn said, leaning forward and getting in their space again. "That'd be awkward. Man, I'd like, see your junk cause we'd both be fucking our wife at the same time, right?" He turned to look at Nix. "Or wait. Do you just line up outside the bedroom or how—?"

"Jesus!" Logan shouted, and not just because Finn was a dumbass.

Logan jammed his foot on the brake, and the truck came to a skidding stop, nearly plowing through a rotted wooden fence.

"What the fuck?" Finn yelled, his body almost launching over the front seat.

Nix turned on him. "How many goddamn times have I told you to put your seatbelt on?"

Finn waved in front of them. "Don't yell at me. It's not my fault Ghost can't navigate for shit."

Logan's jaw locked. "Well maybe if we had a better map or directions I wouldn't be on a road that goes through a damn field and dead ends into a fence."

While Finn was still shouting and losing his shit, Logan went quiet. Then he turned around and jammed his hand over Finn's mouth.

Finn looked even more pissed, but Logan just hissed a long *shhhh* noise while not moving his hand from Finn's mouth. Then he made a motion to *listen,* and Nix immediately went on alert. It took Finn a little longer to catch on, but eventually he calmed down and settled. Logan closed his eyes to hear better.

The noise that had first drawn his attention sounded again and Logan's chest cinched tight.

"Is that a—?"

"Shhh," both Nix and Logan hushed Finn at the same time.

Then all three of them were quiet, and the sound came again.

Logan and Nix's eyes snapped to each other. And then they both shoved their doors open and started sprinting across the field in the direction of the noise.

In the direction of the high-pitched scream.

Logan was solid and well-muscled but not as bulky as Nix, so he ran faster. He jumped the fence like it was a hurdle and ran through the field before hitting the woods. Branches and nettles slapped at his arms and face, but he didn't slow down.

The shouting was louder now so he was going the right direction. *Hold on. Whoever you are, just hold on a little longer.*

When he came around the bend in the trees and saw the rocky embankment, he thought he was too late.

Two men—smugglers Logan would guess—stood over what looked like a pubescent boy, trapped on the ground by a thick meaty hand held at his neck.

"Hey!" Logan shouted, waving his arms over his head. The two men's heads shot up and looked his direction. "Yeah, you, you ugly fuckers. Why don't you pick on someone your own size?"

It was only as one of them raised a gun in his direction that Logan realized he didn't have any weapons on him. *Son of a bitch.* He'd heard the scream and just took off without thinking. He wasn't going to be any help to this kid if he ended up full of bullet holes.

Logan was about to dive into the bushes when the man holding the gun suddenly cried out in pain, arching and looking down at his foot.

Damn. The boy had shoved a wicked looking knife right through the top of his assailant's foot. The man stumbled and fell to the ground. His gun tumbled out of his hand at the same time.

The boy didn't waste a second. He scrambled for the gun, bashed the guy under the chin with it, knocking him out cold—all before the second assailant realized what was happening. The only conscious smuggler reached for the kid but—*Shit!*—the kid was fast. The smuggler's hand closed around air, then an explosive shot rang out, the sound vibrating against the rocks.

Logan was close enough to see the spray of blood before the second man dropped to the ground. Dead. Then the boy was up on his feet, the gun swinging back and forth between the unconscious smuggler with a knife in his foot...and Logan.

Logan's mouth dropped open. Not because there was a gun aimed at his chest. But because the boy wasn't a boy. It was a tiny woman, at least...Logan was pretty sure that's what he was seeing. Her hair was shaved close to her skull, and she was too skinny to have much in the way of breasts, but her eyes were dark, round and beautiful, and her hips... That was no boy.

"Who the fuck are you?" she shouted at Logan, gun still moving.

Yep. Not a boy. Logan put his hands up. "Just someone who wants to help."

She scoffed. "What do you think I am, an idiot?" She leaned over and, gun still trained on Logan, yanked her knife out of the smuggler's foot. He flinched and started to groan, coming to.

Logan took the last ten steps out of the woods onto the embankment. The woman kept her eyes on him the whole time as she leaned over and, using the knife she'd just reclaimed, slashed the smuggler's throat. Ear to fucking ear.

Holy shit.

Finn and Nix stepped out of the woods behind Logan. He held out an arm to keep them back. He didn't know who the woman was but she was lethal, that much was obvious.

She straightened her spine and turned in their direction again. Her face and dark stubbly hair was now covered in blood spatter. With the knife in one hand and the gun in the other, she looked like some sort of miniature avenging Amazonian warrior.

"I asked you a question," she bit out. "Who the fuck are you?" She jerked the gun to make her point that this was her show. "Don't make me ask again."

Logan's hands were already up, but he lifted them higher.

"Holy fuck, you *smoked* those assholes," Finn said excitedly. "That was awesome. I mean, he was like," Finn made a choking gesture with his hand, along with accompanying gargling noise, "and then you were like, *whaaaaa*," Finn made a downward slashing motion, "and then, *boom*, you take him out. Fucking sweet."

The woman frowned at Finn, and Logan felt the urge to apologize. Nix took a step forward. "On behalf of Jacob's Well Township, I'd like to extend our warmest—"

The woman's eyes flared in recognition. "Jacob's Well?"

Nix nodded, eyes wary. "You've heard of us?"

The woman took a step toward them, and the gun wavered just the slightest bit.

"Jacob's Well," she repeated, her voice shaking. And then her eyes rolled back in her head, and she collapsed right where she stood.

CHAPTER 2

RIORDAN

"You're going. Both of you. And that is that."

Riordan ignored his mother, scowled at his *perfect* brother Ross, then ran his spoon through the disgusting slop they called food around here.

Both of you. Always "both of you." Being an identical twin wasn't as awesome as people thought. Which was why Riordan was going somewhere all right—just not the same place his mother was talking about. Riordan was getting the hell *outta* this town.

He wouldn't plan his exodus to death like Ross would. No. Fuck that. He didn't mind taking chances. One day it would all get to be too much and he'd just pull the trigger. He'd pack some hunting gear, steal a truck maybe, then take off.

He'd go someplace where a man could really make something of himself. He'd thought about heading to Fort Worth and signing up for the Army, but shit, that kind of thing was more Ross's style. He didn't want to trade-in their mother's house just for another set of rules.

Don't stay out after dark, Riordan. Don't use that knife, it's too sharp, Rior-

dan. Come home right after school, Riordan. Why can't you be more like your brother, Riordan?

"Finish your stew, Riordan," said his mother, breaking into his thoughts. "It's got real meat in it, and you need the protein."

Riordan pushed the bowl away and slammed the spoon down on the table. "Jesus, Ma. I'm nineteen. When are you gonna stop treating me like I'm six years old?"

"Here we go," Ross muttered under his breath from where he sat at the table beside him. Ross scraped the bottom of his bowl like the good little boy he was, and Riordan shook his head in disgust.

"Maybe I'll stop treating you like a six-year-old when you stop acting like one." His mother put one hand on her hip and stared him down.

She was short and had the rounded profile of a keen-eyed bull terrier. And like a bull, she was prone to plowing down whatever obstacles lay in her path. Including her own sons. Sometimes Riordan thought she'd taken her survival from Xterminate as proof from the Almighty that she should always get her way. Especially since their dad had died not long after The Fall.

"Now. Finish. Your. Stew. And then you two need to march yourselves down to the town square to put your names in for the lottery. A new girl was just brought into town."

Riordan had heard about the knife-wielding wild woman that had been picked up earlier today. Apparently she was practically feral. She'd been brought into town covered in blood, head shaved, and skinny enough to barely count as a woman.

At least that's what he heard. It wasn't like he was ever allowed to be on the front lines of anything.

Riordan shoved his chair back and stood up. "No."

His mother's eyes widened. "What did you just say to me?"

"Riordan," Ross said, standing up with his hand out, obviously ready to play the mediator.

Riordan turned on him incredulously. "Grow up! You don't have to be so damn compliant all the time. What if your name gets called? You don't want to get married any more than I do."

"Ross will do what I say he needs to do," their mother said. "Because he's a good son."

Ross dropped his gaze to the ground.

"You know they don't give out merit badges for being a mama's boy, right?" Riordan asked.

Ross's eyes shot up with a quick murderous look before dropping again to the floor. Ross had always had his heart set on becoming an Eagle Scout. The world had gone to shit when they were twelve and even though the Boy Scouts of America no longer existed, Riordan knew Ross was still secretly working toward it. He was always such a dog with a bone.

Riordan would catch him pouring over all the old scout books and practicing knots or reading about what mushrooms would kill you, or setting up wilderness shelters from scratch. That was the perfect example of who his twin brother was—the kind of kid who loved rules and order so much he spent all his spare time following them to reach a completely pointless goal. So he made unofficial Eagle Scout? So...? Then what?

Riordan was done with all of it. Ma. Ross. Always being compared. Never good enough. D-O-N-E.

"Enough," his mother said like it was the last word on the issue. "You're both going to go down to the town square tonight." She looked Riordan in the eye like she was daring him to talk back.

He smirked but didn't say anything.

"Then you'll put your names in that box. Between the two of you, I've doubled my odds at having a son settle down. I could have a grandbaby by this time next year."

"Jesus Christ. A *baby*?" Riordan exploded.

Was she even listening to herself? They were *nineteen*. They were barely starting their own lives. Give them some time to live before saddling them with the responsibility of marriage and a damn family.

Actually, strike that. That was the kind of shit Ross might want— someday. But Riordan was gonna be a lone wolf forever, making his own damn way in the world. No one telling him what to do. Maybe he'd join up with some smugglers.

Or he could even leave the New Republic and head out West. New

Mexico or Colorado... According to the rumors, they were lawless territories that would be just the kind of place for a maverick like himself.

"Riordan Sean O'Sullivan," his mother came forward and grabbed his ear in an awful pinch, yanking him down so that he was eye-level with her five-foot-four frame, "I ought to wash your mouth out with soap for using the Lord's name in vain. Now. You will go to the square right this minute with your brother and you will put your name in that lottery box. Am I making myself perfectly clear?"

Riordan swallowed, shame and self-loathing rose up to choke him as he adopted the same posture as his brother, eyes to the floor. And then he did what he had done every day of his nineteen years on this earth. He gave in to the domineering woman who ran his life.

"Yes, ma'am."

CHAPTER 3

MICHAEL

Michael sat on the edge of his bed and watched Ana, the woman who lived in the house next door, through the gap in his curtains. The sun had set about an hour ago but she had several oil lamps lit, so he had a perfect view from his garage apartment.

The first time he'd watched, it had just been through the tiniest gap and he'd only taken furtive glances. But as the nights and months progressed, he'd taken to leaving his curtains open wider and wider.

Because Ana? She left her own bedroom curtains *all* the way open, *as per usual*, and the lights on, *of course*.

For tonight's performance, she was wearing a red lace bra and matching panties cut high on her long legs. When she turned her back to the window, Michael sucked in a breath at the sight of her firm ass cheeks split by the red thong.

Ana was twice his age, nearly fifty, but you would have never guessed it to look at her. Sometimes he felt bad about watching, but never for long. She knew he was there. And she gave these shows just for him. They started shortly after she asked him about his clothes.

"What's with the outfits?" she asked one day when they found themselves stepping out of their houses at the same time.

"The outfits?" he asked.

"Yeah." She gestured at his body, drawing her hand through the air in a vertical line. *"White tank top. White basketball shorts. You're like the sixth Back Street Boy."*

"Who?" he asked.

She rolled her eyes. *"Never mind. Ancient history."*

"Oh."

"So you're not going to tell me?" she asked.

"Tell you what?"

"What gives with the clothes? Every day it's the same thing. You must have a closet full of them."

"Oh. I do."

"And..." she said, prompting him to go on.

Sensory processing disorder was not something Michael like to talk about. Not then. Not now. Not ever. There was enough disease, death, and loss in this world to trouble anyone with *his* lame issues. Besides, SPD was kind of a conversation stopper.

The short story was: Michael couldn't bear to be touched.

He didn't shake hands. He didn't go to the clinic. It was the reason he had this garage apartment instead of living in the men's dorms with everyone else—too much chance of being touched or jostled. After one too many panic attacks that ended up with him screaming on the floor in the fetal position, the Commander had taken pity on him and given him this place.

God, even the feel of most clothing was too much for him to handle for longer than a few seconds. How anyone could wear a wool sweater was beyond him.

The only thing he'd ever managed to tolerate for long periods of time were these tanks and loose basketball shorts because—one—they left most of his skin untouched and—two—they were made of one hundred percent silk, no scratchy tags, and no dyes, either. Basically, they were a whole lot of nothing.

Sometimes Michael felt like *he* was a whole lot of nothing.

His mama, *God rest her soul*, had always bought his "nothing" in bulk.

When he took a chance and explained all of this to Ana, she seemed more fascinated than pitying. He was grateful for that. To be seen and not judged, especially by a woman, he wanted that more than anything.

"No interest in a wife, then?" she asked.

He laughed out loud. "Loads of interest. Just no way to get close enough to consummate."

"So if a woman touched you....?" She took a step closer, and he backed up.

Ana was one of the women in town who'd elected not to enter the Marriage Raffle, an option for women who were either too old or for some other reason unable to have children. She'd come with her son, Danny, to the town so long ago both of them were practically pillars of the community. Especially considering the fact that Ana, like several other of the unattached women, became very popular because they shared their favors widely with many men.

Michael held up his hands in warning and took several more steps back. The idea of being one of the men who visited Ana's bed appealed to him, but it was impossible. "Best case scenario, I run. Worst case, I scream and bawl like a baby."

That's what Michael's father had called him: a big baby. "He'll never be a man," he'd said. "Helpless...crying...disappointing...baby..." Michael hadn't seen the man since he was ten but still his words banged around noisily in his head.

Ana glanced up at his window, the one that faced her house. "I hope you've got an old stash of dirty magazines in your room because, bless my soul, darlin', you've got to have some kind of outlet. If you don't, I know some men who have a whole stack in their closets."

"Nah," he said. "That's okay. I'm more of a three-dimensional-woman kind of guy." Ana's gaze moved over his shoulder to look at his bedroom window.

The window shows started shortly after that.

In no time, Michael became the virtuoso of voyeurism, not to mention, the maestro of masturbation. And he developed quite the sophisticated palate for both. At least he could handle his own touch. Thank God for small favors.

He was partial to the solo scenes Ana played, the slow strip teases. He'd work himself up, stroking, grinding against his palm as he watched her lower one bra strap, then the other... He could get lost in the arch of her spine as she unclasped the back... Then mesmerized by the shimmy of panties over sweetly rounded hips. When she'd turn and bend, dropping them to the floor and flashing her privates like a pretty pink petaled flower... *Poetry*.

Other times, one of her gentleman callers would join the show. The men never looked Michael's way. He didn't think they knew about their audience.

He often wondered how it would be, being a normal man and being with a woman like Ana. Or better yet, being one of the men chosen in a lottery. Having a wife of his own.

Tonight, Ana sat on the edge of her bed and spread her knees wide, sliding her hand down over her stomach. Her eyes locked on his. Or at least he thought they did—he only had one oil lamp burning on low.

But the next second he'd forgotten all about it because Ana was sliding her panties to the side and driving her finger into her cunt.

Michael stroked himself faster. Shit, she was so hot.

What would it be like to touch that pussy? To have his cock sliding in between those slick, wet lips?

A fucking fantasy, he knew, but still. What would it be like to have a woman like Ana, all his own...?

Right now, men were in the town square, putting their names in the ballot box for the lottery. Later, names would be called and a new clan would be created.

Michael would be there. Not because he'd put his name in the box. That was out of the question. No, Michael was a journalist. He covered the local stories only, so it was his job to cover the lottery for the *Gazette*. He'd take notes, consider the men who were chosen. He'd imagine himself in their place. Maybe later he'd wonder what it would be like to take their new bride home for the very first time.

He could do all this from the periphery of the crowd—away from the jostling and involuntary touching. He shuddered just thinking about it.

The bedroom door opened behind Ana, and a furry-chested warrior guy walked in. Michael recognized him. He had something of a standing appointment on Mondays.

A sly smile spread across his face when he saw what Ana was doing to herself. He came closer, bent and sucked on the side of her neck.

She tipped her head to give him more access and his hand slid down over her body until he replaced her fingers with his own.

This went on for a few glorious moments.

Michael was ram-rod hard. His ink-stained fingers moved swiftly over his cock, getting closer...closer...when the man suddenly looked up.

Michael froze. Had he been seen?

The man narrowed his eyes and scrutinized the parted curtains on Michael's window. Then the man slowly rose, took a few steps, and yanked Ana's curtains shut.

Michael exhaled with relief—though his orgasm was lost—and thought about the lottery again.

If he had a bride of his own? It would be one thing to share her with four other husbands. She'd still be his to wake up to in the morning. To talk to at dinner every night. To watch up close and personal while she stripped and one of the other husbands—

Too bad you'll never have that, freak. Always the voyeur.

Michael's hands clenched into fists and he jerked his shorts up.

Time to go do his job—reporting about the lives of other men living out what for him would only ever be fantasies.

CHAPTER 4

VANESSA

Everything happened for a reason. Vanessa believed that with her whole heart. She had to. There was no other way to explain surviving for as long as she had, all on her own out in the wilderness.

Luck.

Fate.

Karma.

Whatever you wanted to call it, Vanessa was one lucky girl.

Okay, so a lot of the time it was *bad* luck, but hey, she was still alive. That was more than most women could say. Her life had balanced on a knife's edge one too many times for her to believe in anything other than Fate being on her side.

Take the last twelve hours, for example. In half a rotation of the earth, she'd been almost recaptured by Lorenzo Ramos, one of the scariest human traffickers left in the whole of the Republic, held two of his crew at bay with their own weapons before giving them the only ending they deserved—aaaaaaaaand then she'd humiliated herself by fainting and needing to be "rescued" by some dudes from Jacob's Well.

She came-to in the back of their truck only to be driven the last hundred miles to the exact place she'd been *trying* to get to. Then when she got here, she was fed, cleaned up with actual soap and hot water, then brought to a very pink bedroom for a nap and was tucked into a bed that had—she still couldn't believe it—*pillows*. The soft kind with freaking feathers inside.

Suffice it to say, it was a lot for one girl to take in—even for Vanessa, who in her twenty-three years, had endured more than her fair share of shit.

Now it was late evening, and she was about to find out if all the rumors about Jacob's Well were true.

So far things looked promising.

Earlier in the day, the leader of Jacob's Well Township, Commander Wolford, and his exuberant daughter Sophia (whose bedroom she'd been given for the nap) told her the plan for her continued stay in Jacob's Well. They'd explained the necessity of the arrangement: a lottery to marry her off to five local men, which was when Vanessa'd cut them off, informing them that she already knew all about it.

"I know," she'd said matter of factly. "That's why I was heading this direction. I want to become a lottery bride."

Despite her isolation in the wilderness for the last eight years, Vanessa was well aware the world had changed since Xterminate had wiped out ninety percent of the earth's female population.

Women were vulnerable. She understood vulnerable. She'd lived that for *years,* both at home before the Fall and then afterward, alone and out in the wilderness. Didn't mean she couldn't protect herself, though. She knew all about that, too.

The Commander and Sophia had done nothing to hide their surprise at Vanessa's declaration. They'd obviously been told about the knife fight. Or maybe it was how she looked that had them pausing.

Vanessa passed a trembling hand over her head. She'd once had long, thick, chocolatey locks. Now it was shaved close, in some places *so* close you could see the nicks left on her scalp by her knife.

She'd shaved it out of necessity. Long hair was a stupid vanity when you were out in the wild and too often on the run. And she was determined to look nothing like herself after her last close call with Lorenzo... she shuddered even at the name.

She'd first run into the bastard six years ago. Back then, she'd camp off grid, but sometimes she found a group here or there to hook up with for a while. She'd been hanging out with this group that was camping out just past the badlands of the fallout zone east of Austin. There were several other women in the group and Vanessa had hidden in the trees for several days, watching, and only approached after seeing they were treated well.

No one knew exactly where the fallout zone ended and safe land and/or water began. There was a UT professor in the group who'd done some calculations based on the wind direction and speed on D-Day and he felt confident the area was safe.

It was back before the territorial control had been solidified by the various factions, when the war with the Southern States Alliance was waging and everything was pretty much chaos. So hiding out in an area others would stay away from sounded like a great plan to Vanessa.

They used an elaborate soil filtration system to clean their water, and hunters went out further east for meat and foraging, so Vanessa wasn't too worried about radiation poisoning.

What she should have been worried about, however, was the fact that most in the group were scientists, professors, and Austin hippy types.

When Lorenzo and his gang raided the camp a month and a half later, the inhabitants never had a chance. All the men were slaughtered immediately.

And the women, they were—

Vanessa clenched her eyes shut and took a deep breath.

She'd been spared only because she was a virgin.

Virgins were worth more at auction, you see.

What followed were the most hellish three weeks of her life. The things she saw... Her shudder worked its way down to her bones. She was dragged around with Lorenzo and his crew as they made their way to Nuevo Laredo. That was where the biggest and most lucrative slave market was.

Vanessa managed to escape the night before they arrived at the border.

But Lorenzo Bernal was not a man who forgave or forgot. Especially since she'd killed one of his men and severely wounded another as she escaped. Apparently, he took that sort of thing personally. Or maybe it was just the fact that he'd been bested by a woman.

He'd shot her as she ran away so—frankly—she'd considered them even. Okay...so she stole his truck technically *after* her shot her, but still. Why couldn't he just move on and forget about her?

Lorenzo Bernal was why she'd been forced to live off the grid for the last several years.

She found herself a nice cave by the Pecos River. She woke up every morning and did the grueling work of surviving another day. She talked to no one and avoided human interaction at all costs.

But then she got sloppy—ventured into a couple of trading towns to get seeds and to replace her broken and used-up supplies—and he found her again despite her disguise.

God, she was just so damn *tired*.

Every year she lost more muscle mass. She was getting slower and slower at skinning the rabbits she caught. She was sleeping longer and longer hours. She knew she couldn't keep up that kind of brutal existence forever.

Jacob's Well had been an extreme plan B, but as the months passed, it began to look more and more attractive.

Lorenzo's crew was only at most ten men strong. And he might be vengeful but he wasn't stupid. He was a vulture, picking at the bones of prey only after it was dead. He didn't walk into fights he wasn't positive he could win.

So no way he'd dare enter a well-governed township looking for her. Not to mention, slave trading was illegal now and the President had issued a price on his head.

Even if he was stupid enough to come into town, with five husbands devoted to her protection...

As soon as she'd heard rumors of Jacob's Well, she'd been fascinated. Traders talked about the town like it was a mythical place. An oasis outside of the rest of the war-torn, ruthless Republic. A place where peace and order ruled and women were treated like queens.

Queens who had to marry five men, sure, but still. Apparently there was a law in Jacob's Well that if you raised your hand to a woman, they'd cut your hand *off*.

The first time she'd heard about the township, she'd scoffed. Any time something sounded too good to be true, it usually was.

Even now—after having seen the place, met the Wolfords, and been treated so nicely—she worried she'd got it all wrong. Chances were, it was all a ruse. It would probably turn out to be just like Travisville where they lured women in with lies. Colonel Travis was an evil bastard who trafficked women in his territory right under President Goddard's nose, and nothing was done about it.

But the traders who talked about Jacob's Well were the real deal who usually saw beneath bullshit propaganda.

So yeah, she'd definitely been thinking about Jacob's Well.

When Lorenzo's two lackeys ambushed her at the river two days ago, well, that just accelerated her decision to make the plunge. She'd escape them, then high-tail it to Jacob's Well.

Men from Jacob's Well just happening to stumble on them and providing the perfect distraction so she could take Lorenzo's men out? What were the odds?

Fate was one tricky bitch, that was for sure.

So now she was here.

And tonight, there would be a lottery to choose her five husbands.

Theirs to Wed is AVAILABLE NOW

Want to read an EXCLUSIVE, FREE 45 page novelette, *Their Honeymoon*, about Audrey and her Clan's honeymoon that is available only to my newsletter subscribers, along with news about upcoming releases, sales, exclusive giveaways, and more?

Get *Their Honeymoon* here:
http://bit.ly/theirhoneymoon

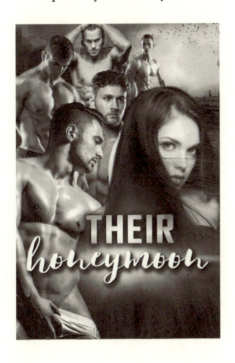

ALSO BY STASIA BLACK

MARRIAGE RAFFLE SERIES

Theirs to Protect

Theirs to Pleasure

Theirs to Wed

Theirs to Defy

Theirs to Ransom

DARK MAFIA SERIES

Co-written with Lee Savino

Innocence

Awakening

Queen of the Underworld

BEAUTY AND THE ROSE

Co-written with Lee Savino

Beauty's Beast

Beauty and the Thorns

Beauty and the Rose

BREAK SO SOFT SERIES

Cut So Deep

Break So Soft

Hurt So Good

STUD RANCH STANDALONE SERIES

The Virgin and the Beast: a Beauty and the Beast Tale (prequel)

Hunter: a Snow White Romance

The Virgin Next Door: a Ménage Romance

ACKNOWLEDGMENTS

Aimee Bowyer, my most fabulous beta! You were the very first person to read this book and I anxiously awaited for feedback. It meant SO much to me that you got it and felt these characters as much as I did. Thank you!!!

Bobby! Holy shit!!!! Thank you for everything!

Zara Zenia – wow, I cannot thank you enough for helping me figure out how figure out some marketing stuff I was being way dumb about. You provided a SERIOUSLY needed wake-up call and now I'm like, wtf was I thinking??? Lol, thank you so much!

Melissa Lee – zomg, thank you for keeping my calendar straight and keeping me on time with all my responsibilities because lol, on my own, I'm an epic mess!

Melissa Pascoe— Thank you for helping me stay on top of All The Things!

Christine Jalili – so excited to have you on the team, we're gonna do some epic shit :)

Riley Edwards – omg, thank you for spending that hour tutoring me on Photoshop and helping me realize I've been doing things the Hardest Way Possible for YEARS now without even realizing it, and

schooling my ass, lmfao! And thank you for your general encourage-
ment and being an awesome voice in our group. Hugs!

Thank you to Alana Albertson and Sara Fields and Harloe Rae Lee
Savino and Sara Fields for your general awesomeness and chatting at all
times of the day and night and super support! And I'm sure I'm forgetting someone here or several someones but it's only because my brain
is pan-fried after this week, I love you all, I promise!

And thanks as always to super hubby. Love you forever.

ABOUT THE AUTHOR

STASIA BLACK grew up in Texas, recently spent a freezing five-year stint in Minnesota, and now is happily planted in sunny California, which she will never, ever leave.

She loves writing, reading, listening to podcasts, and has recently taken up biking after a twenty-year sabbatical (and has the bumps and bruises to prove it). She lives with her own personal cheerleader, aka, her handsome husband, and their teenage son. Wow. Typing that makes her feel old. And writing about herself in the third person makes her feel a little like a nutjob, but ahem! Where were we?

Stasia's drawn to romantic stories that don't take the easy way out. She wants to see beneath people's veneer and poke into their dark places, their twisted motives, and their deepest desires. Basically, she wants to create characters that make readers alternately laugh, cry ugly tears, want to toss their kindles across the room, and then declare they have a new FBB (forever book boyfriend).

Join Stasia's Facebook Group for Readers for access to deleted scenes, to chat with me and other fans and also get access to exclusive giveaways:
https://www.facebook.com/groups/StasiasBabes/

Made in United States
Troutdale, OR
03/10/2024